Sadie Montgomery's Phoenix of the Opera Series

The Phoenix of the Opera

Out of the Darkness: The Phantom's Journey

The Phantom's Opera

Phantom Death

Phoenix of the Opera Novels

Phantom Madness

Phantom Murder

PHANTOM MURDER

Sadie Montgomery

iUniverse, Inc.
New York   Bloomington

Phantom Murder

This is a work of fiction. All of the characters, names, incidents, organizations, and dialogue in this novel are either the products of the author's imagination or are used fictitiously.

iUniverse books may be ordered through booksellers or by contacting:

iUniverse
1663 Liberty Drive
Bloomington, IN 47403
www.iuniverse.com
1-800-Authors (1-800-288-4677)

Because of the dynamic nature of the Internet, any Web addresses or links contained in this book may have changed since publication and may no longer be valid. The views expressed in this work are solely those of the author and do not necessarily reflect the views of the publisher, and the publisher hereby disclaims any responsibility for them.

ISBN: 978-1-4502-2647-9 (sc)
ISBN: 978-1-4502-2648-6 (ebook)

Printed in the United States of America

iUniverse rev. date: 04/30/2010

To Doug, Zach, Betty, and Mom.

As always, with gratitude and love, to those friends who have followed these stories, Marie, Cherie, Chris.

This is the excellent foppery of the world, that,
when we are sick in fortune,—often the surfeit
of our own behavior,—we make guilty of our
disasters the sun, the moon, and the stars: as
if we were villains by necessity; fools by
heavenly compulsion; knaves, thieves, and
treachers, by spherical predominance; drunkards,
liars, and adulterers, by an enforced obedience of
planetary influence; and all that we are evil in,
by a divine thrusting on: an admirable evasion
of whoremaster man, to lay his goatish
disposition to the charge of a star!

King Lear,
William Shakespeare

Poor naked wretches, wheresoe'er you are,
That bide the pelting of this pitiless storm,
How shall your houseless heads and unfed sides,
Your looped and windowed raggedness, defend you
From seasons such as these?

King Lear,
William Shakespeare

Jack shall have Jill;
Nought shall go ill;
The man shall have his mare again,
and all shall be well.

A Midsummer Night's Dream,
William Shakespeare

THE DARKNESS

Murder most foul; as in the best it is.

Hamlet, William Shakespeare

"Here, sir."

The child pointed down the long tunnel of darkness that stretched between the two buildings. The night air was damp and cold. But that was not why the child's finger trembled. On a dare he had gone into the black nothingness. To show his courage he had continued even when the darkness at the end took on a solidity that differentiated it from the air about it. He would have cried out for his friends had he been able to breathe, but when he stopped and unblinkingly stared at the denser black that lay upon the ground, he thought he heard a moan. That was when he no longer cared if his friends thought him a coward. He turned and ran until, carrying in his wake his friends as if the force of his movement had created a vacuum that would suck up even the blackness behind him, he came to a grinding stop in front of a policeman.

The policeman held his light high and out in front to brush the shadows aside. Within the circumference of the light all was visible—the debris of casual foot traffic, the pock-marked stone, the puddles dulled by scum and oil, the furtive movement of a naked tail of some rodent scurrying away—but just beyond the darkness was by contrast impenetrable.

Dead men don't walk and dead men don't talk, thought the officer as he advanced in spite of the short hairs rising along his collar, in spite of the fact that his eyes grew incredibly wide in his efforts to see into the darkness, in spite of the ripple of fear that crawled up his spine to lodge in the shoulders that he unconsciously hunched close to his neck.

Dead men can't harm you, can they?

The sweep of the light spilled over the irregular shape on the ground. Immediate recognition eased the atavistic dread that the policeman had kept at bay. He'd seen many a prostrate body—in the streets, along the gutters, just outside the taverns, down in the gullies at the edges of the city. Most were drunks that had collapsed on their sorry way to home, many were without a home to go to, and then a few were, like this one, no longer on their way anywhere. He could sense that the bulk was no longer a living thing. He restrained the urge to reach out with his boot and kick at it to see if it might move. The boy and his friends were behind him, at the opening to the alley, and they would think him afraid to touch the dead thing with his hand. So he bent, knees crunching in the expectant silence, and reached out for what appeared to be a shoulder. The fine weave of a dark cloak had more life than the bulk it clothed. It gave way to the soft pressure as the officer's fingers gripped more tightly and then pulled the shoulder toward him.

"Good God!" The officer jerked back on his heels. His foot slid out from under him on the viscous surface of the stone. His hand went out to break his fall, but he landed heavily on his backside. Next to him, the lantern clanged against the paving stones, its light wavering, threatening to go out. Eyes fixed on the corpse, the policeman wiped his wet, sticky hands on his pants. Behind him, he heard the startled sound of the boys. In the light of the lantern could be seen what should have been a face.

PART I

CHAPTER 1

Preparations

In his mind he remembered, he rehearsed, the notes of the song of the Phoenix. It began with fire and pain, a staccato of tortured notes cutting across a low ominous field. The sounds would oscillate between fortissimo and pianissimo as if they mimicked the very fires in which the Phoenix burned. Suddenly a sustained rest would, in its absence of sound, take on a corporeal weight as if it were sound and stillness simultaneously—death. Then, the movement of healing, of the gradual rise from nothingness, would begin with one simple longing strain, a note so pure it had always been inside the listener's mind and only now perceptible. Other notes would join until woven together they would fly up like the Phoenix itself, glorious and beautiful, powerful and wise, old and yet new again.

The Phoenix of the Opera, Sadie Montgomery

Preparations are underway for the opera's debut. Stagehands oil casters to silence the transport of heavy props—castle ramparts, rock promontories, library walls, alchemist's desks, and forest sanctuaries. Space is segmented and assigned. Previous worlds are carted off and left to molder in silent resignation.

Musicians rifle through the score, pages flapping across music stands, the slap of gulls' wings. The conductor tests the pitch and tone of the instruments, listens for the lament of one left behind, insists that the notes rise and fall on the currents in unison. Tap tap tap tap. He gathers the flock on the beach. His baton jabs the air.

5

Wings beating, resounding in a maelstrom of notes, upward flies the music that had once existed only inside the composer's mind, tuned to his inner ear, born of the vibrations of his soul.

Scraping wood, the landscape of a distant city in a valley of rolling hills recedes. Wallpapered panels of an inner parlor pivot on their axis and wobble into queue. Sceneshifters, shadowy movers of universes, lock hands and shoulders against canvas and wood, slide spatial illusions, stacked and numbered, to a dark back wall so that the chorus can occupy the vaulted womb of the stage. Eyes directed heavenward, a huddle of workmen in thick, rough clothes with great aprons of heavy metal tools for tightening, cutting, wedging, twisting, stare at the rigging, point, gesticulate, argue, make plans. Confirmed by white markings of chalk upon the cedar floor, the silent troupe of long-legged, supple-limbed dancers, grim-faced, stretch their fingers and tilt their heads, rise on hardened, powdery points, snap and sway to the numbered count of the ballet mistress.

One and two and one and two...toes and spine and elbow and thigh...

Skittering notes, bursts of arias, again from the fifth measure. Oboes and bass anchor fugitive flutes and violins. A snarling rumble of a kettledrum sends vibrations throughout the walls and floors of the pit along the boards of the stage, like a sleeping beast on the verge of waking.

The chorus waits, clearing its throat, pure, limpid notes clearing the path.

Behind the scenes, percussive clacks and muffled clomps, swish of starch and silk, tittering voices compete with the first notes of Act II. Erik Costanzi makes his way through an onslaught of technicians and performers. Dozens of like-outfitted young slips of girls, faces barely distinguishable one from another, smile awkwardly at the composer-director, the tall, dark man whose voice commands them, a voice rich in velvet promises, a voice that seduces as it demands, a voice that leaves behind in their young hearts the hope of pleasing and being pleased. Two, five, seven more white snowflakes flutter by

Erik, by the composer, the man who has written music that tests the very limits of their bodies and souls.

Erik mentally counts the snowflakes on the way to their dressing room to become forest nymphs. One catches his eye, one whose limbs seem stretched against the laws of gravity, arching to touch heaven itself, a glimpse of blond hair, a turn to the cheek, a slice of lip curled at the corner. She makes him recall another dancer, a young blonde, a wisp of a girl, no not a wisp, petite, yes, but shapely, a dancer whose body was molded by a lustful god, not like the thin-boned, paper cut-out dancers who flit by him now, their voices as reedy as their limbs, a dancer whom he refashioned into a singer, a dancer whose body is as complex and elegant as the score of his opera, whose body he knows as well as the notes the orchestra rehearses, whose body is as familiar and responsive as the violin he plays each evening as if the strings were the prelude to the touch between the dancer and him.

Had Meg ever been one of these skittering creatures—divine and whimsical, yet so young and innocent?

Perhaps...

Erik smiles to himself, steps aside and bows indulgently as they whisk past him. Fugitive glances at his chest, his limbs, his eyes, his half mask—shy yet daring in their fear and admiration, such glances no longer torment him. He takes them for the silent homage they are. Meg has taught him to understand the effect he has on young, nubile, impressionable girls. Let them look. Let them fantasy about him. Let them wonder about the half mask.

The mask. A tool, an accessory, it no longer hides him from the world. In the confines of his domain, he wears it as he pleases, like the carnation Meg sometimes fits in his button hole, like the carefully folded silk handkerchief he sometimes displays just above the rim of a pocket, or the gold chain and watch that Marcelo Costanzi has given to him—a watch that has belonged to several Costanzis—as a sign of Erik's acceptance into Marcelo's family, as a sign that Marcelo's protestations that Erik is like a son to him are literal, not just an expression of friendship, but an expression of love, a covenant between them. The mask—his second skin—eases his presence among those that pass through his world. So many.

The mask is a tool, a comfort, a mark of his distinction, no longer a brand, no longer a torment, no longer a curse.

One snowflake tarries. One snowflake with dark blond hair, whose body is not like the others, whose body jars something in the composer-director. It is a body not likely to excel in the dance, a body too voluptuous, too solid, pleasing but too bound to the earth to soar to the heavens. The snowflake hesitates, glances up at him, starts to retreat, without grace, stumbles.

He reaches out his hand to stay her course. He does not think to touch her. He has not formulated the command that his hand grasp her. Her one foot, caught on the warped edge of a board, betrays the other. She is incapable of righting herself. His hand, without his knowledge, grasps her arm and checks her fall.

Stunned she looks up at him. Green, the color of woodland pools of calm water, his eyes show his concern as he helps her steady herself on her awkward and untrained feet.

Down the tunnel of the backstage corridor, Meg watches.

From the wings, Erik walks to the center of the stage, scans the various parties loosely assembled. Out of this riot of movement and sound the opera will come. Standing, silent, by pure force of will he calls them forth. First full rehearsal. What has been honed to perfection in their separate states will now converge. Each will bring forth a new delight, subtle and outrageous marriage of form and thought. Bodies, instruments, and voices will become song and story.

Erik sighs as he considers the complexities of bringing to heel so many diverse and independent wills. No smoke and mirrors, no illusion, no magic, no hidden traps under the opera house stage achieve the majesty and wonder of the ultimate trick—the successful staging and execution of an opera—his opera.

Close they are, so close now to his original intension, and yet the work taking shape is never how he imagined it. As detailed as his instructions may have been, the set designers surprise him, actors move on the stage with a volition of their own that somehow escapes his vision, the lighting is and can never be the imagined haze—the shimmering glow his imagination refracted upon a fantasy stage when everything disappeared except the story and the music unfolding. The music itself is his. That is always his, true and faithful. It alone obeys him, pouring straight from his desires and into the sentient world.

Erik stood just outside the door. The room was brightly lit. The mirrors along two sides of the rectangular expanse heightened the effect of the lamps in their sconces. Overhead a series of four simple chandeliers guaranteed that no darkness could linger, not even in the remotest of corners. Here was where the dancers stretched and exercised. On occasion the ballet mistress would assemble the dancers in the long gallery and put them through their paces, rehearsing bits and pieces of the elaborate performance under preparation. Meg often spent the last hour or so of her day in this room while Erik finished details or sat at his piano in the office, after the crowds dispersed and went their separate ways for the evening.

From where he stood, leaning lightly against the doorjamb, Erik knew she couldn't see him among the multiple shifting images of herself receding along the bank of mirrors. She stood, her back to the doorway, her chin raised, her one arm gently arched in a semi-circle so rounded that it seemed as if the bones themselves had bent and curved. The illusion disturbed Erik at the same time that the beauty of her pose clenched his heart, a sweet pain that seared him for he yearned to capture the ephemeral perfection of such moments and knew it was not to be. He regretted not having at hand his sketchbook. He felt the charcoal in his fingers as they tingled with the desire to trace the lines of her body on paper. No sooner had he caught his breath than Meg struck out her leg perpendicular at the hip, held the pose, and then pushed away from the bar to twirl across the wooden floor. Erik wondered what silent score guided Meg's dance. Was it his she obeyed or perhaps she betrayed him, secretly in these moments, and danced to someone else's notes? He would not ask. He would not risk blighting her silent pleasure.

Unexpectedly he was seized with a yearning to step forth and place his hand firmly on her hip. With the other he would brace the large, taut muscle of her thigh. With ease he would lift her, all of a piece, a statue warm with life, ballasted with dreams, into the air, as he had seen other men do on stage during the ballet. Desire so poignant it felt like pain seized him. He would not be content to partner her dance.

No one would come upon them. The lights in the auditorium had been extinguished long ago. Gentle and distant the odd conversation had melted away even as the chorines and staff had left, dragging their tired bodies behind them. Rinaldo had lingered, departing only when Erik told him in a tone that brooked no argument to escort Carlotta to her apartment and not to return until the next day. So Erik knew the silence at his back was complete. He gathered his patience about him like a mantel and forced himself to relax against the doorway, watching Meg move through space and time like a force of nature, as if propelled by some invisible hand, her body a well-tuned instrument, each pose a visual poem, each movement an act of love.

She turned vertiginously, then leaped, legs impossibly straight, and landed on the fulcrum of one foot, suspended against the laws of gravity and reason on the tip of her toes. Erik held his breath as she performed a series of pirouettes, encircling the circumference of the room in preparation to vault again.

Just before she crumpled, Erik saw her ankle wobble and then bend at an unnatural angle. He rushed into the room as she lurched forward and fell. She landed with a loud slap of flesh against polished wood, palms and knees slamming against the floor. He knelt at her side, drew her up into his arms, and stood with her cradled against his chest before she could complain.

She gripped the fabric of his coat in great wads, her teeth gritted tightly against the unexpected pain.

"Put me down."

Reluctantly Erik slowly released her legs, allowing her to place only the barest weight onto her feet. He retained a firm hold on her torso, his left hand spread across her rib cage just under her breast. He swallowed the impulse to complain that not only had she not regained the weight lost last summer when she had fallen ill but she had continued to lose weight in the past several months. Lately he had noticed that her always-slim figure had given way to tightly stretched skin over the bones of her chest. When he held her, his fingers couldn't resist tracing the contour of each rib. When they made love, he felt himself thrust against the bones of her pelvis as if they were not covered by flesh. He worried that he would bruise her if he was not careful in his ardor.

Meg bit her lower lip the moment her left foot touched the floorboard. The pain shot through her, and she squeezed and pulled against the fistful of Erik's coat that she had not released.

"You've injured your ankle," he said and hoisted her back into his arms. She grunted as he settled her and set off toward the passageway.

"I'll be all right," she complained, but she didn't struggle or beg to be let down. "I just twisted it. It will be fine by morning. I just need to let it rest."

Erik swiveled his face and looked into her eyes. His scowl gave the green of his eyes a dark gray cast. He refrained from chiding her. She would only argue with him. He continued walking along the passageway in spite of the absence of all but a dim light toward the end of the black tunnel. He knew his way, having always had a preternatural ability to move about in the dark, relying perhaps on other senses, the give of the wood under his tread, the thickness of darkness coalescing around solid objects, the acute perception of his hearing.

Meg could make out little of their surroundings, although she knew the theater well enough to realize that he was taking her to the private room off the side of his office. Lulled by the security of his arms, the rocking of his pace, she leaned her head on his shoulder and breathed in the scent of his wool coat, the scorched starch of his collar, the faint hint of musk, the light touch of the cologne she had given him Christmas past. She brought her hand up to his cheek.

His pace slowed and stopped. She felt more than saw his lips turn toward her. Then they pressed, warm and soft across her mouth. His tongue glided over her bottom lip and dipped inside to tease hers. He tasted, as always, sweet and clean. Fennel and mint rose off the warmth of his breath. His lips pressed harder, his tongue demanded, and she opened to him, bringing her hand behind his head, pressing against his soft hair, urging him closer, urging his kiss to deepen.

The kiss went on and on in the darkness until his lips were gone. But Meg could feel the flutter of his rapid breath against her face. He began to walk, his pace brisk, faster than before. He pushed the door open to his office where he had left a light burning. Meg expected that he might place her on the sofa in the study, but he glided past the desk and the sofa, past the piano to the door that separated the office from a small, private room. Inside he laid her gently on the daybed, taking particular care to rest her injured ankle on a small pillow. Then he stood hesitant as if at a loss.

Meg saw the hesitation in his eyes. She wanted to laugh but it would be cruel to take advantage of such an infrequent and unusual situation. She knew what he wanted. She had felt his arousal against her hip before he released her.

"You won't hurt me." She slid her hips over on the silken spread, careful not to jar her ankle unnecessarily and patted the edge of the daybed.

"Your ankle."

"Are you planning to do something to my feet?" She forced her face into a blank mask.

Erik's mouth turned up on one side in a lopsided grin. "Stranger things have happened."

Meg's blankness fell away, and she smiled up at him. "Come, M. Phantom, I want to show you something."

Erik raised his hands to the back of his head where he untied the simple mask that he tended to wear at the theater. He removed it and threw it carelessly aside. It hit the edge of the table and fell to the floor. He eased his weight to the edge of the mattress, but he did not lie down. Instead he brushed Meg's hair from her face and stared down at her.

For several moments they were silent. He bent and kissed her lightly, just brushing her lips with his, then looked again into her soft brown eyes.

"Beautiful," he whispered as he feathered kisses from the corner of her mouth to the soft pulse at her throat. "I just want to hold you."

Meg wrapped her arms around his shoulders as he pressed his face deep inside the pocket of her neck and shoulder. His warmth against her throat moved down along her shoulder. He could not see her furrowed brow, the deep stir of some undisclosed emotion swimming at the back of her eyes.

When he tried to move away, she grabbed his coat in both her fists to keep him intimately suspended over her. "Don't," she whispered and, raising her face, kissed him hard against the mouth. He resisted only a moment before he gave in to the force of her demand.

"I don't want to…"

"You won't. Don't be silly."

He moved away from her, stilling her attempt to unbutton his vest with his hand. "Meg?"

"Don't. Don't talk." She pulled him down again to take his lips, to make it clear what she wanted. He could not resist her. He pushed aside the light fabric of her costume to touch her naked skin, the rounded firmness of her breast, to caress her, to open her body to his. He wedged his knee between her thighs, his eagerness plain in every tense fiber of his body in spite of the barrier of his trousers.

Meg's hands reached down along his chest, his abdomen, and then searched inside the layers of fabric, behind the panel of his trousers, until she encircled him. Erik's fingers, without thinking, slid from the rounded softness of her breast. Running the length of her torso, they counted, one by one, each of his wife's ribs.

Occasionally Erik did attend public performances. He faced strangers' stares and curiosity with apparent indifference. The half mask was no longer what it had been. He no longer hid behind it. Like his vest or the stiff cuffs of his shirt, the molded form that covered his face like a second skin was simply part of his wardrobe. He had accepted the face he was born with because it had cost him too dearly to rail against his fate. He refused to see the disfigurement as a sign, as the mark of Cain, as the revelation of the deformation of his soul. He did not have the strength or inclination to bemoan his fate and stand on guard. He tired of expecting pain. He tired of vigilance. If others were disgusted by him, let them look away. If they feared him and rejected him, what mattered their opinion to him? He basked in the love of a beautiful and kind woman. He was warmed by the trust and love of his family and a few dear friends who had become his mirror. In them, he saw himself whole and worthy. If he wore the mask, it was for the same reasons that he shaved or combed his hair. He liked the way he looked in the mask. He knew that it did far more than hide an unattractive feature. It gave him a mysterious air. It accentuated his eyes. It sculpted his face, brought out the lines of his jaw, and drew the eye to his full, sensual mouth.

Slowly, over the course of several years, Marcelo and Madeleine had led Erik into society. The dinner parties at the Costanzis, which had been limited and rare events, grew more boisterous and more frequent. In time, Erik remained longer, became involved in the conversations, participated in the card games and light performances. Eventually invitations reciprocating the honor lured Erik to similar events among the closer of Marcelo's acquaintances and outside the protective walls of the Costanzi estate. Meg was always by his side, a reminder that his world was solid and secure, a reminder that the man behind the mask was real, substantial, that it was *he* to whom Sig. Valerio and Sig. Conti addressed their praise, their questions, their comments, and their offers of friendship.

Just that morning, Erik had watched Meg read with unveiled eagerness and longing the announcement of the tour of the Russian Ballet. There would be a limited engagement in Rome. Meg gnawed her lower lip as she studied the information. Folding the paper into smaller and smaller blocks, she had commented, as if she wanted Erik to know that it didn't matter to her, that it would be difficult to secure tickets. But he could see the warm rush of blood to her cheeks. He saw how she looked away and pretended to be fascinated by the arrangement of spring flowers that she had selected for the breakfast table.

Slowly the plan took shape in Erik's mind. He might have

charged one of the servants with the task of waiting on queue for the ticket office to open. However if Meg were not mistaken, the usual patrons of the theater would surely have had advanced warning of the special performances and would likely have secured the best seats. The tickets the servant might obtain would be in one of the lesser galleries and probably woefully removed from the stage. Not the gift he wanted for his wife. And if he were frank, not seats in which he would be comfortable. His only and best recourse would be to appeal to the manager of the theater.

Meg had left the folded sheet of newsprint on the table, unable to consign it to a waste bin. Before he left the parlor, Erik covered the paper with his palm and slid it into his vest pocket without Meg's knowledge. Later, safely ensconced in his office at the Teatro dell'Opera, he had taken it out and unfolded it to find the brief notice. He smiled, his lips curling at one corner of his mouth, as he realized that the ballet had been invited to perform at the Teatro Regio. He knew the theater. His own opera had been staged there once upon a time, an opera that he had written under the pen name of Henri Fournier and which he had thought at the time to have been his first composition.

Erik tried to recall the manager's name. He envisioned a man with a long torso and short legs, looking as if he had always been in his middle years. He reminded Erik of a thinner version of one of the last managers at the Opera Populaire, M. André. The latter, as well as his partner, M. Firmin, had been more suited for business than the arts. Their concerns were always with the profits, the calculations of expenditures and receipts. Erik remembered the name of the Teatro Regio's manager, Sig. Rossi, in the same moment that he recalled the night that the man had approached him, in one of the lateral passageways, at the premiere of *The Stranger*, his hand outstretched, thinking to have a chat with the enigmatic composer himself. At the last moment, the enthusiastic crowds had diverted Sig. Rossi. But Erik could not easily forget the look of shock as Rossi glimpsed Erik's unmasked face under the brim of his hat before he could turn away.

It had been, as always, disconcerting to Erik to see the effect of his disfigurement in the way others looked at him. Even so, he would not allow such encounters to dictate his behavior now. Instead of worrying about the opinion of the obsequious manager of the Teatro Regio, Erik would assume that there was an advantage to dealing with a man with whom he'd already established a business relationship. Erik's familiarity with the theater itself also quelled misgivings about his plans. He knew the layout, knew its limitations. Already his mind was working on the exits and entrances, the corners and alcoves of the building. He would easily find his way about should it be necessary.

Should what be necessary? He scoffed at his own paranoia. He had spent too long hiding, too long devising escape routes. It was now simply the way his mind worked. Aware that there was no threat from which he must hide, it only struck him as a curiosity this way of surveying the spaces around him. Even so, it allayed his anxiety to know that the performance would be on known territory.

If for no other reason, it meant that Erik knew which were the best seats in the house.

The next day Erik made his way to the Teatro Regio, requested an audience with Sig. Rossi, and within moments found himself sitting across from the impresario.

They had barely met during the short career of Henri Fournier, but the little man lost in the high-backed, stuffed chair obviously recognized Erik Costanzi as the composer of the opera, *The Stranger*. The card that Erik had given the assistant lay prominently on the desk before the impresario, and Erik was sure that Rossi realized that Henri Fournier and Erik Costanzi were in truth the same person. Erik could tell that Rossi barely refrained from asking him a series of questions about the subterfuge of an assumed identity.

Clearly the manager of the Regio could not fathom why the renowned artistic director of the Teatro dell'Opera had submitted his piece to a different theater and under an assumed identity. Indeed the whole affair of the fire at the Teatro dell'Opera and the following months when Erik was reported as having perished in the blaze had never been fully explained to the public. A brief notice had appeared months later to announce the staging of a new piece by Costanzi and to affirm that he had not died in the fire, but had spent the time convalescing in seclusion somewhere in the Alps. Such cloak and dagger complications escaped Rossi's comprehension.

Erik forestalled any attempt on the impresario's part to pry into the past and went straight to the point of his present visit.

"You have done well, Sig. Rossi. Congratulations."

"Congratulations?"

"On the success of bringing to your theater such a respected ballet corps."

"Ballet?"

"Yes."

"But I thought you were interested in opera, Signor…,"—here the man paused and glanced down at the embossed card before him on the blotter, as if he needed to be sure to whom he was speaking—"…Costanzi."

"I appreciate all the arts, signore. But I come mostly on my wife's behalf."

"Your wife?"

Erik stared at the man who shifted awkwardly in his chair. An image of an auburn-haired beauty passed both men's mind.

"Yes, my wife, Signora Costanzi, began her career as a dancer."

"A dancer?"

"Yes, a dancer." Erik forced the irritation from his tone and continued, "I find myself in need of your assistance."

"My assistance?"

Erik shifted in his seat and sighed. The man's habit of answering each statement with a question was beginning to annoy him.

"Yes, Sig. Rossi, I intend to escort my wife to the ballet. It is a gift, a surprise. I need something special, something more private than what is available at this late date."

"You mean Il canarino, Signora Costanzi? May I say that I have attended and enjoyed several of her performances? She is…"

"I need a box seat for the premiere." Erik needed no one to extol Meg's talent. Only he was capable of judging how gifted and accomplished she truly was.

"For the premiere, did you say?"

"Of course."

"Might the evening performance on the fifteenth suit? I have several wonderful…"

"That won't do."

"The fact is that the premiere is…"

Erik cut the man off. "When may I send my man for the tickets?"

"Uh, Sig. Costanzi, you must know how difficult it is to…"

"Nonsense."

Sig. Rossi stared, slack-jawed, at the man on the opposite side of the desk. It was disquieting to speak to a man in a mask, and yet Sig. Costanzi wore the ivory half-mask as if it were and had always been a part of his face. No, the mask was not unsettling. It was the eyes framed by the mask. They were unwavering, unblinking as if they housed the man's entire will. His jaw line was sharp, solid, and his mouth was set in grim determination. Sig. Rossi was at a loss as to how to explain. There were no tickets left for the much sought-after box seats.

"I'm afraid our regular patrons have secured the box seats."

"I will buy a season pass to all the performances. Not just for the special performances. That should help to remove obstacles. A box near the stage, one or two levels back. I'm not unreasonable, Sig. Rossi. Either side will do, although I prefer the right-hand side."

"But…but…I…can't…"

"I shall send my man later today to pick up the tickets."

Erik rose, turned his back to the stuttering man, and walked out before Sig. Rossi could collect his words.

Erik knew full well that the Mendiotas were patrons of the Teatro Regio and occupied one of the more elegant boxes for each season. They were acquaintances of Sig. Valerio. At a recent dinner party to which the Costanzis had been invited, Erik had overheard that the Mendiotas had taken an extended holiday in England. The box seats would lie vacant for the next several months. Of course, Sig. Rossi may have had plans to profit by selling them for the time being to another patron. But Erik had few qualms exercising the power of his purse to get what he wanted in such a case since it was meant to please Meg. He understood how persuasive money could be and could not regret using other men's greed to further his own plans. Either way, the manager would gain an exorbitant additional profit whether the box seats went to Erik or to someone else. The Mendiotas would not be concerned by the advantage made of their absence.

Satisfied with himself, Erik was oblivious to the stares of passersby on the street as he walked along the avenue toward the Teatro dell'Opera. If he had noticed, he'd have reminded himself that people were, by nature, curious. It did not mean that they were cruel. But he was not thinking about his surroundings when the voice called out his name. He stopped and turned to see a person whose attention he had never sought or appreciated.

Paolo Ricci was not a man that Erik wished to meet. He considered ignoring the journalist, but he would not have Ricci assume that he was trying to escape. So he stood, waiting for the dark-haired man to draw up beside him.

Ricci, out of breath from having sprinted up the block, couldn't speak immediately. Leaning heavily on his silver-knobbed cane, he looked up at Erik's unsmiling face, met the gaze of two guarded and intense green eyes that stared down at him in obvious displeasure. The journalist was used to people not liking him. He had built his profession on hounding and berating important men. Even on occasion, in spite of his natural tendency to flatter them, a few women had fallen victim to his sharpened pen. He had cultivated a surly demeanor and was not accustomed to having to look away from a subject. Usually those whom he interviewed lowered their eyes, overwhelmed by his perceptive gaze.

Before Ricci could speak, Erik turned his back on the man and set off in the general direction of the Teatro dell'Opera. The journalist cleared his throat and said what he had rehearsed the moment he had seen Costanzi disappear inside the Teatro Regio.

"So rare to see you outside your own domain, Sig. Costanzi."

Erik didn't acknowledge the remark, the undisguised reference to his solitary habits as well as the supposed egotistical disregard of any work that was not his own. All these were, of course, themes that

Ricci had nurtured and exaggerated in his columns on the "masked genius of the opera." Erik continued walking away from Ricci as if he hadn't spoken.

"Scouting for a new talent to replace Il canarino?" Ricci tossed the bait out in a tone that was meant to cut.

Erik pulled up short.

Ricci closed the gap and stood to the side of the masked man. He wished that they might have met in a café or in the office where he wrote his column. Then he might have asked Costanzi to sit. He would not feel now so overwhelmed by the power of the man who was not just taller but somehow exuded a strength that did not lie in size or mass.

"Reports are that Il canarino's singing is not up to its usual splendor."

Ricci disguised his momentary fear when he saw the look in Costanzi's eyes.

"The weather is quite pleasant, is it not, Sig. Ricci?" Erik snarled what should have been an innocuous comment through narrowed lips.

"We all know the close relationship that exists between an artistic director and his diva. Tell me, Don Erik, has your songbird displeased you? Have you chosen a suitable replacement?"

Erik stepped toward Ricci. The journalist felt shoved back even though the man had not touched him. He stumbled slightly but found his footing and stood his ground just beyond the reach of Costanzi's arm.

"Good day, Sig. Ricci," Erik whispered and then, just as a carriage approached, he set off to cross the street. Erik easily reached the other side, but when Ricci went to follow he had to step quickly back to avoid being trampled. The driver cursed him as he pulled at the reins, horses neighing their surprise and annoyance. Looking neither to the side nor behind him, Erik disappeared down the street as if nothing had happened.

Ricci took out his handkerchief and wiped the sweat that had broken out across his forehead and along his upper lip. Only several moments later when his pulse had returned to its normal steady gait did Ricci realize that he had seen more behind the mask than Erik Costanzi had wanted to show.

The crowds were, as usual at the Teatro dell'Opera, thick with patrons and aficionados of the opera last night when the Costanzis premiered their latest extravaganza, a piece steeped in horror and pathos with a score that could only be called strained and forbidding. Forcing the principals and the audience to remain at the veritable pinnacle of emotion for the three and one half hours of the performance, not counting two elaborate intermissions so that the ladies might parade their feathers and jewels along the elegant salons of the palatial theater, Sig. Costanzi insisted on betraying his artists with a score that was technically impossible to realize. Had our Masked Genius of the Opera cast the lovely Il canarino in the role of the heroine, as we all expected and wished, perhaps the evening would have yet been saved in spite of the material. Signora Meg Costanzi surely would have managed the challenge. But piling one mistake upon another, Costanzi sacrificed a wobbly-kneed, thin voiced child, Chiara Greco, in a role that had clearly been meant for the talents of Il canarino alone. The tenor of the company, Grimaldo Tessari, without the support of Signora Costanzi proved lackluster and uninspiring. What should have been an enjoyable experience, a pleasant way to pass the evening, proved exhausting to both the audience and the performers. The Masked Genius of the Opera may wish to write inimitable masterpieces but without his songbird the results are far from melodious. Paolo Ricci

She was tired. She had not recovered fully from the illness she had caught last summer from Raoul and Etienne. The twin boys had both fallen ill at the same time—even in this they were reflections one of the other, inseparable. Erik and Meg had taken turns sitting with them. Meg had exhausted herself tending to each of their children as the fever and fits of coughing raged through the household. Only Erik and Laurette had somehow resisted the illness's assault.

Although the fever had spiked dangerously high in each of the children's cases, the illness itself was spent upon the fourth day and the recovery among the young was remarkably swift. However with Meg, the illness had hung on, keeping her in bed for a fortnight. Erik had never come so close to losing her as he had during those feverish nights. Each night, Erik heard no sound but his wife's hoarse and repeated cough. He counted the silences between, knowing that they were illusions, knowing that the truth was only audible in the rasping and tearing of Meg's throat as she fought against the desperate attempt of her lungs to breathe. Not until one night when he fell into a sleep that was so deep that not even his dreams could find him did he wake the next morning to find her watching over him. She was breathing more easily. She, too, had slept through the night, she informed him. Although still pale, she smiled and for the first time, Erik felt hope.

But although the fever had abated, the tenderness in her chest did not lessen over the course of the next days and weeks. A persistent cough took root in her lungs and punctuated her waking moments. Only when she slept did the percussive bursts of air cease to chip away at her strength. Even so, Erik could not ignore the rattle of phlegm that accompanied her uneasy breathing. When he thought that she would rally, her ongoing weakness seemed to threaten a relapse at any moment.

Since that bout, she had not sung. Erik had insisted that she not strain her voice. They commissioned a run of light operettas to inaugurate the next season. He paid only partial attention to the playbill, uninterested in the mediocre story and music. He passed them to Rinaldo, whose efficient and intelligent direction brought out nuances that Erik had not seen in both the staging and the score.

Then he had convinced himself that Meg was recovered. She, too, insisted that she was well. Having come so close to losing Meg had made him reluctant to leave her side. He had hung on her the rest of the summer, even into the autumn, unable to sequester himself away for the discipline that he required in order to compose. Finally his vigil began to wane. She took her afternoons at the Teatro, preferring, she said, to practice her scales with one of Sig. Bianchi's assistants in the quiet moments before the evening performance.

Erik breathed a sigh of relief to know that the crisis had passed and opened his mind to inspiration, turned his hearing inside to invite the building tumult of notes.

Silence mocked him. So long had he listened to the irregular tide of his wife's breathing that now he heard only its absence. For days he prowled the corridors of the estate in a mood as black as any he'd ever felt. He walked, his boots striking the wood, the marble, the tiles with a dull, sharp, slick insistence. He climbed stairs and stood glaring down the corridors at the servants' closed doors, turned and clambered down to the very heart of the domestic soul of the estate, awash in the sounds of industry, the spray of water, the clatter of pots and pans, the chink of fine crystal, the soft swish of chambray on leather, the multiple voices of those who worked at the estate going about their business, chatting and barking instructions, asking questions. He ignored the sharp intake of air, the sounds of surprise when two women, laundry baskets perched upon their generous hips, stopped, amazed to come face to face with a glowering, self-absorbed man with half a face.

He mumbled excuses, nodded a respectful greeting to Signora Bruno, and tripped loudly up the flight of stairs to the main floor. Finally after several nights of fitful sleep and days of anxious irritation, he heard the first theme dance across his mind, a sweet and lovely sound full of laughter that his fingers twitched to commit to the keyboard and then to paper.

For nearly three weeks, he closeted himself away from everyone— forgetting his family, forgetting his surroundings, forgetting even his own name—while he wrote the score dictated from his inner imagination to his fingers.

It wasn't until he pulled Meg to the piano—barely glancing at her fear-struck face as he handed her the aria—that he had realized that she could no longer sing.

Swinging his arms as his stride lengthened and quickened, Erik walked away from the Teatro Regio. Behind him he imagined Paolo Ricci, frustration darkening his already somber features, cursing after his elusive prey. Erik was vaguely aware that he was passing others as if they were standing still yet he felt no hurry, comfortable with the exertion, needing it to still the rising annoyance that the journalist's probing always goaded. Erik kept to the shadows of the buildings, following the road itself. At some point he would need to change direction if he meant to return this day to the Teatro dell'Opera. His mind was not on his destination but rather had gone back to the past summer, the summer when he had nearly lost her.

CHAPTER 2

Last Summer

And ere a man hath power to say "Behold!"
The jaws of darkness do devour it up:
So quick bright things come to confusion.

                    A Midsummer Night's Dream, William Shakespeare

Last summer...

The twins awoke with a high fever, delirious, sucking at air, unable to breathe for the rattle of congested airways. The doctor had come and left, leaving instructions and concoctions whose names made Erik cringe with superstitious dread. They evoked dank mossy banks, cauldrons, and three weird sisters cackling on the heath. Erik had been pushed aside by the nursemaid and Meg. Madeleine took pity on him and tried to get him to retire and leave the women in charge of the sick room. But Erik could no more easily remove himself from his sons' side than could Meg. Madeleine strained against a granite wall of determination. He scowled and gently but decidedly brushed her hands aside and took his place near Etienne. He stroked the child's forehead, raking the light brown hair from his damp skin while Meg tended, with the nurse's help, to little Raoul.

Later Madeleine would tell him how close they had come to losing one of the twins.

Etienne seemed somehow to have been struck more fiercely by the illness. Lying against a bank of pillows, little Raoul managed to quell his coughing and to fall into a fitful sleep. Unlike his twin, Etienne wheezed so pathetically that his parents feared he'd not be able to breathe at all. As those first hours passed, his condition worsened. Meg and Erik took turns sitting with the child propped up in their arms.

The crisis passed several days later, and Meg wept in Erik's arms the first night the boys were able to sleep through the night without waking in a fit of convulsive coughs, choking and sputtering for air.

But the illness was not ready to admit defeat.

Madeleine was the next to succumb. Within a week of the boys' recuperation, she woke with a tight chest and a cough that had everyone, especially Marcelo, concerned. She made light of it, blaming the dust in the rooms from the open windows and the dryness of the season. Within a few days, in one form or another, the illness marched its way through the household, affecting all but Laurette and Erik.

At the height of the illness, the nursemaid took to her bed, exhausted and feverish, leaving Erik and Meg to attend to their children. In spite of Erik's insistence that Meg, too, should rest—for he had been awoken by her coughing the previous night—she hovered over the older boys, administering medicine, wiping the sweat from their limbs, humming an endless litany of lullabies.

"Meg," Erik whispered, interrupting her children's song. "Come to bed." A few hours. He knew neither of them would be able to sleep more than that.

François turned onto his side, away from the damp rag. His body curled convulsively, his chin dug into his chest as a wave of coughs came and went. Slowly he drifted back to sleep.

"Meg, come," Erik repeated.

"No," she answered, her voice scratchy and stern.

Erik scowled but said nothing for several moments while he watched her. Then he laid his hand over hers and folded it—rag and all—into his grasp. He could see that she meant to resist, but her pallor worried him. He pulled her from the chair at the side of the bed and forced her to her feet. She floated up toward him, a feather caught in a draft, and his heart clenched in fear at her weakness. He could see the struggle against him in the set of her lips, the shadowed eyes under her lowered brow, but there was no strength in her body to back her purpose. She was a ghostly white. A dew of sweat glistened on her forehead, condensed, and ran down from her temple across her cheekbone as if it were a tear.

"No," he growled as he swept her up in his arms and rushed her through the door, down the hallway, to their room. He settled her, reluctant to let her go, on the mattress. "You are not to move from this spot," he demanded in a low rumble of thunder.

But there was no need. She had closed her eyes and now slept. He stood, a stone sentinel beside their bed, watching her breathe, counting as if keeping the beat of a measure. As the sleep deepened, he made out the faint strangled stutter of a wheeze.

Before the first notes had died, Erik was in the hallway, barking orders. No one was about. Half the staff had taken to their beds. The others managed to complete the barest necessary tasks to keep things in order. Madeleine was still ill. Marcelo and she remained sequestered in the opposite wing of the estate. The twins were on the mend and were being attended by a scullery maid who had a strong constitution and an easy manner about her. Erik pounded down the stairs and found one of the servants cleaning the fireplace in the east parlor. He sent him in search of the physician. Then he went to the kitchens and the downstairs rooms where most of the staff worked.

From one of the small offices along a gallery of rooms stepped out a tall, straight-boned matron. As head housekeeper, Signora Bruno managed the tasks behind the scenes and dealt with her staff much the way Erik handled his staff and performers at the Teatro dell'Opera. Like Erik, she was fiercely dedicated to what she did.

"Don Erik?" She could not disguise her concern at the master's obvious disquiet. He rarely came to this section of the house. "Are Masters François and Mario recovering?"

Erik was without his mask. He no longer wore it when at the estate. The servants had grown accustomed to his strange visage and rarely were shocked or disturbed by it. But it was another thing altogether to see him distraught.

Signora Bruno calmed her initial impulse to look away and step back into the relative protection of her office. She forced herself to stand toe to toe with the man who towered a good head above her and to look him in the eyes.

"They're improved," he said, then stared at her in silence for several seconds. "My wife." Here he paused, lips parted, silent.

She understood immediately.

"The doctor has been fetched?"

He still could not muster the words, would not put his dread into form, feared that to say it would make it real. He nodded.

"Mariana and Simonetta, they're young and strong. They've been in and out of the sick room and shown no signs of the illness. I'll send them to tend to the boys and to Donna Meg."

Relieved by Signora Bruno's efficient tone, Erik let out the breath he'd been holding. He recovered his former determination.

"Grazie. I'll return to my wife."

He watched over Meg, only leaving her side on occasion to check on his children. Laurette was miraculously as healthy as ever, somewhat vexed to be abandoned by all. Erik could tell that her petulance was only a protective veneer. The child was frightened to distraction to know that all but she and her father had succumbed to the illness. When Erik told Laurette that her mother had also taken to her bed, the child had cried to be allowed to be with her. But Erik was adamant. He would not risk that Laurette, too, become infected. She would remain safely away from those who were ill.

Unwilling to admit to her weakness, Meg had tried to rise the next morning only to collapse into a fitful sleep laced with delirium. The young servant, Mariana, came and went without Erik's notice. He remained at the bedside, soothing Meg as much as he could with cool compresses, sips of sweetened lemon water, and melodies from written and unwritten scores.

Reluctant to sleep himself, he kept vigil as his wife slept. However even his fear could not keep him from drifting off to sleep on the second night. He sat in the chair next to the bed, his head supported by his arms folded across the bedcover. His head abutted Meg's hip, one hand rested near her thigh. He was dreaming of Diavolo Rosso. The stallion deserved its name for its russet coat and evil disposition.

He was one of a stable of horses that Erik maintained at their island estate, off the eastern coast of Italy. Erik had won the animal's begrudging respect. In his dreams, Erik rode across the sloping meadow that led to an escarpment overlooking the bay below. In his dream, however, the stallion and he never reached the edge of the cliff. They galloped at an impossible clip across an endless sea of verdant, silky grasses. Each hoof gouged the earth and sent clods of dirt spraying in their wake. The sun warmed but the wind cooled, wiping the sweat from their bodies. As the sun dipped behind the horizon, the exhilaration of the ride gave way to urgency. A black shadow spilled across the field engulfing both rider and mount.

The silence in the dream was interrupted by a rasping sound that surrounded Erik. Its origin was uncertain. Wind and sand funneled by gusts from the sea whipped past Erik's face, pebbles tossed and turned against each other in the froth of eddying waters, the sound of his own breathing beat inside his head. Then it struck Erik in his half sleep that he had heard these wet, rustling noises before. His mind filled with dread as he twisted the rope round Buquet's throat. The man scratched at Erik's gloved hands, at the hemp rope, at the fabric of his assassin's vest. As the life was choked from him, Buquet stared up into Erik's cold eyes. The strained, gurgling notes of a dead man were those that now disturbed Erik's dream.

His eyelids twitched as the sound became an alarm that wrenched him from the dream. He opened his eyes and raised his head from the warm coverlet. Diavolo Rosso and the green fields of the island had evaporated leaving only the sensation of urgency and the fatigue of their phantom ride. Yet the sputtering sounds of the dream had not gone with them, but had grown louder.

Meg's chest rose and fell in jerky, rapid tremors unequal to her need to breathe.

Erik was on his feet, bending over his wife, his hands fisted on either side of her shoulders.

"Breathe," he hissed at her, his mouth set in a tight grimace just inches from hers.

Her pallor made her ghostly against the ivory pillow. Her hair lay like a tangled weave of yarn, darkened by perspiration. Erik could see her throat stretch and shudder at her attempt to suck in air. The tightened airways strangled her on both exhalation and inhalation. Her chest rose and fell unevenly in its efforts to expel the stale air and make room for the breath her body craved. He swallowed an involuntary groan and pulled Meg from the pillow into his arms.

"Breathe, damn you! If you've ever obeyed me, do so…do so, now."

He rocked, Meg's head cushioned against his shoulder, holding her up nearly in a sitting position. His ears twitched with each reedy course of air. He felt Meg's hands rise and come to rest on his back. Then she expelled several bone-crushing coughs. Her body convulsed in Erik's arms, but he held her secure in his gentle embrace. After several moments of choking, the violence of the coughs lessened, and Erik moved back to look at his wife.

Her cheeks burned from the force of the seizure; her eyes were wet and bright. She breathed, the sound raspy as it cascaded through congested pathways. But she breathed. He could see that she wanted to say something to ease his anxiety, but the effort was beyond her strength.

"Rest," he said as he eased around behind her on the bed and dragged her back to rest against his chest. It had eased the boys' breathing when they had propped them up in their arms. Lightly she lay back, sheltered by his body, against his beating heart, her damp hair crushed under his chin.

In this position, Meg managed to sleep. Erik felt himself residing somewhere between waking and dreaming, unable to stop listening to the rhythm of her breathing or to avoid seeing Buquet's blue lips and white upturned eyes.

"Papa?"

A hand squeezed his shoulders. Erik had been climbing the endless, spiraling stairs—steps roughly hewn and pocked from years of condensing damp dripping from the cool stone surface above—that led to the hidden fissures between the walls of the Opera Populaire. No matter how fast he took each step, each bend in the stairs—which folded like the coiled rings of a cobra—he was led to another steep ascent disappearing just beyond his vision in yet another curve of the stairwell.

He shook off the fatigue of the dream and raised his head to find that he sat at the piano. The light was diffused, night having barely released its hold to the morning. The discomfort of Erik's position awoke with him, and he bit back a groan as he straightened the aching muscles along his spine.

"What?" he asked, the sound rough and raspy. The momentary disorientation gave way to a sharp goad of anxiety. "Your mother?" he asked as he gripped François's arm.

His son held back a complaint. His father eased his grip, seeing the tight-lipped grimace the boy could not avoid.

"No, Papa. Maman is still asleep. Grand-mère is with her."

Erik released his son and wiped his hands roughly over his face, rubbing to clear his eyes, his palm raking over the stubble of his morning growth of beard. Fortunately, his older children had recovered, as had Madeleine.

"Did Madeleine send you for me? Does she need me?"

"No, she says you're to get some rest."

Erik studied François. Incredibly it seemed as if the boy had grown over the course of the past few days, in spite of the illness, and had suddenly turned into a young man.

"You're taller," Erik said.

François straightened his posture to enhance the effect. "You're sitting down."

"Even so."

Meg had been so young. So young to do what she did. How had she found the courage to risk getting lost in the labyrinth below the Opera Populaire. Hadn't she seen the madness seize him? He had killed. He had dropped Buquet's worthless body from the flies to the stage below while she and the others danced a bucolic round. She had known how obsessed he had become with Christine. She had witnessed him drag Christine from the stage to the underworld below. Surely she must have guessed what he meant to do. She had seen his blatant desire. She had seen the consequences of his rage and determination. He had unleashed the chandelier without regard for those trapped below, those unfortunate enough not to avoid the weight of metal and broken glass. So young.

Erik turned away from his son to mask the sudden rise of tears to his eyes. She might have died. She might yet die. He could not shake the fear.

"Papa?"

"I only left for a moment. I guess I dozed off."

He had risen and found her calm. His muscles were knotted. He had thought to walk about to ease his cramped muscles. He had alerted the servant Mariana to his departure, had expected her to sit vigil for only the few minutes of respite he had needed. Erik rubbed his hand over the dark varnished surface of the piano as if it were a sentient being.

"Is Maman going to come down today?"

Erik heard the anxiety in his son's question. François wondered how grave his mother's condition was. Erik considered lying. Was that not what parents did? Did they not protect and reassure their children in the face of possible pain and sorrow? But he could not lie.

"She...managed to fall asleep last night. That's why I came down. I didn't expect to stay away for more than a few minutes." What if Mariana had fallen asleep? What if Meg had needed him?

François frowned. He was used to his father being more direct. It was not like him to avoid the question.

At that moment, Mario rushed inside the room.

"Papa, something's wrong. It's...."

Not waiting for Mario to finish his sentence, Erik pushed away from the piano, brushed past both boys, and ran to the stairs. Taking the steps two at a time, he climbed to the second floor. He jerked open the door to his and Meg's chamber. The sight of Madeleine holding a shuddering body in her arms struck him speechless. The older woman's crying sucked the air from the room, and Erik felt the world tilt. He might have slid from the room into a gaping abyss at the edge of consciousness had he not realized that to give in to the vertigo would be to let Meg die.

He found his bearings and in two steps had reached the bed. Without a word or glance at Madeleine, he wrenched Meg from her mother's grasp. He ignored Madeleine's anguished pleas. Holding Meg's twitching body in his arms, he carried her down the stairs to the grand hallway. For one moment he stood indecisive. Her eyes had rolled back inside her head, leaving only the white half moons visible. Waves of heat beat against his face, rising from his wife's fevered skin. Then he decided.

He went to the back of the building and down the stairs, shoving past frightened maids, kitchen staff, ignoring the startled cry of Cook who stood in the kitchen doorway, wiping her large hands on the stained apron. She stepped aside in time for him to enter the warm enclosure of the kitchen. It was aglow with breakfast fires. The heat rising from coals and braziers trapped inside the room competed with the fever that he held against his chest. Then down the narrow stairwell at the corner of the kitchen to the dark cellars below.

"Light!" he growled. As he felt blindly for each step, a taper blazed behind him. Its light was sufficient to see the rows of carafes and bottles lining the far wall. At the back of the cool, underground room were vats of wine in various stages of preparation. He laid Meg gently on the cold stone floor, took a metal strip left for the purpose, and wedged open the rounded lid of the nearest barrel. Inside the dark purple liquid churned and frothed from Erik's agitation. He dipped his fingers into coolness. Satisfied, he lifted Meg and slid her over the lip of the vat and submerged her in the cool wine up to her neck. Her blond hair darkened and threaded into cobwebs across the surface. His arm up to his shoulder had disappeared in the liquid, bracing her, keeping only her face above the wine.

The smell of grapes and tannin filled his nostrils bringing tears to his eyes. The purple spray stained Meg's cheeks with a bluish tinge that quickened Erik's pulse as it brought to mind the deep pallor of a corpse. The heat fused with the coolness of the wine and within moments the jerking of Meg's muscles stuttered to an end. She floated calm, still, too still in Erik's arms. He was muttering words over and over that he hadn't realized that he was saying out loud—her name over and over, words of love, words pleading for pity, curses demanding the recovery of the only person without whom he could not, would not live. He kept up this litany as he watched her features soften, her lips part. The constant sound of his chant disguised the hiss of her breathing. Then her eyelids fluttered, fluttered and stilled, and then finally opened. It took a second for her eyes to focus. When they did, they fixed on him.

She smiled.

"Meg?" he dared to whisper.

Then she curled in his embrace and coughed. He held her tightly to keep her from slipping farther into the vat. Then he lifted her drenched in wine from the barrel and sat on the stone floor holding her, cool and aromatic, until the coughing lessened and she seemed to rest.

The next several nights Meg flowed in and out of feverish dreams. Erik refused to leave her side for more than a few moments. Not even Marcelo could convince him to allow Mariana or Simonetta to take charge of Meg. In a chair so close to the bed that he could drape his arm over Meg's hip or rest his head beside her, Erik kept vigil and slept only fitfully. The least tremor, the softest convulsion of a cough, crawled up his limb and woke him until he was so exhausted that the modest, almost regular, bursts of air lulled him into a half-sleep.

Madeleine, thinned and washed out after her own bout with the illness, stood vigil with him for several long hours in the day. She encouraged him to sleep more deeply while she was on watch, but she could not convince him to lie down in the next room on the cot that she had instructed be set up. At times Madeleine accompanied him for several hours into the night. They barely spoke, but when they did it was about Meg.

Madeleine tried to distract him from Meg's illness, the catalog of her symptoms, the reading of her pulse and color. She spoke instead of Meg's childhood.

"She thought you were a dragon, you know." Madeleine let out a series of sounds that could only be called a giggle. Erik chuckled in spite of his anxiety and exhaustion to hear such an unguarded reminder of the girl Madeleine had been when she rescued him from the cage.

She smiled, her eyes warm and tranquil. The moment stretched out between them, and Erik felt time slip backwards. She reached out her hand, at first hesitantly. When he did not move away, she smoothed the hair that had fallen across his forehead. As she stroked his hair, she studied his face. The hair that had partially covered the uneven and reddened skin of his face lay against his scalp, and Erik remained unmasked and naked under her steady gaze.

"A dragon," she said, her tone rueful. "Can you imagine?"

Erik smiled and took her hand and kissed it gently along the fingers.

"And what gave her that idea?" he asked.

"Oh, who knows where she got such ideas! She had a vivid imagination, was always rifling through my things, poking her nose into corners of the opera house. I lost her once. For more than an hour I searched frantically until I found her standing in front of the wardrobe in the room she shared with Christine."

Erik stiffened in his chair. Madeleine couldn't help but notice. "What?"

"What was she doing?"

"Well, first of all she was talking to it."

"What was she saying?" Erik urged her to answer, and Madeleine guessed at the cause of his curiosity.

"That was one of your portals, wasn't it?"

He nodded. "She must have heard me one night."

"Singing to Christine, no doubt?"

He nodded again.

"Well," Madeleine continued her story. "She had taken all the clothes and dumped them on the bed. She didn't hear me come in. She stood, feet splayed, talking in a most angry tone of voice to the inside back panel of the wardrobe. I couldn't make out the words, but the emotion was clear enough. Then she reached in and felt all about the space."

"Looking for the lever."

Madeleine's smile grew. "Yes, I'm sure."

"She didn't find it."

"No, she didn't." Madeleine sighed and turned to look at Meg's white face. "She was so determined," she whispered as if to herself.

"She...she...can be stubborn." Erik squeezed Madeleine's hand, bringing her attention back to him. In a voice meant to reassure, he added, "She'll fight this off."

"Yes. She will."

Madeleine and Erik were quiet for some time.

"Was she afraid of the dragon?"

Erik's question startled her. They had been quiet for so long that Madeleine had lost track of time and place. She had been lulled by the respite in which Meg slept.

"Afraid? I don't think so. She had heard you in the vaults. I'm sure that she followed me on more than one occasion when I came to leave supplies for you. She knew better than to let me see her, so she hung back." Madeleine chewed her lower lip and hesitated to confess that she had perhaps been wrong to keep her daughter so in the dark as to Erik's presence. "I told her stories...to keep her from... coming down the stairs and exploring the underground vaults."

Erik could sense Madeleine's uneasiness. "You were only trying to protect her."

"Not just her," she added. "I was also trying to protect you."

"I can see that."

"She was just a child. It was impossible to tell her and expect her to keep quiet. She would not have meant to cause harm, but she would have. They would have gone to find you."

Erik sighed. It was true. Hadn't Madeleine and he done the best they could to create the Opera Ghost? Several mishaps—mostly harmless—had given rise to rumors about a ghost that haunted the dark corners of the Opera Populaire. Those who knew of the underground vaults, the series of stone staircases that wound their way down to the black waters of the subterranean lake, spoke of the cadaverous thing that lay at the bottom of those waters and that dragged its soggy dead flesh up those stairs to walk among them. Fear of discovery had kept Erik hidden, a prisoner, and fear of the Opera Ghost had also protected him, keeping the idle curious from venturing down into the depths where he made his home.

"So she *was* afraid of me," he said only to encourage Madeleine to talk. It was less frightening to hold vigil over his sick wife when Madeleine spoke of the bright and curious child Meg had been.

"Afraid? No, you don't understand. I had done what I could to caution her away from your hiding place, but she was no fool. She knew I visited you. So she knew you couldn't be that dangerous. But she couldn't ask me about you without revealing that she had disobeyed me. She reasoned you were not an evil monster or a vengeful ghost. Instead she made you a dragon."

Erik looked questioningly at Madeleine and waited for her to explain.

"You see she had read these stories about dragons. The book had beautiful illustrations of the beasts—all glittering green, red, purple, and gold with long sinuous necks and spiked tails, huge wings that unfurled and filled the pages with the kind of graceful delicacy that butterflies have, dark and intelligent eyes. They were majestic."

"I see," Erik smiled, his lips twisted up in the corner.

"Yes, they were beautiful. Like you."

Erik lowered his eyes, but he did not turn away.

"She said to me one night that she had heard the dragon moving about in the tunnels and behind the walls."

They both knew how the deep cavernous spaces amplified noises and played tricks on one. Sound echoed against the stone walls and off the surface of the lake, making it impossible to know its source or direction.

"When I asked her what she meant by the dragon, she went on to tell me that I must have found the entrance to a cave beyond the vaults and that there I found the dragon prince. I couldn't think what to say to her. She didn't ask, she told me. She described you down to the number of shiny scales along your flanks and the fact that when you breathed your flame ran blue and cold. Only when you were angry or trying to protect yourself did you breathe true fire, and then it was bright orange and red. She said that you were a prince and that you shifted forms. At times you were human, but at other times you had to resume your dragon form."

Madeleine stopped, her lips pursed shut. For a moment, Erik thought she was about to cry. Tears welled up in her eyes, but she saw his concern and smiled. In a small, high voice, she explained,

"She told me it was our secret. That it was our destiny to protect the dragon king because he was the last of a mighty race. 'After he goes,' she said to me, 'there will be no more magic in the world.'"

Meg wrestled with the blanket, shifted, and twisted in an effort to turn onto her side. Erik brushed her hair from her forehead and soothed her with his deep rumble of sounds meant to comfort, senseless sounds, like notes, like melodies. She smiled and cleared her throat. Then she opened her eyes and spoke to him for the first time in four days.

"Why aren't you in bed?"

Erik felt his lips tremble as they tried to form a smile. Then he doubled over the edge of the mattress, his head buried against her soft upturned palm and wept. He cried unchecked in great bursts of painful sobs as he hadn't done for years. Meg rested her other hand lightly on the back of his head and stroked him, smoothing the dark hair that curled over the rim of his collar, stilling the jerky spasm of the intense emotions he could no longer beat down.

When the violence of the reaction eased, Erik wiped his face with the bed cover. He gulped against a tender knot at the base of his throat, and looked into Meg's soft brown eyes. They were glistening and tender with such concern for him—concern and love.

"I thought," he whispered, but he couldn't go on. His throat tightened even now against saying what he had feared would happen. He bit the inside of his lower lip to refrain from a new burst of sobs that threatened to overtake him. Instead he gained control enough to ask, "Are you hungry?"

She muffled a cough and nodded. The sudden inhalation of air was cold and teased the sensitive tissues inside her lungs and throat. She consciously regulated her intake of air, fought the impulse to cough, and asked for water.

CHAPTER 3

Ballet Slippers

he forced the air from her body, her soul rose through that gasp and begged him to trap it, to keep it forever in a gilded cage, in a scarlet prison, the scarlet prison of his heart, and she sang and just a brief moment she forgot him, her prison, her iron dwelling, her crimson love, and he was gone

Phantom Death, Sadie Montgomery

The manager had worked a minor miracle to secure a private box for the eccentric composer, Erik Costanzi, and his wife, Il canarino. The trouble had been worth it. So rarely did Sig. Costanzi appear in public that it would soon be the talk of the town that the performance at the Teatro Regio had captured the interest of the masked genius himself. The next day, Sig. Rossi was sure the remaining seats for the season would quickly disappear. He stored away in the back of his mind a note to speak with the director of the ballet about an extension of several weeks. The profit should far outweigh any cost or inconvenience.

Moments before the performance, the Costanzi coach drew up before the entrance and the striking figure of a tall, elegant man stepped out amid the crowds. The manager had anxiously awaited Sig. Costanzi's arrival, thinking to escort him and the lovely chanteuse to their special box for the performance.

Erik Costanzi stood nearly a head above most men in the

crowd, but that was only one of the reasons for the agitation. He did nothing to attract their attention. Indeed he stood with a stillness that was nearly preternatural. An ivory mask framed his green eyes, drawing them out as if everything he was might be seen therein if only one understood how to read them. He glanced at the men and women who had gathered just outside the theater doors, surveying them with serious, unblinking eyes. Several moments passed as he inspected the crowd, took the measure of each soul, its perfidies and its treasures. Then in one fluid movement he turned toward the dark interior of the carriage, his gloved hand raised. A white flutter of fingers perched on the dark harbor and from within emerged Il canarino. The previous cautious attention of the crowd was overwhelmed by spontaneous applause as the diva, Signora Meg Costanzi, alighted from the coach. Her dark companion folded her arm inside his own and without regard to the reception afforded his wife led her up the steps to the grand entrance.

Many in the audience had come to see and be seen. The performance itself was a mere backdrop at best or an annoyance at worst for the swaggering youths, the bored and complacent gentlemen and their ladies, the dashing bachelors who attended functions of this sort as a sign of their rising importance in society. The music barely drowned out the twittering sound of hundreds of mouths whispering endlessly, asking questions not aimed at the truth but at the bizarre and the scandalous. Eventually as the lights dimmed and the performance itself began—always with a stunning extravaganza of color and spectacle—in an effort to compete with the audience's own self-important dramas, the voices would quiet.

Erik had felt the curious stares, heard fragments of conversation in which the spectators had conjectured about his mask, about his face, about the beautiful woman trapped beside him. Yes, he could imagine the thoughts and whispers, the story they would construct about the cruel tyrant, a man who wore a mask to hide an evil, twisted countenance. How had such a man carried off a woman as beautiful, as graceful, and as talented as Meg Costanzi? What horrible pact had the young woman's family made with a faceless demon? He could imagine the dowagers as they wondered about the private moments, the songbird locked away in the darkness as the disfigured man grasped her in his lecherous embrace. Did they leave one candle lit or did they only touch in the dark so that she could be saved seeing his face so intimately close to her own?

Erik tried to hide the sneer the truth brought to his lips. The truth was beyond their small imaginations. They could not know how soft Meg's hands were as they took possession of his body, awakening and guiding it, as they swept across his skin, as they stroked and caressed. They would be scandalized and bewildered to think that she left warm, hot kisses across the tender flesh masked in ivory against the invasion of strangers' curiosity. They would perhaps refuse to believe that Meg's eyes were moist and bright with desire as she stared up into his face—yes, his face that was only partially a face. Had they known the power with which she pulled him to her, the fierceness in those tiny fingers, the hunger in those lips, they would not credit it.

Erik could not stop them from wondering, but he would not let their impertinent stares deter him. He had not come to parade his wealth or to beg their approval. On his arm was Meg, and he could feel her excitement in the gentle rhythm of her hand on his coat. Too long had she lived hemmed in by his reluctance to be seen outside the protective spell of the opera house. She hummed. She glowed golden with light, iridescent. Before them the crowd parted, stepped to the side to allow them to pass. He glanced at the marble columns, the thick brocade hangings, the regal staircase that he now ascended with Meg by his side. He could see her pulse quicken in the rapid rise and fall of her bosom, sensed her pleasure in the warmth along his palm where her one hand now rested. For he had removed his gloves and was leading her up the marble staircase that would take them to the box seats from which they could admire the crowds and anticipate the performance.

His eyes trained on their destination, Erik only vaguely felt the rearrangement of bodies behind him, barely sensed the tension, the rush of movement just seconds before the man's voice reached his ears.

Meg pulled at Erik's sleeve, anything to intercede between him and the insolent and stubborn journalist, Paolo Ricci.

"Erik," she whispered at his elbow, aware that for both men she was an abstraction.

Not now. Not here, she thought as she stood staring up at the green fire that had caught in her husband's eyes. If only Paolo Ricci would stand down. He stood too close, and Meg felt Erik's instinctive reaction. If only the intruder would turn and walk away, everything might yet be all right. Her fingers on Erik's sleeve felt the muscles, taut and thick under the elegant weave of the fabric, prepare for exertion. From his grim expression to the tension along his back, Meg could tell that Erik was restraining his impulse to rip Ricci limb from limb.

Oblivious to the nature of the man that he was baiting, Ricci smirked, gesticulated, and persisted in berating Erik for his sullen refusal to grant him an interview. The curtain would rise in ten minutes. Meg kept a firm hold of Erik's arm, knowing that as long as she did so he would control himself. She wondered if Ricci had any idea how dangerous his intrusion was. Did he realize that had he met Erik under other circumstances and approached him so rudely Erik might well have throttled him? Yet in spite of the ominous tension Meg wondered if that were true.

Was it only her presence that restrained the violent tendencies that still lay somewhere under the surface in Erik? She put aside the thought to examine at another time. She selfishly understood that she cared little about what Erik might do to Ricci. At this moment all she could think of was how much she longed to reach the safety of the box seats. She wanted nothing more than to take her seat and prepare herself for the performance itself. She had had little chance to see professional ballet. Work consumed much of her time. And then there was Erik's reluctance to attend public events where the crowds would be large, filled with strangers. He had never suggested that she could not attend events on her own, but it had not occurred to Meg to go without him.

She sighed and listened as Ricci spouted false praise, taking away with one hand what he gave with the other. When Ricci's gaze switched to take her in, unsettled she looked away. But the man would not be ignored.

"Signora Costanzi, surely you have no objection to…"

Erik's arm jerked forward under Meg's hand, but she moved quickly and stepped between the two men.

"Sig. Ricci, they have called the curtain twice. Let us assume our seats, shall we? It was a pleasure to see you again." Meg pivoted on her heel to come up against the solid barrier of her husband's chest.

Erik stared at Ricci, but Meg's upturned face drew his eyes down to hers. Silently she grimaced at him in an effort to move him along. For one second, she thought he'd push her to the side and grapple Ricci to the floor. She could imagine Erik's hands clasped like iron around the other man's throat. Ricci had not given up. But Erik must have understood her attempt to deflect the potential violence. He turned, folded Meg's arm over his own, and led her briskly down the corridor to their assigned seats.

Ricci, for once, understood and did not follow.

Ostensibly, as if nothing had happened, Erik led Meg to the foremost seat, arranged the skirts of her gown, and drew his own seat close beside hers. He sat stiffly for several moments until his anger subsided. Then slowly he relaxed against the plush velvet cushions, letting himself be seduced by the sheer pleasure of the sensations around him. He glided his hand across the smoothed, polished oak of the arm rests, leaned against the firm support of the embroidered chair back, stretched his right leg slightly forward across the thick woven pile of the carpet, and took in the vast auditorium before him. The tenuous light within the small alcove lay across his shoulders like a warm blanket, and he felt invisible and safe, soothed by the growing anticipation of the music and spectacle to come. Then he felt Meg's hand on his knee. He glanced at her to find her attention fixed on the stage. The lights below dimmed and were extinguished as the heavy pleats of the curtain were gathered and pulled aside. A collective gasp of delight sent a shiver of awe up Erik's spine, all thought of Ricci gone, as the music rumbled through the dark vaults and the ballet began.

The glitter of tiny arabesques spun across the stage, trapped in Meg's memory and enhanced by her imagination. Her muscles twitched with the sympathetic response to each glorious movement of the past performance. She felt as if she, too, had danced this evening. She moved about the room, her mind wrapped in chiffon and silk, rubbing a lightly scented cream into her hands, along her elbows, then in wide strips up from her feet to her thighs. Her skin tingled from the coolness of the deft touch of her hands. Behind her, she heard the rustle of clothing as Erik prepared for bed.

He had been quiet in the coach as they wound their way home. She prattled on about the grace and stamina that certain movements—poses and pirouettes—required, remarked in particular on the talent and panache of the leading ballerina. Erik smiled and listened. Only when she had touched upon the music had he spoken at any length. Had he enjoyed the ballet? she had asked at last, concerned that his silence was a sign of his disapproval or the effect of a lingering annoyance from Ricci's intrusion earlier that evening. Instead of answering, he had asked her if she regretted that it wasn't she who danced upon that stage or another in this ballet or its kind, in Paris, perhaps, if not here in Rome.

Her rush to assure him had not convinced him. She had stared into the reflected glimmer of a streetlight in his eyes. The coach was dark, but she could see just the faintest hint of green as the light waned and glowed as they passed along the streets. He watched her, and she knew what he was thinking.

Although the hour was late, Erik reached out to her when she doused the light. His hand slid inside the opening of her bedclothes, peeling them away from her shoulders. His mouth, hot and moist, lingered at the base of her neck, trailed to the gentle spirals of her ear, and found its way to her lips. She felt his hand, large and broad, spread across her naked back, resting low at the base of her spine, in the hollow just at the rise of her buttocks. The other dipped lower, cupping her, cuddling her to his fevered flesh. Then, as the remembered music of the evening built, she was lifted by strong, agile arms and raised into the air, a moment of sheer beauty, suspended between heaven and earth. Her fingers stroked his face, teased the corner of his mouth even as he deepened his kisses and tasted her tongue, her palate, grazed across her teeth, washed the tender inside of her lips. She came to rest across his hardened muscles. Her thighs spread to either side of his hips, a yearning pull of sinews and tendons, a softened opening of warm lips over the length of his arousal. She stretched and opened and took him inside her. She gasped at the completeness as he filled her. They glided together, moving and pulsing to a silent score played in the deep recesses of their entwined soul.

Later she drowsily kissed the edge of his jaw, her tongue rasping across the prick of his stubble. She felt him drifting in and out of sleep. Pushing herself up along his body, bringing her mouth to his ear, she whispered that she loved him. If she could live it over again, she would not change a single moment. She would still have gone in search of him, brazen and fearful, innocent and naughty. She would still have bowed to his demands as her teacher. She did not regret all those roads, those decisions, and the painful missteps as well as the fortuitous ones, that had led to this moment.

But Erik's breath came in slow, even sighs. Already she saw dreams take hold of him, a flutter of movement just beneath his eyelids.

No, she would not regret her choices. She would not regret what they had—even though it was all slipping away.

Patrons and aficionados of the opera will be relieved to know that Il canarino yet lives. My own eyes attest the fact. The enigmatic Masked Genius of the Opera released his songbird from the gilded Teatro dell'Opera and allowed her a modest excursion to the Teatro Regio last night. There the composer and Signora Meg Costanzi, his wife and cantante, attended the premiere of the Russian Ballet, choreographed by the famous Lev Ivanovich Ivanov. Needless to say, the performance was a unique delight. However, the presence of the Costanzis was such an unusual event that it quite distracted your humble servant. I made every effort to approach the darling of the Teatro dell'Opera to ask the question that is most present in all our minds, "When will you once more sing for your adoring public?" Except for the jealous vigilance of her husband, Signora Costanzi, always generous, seemed willing to speak. Our question might better be revised to ask our Masked Genius when he intends to allow Il canarino once more to perform. For until Il canarino sings, the mediocre works at the Teatro dell'Opera shall certainly not soar. Paolo Ricci

Erik led Meg to the piano and handed her the score. The aria was complete. He had worked on it for days, ever since he watched her enthralled by the music and movement of the Russian Ballet. It was in her key, and he felt sure that she would love it. The ghostly echo of a Slavic folk song played at its foundation.

Meg studied the sheet music that Erik had crammed into her grasp. He had not given her a chance to object or explain. Her brow shadowed her darkened eyes, her lips disappeared in a tight grimace. Frustration rippled off her skin like heat.

Apparently unaware of her reaction, Erik sat at the keyboard and ran his fingers over the first notes.

"The orchestra leads into the first measures, the one giving way to the other. After the last note of the overture, you open a capella. But there is a pause before the cavatina." Erik played allegro the last several bars of the overture, his fingers having already committed the music of the sinfonia to memory. Then he slowed the rhythm until his fingers came to a rest. The last note lingered waiting for Meg to pick it up and begin the first half of the double aria Erik had composed. But Meg did not begin. The note dissipated existing only vaguely in their memory.

Erik looked up at his wife and wished that he hadn't.

"It's a simple piece, Meg, meant to be sung legato. I admit that it lacks coloratura, but it's...beautiful. Almost a lullaby." He searched her eyes, hoping the anguish he discerned would abate.

Meg laid the papers on the smooth polished surface of the piano. Her voice rose barely above a whisper. "It's lovely." Then more forcefully, she added, "You should have Chiara sing it. She'll love it." She stepped back from the piano, her eyes studiously avoiding his.

"I don't want Chiara Greco to sing it. I want..."

"She has a lovely voice."

"It will come..."

"Yes, I'm sure after her instruction with you, she'll..."

"Meg, I swear, it will come back. Your voice..."

"She has already improved under Rinaldo's coaching. When you..."

"I've no intention of instructing her." His voice had deepened, ominous and thick. He had meant to remain calm, to cajole her tenderly back to the music. But her constant deflection of the issue unnerved him.

"And why not?"

Erik stared incredulous at the question, her tone of challenge.

"You trained me, did you not? Before me, you instructed Christine. What is so different about taking Chiara on as a pupil?"

"You can't be serious."

"Why not?" Meg's voice had risen slightly in volume. Erik could not understand the emotion evident in her insistence. "She's young. You picked her out yourself, said she was exceptional, that she has an unusual gift that only needs to be brought out by the right teacher."

"She is. She does. But I am not that teacher."

"You did it before. You can certainly do it again."

She was baiting him. He could not understand why she would urge him to take Chiara on as a pupil. That in and of itself was not unreasonable. But Meg's reference to the time he had spent training Christine and subsequently herself was laced with a biting undercurrent of accusation. She taunted him, he knew not why. He had done more than instruct Christine. Their souls had woven themselves together. He had not been able to discern how she could exist beyond his will or he without her presence. The parting had nearly destroyed him. The wound was still bleeding when Meg forced herself into his life. The months that had followed had been excruciating. Then at some point—he could not know when—he had found himself calmed and soothed in Meg's presence. He had begun to hear her voice instead of Christine's, echoing the latest aria that he had taught her. Afraid, he had resisted, but Meg had burrowed deeply into the open wound, weaving herself into the scar tissue, impossible to extricate without ripping his very soul from his body.

Softly he finally answered, "I can't."

"Is it so easy for you to imagine falling in love with her?"

"Don't!" He rose to his full height and faced her. "What are you doing?"

Meg tilted her chin up and stared into his somber eyes, the green so dark, so rich, so compelling. The young girl would inevitably fall under his spell, whether or not he wished it. He was a force impossible to resist. Even Christine had fallen under his spell for a time.

"The aria is lovely, Erik. It is perfect for Chiara. You'll see."

Erik gathered the staff papers in one fist, wrinkling them carelessly. Without a word he went to the fireplace and threw the sheets into the flames. He did not hear Meg gasp for the crackling roar as the papers caught and burned.

"I wrote it for you, Meg."

Meg ran from the room. Her skin burned as if she, instead of the aria, had fallen into the flames. She choked back her tears. Still she could see him, his hand firmly latched onto the edge of the mantel, his knuckles hard and white with the pressure, his back a massive wall, his head tilted forward as he watched the bright orange and red flames surge and engulf the carefully drawn notes. His music. He had thrown it away.

She felt her throat strain in memory of the melody she had read in the few moments before she had left it, abandoned, on the fine polished surface of the piano. She let it play in her mind, her throat muscles mimicked the rise and fall of the melody. Silently she sang what she could recall. If only she could transcribe it to paper, to rescue it, to resurrect it from the ashes. The details had already blurred, and she began again at the beginning, half recalling, half guessing the path Erik would take. She knew his music well. She knew the sounds that pleased him, but she could not second guess him. The aria was like and yet different from other pieces he had composed.

She insisted. She closed her eyes, feeling the wetness of tears seep along the sealed rims, never gaining the momentum or weight to run unchecked down the plane of her cheeks. Blind she saw the sounds like steps, a staircase, winding paths leading forward, tracing back, breaking off to resume two steps higher just around the bend. She followed, danced, sang silently, the notes leading her, carrying her along. Such lovely sounds those that she had fortunately read and stored before so foolishly she had sacrificed them. Her throat constricted, her breath caught, and she felt the convulsive clutch of a cough. The path came to an abrupt end. Before her darkness and silence. Somewhere inside that darkness and silence lay Erik wounded and betrayed.

She covered her face with both hands and fought back the tears and the choking sensation that even now threatened to take hold of her.

CHAPTER 4

Il cuculo

Lord, what fools these mortals be!

A Midsummer Night's Dream, William Shakespeare

Carlotta Venedetti folded her arms under her ample breasts and stared at Rinaldo's back. Such a wonderful back, too, she thought as she gritted her teeth and watched him coach the dark-haired soprano that the Phantom had put on the stage in Mig-Mag's place. Erik Costanzi himself had coaxed her away from a smaller company to replace his wife. It was only temporary. No one was sure why Meg Costanzi had, at least for the present, withdrawn from the stage. Carlotta was thrilled when Erik announced that Meg was taking a hiatus from performance. But before she could step forward and generously accept the position of lead soprano, the awful man had presented Chiara Greco to the company. It little pleased Carlotta that Greco's performances were less than satisfactory. For Erik had insisted that the girl required special guidance from Rinaldo. Carlotta muttered sotto voce as Rinaldo and Greco rehearsed, heads together over the same sheet of music, the more difficult aspects of the first aria. Carlotta did not like Chiara Greco. Why would she? She disliked Chiara Greco even more than she had ever disliked

Meg. And she disliked her more with every note the younger cantante sang.

"Impossible." Carlotta hissed and swiveled to find Erik Costanzi in close consultation with the maestro, Sig. Bianchi, near the pit.

Although she had not meant to speak out loud, the man had sharp ears. Erik glanced over at her at that moment and scowled. That was nothing new for Carlotta. She saw Erik scowl more often than not. Having caught his attention, she marched over to where he stood and stepped between him and a surprised and slightly offended Sig. Bianchi.

"She's too fat."

Erik stared unblinkingly at Carlotta. Even though he wore a mask, Carlotta had the distinct impression that he had arched one sarcastic eyebrow over his left eye.

When he didn't respond, Carlotta jabbed her finger in the general direction of the new soprano. "Her!"

Erik's gaze followed Carlotta's finger to come to rest on Rinaldo and Chiara at the very moment when Rinaldo must have said something humorous. In the middle of a measure, Chiara burst out laughing in perfect pitch as if it were part of the aria itself.

"Nonsense." Erik stepped slightly to the side to resume his discussion with the maestro.

"Fat! Fat! Fat! The costume she will not fit."

"I didn't realize that you were now working in the wardrobe, Signorina Venedetti." Erik pointed to the key signature and was about to say something to the maestro when Carlotta once more interposed herself between the two men.

"Always the jokes with you."

Sig. Bianchi looked as surprised as Erik.

"She sings like a cow. She moos. Her voice it disappears. Only dogs can hear her!"

"Signorina, I have work to do with the maestro. Since your feelings on this matter are so strong, perhaps you might wish to help coach Signorina Greco. However, I believe Rinaldo is doing a competent job correcting the few weaknesses Signorina Greco has."

Carlotta made a sound that expressed perfectly her displeasure and doubt. "The other one should come back."

"Other one?"

"Her. You know. Her. The wife." Carlotta ignored the half smile that teased at the corner of Erik's mouth. "These operettas are not interesting. They are like feathers, too light. They make me sneeze. When are you going to write an opera? Why is Meg not here instead of that fat cow?"

"Temper, temper, Carlotta," whispered Erik. He glanced at Chiara and Rinaldo who fortunately were far enough away not to pick up Carlotta's words over the accompaniment of the piano. "Chiara Greco is charming and talented. She lacks a bit of training. And she is quite attractive."

"You have not answered the question. Is this not so? You think that I will forget what I have asked you because of the foolish things you have said about the...cow?"

"I've no intention of answering your question. I'm the artistic director. You are a member of the company."

It wasn't as if the Phantom did not remind her weekly, nearly daily, that he was in charge and that she was supposed to obey him. But there was an ominous undercurrent she picked up in Erik's tone that suggested that their conversation was at an end. Even so, Carlotta was used to ignoring warnings, even those made by the Phantom.

At that moment she saw Erik's eyes dart toward the back of the stage where Meg Costanzi stood among the dancers, speaking animatedly with several of the older women.

"She is here every day, yet she does not sing." She had meant to go on and give the director the benefit of her opinion except that when she looked back at the Phantom's eyes there in the green depths she glimpsed something that she had not seen for some time.

The moment Erik realized Carlotta stood slack-jawed staring up at him, he tore his gaze from Meg and trained his eyes on the sheet of music that he still held.

"She...my wife has requested a brief hiatus from the stage. That doesn't mean that she has lost all interest in the company."

"She was, after all, a silly little dancer when you switched your attentions to her, was she not?"

Erik closed his eyes as he pressed the white half mask tightly against his face. His voice was a low rumble behind his hand. "Carlotta, please, could you, for once, control yourself?"

"Humph. What did I say?!"

"I need your support." His voice was quiet and without inflection in spite of the unusual admission.

"When have I ever been anything but supportive? I smile. Everyone appreciates my presence. I fill the auditorium with my…"

"Yes, I'm sure," he interrupted. "Please keep your distance from Meg. And give Signorina Greco the benefit of the doubt."

"Doubt? What doubt?"

"Carlotta, just…" Erik pushed his lips shut, bowed his head slightly in sign of departure, and left Carlotta alone on the stage.

"What? What is that? We were talking," she complained to Sig. Bianchi. But the maestro had long ago retreated to the safety of his pit. "Humph!"

Erik had stepped out the side door of the theater into the shaded protection of the alleyway. He had needed to get away for a few moments. Even in the wings, he could hear Carlotta's voice, and it would not have surprised him had she followed him through the labyrinth of the theater, reciting her litany of demands and complaints. He stood, his masked face turned up toward the low-hanging sun, eyes closed, and wished he could feel the warmth against his skin. There was no one in the narrow space between the buildings. He was well back from the public street, the sidewalk. He reached up and hooked his finger under the edge of his half mask and removed it. At any moment someone—a performer or one of the staff—might come rushing out the same door. *Let them come.* Erik contented himself with the feel of the sun on his face and the gradual spreading of warmth throughout his body.

Carlotta was mistaken about Chiara Greco. The woman was lovely. She had a decent voice, untapped talent, and surely she was aware of her good fortune. She had been given an opportunity to sing with the premier company of Rome. Milan may well surpass Rome as the center of opera, but Erik had made the company at the

Teatro dell'Opera the rival of any and all the best houses in Milan, Rome, or Paris. He was justifiably proud of his achievement. He was also aware that, without Meg, the company was severely weakened.

Signorina Greco was young. She had potential, but she needed to be trained—trained by an implacable master. Rinaldo was not that master. He was too kind; he lacked cruelty. Erik knew kindness did not push one's student past what was possible, what was…natural. It took pain, the ability to work through obstacles, to touch the truly extraordinary, to reach the truly sublime.

What Chiara Greco needed was for Erik to take her on as a pupil. But although he convinced her to join his company with every thought to shape her into the singer, the artist he had glimpsed in her, once he found her on his stage he knew he did not have the energy or the interest to commit himself to the work that would be required to transform a competent singer into a sublime artist. He had done it twice in his lifetime, and to a lesser degree he had sweated blood to whip Carlotta into shape. He wasn't sure that he could ever expose himself again to such an intense relationship. For the experience had changed both him and his pupils. He would not risk his soul again, not for Chiara Greco.

Meg Giry stood as if chained to the stone floor. She could not disguise the fact that she trembled. Was it fear or exhaustion? Or was it some other intense emotion?

He looked away. Something tightened in his chest. He could no longer differentiate between the pain and the anger, the loss and the fear of facing the long years stretching out into the narrowing tunnels of his loneliness. To live the same life over and over, here in the darkness, with only his heartbeat to fill his ears, his heart broken, stuttering, and his own empty voice.

You are not alone, Christine had said to him even as she stepped into the narrow boat, rested her hand on the count's shoulder, and floated down the dark, oily waters of the submerged lake. Even as she left him. Alone.

Oh God, the pain had not gone. He knew it well—a white brand cut straight through his chest! If he had a soul, it most assuredly would not survive this trial.

Erik circled the young girl, the other one, the blond one, Madeleine's child. She stood, silent, obedient. Obedient? How could he think her obedient? She had disobeyed all the most important rules, broken all the prohibitions, risked her body and her soul.

How old could she be? Perhaps she was a year or more older than Christine. Christine. The name burned. Christine. He squeezed his eyes shut. He had banished the name as well as the image—her long brown hair, her lithe body, her eyes full of…

He would not give in to misery. Had he no witness, he might have sunk to the cold stone and wailed like a child. But the solitude that would have been his prison and might have also been his consolation had been breached—breached by this other one.

She trembled, silent, watching him, her blond hair tied back with a powder-blue ribbon—a blue like the sky he would never see again. Her brown eyes rounder and wider than Christine's.

Christine's eyes. He had waited so long in the dark for the moment that those eyes might look into his—with love, with passion, with understanding. He had seen those eyes through two veils of tears. She, too, had cried for him. As the count pushed the narrow boat along the channel toward freedom, Christine had looked back at him, tears in her eyes, tears for the abandoned beast, tears for the man that would never be.

This one fair, this one more petite, but not delicate. Her body already the body of a woman. This one, too, he had seen. This one, the one he had turned away from, the one Madeleine had kept apart from him. The child had stolen from him Madeleine's time and affection. The near-sister that he knew he must not admire as he now admired her. Desire, kindled cruelly, would not abate.

Why did she tremble? Oh, yes. He had interrupted her competent, but uninspired performance. He had shouted at her, demanding that she be silent. In this one thing, she had shown herself obedient.

Each day she had come, led reluctantly by Madeleine, to the beast's lair. Each day she descended into hell, a gift to drive the other from his mind, his heart, his body. Yet he suffered still when his eyes fell on her and knew her not to be Christine, nor did it assuage him to know, upon her departure, that he had forgotten, for a few moments or even hours, his obsession with Meg's dark-haired friend.

She trembled, and Erik felt a stab of regret, a wave of pity for someone other than himself. Why had she insisted on following him that night? Why did she now insist on coming day after day, for months, to this dank underground lair of a monster? What treasure did she come to steal? What could he give her? What had Christine not already taken?

He circled her, his eyes darkened by pain and something else— something that had been growing, shifting inside him. She was small yet powerful. Her limbs were smooth and strong, muscles and sinews trained over years by dance. He had seen her on the stage, in the rehearsal rooms. Madeleine had taught her well. He stopped behind the young blond woman, for she was not a child but a woman, with a woman's body, a woman's will, and a woman's heart.

He stood behind her, close enough that he saw stray strands of her hair vibrate in the warm exhalation of his own breath. Like her shadow he felt fixed, attached to her body. His hand rose and reached out toward the soft expanse of her neck. He imagined it gliding along the contour of her throat, down over the edge of her collarbone, lower, dipping to the rise of her breasts. He stopped himself before he touched her. Her head turned just barely as if she wished to peer over her shoulder at him. Desire twisted in his gut, and he could not tell if it brought him more pleasure or more pain.

He stepped away, willing himself to feel nothing. Coldness seeped into the fissure, the wound created between them. Coldness tempered the pain, tamped down the longing. He must not want. Wanting would only bring madness.

Her trembling had eased.

He approached her from the side. Close to her ear, he whispered, cold emptiness bringing the desire to hurt, to see someone other than himself in pain, "You think you can learn to sing like her?"

Her eyes grew wide. Their soft rich brown threatened to melt. She turned to stare up at him. There was no pain in those doe-like eyes.

"Are you saying that you can't teach me? You? The Phantom?"

No, there was no room for pain in those eyes, only challenge, defiance, determination.

Her tone matched his. One challenge met by another. But he was a more experienced monster than she could ever hope to be.

"Christine had talent."

For one moment he thought he saw defeat in her eyes. He had meant to destroy her. Yet that one glimpse into her eyes, that glimpse of pain that he had caused did not soothe or please him as he had expected it would.

In that brief moment, he felt terror, realized that if he were successful in discouraging her, she would leave him down in his lair, in the dark and the silence for eternity. He would again be alone to lick his wounds, to…

But Meg did not crumple in the face of his cruelty.

"If you're incapable of teaching me, then have the courage to admit it."

The cool air robbed the last vestiges of warmth from his face. Erik had been oblivious to the passage of time. How long had he been standing outside the theater, his thoughts immersed in memories? It had seemed only moments, but it had to have been longer. The sun had dipped, its rays cutting obliquely down the tunnel of the narrow space between the buildings.

He traced his thoughts back to Chiara Greco and Carlotta Venedetti. Rinaldo was competent. Chiara had already shown some improvement. Carlotta would simply have to learn to control herself. Meg's health would improve. He would not entertain any doubts. The work they had done would not fail them. And once Meg returned to her rightful place in the company, they would reconsider their options.

Erik was about to step back inside the theater when something caught his eye at the far end of the alley. People were walking to and fro along the street, except for one lone figure who had stopped and turned in Erik's direction. Even at this distance, Erik could see that the man was impossibly tall and thin, the bones jutting out at the shoulders, the arms longer than one would expect. What was it about the unusual figure that immediately sent a shiver down Erik's spine? The stranger stood, looking at Erik, for several heartbeats. Before Erik could react, the figure had retreated and disappeared behind the edge of a nearby building as if to hide.

Only one man had Erik ever known who was that tall and angular—unnaturally tall, disproportionately so. Erik couldn't shake the memory of a caravan of painted wagons, a temporary settlement of tents and cages in the Italian countryside, a riotous assembly of misfits and freaks of which he himself had once been a member.

From the far corner of the stage, dressed in green leggings and a skintight sheath upon which were pinned gold, orange, brown, and red leaves, watched one wood nymph. She studied the tall, foreboding Sig. Costanzi. He was an impressive man, what her mother would have called "well-formed." Velia chewed at her ragged nail until the tender flesh beneath reddened and bled. Annoyed with herself she licked the wound to soothe it and glanced to see if anyone had noticed her gnawing away at her finger tips, like an animal at a paw trapped in a vice. Fortunately, she stood on the periphery and towards the back of the dance troupe, hidden from everyone's view, including that of the diva, Il canarino.

Velia couldn't help but admire the beautiful Meg Costanzi. Her husband couldn't possibly be hideous, could he? Yet Velia had heard snatches of conversations among the dancers and the chorines. There were those who had glimpsed his face. Their descriptions were imprecise. Velia glanced again toward the tall, darkly elegant profile of Sig. Costanzi. She could see the strong line of his chin, the definition of his lips, the contours of the mask. Her desire to know what he looked like behind that white molded material puzzled her to distraction. He didn't carry himself as if he were ugly or deformed. The lines of his body suggested he was strong and healthy, no curvature of the limbs, no unsightly growths bulging against the perfect lines of his trousers and coat. His posture spoke confidence, privilege, even pride. How could someone reportedly marked by disfigurement give such an impression of beauty?

The signora, his beautiful French wife, spoke excitedly with the ballet instructor, Renata Cossa, and several of the more experienced members of the dance troupe. The ease of their conversation suggested a long and comfortable association among these women. Velia envied their camaraderie. Since the death of her mother, she had been immersed in a world dominated by men, most of whom were stern and rough, molded and crippled by circumstances of loss, poverty, and the brutality of hard physical labor.

Even now, after nearly a week at the Teatro dell'Opera, Velia was amazed by the beauty and luxury surrounding the staff and performers in the palatial confines of this building. When one or another of the dancers complained about a dusty corridor or the cramped dressing room or slippers that were too tight, she wanted to laugh incredulous that these women could not recognize the advantages they had. The colors alone, the music, the sweep and drama of the story as it unfolded piece by piece on the stage filled her with excitement and joy. This was nothing like the inns, nothing like the dark streets, the filthy rooms let by the night or the hour.

She had only recently been admitted into the company. With no training as a dancer, she kept herself well out of the way of the ballet mistress, shuffled among the less trained and younger dancers in the back rows. Even among these less seasoned performers, Velia sensed their dismay at her awkwardness, her lack of training, her inability to keep in step. Soon it would be so evident that not even the arrangements made between her brother Adamo and the ballet mistress's assistant would protect her from dismissal.

She swallowed against the loud rumble of her empty stomach. Adamo had warned her to shed some weight, to fit in better with the other dancers. Little did he realize that her ribs stuck out already, and there was barely any excess to sacrifice. She simply wasn't built like most of the other dancers. They were taller and slighter of build, with small busts and narrow hips. On the other hand, she had a tiny waist accentuated by her broad, round hips.

As early as the age of twelve, her bust had filled out to the point that she began to wrap a large swatch of cloth around her chest. She fastened it tightly to cinch down her breasts. Her precocious development had made her the target of older men who no longer chucked her under the chin, but looked at her with hungry eyes that frightened her. Youths tormented her, too. Growing up in a world of men had sharpened her tongue, and she was not hesitant to use it against the young men that she came across.

Now she studied the girls and women around her on the stage and saw that their limbs stretched and pulled away from their torsos, bringing the eye up and out toward the air as if their bodies were constantly in danger of flying off towards the heavens. Whereas her body seemed permanently fixed to the earth itself, no less secure than if it had roots like an oak tree burrowed deep into the damp soil.

Yet Velia had felt elated to see the famous Il canarino, who had once been a dancer herself, so the story went, and whose body was no less voluptuous than her own, execute with remarkable grace and precision several jetés and pirouettes. Clearly it was possible, thought Velia, with training and determination for someone like herself to dance. But she had never aspired to become a dancer. That had been Adamo's idea, a ploy to get her inside the company, a foot in the door. He had chided her when she complained. The singing would come. Eventually she would find a way to get the attention of someone important, someone like…

The older soprano was waving her arms about her head, like she often did. Velia wondered what the tall, imposing artistic director, was thinking. "Don Erik," the others had the confidence to call him, but not she, not now, not yet. The discussion between Signorina Venedetti and Don Erik Costanzi seemed to have come to an end. Velia was disappointed to follow the retreat of Don Erik from the stage. One glance at the older singer told the story. The irascible woman had been dismissed. She had not gotten what she had wanted from Sig. Costanzi for she was clearly still agitated. Velia smiled to see her stand with her fists pinioned to her waist. Her very body shook. Velia imagined that under the long skirts of her costume she was tapping her right foot vigorously in annoyance. Don Erik was not an easy man to manipulate, not someone that could be twisted around one's little finger.

This was only one flaw in Adamo's plan.

Velia had listened in horror as her brother had worked out the details of a scheme in which she was simply a tool, a tool that was to be used, material that was easily sacrificed in the achievement of a goal. Yes, she would also benefit should the plan succeed. But the dangers and the immediate consequences would be hers and hers alone to bear. Adamo carried little or no risk. Was this the boy who had carried her on his shoulders across the piazza to the fountain to search for coins? Was this the same person who had washed the dirt from her face before dressing her in the one proper dress that still fit and had led her by the hand to mass? It pained her to doubt. Adamo would share his sweetened cannoli with her, had poured half his milk into her emptied glass when she had looked on with hungry eyes at his as yet untouched glass.

She had adored her brother. He had been a handsome boy, six

years older than she, generous and loving. But that was before their father had lost his work and even his will to live, before his drinking had taken over all their lives. Adamo had gone off to sea to work on a frigate bound for the Orient to make his fortune. He returned, with a few lira in his pocket, crippled and bitter. He had gotten caught in the rigging—his left side crushed by a falling mast—and nearly dragged into the sea before they had managed to cut him loose. His knee mangled and his arm hanging limp and useless by his side, Adamo was no longer fit for adventure at sea nor was he likely to find work on dry ground. Suddenly their only hope had seemed fixed on her.

Velia was unsure how Adamo had managed to get her a position among the dancers except that she had seen the ballet mistress's assistant, a younger woman who dealt with all the mundane and material matters unrelated to the actual choreography and performance itself. She was plain to a fault, especially in the context of the performers. Velia imagined that her brother, handsome even with his injuries, had impressed the woman, and it was she who handled the details of the troupe. All she had to do was add Velia's name to the list. No one would question the addition of yet one more wood nymph, one more discreet snowflake.

The rest was up to her, Adamo had said. Velia had asked him to explain, but the words had seared her ears, burned her eyes. She had not been able to speak. He had insisted that she agree, that she admit that this was their only choice. Her throat had clamped tight. No longer listening to his explanations and urgings, she turned away and could only nod.

A dark-haired woman with gold coins ringing her neck and wrists, the chink of metal a constant accompaniment to her limping gait. Dark hair, dark thoughts, old eyes, she had once been Belle, beautiful like the name he gave her when she used to come and distract him from the cold corrosive edges of the bars, from the sting of lashes as they began to heal. She had worn bells then, tiny cymbals that made music when she performed for the Devil's Child.

Each of them had had a name back then—before the vaults, before sanctuary, before disaster. She had been Belle, and he had been the Devil's Child. Each had abandoned previous lives to live again in another land.

The Phantom had returned to the caravan of gypsy performers, the grotesque spectacle of the bizarre, the strange, and the wondrous. In his travels, when he had fled from Meg, he had come full circle and in the Italian valley he had found the dark-haired woman who had once been Belle. Sabia, she called herself then, and she had lost the innocent beauty of her youth. She reminded him of the brutality of the cage, made him remember moments deeply buried that he had longed to forget. Sabia destroyed Belle, for Belle had been a child's understanding, a shared illusion. Belle, the playmate and sister he had never had, the first love that he had wished to keep untouched, a symbol of everything that Abel, his master had denied him.

Sabia, the one who knows, like Circe, wise and wicked sorceress, bewitched and cursed him. For months he labored under her spell. For months he returned to the cage and performed his pantomime of good and evil.

It had not been easy to break Sabia's incantation, Sabia's fleshy chains, Sabia's dark desires.

Erik could not easily shake off the memories. He had gone to the edge of the street and surveyed each direction to catch sight of the tall man. Nothing. He had disappeared, and for a moment Erik had doubted his senses and wondered if he had fallen asleep and drawn the specter up from the dark hidden vaults of his mind. He ignored the sensation of being watched and returned to the safe darkness of the backstage corridors. As he approached the stage, the uneasiness that had dogged his steps lessened its hold on him.

In the center of the stage, Meg stared off toward the empty seats of the auditorium. Erik followed her gaze and wondered what she might be thinking. Was she imagining a packed house? Was she remembering past triumphs, the sound of hundreds of hands clapping, the admiration of her public? She was so thin that he felt a pang of sorrow cut through his chest. She stood, frail and abandoned in her own thoughts. He felt drawn to her, wanting to hold her, to protect her, to keep her from disappearing. She was the one to whom he had returned. She had always been his home, his sanctuary. He would always be that for her, if she let him.

She was momentarily alone. The dancers were lined up against the back of the stage, learning a complex sequence for the ballet in the final act. He came alongside Meg as she watched them.

"You look tired," Erik whispered next to Meg's ear.

She disguised the deep blush that darkened her cheeks and lips with a hand that brushed a stray strand of her blond hair back behind her ear. She turned slightly away from Erik.

"I'm fine," she answered. The words snapped back at him, crisp and sharp.

When she walked away, he checked the impulse to march after her. He watched until she stopped at the far corner of the stage just feet from the queue of dancers. The ballet mistress approached her, and the two women became involved in a conversation. The dancers completed the set and stretched and fell away from the rigid order imposed by the sequence.

Erik had the distinct impression that Meg had only wanted to get away from him.

There was not an inch of space that was not occupied in Il Café di Mondo. The after-theater crowd had wedged itself into the establishment, taken every seat along the mahogany bar and at every table. In the spaces between stood rowdy customers bumping unapologetically into the shoulders and backs of those who were fortunate enough to have secured a seat. From several of the best known theaters including the Teatro Regio, Teatro Argentina, and of course the Teatro dell'Opera the workers among the staff, costumers, set designers, musicians, as well as those who had performed that evening on the stage, had filled to bursting the favorite haunt of their world. This was where they came to drown their disappointments when the audience was indifferent and where they also came to celebrate—toasting their wines and champagnes—when success crowned their efforts. Although many who came together in the relatively small space of the café were rivals on the stage, here at Il café such concerns were mostly forgotten.

The air was rank with sweat and the sour smell of strong drink. At this late hour of the evening, when the theater people came tripping over the threshold, the waiters served only a simple fare. The salty aroma of cooked meats, the sharp, acrid tang of tomatoes, onion, and herbs came in waves as the servers wedged their way round the congested tables.

Carlotta wiped her lips deftly with a handkerchief and sighed as the wine warmed her from the hollow of her stomach out along her limbs. Rinaldo would regret his decision to escort il cuculo home from the Teatro dell'Opera. Carlotta had christened Chiara Greco il cuculo or cuckoo, not only to deride the repetitious arpeggios through which the entire cast had been forced to suffer but also because she had remembered her nonna telling her stories about the wicked bird who stole other birds' nests, kicking out the newly laid eggs and replacing them with her own.

Her nonna, her mother's mother, had raised her until Carlotta's rebellious temperament had gotten the best of both of them. She had been fourteen when she accepted the tall, handsome man's offer to take her to Milan so that she could make her fortune on the stage. Carlotta hadn't thought of her nonna in years. She didn't like to recall that she had waited too long to send for the old woman to join her in Milan. Her nonna had been buried a year when Carlotta received word. She had thought the woman would live forever, so strong and hardy had she been when Carlotta displeased her and deserved a thrashing.

Such memories! She blamed these, too, on il cuculo. Just like a cuckoo, Greco has stolen another's nest and meant to lay her eggs if someone didn't stop her soon. Acting the delicate flower, Greco didn't bat an eyelash when Rinaldo had offered to call a coach for her. No, no, no, she could not put him to such trouble as to pay for her transport. Then without so much as a breath—in that bovine plaintive—she'd mooed that she preferred to walk. It was slimming and good for the lungs.

"Bah!" spat Carlotta, remembering the coy half look il cuculo had sent Rinaldo. *Her* Rinaldo. Who preferred walking when there were perfectly comfortable modes of conveyance that circulated the city at all hours of the day and night? One could lie back on the stuffed cushions and stare out into the lights of the fountains and listen to the street sounds. One could even slip off one's shoes and wiggle one's toes without worry that anyone would notice the bunion on the side of one foot. "Bah! Quella vacca! The cow! Slimming?" All walking had ever done for Carlotta was tire her feet and darken her mood. "Cuculo-vacca-cuculo-vacca-cuculo-vacca!" She couldn't make up her mind which insult was more apt.

Carlotta had dismissed Chiara Greco to her walk with a curt farewell and had taken Rinaldo by the arm with every intention of steering him to a barouche that would take them to Il Café di Mondo to join the others from the company, to relax and unwind after the evening's performance. She'd not pulled him more than a step when he gently took her hand from his sleeve, apologized, and addressed Chiara Greco.

No, he couldn't allow her to walk unescorted the streets of Rome. Carlotta growled under her breath to let one of the stagehands do the honors. She was not about to walk the cow home. But Rinaldo had no intention of asking her to accompany them. Dismissed. Unaccompanied. Sent on her way. He'd join her…later. Later?

After he made love to il cuculo. After he bedded the vacca impertinente.

"Eh, you. You with the tray. Where do you hide the bottle?" Carlotta waved her empty glass at a passing waiter. No sooner had he served her than Carlotta upended the glass and drained it.

Sig. Bianchi sat among a small group of musicians toward the back of the room. He cast disapproving glances Carlotta's way every few minutes. It was beginning to irritate her. She waited for Bianchi to look once again in her direction. Then she stuck her tongue out at the old goat. He mouthed a choice word or two and gave her his back. She cackled and slammed the glass down on the table.

A man's voice coming from behind her left ear startled her. She clasped her hand over her heart and cursed.

"I'm sorry, Donna Carlotta. I didn't mean to frighten you." She recognized the voice as that belonging to the tenor at the Teatro dell'Opera, Grimaldo Tessari. "Is Sig. Rinaldo Jannicelli not here?" he asked.

"Rinaldo Jannicelli is milking a cow," she said. Seeing the puzzled look on the man's face, she burst into laughter, but her glee did not last long. "I do not need milking. I am not a cow. Not like some people I know."

"Perhaps I should…" Grimaldo was about to reach out to help Carlotta to her feet when Paoul Ricci stepped directly in his path.

"Well, what have we here?" said the journalist. Ignoring Grimaldo, Ricci leaned forward and looked into Carlotta's unfocused eyes. "Carlotta Venedetti, the tragic and murderous Lady Macbeth?"

Grimaldo tapped Ricci on the shoulder to get his attention.

"Sig. Ricci, I think I should…"

"Everything's fine, Don Grimaldo. You should go back to your seat. I'll make sure our lovely diva gets home safely."

Carlotta fought down a belch, turning and letting it burst silently through her lips. As Ricci took a seat at her table, Grimaldo hesitated and then retreated to his place by the window.

Carlotta opened and closed her eyes several times to dispel the image of Paolo Ricci sitting across from her at her own table. A moment before, she could swear that he had not been there. She recalled having spoken to Grimaldo. He had been worried about her. He had asked her something, but she couldn't remember what it had been. Not given to imagining things, she still wasn't sure how Grimaldo had metamorphosed into Ricci.

"You," she accused.

"Signorina Venedetti, are you speaking to me?"

The man was laughing at her. *How dare he?* His lips were thin and stretched across his broad face in a sarcastic grin.

"You! Who else is seated across from me? At my table?" He did not answer but his merriment seemed undaunted. "Your face is sly, Paolo Ricci. I don't trust it." She squinted at him and frowned. "You…you…"

"Yes, I?" he encouraged.

"Wrote that review." He cocked his head as if intrigued by what she might say next. "Did you forget? Did you run out of paper or ink? Not one word. Not one."

Undaunted, the smile lingered. Ricci leaned forward across the small round of the table and in a stage whisper, loud enough to compete with the ambient noise, remarked, "Signorina, I trust it is a compliment not to be mentioned when the review is not favorable."

"Humph. You write just to see your name in print. To see how clever you can be. Mediocre, you said the performance was mediocre."

"And you don't agree?" He folded his hands under his chin. The fact that he was enjoying their little talk set Carlotta's teeth on edge even more than the review had.

"Il cucu…Greco's performance, sí, it is a compliment to call it mediocre. Did you not hear my aria in Act II? Or had Greco deafened you to everything of merit by then?"

"As always, Signorina, your performance was…energetic." Carlotta scowled suspiciously as the proud man hesitated and added, "As well as memorable."

She still felt as if he were laughing over some secret joke at her expense. His dark hair curled around the sharp bones of his cheeks. He was perhaps only slightly taller than she. His eyes were large but set too close together, his nose a straight line that segmented his face too neatly down the middle. But they stared across the table eye to eye. He was not unattractive.

"Speak."

"And what do I say, Signorina? What is your pleasure?"

Pleasure? The word rippled through her soggy imagination. His voice was not deep. It was vaguely pleasant like most men's voices. She liked men's voices, wished she could sing like a man and shake the walls of the theater. Men's voices reminded her of men's cocks— velvet, smooth and thick, powerful.

"Home. Take me. We will go now." Carlotta stood. The sudden change unbalanced her, and she tilted to the side. Ricci rose and stretched out a hand to steady her. His hand on her arm was only meant to save her from falling, but she quickly took it and moved it to the front of her bodice.

Ricci withdrew his hand as if it had been burned. Carlotta could not stifle the spontaneous burst of laughter as the journalist looked about to see if anyone had noticed.

Most were talking, arguing, even singing. Spirits ran high and mischief was the rule, not the exception. Ricci, the barman, and Grimaldo Tessari, who sat in his corner by the large picture window at the front of the café, were most likely the only people not lost in their cups or nearly so.

Carlotta cocked her head at a nearby scene in which a man had pinioned a woman to the table and pushed down the neckline of her dress to free one breast. He held it tenderly as if it were a child and was trailing long, wet kisses along its slope. The woman's face was aglow with pleasure, oblivious to the fact that Carlotta and then Ricci were watching them.

"Well? Aren't you game for a private performance?" Carlotta grinned and placed her hands on either side of her hips.

CHAPTER 5

The Night After

You spotted snakes with double tongue,
Thorny hedgehogs, be not seen;
Newts and blind-worms, do no wrong,
Come not near our fairy queen.

A Midsummer Night's Dream, William Shakespeare

That was it? Carlotta poked her finger into the sleeping man's chest. He sputtered but did not wake. He rolled to his side, facing the opposite side of the room, and let out several hoarse, staccato bursts of noise that made the fine hairs along Carlotta's neck ripple and stand at attention. For several moments she studied the man's back as she listened to him snore. The pre-dawn light cast milky shadows that allowed Carlotta to make out the coarse dark hairs growing across the upper plain of Ricci's rounded back. There, too, stood out dark and thick several warts between his shoulder blades. In the last moments of their tryst, her fingers had stumbled upon the raised and knobby growths, distracting her from the pleasure that constantly evaded her determination.

Carlotta tensed in the half-light with each rattling intake of air that Ricci took.

"Dio mio!" she said out loud. Oblivious to her frustration, Ricci snored on. She would never get to sleep now. Not only had she been left merely on the verge of satisfaction, but she was wide-awake and restless. It had taken her by surprise when Ricci ground his hips, stiffened, groaned, and then slumped with a smug smile on top of her in complete and blissful release. She had barely gotten the rhythm of the man when it was over. Now to make matters worse, she could not sleep for his snoring.

She wanted Ricci out of her bed. Perhaps even out of Rome. The man was an insufferable bore in bed.

Wrinkling her nose in disgust, she stuck her fingernail into the spongy flesh at the center of his back.

"What the hell!" Ricci woke and sat up in bed. He bent his arm behind his back to brush away the annoying sting.

"Ah, you are awake?" Carlotta asked, her voice falsely cheerful.

"Something bit me." Ricci rubbed his hand along the wrinkled sheet where he had lain.

"Now it is time for you to dress."

Ricci rubbed his hand across his face and blinked.

"Now," she added.

"It's the middle of the night."

Carlotta rose from the bed and pulled the covers with her, leaving her lover exposed. She dropped all but the light sheet to the floor. She wrapped it Grecian style around her torso. "It is time you should go." When Ricci didn't move, Carlotta sighed heavily and pointed toward the door.

At first, Ricci hesitated. But when Carlotta showed no sign of changing her mind, he grabbed his clothes and pulled them on. Carlotta was not moved by his sullen mutterings. She wanted him gone. If she had to listen to anyone snore, she preferred it be Rinaldo. Rinaldo's softer rasping lulled her to sleep. Ricci's drove spikes through her eardrums. The journalist had been an unexpected disappointment, a mistake.

"Out," she repeated even as Ricci pulled up his trousers.

"Signorina, may I put on my shoes first?"

Carlotta folded her arms in evident displeasure, but she nodded her reluctant permission.

Ricci fastened his trousers, bent, and retrieved one of his shoes. He kicked the stray piles of Carlotta's clothing aside until he came upon the other one. He sat on the edge of the bed and began to put them on. Before he had tied his laces, Carlotta walked to the door and opened it.

"Now. You are complete. You have your shoes. Go."

Barely a moment later, Carlotta lay down and dragged the covers up to her shoulders. As the door to her apartment slammed shut, she snuggled into the pillow with a contented sigh.

The young man rubbed his hands over the spikes of a beard that he had allowed to grow the past several days. Its stubble dirtied his face, the beard standing out like a smudge of coal dust against a weathered and sun-darkened complexion. A year at sea would do that to a man. His hands, too, were callused, scoured from hemp rope and roughened by knotted wood. He barely recognized them.

He flexed his right hand, the only one that still served him well. It was larger, stronger than it had once been. The other had already begun to wither, the muscles softened and wasted from disuse. He gritted his teeth and concentrated his will on moving the digits, twisting the wrist, bending or extending the forearm, but the limb was dead. He wanted to believe that he had seen it move, even if only infinitesimally. Perhaps the fingers had curved in more? He held his breath. Sweat broke out and dotted the line above his upper lip. The tension became unbearable, and he let out a frustrated gale of oaths he had learned from the rough lot on board the frigate.

To lose mastery over one's body! There could be nothing worse. Nothing except its consequences—abject poverty and starvation.

He had explained the situation to his sister Velia. She had pretended to ignorance. She would have Adamo state the details, what he expected her to do and why. It had angered him to see her shock. What had she thought would happen to them when he came back broken and crippled?

It galled him to admit that he could not support them. It shamed him to know that their father was nothing but a drunken parasite, nothing like the man he had once been when their mother had been alive. Now that Adamo could not make their living, Velia was their only hope.

She was talented. She had the voice of an angel. But she would not make her fortune singing for the drunks in the taverns of Rome. She would only have a chance if somehow she could get an audience with someone who had power, the power to put her on stage. That's where she belonged, not in the dingy inns and taverns singing for the price of a meal, hoping for a few extra lira should the men fancy her.

And where would that road lead? She blushed now when he told her, explained to her the crude reality of what she might have to do to get a man like Sig. Costanzi to notice her. What would she do when it became necessary to take one of the drunks in the back room and spread her legs for him? Oh how she would blush then, but it would be too late.

He waited for her to come out of the side entrance of the Teatro dell'Opera. He waited for hope. He waited to hear her tell him that Costanzi had noticed her eyes, her long legs, the soft contours of her body. He waited to know that perhaps Costanzi would treat her well, would give her a modest gift for favors rendered.

Perhaps Costanzi would take her in some dark corner of the backstage. And as Costanzi writhed in the throes of lust, she would remember what her brother had instructed her to say and ask for a boon. In the heat of passion a man would do almost anything. Adamo remembered. He recalled with bitterness and longing the utter enslavement to the moment. Costanzi would say yes. He would grant her the chance to sing for him. And once Velia sang for Costanzi—Adamo squeezed his eyes shut and pressed his hand against his forehead in fervent prayer—he would know her talent. God willing, she would not have to debase herself further.

Once Costanzi tired of her body, he would still desire her voice.

"You there."

Velia's heart stopped beating. The ballet mistress was pointing her finger directly at her. She held her leg just as straight as the dancer in front of her. What had she done wrong this time?

"Stop wobbling. If you fall over, the whole lot of you will collapse like a house of cards."

Velia blushed and prayed the mistress would release them before she crashed into the woman to her right. Her thigh muscle burned. The heat and pull was rising into her left buttock and any moment she was sure that it would tighten into a cramp.

"Relax. That's all for the moment."

With general sighs of relief, the nymphs around Velia gracefully lowered arms and legs and disbanded toward the backstage dressing rooms.

"Stretch, signorinas!" The mistress called back over her shoulder as she walked away.

If Velia stretched any further, her joints would separate and she'd fall onto the stage in a puddle of loose bones. The body was not meant to be folded in upon itself and then thrown out to the four corners of the world. Her leg was not a third arm to be waved about in the air over the top of her head as if she were greeting someone. It was not physically possible to do what the ballet mistress wanted her to do.

Velia felt the tension in her backside melt as her leg reached firm ground. She rubbed her buttock, unconcerned that the painters working away at the trompe l'oeil of a forest on the huge panel at the back of the stage snickered, their paintbrushes dripping at half-mast.

She followed the stragglers toward the dressing rooms but at the last minute changed course to circle back toward the stage. She made her way toward the panel of scenery the men were painting. Blending in with the dark green hues of the forest, she looked as if she had stepped out of the canvas itself. She ducked behind the panel to avoid the painters as they touched up the final details of the scene. Just beyond, across the stage and near the orchestra pit, Sig. Costanzi often consulted with Sig. Bianchi.

"May I help you?"

The voice startled her, and she jumped, crashing into the edge of the panel. A curse exploded on the opposite side as one of the painters perhaps made an inadvertent splash of brown across the budding leaves of a young sapling.

"Sorry," she projected to the invisible artist on the other side of the backdrop.

The voice that had addressed her belonged to a handsome young man with dark curly hair and kind eyes, a warm soft chocolate in color. He was of moderate height with a frame that was already sturdy but promised to fill out even more in the next few years. Velia tried to place him among the performers but couldn't. Then she noticed that he was dressed too well to be one of the staff or even one of the performers that made up the chorus. The suit he wore was similar in weave and style to that worn by the artistic director.

"Are you looking for something?" he asked, his mouth lifting in one corner in an ironic, but strangely warm grin. He looked at her sideways, his eyes laughing.

"Trouble," she muttered to herself. She bit into the soft fullness of her lower lip when she saw him raise an eyebrow and chuckle in surprise. She hadn't meant for him to hear her. "I'm sorry," she rushed to say. "I was just curious. I wanted to see the painting up close."

The young man glanced at the untouched reverse side of the canvas and back at the girl.

"It's hard to tell much from the back of the panel, don't you think? Wouldn't it be better to go around to the front where they're painting?"

Then it came to her. There was something in his manner that reminded her of Don Erik.

"You're…you're one of Sig. Costanzi's sons, aren't you?"

"Yes, the handsome one. Mario, Mario Costanzi, at your service. And you are?"

"Velia." When he seemed to be listening for more, she added, "Just Velia. I'm a dancer."

"Yes," he said, keeping his tone carefully even. "I think I saw you just a while ago."

Velia winced to think he'd seen her clumsy attempt to keep up with the others.

"Well, I'm not very good. Not yet."

Mario grinned and stepped forward. "Yes, but you have very nice...eyes."

"I...I..."

"Yes, your eyes are quite nice. Both of them. Are they hazel?"

"I...suppose."

Velia felt as if she might reach out and touch the young man. He was just within reach. She vaguely noticed that he held his hands clasped behind his back. The pose struck her as one in which he held back his own inclination to do with his hands what his eyes were now doing. They teased along her body as if lost for a moment only to find their way again to her face.

Mario stepped back and bowed his head slightly.

"Signorina. I've an errand to run. It was a pleasure to meet you. I suggest you go to the other side of the panel so you can get a... better...view of the landscape."

Velia watched him disappear down the narrow passageway toward the side exit.

"Why wouldn't it be a good idea? He's his son. He...seems to be interested in me already."

"Son? Good God, Velia, you can't be so naïve. Costanzi's sons fuck any woman they want already. You don't think they take their enjoyment in the dark alcoves with the dancers, the chorines? Why there must be any number of young girls willing to service Costanzi and his boys. I'm sure they think it will bring them some advantage."

Adamo stopped when he saw Velia's expression. She seemed locked somewhere between shock and disappointment. He sighed and made a concerted effort to gentle his voice.

"The son won't come into money until Costanzi's dead. And... as beautiful as you are, my sister, no man of Costanzi's position is going to allow his sons to marry a gutter rat turned dancer."

"But..."

"He may turn a blind eye to his sons' dallying. I'm sure you could be Marco's whore..."

"Mario. His name is Mario." Velia could not look at her brother. The heat that came off her skin was unbearable. She knew she was on the verge of tears and refused to give in to the urge. "Besides, you're wrong."

"About?"

"I've heard the girls talk about a lot of things. You don't know the gossip that goes round. None of it includes Costanzi or his sons."

That was not quite true. Velia didn't need to share everything with her brother. There was heated speculation about Sig. Costanzi—from what had happened to his face that forced him to cover it with a mask to what talents he had other than his music that kept Donna Meg satisfied. Half of the girls in the corps were in love with him and the other half were terrified of him. Recently she had heard rumors that there was tension between the diva and her temperamental husband. But no one said an unkind word about the sons. No one whispered sordid tales of seduction involving any of the Costanzis.

Velia could see that Adamo didn't believe her.

"Forget the boy. There'll be no money from that one, and if Costanzi even suspects that his son has had his way with you, we'll be lucky if he doesn't dismiss you from the company."

"Adamo, I think Mario likes me. And I…"

"The father won't take you as a lover if he thinks his son has had you first."

"A lover?"

Adamo ran his hand through his thick hair, leaving it awry and standing up on his scalp at weird angles. "You don't seriously think that we're talking about marriage, do you?"

"Of course not." She knew from the beginning what her brother expected of her. Yet, she had believed that the ultimate goal was to get a chance to sing for the maestro. If they were talking about an affair, why couldn't she encourage the son rather than the father? "But how is the one so different from the other?"

"Because Costanzi has power and money. If he makes you his mistress, he won't throw you over in a fortnight after he's satisfied his lust. A young man catches fire quickly, but he cools just as fast.

Costanzi, if I'm right, will want your discretion. He'll pay for it. And when he's done, he'll continue to pay."

"Adamo, I've a salary now. Isn't it enough that we have money coming in?"

"Father would drink it away in a night. After Father comes begging his drinking money, your salary barely keeps a roof over our heads."

He took his arm and laid it across his lap. The motion brought her attention to the dead limb. She knew that she was all they had.

"But I thought that the goal was to get Sig. Costanzi to listen to me sing."

Adamo looked away, embarrassed.

"Yes," he whispered. "But if that fails, mia sorella, what else do we have to bargain with?"

She fought to retain the memory of Mario's grin, but her tears seemed to flow inside rather than down her cheeks. They washed Mario's image from her mind.

"You bitch!"

Rinaldo stood in the narrow passageway at Carlotta Venedetti's dressing room door. He was unshaven, his vest hanging loose, his shirt unevenly tucked into the band of his trousers. No sooner had she stepped out into the passageway, on her way to the stage, than he had thrown his curse at the surprised diva.

Had he not gone to Il Café di Mondo only to find she had already left with Ricci? Had he not hailed a carriage and directed it to her apartment, sat back against the cushion and gone over a thousand times what they had told him at the café? He didn't even remember alighting from the carriage, paying the driver, walking to the door of the mansion where he had made his intermittent home with Carlotta Venedetti. Only at that moment had the shock melted away and in its place left a searing brand of anger.

Startled by the vehemence of Rinaldo's insult, Carlotta stepped back for one moment. Quickly she recovered, her hands firmly lodged in the curve of her hips. She withstood his angry tone and the sulfurous glare of his examination.

"I don't need to explain to you or anyone what I do with my life. My life! Do you hear me, you…two-bit gigolo?" She waved her hand in front of Rinaldo's face and stood her ground.

Rinaldo was stunned by her brazen lack of remorse or shame. He jutted his hand out to the side to brace himself against the wall. He fought the light-headedness that warned he was on the verge of a swoon. A swoon, for God's sake, how far had this gone? Had he lost every fiber of his manhood to this braying, bottomless, devourer of men?

When he next spoke, he didn't recognize his voice. It was airy and quiet, and yet there was a horrible certainty in its resolve.

"I don't know you," he said to himself as much as to Carlotta Venedetti.

He would not have believed it if he hadn't stayed outside that mansion, unable to force his hand to knock upon the door to which he had never been given a key. He had stepped back and looked up to see two figures, not one, in the rectangular eye of their—no, her—bedroom window. He cursed his faith in her. If he had not, with his very own eyes, seen Paolo Ricci step outside the doorway of Carlotta Venedetti's residence barely before the sun rose, he might yet have stayed a fool. But Ricci *had* come out onto the street, adjusting his coat. The journalist slapped his palm several times with the limp fingers of his gloves, hesitated as if unsure of which direction to take, and then set off down the deserted street toward the heart of the theater district. Ricci. The realization that Carlotta had betrayed him was only the beginning of Rinaldo's torment. To know that she had done so with a man that she had constantly berated, a man that she loathed, drove him to distraction. Had he been so blind that he could not see what Carlotta was?

"Don't you walk away from me!"

Carlotta's strident voice made Rinaldo's ears twitch as he walked down the dark passage that led to the front vestibule of the theater. He had been waiting since dawn at the theater, waiting since he had seen Ricci leave the apartment, waiting for Carlotta to arrive. He had done what he had come to do. He had faced her and found her unrepentant, unashamed.

"You!" she screamed after him, watching as he receded down the long, narrow corridor. "No one walks away from Carlotta Venedetti. Boy! Come back here, now!"

Rinaldo came across no one on his way to the grand entrance. He could hear the percussive echoes of Venedetti's metal tipped heels upon the cedar boards of the passageway. He could still hear the anger in her voice as he opened the front doors wide and stepped out into the clean white light of day.

He welcomed the rumble of voices on the street, the hoof beats upon the paving stones, the chinking sound of metal against wood, leather soles against brick, the odd shouts of vendors and tradesmen as they set out about their daily business. He only escaped the final, lingering sounds of Carlotta's voice when he let go of the heavy doors to the Teatro dell'Opera and let them slam shut in his wake.

CHAPTER 6

Doppelgangers

...once I sat upon a promontory,
And heard a mermaid on a dolphin's back
Uttering such dulcet and harmonious breath,
That the rude sea grew civil at her song,
And certain stars shot madly from their spheres
To hear the sea-maid's music.

A Midsummer Night's Dream, William Shakespeare

Sig. Cuomo was an ardent aficionado of opera, a particularly fervent and vocal admirer of Il canarino's performances. The moment Meg saw him force his way between the press of bodies in the large hall, she knew what he would do. There was no retreat open to her. She searched the room for Erik, not sure if she wanted him to rescue her or if she hoped he was far out of earshot and therefore would not witness the scene she imagined would soon take place. But the latter would have been a vain hope. Sig. Cuomo's voice was a loud and deep bellow, the kind that one expects from a man in public office. Even if Erik had been in another room, there was little chance that he would not hear Cuomo's good-natured bluster.

"Donna Meg, Il canarino, let me kiss your hand."

It would not have struck her as so comic had he not been several feet away. He strode forth, his hand extended, until he came within reach. He took her hand in his with an exaggerated flourish and yet barely touched his lips to her glove. Around them everyone had paused in their own conversations to watch the comedy unfold.

"It has been too long that you have kept from us your beautiful voice," said Sig. Cuomo. "I fear the doors to paradise have been forever closed unless we hear you sing this very night."

"Please, Sig. Cuomo, you are a most dear man, but you are prone to exaggeration."

Meg kept her voice low and modest, hoping that her host would follow her example. But Sig. Cuomo enjoyed an audience. He even looked about him as if to invite others to join him in encouraging Meg to sing for those present.

"There is no exaggeration possible. For anything that I might say falls woefully short of its mark. You must, Donna Meg, grace us with song."

The guests nearby pressed in on either side. Others beyond the inner circle caught the drift of the theme and pushed closer until most in the room were silently listening for Meg's answer.

That was when Meg caught sight of Erik. He, too, had heard Cuomo. He, too, watched her, tense with expectation. She blushed and cursed her complexion for its inability to disguise her embarrassment.

"You must pardon me, Sig. Cuomo."

"But surely," he said, as he blocked her intended retreat, "a song, a ditty, a refrain or two, just to remind us of past delights and future joys?"

The murmurs of encouragement closed in on her. Meg felt her throat constrict, a warning tickle, the feathering sensation that indicated that she was on the verge of a coughing spell. Meg cleared her throat in an effort to dispel the familiar tickle at the back of her throat.

Erik began to push his way toward Meg. But Signora Cuomo must have seen Meg's distress. Before he made it halfway across the room, their hostess had come and hooked her arm into her husband's. The two of them effectively blocked Meg's view of Erik.

"Stop making a spectacle of yourself and harassing our guest," Signora Cuomo said to her husband as she gave Meg a conspiratorial wink. "Anyone can see that Meg is enjoying a quiet conversation. She's not here to entertain us. It is we who should entertain her."

Chiding Sig. Cuomo for his bad manners, the matron guided her husband toward the piano, diverting the attention of their guests away from Meg. Within no time, she convinced him to play. An attractive man with a rather haughty expression on a surprisingly plain face took his position next to Sig. Cuomo and in a rather pleasing, but not remarkable, tenor began to sing.

Meg sighed in relief to know that she was no longer the center of attention. As the crowd settled in to listen to the light strains of popular ballads, she looked in the direction where Erik had been just moments before. He wasn't there. She scanned the room and could not find him.

"She's much younger than he is. What do these men think? That a young girl knows what she wants at that age?"

"But he's a powerful man, and I've heard he has a temper. She'd be wise to cover her tracks well."

"Oh, as far as that's concerned, he's no idea she's having an affair."

Erik's ears twitched in an effort to hear more clearly what was being said. However the women who were now responding had their backs to him and he could not read their lips or pick up the light strains of their voices. Facing him obliquely in the corner of a parlor teaming with guests, Signora Beauchamp had no idea that Erik could hear her.

He had bored of the conversation with Valerio and Conti. Usually they were more engaging. But tonight all they could talk about were the levies and taxes and cost of transport that were adversely affecting not only the reconstruction of the Roman baths but their businesses. Erik only half listened to their prattle about silk and muslin and the exportation of olive oil. The moment the talk turned dull he peremptorily interrupted Valerio and took his leave. He knew it was brusque and impolite, but he at least excused himself—something that he would not have considered important until Meg argued with him over what she called "the social graces." Nonsense, most of it, but Erik knew that his behavior was odd, arrogant at best. Indeed he was intelligent enough to imitate the manners he saw others practice, knew the expectations of the aristocracy and the wealthy. It was not a matter of training or understanding—it was a matter of disdain for the hypocrisy.

"I heard that she met her lover at the theater, and it was there in the back of a closed box that they made love." Signora Beauchamp's voice lowered and slowed for dramatic effect, making it even more audible to Erik's sharp ears.

The woman beside her blinked wide-eyed and drew her hand to her mouth in apparent shock.

Erik's heart beat too fast. He stood, somewhat hidden in a nearby recess, behind a garish faux-classic column that had no structural or aesthetic merit. Sweat broke out as his blood rushed up his throat to his face. His mask weighed heavily, like stone on the surface of his skin, and he would have sought a private chamber to remove it and wipe his brow had his feet not been nailed to the floor.

"I'm told she meets him often, mostly at the theater."

"Well, it won't last. These things don't."

"So right, Fabrizia. At first it's all exciting. But sooner or later the secrecy and danger will lose their appeal."

"Especially when there's money involved. She's a fool to let the golden goose slip through her fingers."

"For a fleeting romance. We all know what happens to passion."

Do we? The question repeated in Erik's mind. What does happen to passion?

His passion had not abated. It did not always overwhelm him as it once had done. It had lost its sharp, hungry edge, an edge whose intensity had at times bordered on pain. His passion had grown, matured. It had permeated his life and fueled his every thought and action. He felt it in the smallest things. It sat between him and his beloved at the breakfast table and between them in the carriage on their ride to the theater. It glowed soft in the moments of distraction and blazed hot when, after a long day's work, he came upon Meg alone in their room, as he watched her pull the teeth of the comb through the silken threads of her hair, when she let the gown slip to the floor and stepped out naked into his arms.

These women knew nothing of passion, nothing of the passion that he knew.

He yearned for the women to speak her name, the name of the unfaithful wife, the wife who married too young and too quickly, who had tied herself to an older man that she could not love, who met her lover at the theater and felt passion perhaps for the first time in her young life. If not the traitor's name, then the unfortunate husband's. But they had gone on to other matters.

No, he told himself. No, it was not Meg. Even so images of Meg wrapped in another's arms played across his mind's eye. Choppy and insistent the same image pounded away at his denial. Too young and too unwise to make that decision. What had driven Meg, so young, to risk tracking a madman to his final sanctuary? Had she been a green girl, ignorant of the dangers she ran, swept away by wild romantic fantasies? No, she could not have blinded herself to what he had become. It had not been a wise decision. More than unwise, it had been dangerous and foolish.

How could she have known that he wouldn't knot the rope around her graceful neck and twist it until the bones snapped? How could she have known that the beast would not devour her whole? Christine had left him. Her kisses had seared his soul and with them had come the realization that he would never demand of her what he desired. She had held the glass for him to see the beast that he had become. She had ripped all his illusions to shreds and made him ashamed of what lay behind them. Christine loved another man, and yet she had kissed *him* and had been willing to wed herself to her tormentor.

Christine's kiss had crippled the raving beast inside him. He understood that he loved her more than his own soul and could not bear to see her suffer. Instead *he* would suffer.

No, Meg had not been safe. But she had come after him in spite of the dangers.

Erik forced his feet to move forward into the parlor. The air about him swirled and shifted. He must find Meg. He pushed his way through the clutches of men and women. A straight path opened before him, and there he saw his beloved, the woman who had braved death to follow after him. She was surrounded by her admirers.

Erik was on the verge of marching through the crowd and dragging Meg from the room. He had lost his taste for the inane conversations, the vanity and superficiality of the assembly. All he could think of was Meg's recent coolness, her seeming indifference, and even her avoidance of him.

Before he crossed the space between them, their host stepped into his path. Erik listened as Cuomo exhorted Meg to sing for the party. For one second he was buoyed by hope. She would take her spot by the piano, and she would sing. He prepared himself for the possibility that he would hear some weaknesses, perhaps some permanent flaws in her voice left by the ravages of the illness. It would not matter. What mattered is that, even flawed, her voice would move him.

But Meg did not rise and accept the admiration of her public. She shook her head. Erik could imagine her words, could nearly make them out as he read the sounds on her lips. He saw her blush crimson, felt Cuomo's insistence, knew that she was uncomfortable with the rude refusal to accept her initial answer. His body stepped forward even as his heart squeezed tight in his chest with anger and frustration.

Cuomo's wife came to rescue Meg. Erik willed himself to stop. He could not remain in the room.

When would she sing? What was she waiting for? If she could no longer sing, so be it, but he could not bear that she would not try.

He walked out into the long corridor beyond the drawing room. He leaned against the wall and waited for his breathing to return to normal.

Snatches of the previous conversation among the women came back, insistent and demanding. How often did lovers fall out of love? Was it so rare that two people would continue against all odds, including the passing of time, to find everything that they needed in the eyes, arms, and heart of their beloved?

He must drown these thoughts. He must get away from the

magpie voices. Erik gathered his determination and returned to the drawing room to search for his wife.

She sat on a low settee. Next to her, Sig. Conti. Was it Conti's wife of whom the women had spoken? A second wife—Conti's first having died in childbirth—was perhaps twenty-one or twenty-two, at least twenty years younger than Conti, a man in his mid to late forties.

Having lost all patience for the social graces, Erik briskly made his way through the congested parlor to stand before Meg. Ignoring Conti altogether and without preamble or apology, he held his hand out to his wife and demanded that she come.

Meg's lips straightened into a thin line. Before she could express her excuses to Sig. Conti, Erik took her by the hand and pulled her to her feet. Around them the guests hushed and watched as Erik led Meg through the crowded room. In the vestibule, he held Meg's hand firmly in his while the servants, having sensed the strange man's determination, fumbled with the wraps.

Only once they were in the carriage did Meg complain. Erik sat sullen, his body turned away from hers, his eyes staring out the window into the night.

What she said was true. He had acted a brute. He had no right. He had insulted everyone in the room. Don Marcelo, had he been there instead of touring Europe with Madeleine, would have been appalled.

She must have sensed his discomfort, for she stopped speaking. He felt her scrutiny on the back of his neck. Only to disrupt her silent examination, he turned to face her.

When he said nothing, she whispered, "I don't understand you."

Was she wondering why he had not gone to her earlier when Cuomo was pressing her to sing? Was she thinking of his recent show of bad manners, his brusque insistence that she obey him and follow like chattel?

Erik swallowed to dislodge the knot that blocked his throat. He could not fathom why her words had so unsettled him, weighing like a stone on his chest. He blinked to relieve the sting building behind his eyes. *She doesn't understand you*, he repeated to himself in an effort to grasp the meaning.

Had the filament that stretched from her heart to his broken? After all they had been through, how could she *not* understand him?

Then, again, did he understand himself?

The carriage stopped in front of the main entrance of the Costanzi mansion. The lights had remained lit for their return. Erik handed Meg down and led her to the door. But when she stepped across the threshold, he slipped his hand from hers. She glanced over her shoulder to see him back away into the darkness, just beyond the farthest reach of the light that poured from the vestibule. She stood, the glow from the lamps framing her, as if waiting.

Without a word of explanation, Erik set off, his pace brisk, down the street.

He would let her go. He would let her go. Should she ask for her freedom, it would kill him, but he would let her go. His light would go out. The darkness would return, but he would let her go.

As he had Christine.

Barely aware of his surroundings, he walked. His mad thoughts changed with each step he took. Echoes of tawdry infidelity sounded in the silence between his footsteps. Had Meg's passion for him spent its course? Had she fled to other arms?

Giving himself over to his imagination, Erik swore to find her lover and bury him alive in a pine box. He would exhume him only when suffocation was imminent and then bury him again. He would sit on the damp, overturned dirt and listen to the muffled screams. He would listen until his own pain abated or the cries ceased. Such thoughts clouded his pain only momentarily with an anger that almost felt like pleasure.

Anger brought distance between him and his pain like the distance his steps were even now placing between him and his home. The rhythm of his footsteps began to work its magic. The pitch of his anger lessened, and reason reasserted itself.

The clutch of women at the dinner party had spoken of a young woman. Meg was not a foolish girl. The affair had nothing to do with him and his wife. Then why had it seeped inside his thoughts and jumbled his emotions? It had brought to the surface every doubt he had ever had.

He walked blindly down the street. In the piazzas he came upon boisterous crowds, pockets of activity, but he kept his distance. He pulled up the collar of his coat and lowered the brim of his hat to avoid meeting their eyes. Long stretches of road were darkly lit and sullenly quiet, bereft of company. His shadow as he passed the sporadic gaslights urged him on; it pulled at his feet, drawing him toward the next pool of light, shortening as he approached. Swimming through intermittent darkness, he followed without question.

Doubts. The word resounded with the heavy thud of his boots across the flagstones of the road. Not about Meg. About himself. Doubts that he deserved her love. Doubts that he could retain it over time.

His passion for her, his love, certainly his need of her had not lessened. If anything, they had increased. But she had changed. She had grown cold and distant over the past months. He could not remember the day, the hour it had happened. He searched his memory for the exact moment when he had felt her slip away from him.

She had never refused him. Even now he dared to think, should he return and find her awake, if he reached out for her, she would welcome him. Their bodies had always found pleasure in one another.

Yet he had noticed her turn away when he had looked in her direction as if she didn't want him to see that she had been watching him. On more than one occasion he'd started to go to her only to see her walk off if she had not seen him. Their conversations had lost their intimacy. They spoke only of family concerns—the children and the household—and of the business of the theater.

Erik stopped short and nearly staggered. He could not remember the last time they had spoken of music. They had discussed the placement of this or that piece in the opera. They had spoken of the part for the soloist, the need for a stronger melodic thread and cues for the chorus, and the number of violas in the pit. But nothing about the music itself—the way it built and burst through its limits, the way it flowed through one's body, the emotions that it carried in its wake. Its beauty was irrelevant. Meg did not hum the melody, did not stumble, laugh, stumble again, then sing flawlessly a particularly complex measure Erik had purposefully included, knowing that she would love the challenge, admire the timing and proportional beauty of the cadence.

He leaned, his chest tight, a horrid sense of certainty squeezing his heart in its grip. She had not sung for months. She would never sing again. Not his music, perhaps no one's.

Grief bowed his head. His songbird languished silent in her golden cage. He had assured her that she only needed to rest. He had pushed her too soon after her illness to return to the music. That first day, when he thought her recovered, he had sat at the piano and played. She had not completed a scale before a series of violent coughs had forced her to stop.

He had been patient, hadn't he?

But was that true?

Each day he asked her how she felt. Each day he invited her to practice at his side. Had he not suggested in a thousand ways that she was remiss if she didn't push herself? Surely the scales were something anyone could do. Surely she was not doing herself any good by not trying. He had ordered Cook to bring Meg hot tea and honey and to make sure that she drank it each morning even though she preferred her tea bitter. The honey would soothe her throat, he had insisted. When she refused to join him in the music room for a light practice, he had not disguised his irritation. He had barely kept his tongue when she came and did nothing more than sit and listen to him play.

Was that patience?

Yes, he admitted that he had been angry the night François and Laurette played several of their own compositions on the piano— melodies modeled on folk songs and lullabies requiring no exertion or special skill—and everyone except Meg had participated. He had ground his teeth in frustration, but he had not said a word even though it had wrung his heart to hear Meg refuse their children's encouragement to join her voice to theirs. She excused herself to go off to bed. Hadn't he shown restraint? Yes, he had remained silent. Yet he had not joined her in their room. Instead, he had stayed behind, ruminating over his anger, and fallen asleep in the chair next to the fire. His displeasure would not have gone unnoticed by Meg.

Erik took several deep breaths, ignoring the rising stench of the sewer and wet paving stones. The silence was unbearable. He would welcome even the rattle and clang of a passing carriage to fill the night with noise. The deep quiet around him reminded him too much of other silences—the deep silence of the grave.

He forced his feet to take one, then another step forward. Again. Again. The only sound, his footsteps and his memories.

She may never sing for him again, his canary.

He sped his steps in a useless attempt to outpace his thoughts. His foot caught on an uneven stone. He stumbled but caught himself before he fell. He leaned against a lamppost, unable to escape the truth.

This had nothing to do with betrayal. Meg had ever been loyal. If there was betrayal, it was his. When their hosts had clambered for Meg to entertain them, as if her voice and talent should be at their disposal, he had not come to her side to support her.

Sing for your supper, his father had said.

Erik had not recalled Abel's voice with such clarity in years. The memory wedged like ice in his heart. The guests at the dinner party had circled Meg, caged her as effectively as the bars had once closed in on him at the fair. And he had let them cajole and tease her. As if she were a canary in a golden cage, they had demanded that she perform for them. And hardened against her distress he had fled to another room in anger at her more than at the crowd that harassed her.

Erik shivered. He swallowed the bitter taste of gall. The memory of his cruelty to Meg did little to warm his heart. The exertion of walking had kept the cold at bay. Now leaning against the metal lamppost, Erik felt the cold seep through his coat. With it came a degree of calm and the beginnings of a plan. He turned and began to walk, this time in the opposite direction, this time with a destination in mind.

What would ease her disappointment? How could he make

amends for his obsessive insistence on her singing, his unthinking tyranny?

Erik had not realized how far he had walked. The exercise had calmed him, but he was anxious to be home.

The notes of a badly tuned piano drifted toward him from a narrow side street. He would have walked on had he not heard the first few strains of a voice. In spite of the poor quality of the instrument that accompanied it, the voice was not only in tune but of a purity that fixed Erik to the spot. She held a note so lovely, so seamless that Erik held his breath to sustain the impression in his mind. Well past the moment he knew most singers would tremble and let the note crack or fall silent, this chanteuse maintained control. The note held strong until it gave way to a cascade of notes, each crisp and clear, each divided with the care of a mathematician or wizard, each one full of grace and magic.

Erik followed the notes, with each step convinced that the voice was unique. The song was a raucous example of the kind one hears in taverns and inns. Usually such songs were simple compositions based on a repetition of melodies easily remembered, within the limited range of most untrained singers. But this woman played with the notes, adding her own signature to the melodic strain. She was not trained and yet her style showed an impressive range and a comfort with counterpoint.

The street was narrow. On either side were various establishments many of which were dark and closed. At intervals bright light and boisterous noise spilled from open doorways. The music was coming from one of these. Erik glanced above to see the sign over the paved street, the Boar and Bow. The name sounded familiar. Then he recalled that it was one of various inns where Raoul, in disguise, had boarded while they waited for Inspector Leroux to make his move against the Phantom.

At that moment, the song came to an end. A party of drunks stumbled over the threshold, weaving as if on one pair of legs. Erik stepped to the side into the darkness beyond the reach of the light from the doorway. The men tottered and wove their way past him, talking loudly, switching easily from rants to sentimental gushing to goading insults.

Erik felt drawn to another time, another place—a seedy inn and brothel called Roderigo's. Giovanni's pale face rose from a memory long buried, but Erik easily put it to rest. That was one ghost that he would not abide. If he had to skewer the rake again, he would. Even so the uncomfortable memory of past debauchery eased, but didn't completely recede. He firmly locked his jaw against it and stepped across the threshold into the bright light of the Boar and Bow.

The first eyes that lit on Erik were followed by others until each of those present stared up at the tall, still figure of a masked man. Even if Erik had not worn a mask, he was sure that his appearance—in formal evening attire—would have stopped the conversations. Glassy eyed or clear, every gaze was fixed on him. The silence hit him almost as hard as their curious and suspicious regard. Movement distracted him.

Toward the back of the room a raised platform, a piano to the side, a young woman of indeterminate age collected coins from those nearest the rustic stage. She, too, glanced up at the intruder. Their eyes met only briefly for she seemed surprised and in the same instant turned and rushed through a curtained doorway.

Erik went to follow, sensing that she was the one whose voice had lured him to the tavern. His movement broke the strange stillness that had taken hold of the crowd. The sound of wine pouring into glasses, the scrape of bottles and mugs across rough wood, the baritone rumble of voices returned softly then built as Erik reached the back of the room. Something familiar had struck him about the young woman's face, the way she stood, but he couldn't imagine how or why. He did not know her. Yet he was convinced that he had, must have seen her before now.

He pushed the curtain aside to find blocking his way a slim man with dark features. His brown hair was long and unkempt. Thick lashes framed his black eyes. The man stood as if to bar Erik's path, and there was a strange intensity in the way he returned Erik's gaze. Erik could not shake the feeling that the man knew who he was and meant to keep him from following after the woman.

"May I help you, signore?" the young man asked.

Although the stranger stood in Erik's way, there was something awkward in the way he held himself. Erik noticed the stillness with which the man's left arm hung by his side and his uneven stance. He seemed to lean to one side.

"The girl who passed this way?"

"She's gone." The young man did not step aside, did not explain further. Erik had the distinct impression, even so, that the young man knew more than he was saying. He felt his hairs bristle as he sensed a challenge in the young man's clipped words. But Erik, too, understood the value of silence. Finally, the man added, "I could get her name for the signore if he's interested."

Erik heard the veiled offer. The young man was baiting him, luring him toward something. Erik scowled. He wasn't sure what the game was, what was being offered, or the terms involved. Was the girl a whore? Erik looked past the man's shoulder in the direction the girl had taken. The memory of her voice reverberated in his mind.

A shame to let her go, a shame to think such a gift would go to waste, a shame to think that she would be bartered for her flesh rather than groomed for her talent. Erik swallowed the bitter taste of ashes. It galled him to play into the young man's sordid plans.

"Bring her to me, Costanzi, tomorrow afternoon, at the Teatro dell'Opera." Erik turned to go. Over his shoulder he added, "Don't disappoint me."

Erik pulled Meg into his arms. She had been sleeping only fitfully, waiting for his return. When he slipped into bed, she shifted her weight slightly, her back to him, so that he would know that she was not deep in slumber. Then she felt him, a solid wall of warmth and flesh, his breath fluttering over her ear. His arm encircled her waist. She fell backwards, turned so that she rested on her back, cradled against his shoulder. He moved with her, wedged an arm beneath her neck, until her body leaned against his, her small hand on his chest, her face tilted up toward his.

They lay locked together in each other's arms in the dark room.

Meg felt more than saw his eyes on her. Only a glint of reflected light gave away that he was staring at her. Slowly the shape of his face became visible to her, then the features she knew so well, the long line of his nose, the curve of his mouth. Without thought she touched the full lower lip with the tip of her finger; lightly she traced the sunken line between until his lips parted and she dipped inside to feel the warm, tender flesh. His lips pressed round her finger, holding it just inside his mouth. His tongue licked and savored the salt taste of her skin.

She had vowed not to speak. Let him explain his actions when and if he chose to. She would not question him. She was not his keeper. This was not a prison, but a home.

Erik released her finger from the warmth of his mouth, kissed the tip, and folded her hand inside his fist. He lodged their bound hands between them, nestled against their hearts.

The gesture made her ache to hear his voice. But he remained silent. In spite of her vows and determination, she was the first to speak.

"What happened at the dinner party tonight?"

"Nothing," he lied, and she knew it was a lie. "I was restless."

If he didn't want to talk, there was little that she could do to make him. She couldn't shake off the feeling that he had been displeased with her this evening.

"Are you angry with me?"

Nor had she meant to ask him that question. And yet the moment the words left her mouth she knew that his possible answer was what had kept her awake in bed. She had told herself she was worried about him. But that had been smoke and mirrors. Erik was not the kind of man one worried about when he walked the streets at night. Anyone foolish enough to try to assault or rob Erik would soon rue his choice of mark.

"Well?" she asked, when Erik did not answer. The shock of his silence filled her with dread. She could think of only one reason for his anger. She had disappointed him.

"No," he said. His voice was low and soft. She could not read the tone in the one flat syllable.

She had not sung for him. She had seen the expectation in his stillness as he had waited on the periphery of the assembly at the dinner party. When Sig. Cuomo and his wife encouraged her to entertain them with a few melodies, she had still refused to sing.

He brushed his fingers along the soft curve of her cheek. They lingered at her temple and disappeared among her blond strands. Cupping the back of her head in his hand, he brought her face up to his and tasted her with his lips and tongue.

Words unspoken lay thick between them.

My Dearest Christine,

I have but rarely written to you. It had not seemed appropriate for me to do so. It is not that I do not think of you or do not care to know that you are well. Meg reads your letters to me, sometimes reserving sections that she pretends would not interest me. All news of you and Raoul interests me. Because I know that your regard for us is as strong as ours for you, I risk taking up the pen and begging of you a favor.

Since last summer, when Meg became ill, she has not sung. It may well be that she can't and that her career is over. I have handled the situation poorly, adding to her distress rather than allaying her fears. Inpatient and incredulous, I have pushed when I should have comforted, I have scolded when I should have sympathized. And yet, being who I am, Christine, I cannot seem to admit to myself that there is no hope.

I am losing her. And if I do, it will be largely my own fault.

I write to beg that you come. Meg needs you. She needs your comfort and friendship, your softer ways, and I need your guidance. You, my first pupil, understand my music; you understand me. My way will not succeed in this case. It will not bring Meg back along the road to recovery. You have the skills, the knowledge, and the talent to help her. But more importantly you are kind where I am cruel, you are patient where I am demanding. As her friend—as our friend—you will ease her way.

If it is meant to be that she will not sing again, you better than anyone will be able to tell. Christine, if you tell me that my songbird will no longer sing, I will accept it. If you cannot lead her back—with your gentle and loving ways—to the music, no one can. I will be resigned, I promise you.

It pains me to admit that I am not what Meg needs. She needs her friend, her sister. She needs you. As so do I. For I need you to help me understand her. If our lives are yet to change again, I will require some guidance.

With great affection, Erik

CHAPTER 7

Nymphs and Sirens

"I write...I write, I compose what I can't...can't have. It is music, and it must be perfect for that is the only perfection I can ever have!"

Phantom Death, Sadie Montgomery

It was not like Rinaldo to take the day off. A stagehand murmured that he had caught a glimpse of Jannicelli sometime early that morning in the theater. Another mentioned that he had seen him leave. It was nearly two o'clock, and he was nowhere to be found. Chiara Greco was taking her instruction from Sig. Bianchi for the moment. Erik only half listened to her. From somewhere off to his right, he could just hear Carlotta complaining to the stagehands, her voice piercing even the combined force of the piano and Chiara's rehearsal. She was arguing over the blocking for her aria. When he glanced in her direction, she hastily turned her back, pretending to ignore him. Something was afoot. His intuition told him that Carlotta had something to do with Rinaldo Jannicelli's absence.

As Erik started across the stage to confront Carlotta, he caught sight of Jacopo speaking with someone in the wings. The curious young man from the previous night stood unsteadily, leaning his weight on his good leg.

For the moment, Carlotta could wait. He went to the wings, instead.

A glance from Erik told Jacopo that he would deal with the intruder. Jacopo stepped back and leaned against a crate. Without preamble or greeting, Erik addressed the man.

"Where is she?"

From behind the young man stepped a wood nymph.

"You?" Erik accused. Now he recognized her as the clumsy snowflake that had run headlong into him one day in the corridor. Renata had mentioned her, saying that she was hopeless as a dancer. Even though he agreed, he had accepted Renata's generous suggestion that the girl be allowed to remain among the dancers as long as she could be kept in the background.

"Sig. Costanzi, Adamo DeVita is my brother. He said you wanted to…"

"Velia is wasted in the ballet corps." Not nearly as tall as Erik, DeVita straightened his back and stretched in an effort to meet him eye to eye.

"With that I agree," answered Erik.

It hadn't occurred to DeVita that Erik might, for that very reason, dismiss his sister. The subtle threat was not lost on him or the young girl.

"She has talent. She sings…" the man protested, but he had lost a bit of his former arrogance.

"Like an angel. I know. I heard her."

Velia blushed red from the roots of her dark blond hair to the shallow of her throat.

"Then you'll give her a part in the opera?"

Erik studied the young man. He wanted too much, too quickly. Erik ignored him and spoke instead to the girl.

"Are you willing to devote yourself completely to the training?"

DeVita answered for her. "Yes, she is."

"I did not ask *you* the question, signore."

"I am my sister's guardian, Sig. Costanzi."

Erik ignored him. "It will take all your attention, all your energy."

"I would become a great singer?" asked Velia. She, too, acted as if her brother were not by her side.

Erik hesitated. "If it's meant to be."

Before the girl could respond, DeVita once more intruded. "What will you pay?"

"Money? You're interested in the money?" For the first time, Erik let the full force of his gaze fall on the impertinent young man.

"I want what's due."

"Are you the one who will sing?"

The man's jaw clamped shut against an angry retort. Erik, too, was as tense as an E string on a violin. Both men stared at each other as if considering coming to blows.

"I will do anything, Sig. Costanzi, anything you wish." The girl's answer defused the moment, bringing Erik's attention back to her.

Erik studied her. Anything, she had said. He was not sure that he liked her desperation.

In the silent moment, Erik knew Adamo DeVita watched him. The man's eyes were riveted to the mask. He shifted his weight from one side to the other, a lopsided gesture that made him look awkward, that made more, rather than less, evident his damaged leg. It would be a mistake to let pity cloud his mind, a mistake to underestimate this young man. Even though his leg was twisted, he was not weak.

"Tell your brother I don't wish to see him anywhere near me. You'll join the chorines. Gather your belongings. From now on, you live here at the dormitories." With that Erik nodded his dismissal to them both and started to walk away.

"A chorine?" DeVita blurted, his voice loud enough to draw the attention of several nearby members of the company. "My sister is not a chorine."

Erik ground to a stop.

"Don't presume to tell me how to run my opera house, signore." Erik's voice was deceptively calm, but anyone who knew him could hear a clear note of warning. "Jacopo will see you out. The child's voice is good, but she has much to learn."

Before DeVita could protest, Jacopo stepped forth to usher him toward the exit.

"Jacopo, have you seen any sign of Rinaldo?" Erik had watched Chiara Greco go through the motions of practicing her scales. When she had arrived that morning and not found Rinaldo, she had stood in the middle of the stage like a castaway in search of land.

Over Don Erik's shoulder, the sceneshifter could see Chiara rehearsing with Sig. Bianchi. Her head swiveled like that of a dove in all directions. Obviously she was still searching for Rinaldo.

"That one's been looking high and low for him. I imagine she'd have found him by now if he was anywheres about."

"Still no word?"

"Calvino thought he saw him early this morning but not since. Want I should send one of the lads to his rooms to see if he's ill?"

The thought had not occurred to Erik. Rinaldo was a strong young man, not given to illness, real or imagined. Surely he'd have sent word if something serious had delayed his arrival. Yet it was unlike Rinaldo not to inform someone that he might not come.

"Yes, send someone to see. Tell him to ask around if he doesn't find Rinaldo home."

"Sí, Don Erik."

At first Erik couldn't put his finger on it, but there was something else amiss. Then it occurred to him that Carlotta was studiously avoiding him. For once, Erik would have liked to have had her at his heels, demanding and pestering him.

Something was wrong.

…apologize…taken my leave…try my fortune…humble student…

No sooner had Erik tossed the brief note onto his desk and let out a torrent of curses than a knock sounded at his door.

"Come," he said a bit too harshly. Rinaldo's decision to leave Rome in search of another position, perhaps in Milan or abroad, had displeased him more than he would have expected.

Chiara Greco stepped inside his office. Since he had sent Rinaldo to offer her a temporary position as lead soprano at the Teatro dell'Opera, Erik had not said more than five words to her on any given day. He had no idea of her character. He was only concerned with her ability to perform. What he had heard so far on stage had been competent, sometimes impressive. Erik rose and beckoned for the young woman to take a seat opposite his desk.

"Where is Salvatore?" she asked even before he had resumed his seat.

"Excuse me?"

"I mean, Sig. Jannicelli, my instructor. It has been several days. I was wondering…"

Erik had not heard anyone address Rinaldo by his middle name. Was this a sign of intimacy?

"He has left my employ."

Chiara bounced up from her seat, her jaw lax and her mouth open wide.

"But he…." Evidently at a loss as to what to say, she hesitated. Seeming to marshal her thoughts, she began again, "My practices, they're impossible. Sig. Bianchi is a wonderful maestro, but he cannot be expected to…guide me the way Sig. Jannicelli has."

"You're right. Sig. Bianchi has more than enough to do without taking on your training."

"Training?"

Erik caught the surprise and challenge in the young woman's tone, but he ignored it.

"Yes, training."

This was exactly why Erik had sent Rinaldo to negotiate with Chiara Greco. He had no time or inclination to soothe fragile egos.

"You're competent. You have a nice voice."

"Competent?" Chiara sank into the chair. Her voice, tight and strained, floated away.

Indifferent to the possible effects of his frankness, Erik went on, making Chiara shrink even farther into the soft, purple brocade of the cushion.

"Let's see what Rinaldo has managed to do with it, shall we?"

Erik pointed to the piano at the far end of the room. He rose, expecting Chiara to rise, too. Slowly she pulled herself forward and with leaden feet followed Erik Costanzi to the instrument.

Erik gave instructions regarding the salary for the new chorine. In addition to the regular amount given to a new member on probation, he stipulated that a sum was to be added to compensate for extra hours of training. He fought down his distaste for the brother. Perhaps the additional funds would placate him and free the young girl of his tyranny. For that was how Erik saw it. The man may pretend to be looking out for his sister's welfare, but it was obvious that Velia DeVita was meant to work for more than her own upkeep. Thinking better of it, Erik called Mario into his office.

Mario's talent had not been discovered in performance but rather in the financial sphere of the business. It had been purely luck that alerted Erik to his son's proclivity not only for numbers but for organization. When Erik had yelled once too often at the accountant in charge of the financial heart of the opera house, the latter gathered his charts and pencils and left, in the middle of a season, without warning. While Marcelo and Erik discussed their options—the need to find someone immediately to take care of the enormous influx and outflow of money, the complex accounting for materials and salaries—Mario had sat at the desk and had examined the figures in their columns, opened the box of receipts, and begun to enter each one methodically in its proper place. The two older Costanzis had only stopped arguing when Mario interrupted to ask them why they had needed so much saddle soap. There were horses in the stable, but it was hardly an equestrian school. Although Erik had no interest in keeping the books for the opera house, he could read the columns as easily as Mario could make them. He glanced over his son's work with an approving eye.

Although Erik had told Mario that he did not have to work, Mario wanted to be part of the opera world. On occasion François would play in the orchestra alongside the older musicians. He sometimes also assisted his father with the transcription of scores, the revision of certain pieces, and had even helped with rehearsals. Mario yearned to prove that he, too, could make his contribution. So Erik had reluctantly allowed Mario to take over the accounting for the theater with the condition that he hire and train one or two assistants. Under no circumstances would he permit Mario to discontinue his studies in order to devote himself full-time to the task. Instead Mario supervised two clerks—men older than himself—and periodically reviewed the complex financial records. He also streamlined several lines of expenses and proved himself to be a skilled negotiator with the local tradesmen, a task at which Erik was less than hopeless.

"You wanted to speak to me, Father?" Mario closed the door behind him and sat casually, his leg thrown over the arm of the stuffed wing chair near the fireplace.

"The young woman I just hired," he began.

"Velia."

Erik stared for a moment at Mario who shifted nervously in his seat, then smiled at his father.

"She's got nice legs."

"You won't be seeing as much of them now that she's in the chorus." Erik's voice held a touch of reproof in it. He resumed searching through several sheets of music on the piano. "At any rate, Signorina DeVita will be paid as a chorine with a modest additional payment to cover her time for training."

Had he not been browsing through his music, he might have noticed that Mario's attention was more concentrated than usual and might have asked the cause.

"Si, Papa," said Mario when Erik glanced his way to make sure the boy was listening.

"Another thing, Mario." Here Erik paused and faced Mario, but Mario had had time to school his expression and cover his interest.

"Yes, Papa?"

"I wish you to find a way to put aside an amount in a special fund. I do not want her or her family to have access to this account without my permission. Let it be a portion of the money that I've stipulated for the extra hours of training."

Mario's dark lashes shaded his eyes, and his eyebrows gathered over the bridge of his nose. Erik noticed the sudden change in expression.

"It's to protect her, Mario, from her family's greed." Mario's eyes lifted and with them his mood. Erik was not inclined to ask his son what he might have assumed about the special account set aside for a young woman in his employ. "I've no doubt that she'll see little of her actual salary."

"I see." The relief had been replaced by open concern.

"Do you know the child, Mario?"

Mario grinned. "I'd hardly call her a child, Papa. She must be… at least sixteen or seventeen years old."

They could not guess at Mario's true age. He had been living alone on the streets when Erik took him in. Birthdays, had he had any, were a thing lost in Mario's past. In recent months, the boy had far outstripped François and now appeared to be on the verge of adulthood. Erik judged that he could be anywhere between fifteen and eighteen years old. In marked contrast to Mario, François still retained the ungainly disproportion of adolescence.

"Did you shave today?" Erik noticed the dark shadow along Mario's jaw line.

"I've been shaving daily, Papa, for several months." Mario rubbed his hand along his chin with evident pride.

Erik didn't point out that there were sections that had still not darkened and would come only in time, such as the line that would eventually connect Mario's mustache to the beard on his chin.

"Can you set up the account as I asked?"

"Of course."

"Good."

Realizing that his father had finished the instructions, Mario started to leave. Erik called to him again.

"Mario."

"Yes, Papa?"

"You must not do anything foolish."

Mario's face turned a bright shade of red. "What do you mean? What do you think I would do?"

Erik ignored the challenge. He had come to realize that both his sons were easily offended and often responded in an aggressive and irrational manner. At times they continued to be as malleable and compliant as they had been when they were young children—indeed much like Raoul and Etienne were now—but one could never anticipate when they would become surly and answer back in a fashion that verged on impertinence or downright rudeness.

"The child," Erik used the word intentionally, laying an emphasis on it that Mario couldn't miss, "is under our protection."

"Yes, Father," said Mario, with some resentment, before he left the room.

"Jacopo, what's that racket?"

"Oh just some old drunk looking for a handout so he can buy another bottle."

Erik noticed Velia DeVita come in through the side door, the one that led to the narrow way between the buildings. She disappeared down the corridor. Something furtive about her movements struck Erik.

"The girl? What did she have to do with it?"

"Oh, that one?" Jacopo caught sight of her just as she turned to climb the stairs at the far end. "Seems that the old man is her father."

"What was she doing?"

"Doing? Well, she gave him something. Money, I think it was. Must have been a fair amount because the old goat smiled and patted her on the head."

"Then what happened?"

"She kissed him on the cheek and waited for him to leave."

"Then what was the ruckus about?"

"That young man—the one with the game leg—came up and started yelling and pulling at the old man's pockets."

"The girl's brother. He has only one good arm, too."

"Well, that may be, but he's a fierce one when angry. Paolo and I held him back until the drunk got safely down the street."

Erik nodded. Jacopo went back to his duties.

Carlotta had been as surprised as anyone when Rinaldo disappeared the morning after their fight, the morning after he had taken Chiara Greco to her rooms, the morning after Carlotta had led Ricci to her bed. She had been prepared to meet Rinaldo the next morning and throw it in his face that she was not a woman to be left waiting. If he expected to be her lover, she demanded his full attention. She would not take him back until he crawled on his hands and knees and begged her. She was prepared to make him suffer.

The scene had played over and over in her mind. She had rehearsed it as she dressed for the event in her most flattering gown, rosy pink with black fluting, as she rode in the carriage the streets winding back to the Teatro, as she prepared to take her place on the stage. At her dressing room table, she imagined Rinaldo Salvatore Jannicelli coming as a supplicant to her. However, when the moment finally came, before she could deliver her carefully planned speech, Rinaldo threw out *his* accusations, turned his back on *her*, and walked away. She was struck dumb.

He had given no explanation for his cruelty. Before she could even speak, he had insulted her. He had left her speechless in the corridor outside her dressing room.

When Carlotta dried her tears of frustration, put on new make-up, and marched off to the stage, the cuculo-vacca had already been there, doing her incessant cooing, mooing. But Rinaldo was not with her. Carlotta forgot to be angry and went from person to person, group to group, from the stage to the wings to the offices and rooms at the back of the theater, asking for Rinaldo, unable to believe that he had actually gone so far as to leave the building.

"Where, where, where?" she had called, exasperated and incredulous not to find him.

Convinced that Rinaldo was nowhere in sight, she had almost considered walking over to the cuculo herself and demanding that Chiara Greco explain what she had done with *her* Rinaldo. As frantic as Carlotta had been to know his whereabouts, she would not give the woman the satisfaction. At that moment, Erik had come on stage. He, too, saw Chiara Greco alone. He, too, seemed to be looking for Rinaldo.

Then it had dawned on her. Rinaldo had left her. A wave of crimson swam up from her gut and engulfed her face. Hot and bitter, she could not at first name the emotion behind the sudden shift in her bodily vapors. Could that burning sensation be shame?

Erik's eyes had darted in her direction. She had turned away so as to avoid them, as if their weight would crush her. He would see and know what she'd done and then there would be no way for her to brush aside the realization that this time she had gone too far.

Rinaldo had found out. Hadn't he said he'd meet her later at Il café? Hadn't he spent every night for months in her bed? Even as she had lain inert, pinned to the mattress by Ricci's sweating body, she had listened for Rinaldo's approach. He had not come knocking on her door. Had he come demanding entrance to her rooms, what would she have done? She would have extricated herself from Ricci's inept attentions and pushed him out the door. She knew with a certainty born too late that she would have thrown herself in Rinaldo's arms, grateful and relieved that he had kept his word and returned to her.

But he most certainly had come to her apartment that night. She knew it as if she had witnessed it. He had not stayed with Chiara Greco. He had made his way home to her only to find the door barred, and somehow he'd found out that she was not alone in their bedroom, in their bed. Oh, he might have been told at Il café that she had left with Ricci. He might have caught a glimpse of them in the window. Could he have heard their words, Ricci's animal grunts of pleasure? He certainly had not heard hers. Not that the absence of her pleasure would assuage his sense of her betrayal.

Carlotta had felt all eyes upon her the next day and the day after that when Rinaldo still did not come to work, did not send word. Erik studied her, but did not approach. Not until several days had passed, several days in which Rinaldo Salvatore Jannicelli punished her with his absence, did she realize with sinking doom that she had lost him.

"I just received a letter from Christine. They're coming to visit." Meg slipped inside the room and waved several sheets of stationery at Erik.

Erik looked up from his book and smiled as if surprised.

"That will be nice. You'll have more company."

Meg didn't answer. She folded the letter and stuffed it inside a large pocket of her gown. She took her seat in her favorite chair by the hearth. Erik laid the book on the side table and considered his wife. He regretted the unfortunate tension that had built between them. At the Teatro dell'Opera, Meg spent less time with Erik and the musicians. She came to practice but not her scales. Instead she danced. When not exercising, she could be found with the ballet corps, side by side with Renata Cossa or even among the dancers themselves, in line.

"Shall I tell Signora Bruno when to expect them?" Erik asked, keeping his voice light and pleasant. He had had enough strife at the Teatro and wanted at all cost to have a tranquil evening with his family.

"No, I've already spoken with her." Then as if she had picked up his recent thoughts, she asked, "How is the training going?"

Chiara Greco. It was barely a week, and he already dreaded their sessions.

"Fine," he lied.

Meg studied him. "That's peculiar."

"What is?"

"You say fine, but you don't look particularly happy."

"Why wouldn't it be going well?" he asked. *Did she doubt that he could handle the woman?*

"Why did you make her cry?"

Erik rose from his chair and began to pace the length of the room. After a moment, he came to stop before her. He scowled, his hands locked behind his back.

"When?"

"Was there more than one occasion?"

Erik's jaw muscle tightened as if he were chewing nails.

Meg disregarded the tension in the air.

"There have been reports of voices raised in anger, too."

Wednesday had been a particularly bad day. Chiara had reached a wall and would go no farther. Erik had encouraged and then berated her. Yet she pretended that what he required of her was impossible.

Then, in anger, he had called her a mediocre student, a coward. He had been a bit harsh, he would admit. Her reaction was a tantrum complete with tears. Instead of apologizing, Erik had demanded that she stop sniveling. When that brought an even more fervent burst of sobs from Greco, Erik had had no choice but to call an end to the lesson. The woman's sinuses had filled, and her nose was plugged. He knew he'd get nothing of worth out of her under those conditions.

"Like most prima donnas, she believes she has no more to learn. She stares at the door from the moment the lesson begins as if she'll bolt the first chance she gets. In the beginning, she held back, but I soon found her limits."

"She's already a good singer," Meg said.

Erik leaned over Meg. His arms on either side of her were braced against the chair.

"She would be great if she had any drive."

"You're so demanding, Erik. Not everyone can live up to your expectations."

"You did, Meg." Bending even closer, Erik took hold of her upper arms. "You met every challenge, crashed through every obstacle." He held her in place as if, like Chiara, she, too, might intend to flee from him.

"That was in the past," she whispered.

Erik's hands dropped, and he took a step back.

"The past? Is it all in the past, Meg?"

Meg fidgeted with a loose thread on the damask weave of the winged chair.

"What about the new girl that Mario's been talking about?" She spoke as if she only wished to distract him from what she had said. "I hear she didn't even audition for her place among the chorines."

"She didn't need to." Erik's tone suggested that the change in subject had not improved his mood.

"What does that mean?" she asked, unable to keep the coldness from her voice. "From what I understand, a pretty face and a nice figure are far less important than the ability to sing in tune. Or is it that you can spot talent now just by looking at a girl?"

"Why are you upset?"

"Upset?" Meg lowered her voice. It had grown loud and somewhat shrill even to her own ears. "I'm...not upset. Just curious and perhaps a bit perplexed."

"Are you accusing me...?"

"Of what? Is there something that I should know?"

He might have explained. He was on the verge of describing the voice he'd heard that night weeks ago when he had been walking the streets of Rome, alone with his thoughts, beleaguered by his foul temper. But Meg's accusation stung as unjust, and he would not give her the satisfaction.

Meg glared at him, angry at his silence. He stood—a wall, impenetrable and just as cold and unmovable.

"You can be so cruel, Erik. I remember your cruelty." Her lips trembled, but her eyes were dry. "What are you looking for? What is it in Chiara that you demand so fiercely that you drive her to anger and to tears? What does this girl you placed among the chorines promise you? Have you spoken to Mario?"

"What does...?"

"He's smitten with her. Our son thinks he's in love. And you move these people around on the stage as if they were pawns on a chessboard. For what? For your pride? For art?"

"Don't," he whispered, his voice nearly mute.

"Always demanding. For what? For something impossible? For...?" Meg left the words hanging in the air between them.

"Not impossible, Meg." He could not look her in the eye. "I found it. Once."

Before she could react, Erik left the room.

He was a beast, not a man.

Maman had warned her not to search for the Phantom. She had told Meg that he had perhaps lived too long in the subterranean caverns under Paris. How could a man live like that without going mad? Best to let him fade away into the past and the dark.

Meg would not, did not listen.

She had seen him slipping among the rooms in the opera house. She had watched him standing off in the shadows, barely a glint of white mask, a reflection glancing off his eye. He would stand so still. Hidden.

Something terrible and wonderful hidden inside him, too. She had even witnessed his transformation when he donned his disguise in the wardrobe room, trying on the masks, looking at himself in the mirror from behind the carnival faces, finally settling on the simplest and most elegant of masks. They shielded him, hid his strange disfigurement, drew one's attention to the deep intense green of his eyes and the marked line of his jaw, the sensual beauty of his mouth.

She had not listened to Maman. Instead she had sought him out, the beast in his den. He would not have let her remain. He had demanded that she leave. She had to trick him into becoming her teacher, a teacher like he had been for Christine. As long as he taught her, she could be with him. He would not cast her out.

"Can't you read the notes?" His voice thick with sarcasm, his eyes no less cruel, his finger stabbed at the score she sight-read.

Not trusting her voice, she nodded her head and tried to read the note through the film of tears that fell like a curtain over her eyes.

He stood behind her, peered over her shoulder, and in his rich baritone, sang the measures for her, once and then again.

"Simple. It's as simple as I can make it." He taunted her, his scorn evident in the hiss of his sibilants, the clip of the harder consonants, his enunciation so crisp that it felt as if the sounds were slapping her. "Sing!"

Meg fought to inhale, to get beyond the hitch in her breathing. She tried to recall the sound of his voice, to follow it as if it were a shining path laid out before her, the notes nothing more than a map. She could not focus on the notes he had scratched in his rush to commit the melody to paper.

"No! No, no, no, no. You are not allowed to leave these two notes out. It is not your music, it is mine. I say what is sung and what is not sung."

Meg's heart pounded a staccato beat behind her left breast, and yet she was not in her own body so much as somewhere between hers and the dense swirling presence that hovered at her back.

She nodded her head, wordless before his tirade. She knew that she had improved. Maman had been astounded when Meg sang a capella the aria Erik had demanded she learn. She had sung it flawlessly, each note bursting forth as if it had always been inside her and only now had she discovered it.

Yet under his dark gaze, her throat had constricted, strangling the sounds.

His arm suddenly wrapped round her waist, just under her rib cage, pinning her back against his solid wall.

"Breathe," he whispered, hoarsely, next to her ear. His breath had come hot and thick, teasing at her skin, sending chills along her throat that had nothing to do with the coldness of the vaults.

Too startled, too amazed to take a breath, she panted high in her chest, her bosom rising and falling with the rapid percussion of her pulse.

His face was still near her side, his mouth hovering just above her ear, his head tilted down. His breath warm and strange brushed against hair and skin. On its current was exuded the scent of fennel and mint, sweet and fresh.

"Breathe," he whispered, but this time the voice was different. This time the anger was gone, replaced by need. He did not demand but entreated. The palm of his hand flattened against her, the fingers splayed. His arm pressed in and up, forcing the air from her lungs.

Meg bent slightly at the waist from the unexpected force of the exhalation. Her hips pivoted back. Wedged against his solid body, she pressed into hardness.

The arm released her, the wall gave way. Had she imagined the groan? She turned her head to look over her shoulder but stopped when his voice demanded that she remain as she was.

"Don't," he had said. "Don't." And in that word Meg had understood what lay hidden between them—a need so dangerous that it might destroy both of them if it remained too long unsatisfied.

Carlotta had gone well beyond angry. Her cultured Italian had slipped into a gutter dialect more common to the streets of Milan than to the world of high art.

Ricci, too, was answering her word for word, but he was keeping his voice low as if aware that they had become the focus of everyone's attention. The dancers were having a hard enough time following Renata Cossa's instructions without having her drowned out by the piercing voice of Carlotta Venedetti.

"Snake, viper, worm, lower than a worm, maggot…" With each

word, Carlotta stepped forward and Ricci took one step backwards. "Maggot, maggot, maggot!" Having come to the lowest worm-like creatures of which she could think, Carlotta was momentarily speechless. But by then Ricci was at the edge of the stage, just at the lip of the stairs that descended laterally to the auditorium itself. Erik made his way briskly toward them just as Carlotta got her second wind. "Flea! Parasite! That's you, Ricci, a parasite. You cannot make art so you destroy it!"

At that moment, she raised her index finger as if it were a weapon and jutted it out into Ricci's stunned face. Just as Ricci tottered backwards, arms flailing to recover his balance, Erik reached out a hand and grabbed at the journalist's coat sleeve. His fingers felt the textured weave of the woolen coat and the slick surface of the brass button at the man's cuff just as both slipped from his precarious hold and along with them Ricci. The expression on Ricci's face was one of sheer surprise and terror. He tumbled back and down the stairs to the auditorium floor below.

Carlotta leaned over the edge of the staircase. Her head nodded as she counted each step. Ten. Not so bad. Most staircases had nearly thirty steps. But when she saw the look on Erik's face, she let out a curse, and then protested, "Look! He moves. He's not dead!" Looking out over the stairs once more, Carlotta raised her voice. "The maggot does not die. Not until the entire carcass she is eaten!"

Several of the staff in the auditorium had rushed to the fallen man and were helping him stand.

Carlotta didn't wait to see Ricci regain his feet. Maggots have no bones to break.

Erik stared after her, secretly admiring her nerve. He had no respect for Ricci. But antagonizing the man would do little to soften Ricci's acerbic tongue. The journalist had long ago determined to be Erik's enemy and goad. And Erik had never concerned himself with trying to please a man who would never admit that Erik's work had merit.

No, the only way to silence Ricci would be to kill him.

A shame that all things must pass. A worse shame when such a truth is not acknowledged. Fresh faces, new ideas, youthful vigor, that is what keeps our arts alive. No less true for opera than for drama, perhaps more so. The face can be painted with the mask of youth. Do we not look upon castles made of pine and pigment skies and accept the illusion of stone and air? But the voice, my dear readers? The voice has no mask. There is no paintbrush that can color it, no carpenter's skill that can sustain it. The voice does not lie.

Unfortunately it does age. Just as the mirror reflects one's face imperfectly, one cannot truly judge one's own voice. That is the duty of the artistic director. Woe to the one who has stopped his ears with wax! Take for example, Sig. Costanzi, our masked genius of the opera. Strange to think that his criteria are not as rigorous as they might once have been. But then that's why we critics perform a severe duty. For the good of the public, it falls to us to evaluate and to condemn when artistic directors pretend that they have gone deaf! Paolo Ricci

PART II

CHAPTER 1

Gilded Cage

Still he could hear the notes, echoes and memories converging from long ago.
Phantom Death, Sadie Montgomery

The smells of burning oil, the pungent odor of too many bodies enclosed in small spaces over time, the odd whiffs of food from vendors along the edge of the wooden platform assaulted Erik's senses. Only mildly disgruntled by the inevitable stares of strangers passing on either side of him, he winced at the clatter of their voices and the shrill screech of metal on metal as the train's wheels ground against the rails. The vaulted ceiling caught the humid exhalation of the iron dragon as it came to rest beside the congested platform.

Erik had insisted on coming to the station to greet Christine and Raoul. They would be among the passengers alighting from the train. Mountains of luggage sprang up creating bends around which the waves of travelers rushed. There was nowhere Erik could stand that did not obstruct someone's progress. So he planted himself where he could easily see down the platform and waited.

As he had imagined, he sensed her before he recognized her—Christine Daaé. Raoul had stepped down to the wooden platform and helped his wife to descend the steep steps. To Erik's eyes, she stood out as magnificent as she always had on the stage. How could the others not remark on her presence? How was it that other passengers walked past her without regarding her?

It wasn't only relief and hope that he felt upon seeing Christine, it was also a rush of sheer pleasure. Behind Christine, one by one, their children descended to stand beside Raoul. Victor was as tall as his father. Raoul was a slim man, but his son had that look young adolescent boys had; he had grown tall without adding weight, all bone and sinew. The young girl who followed stepped out of Erik's memories. This was the Christine he had come upon in the chapel years ago. This young girl, who must be Elise, resembled her mother as if time had folded back upon itself. Next came a child, a girl, who Erik was confident would be as beautiful as the other. Erica had been named for him, but he could already tell that the child would take after her father, her hair golden, lighter than Christine's or Elise's, her face somewhere between Christine's and Raoul's.

Raoul saw Erik first. He raised his arm just above his shoulder in greeting, and Erik nodded in return. Within moments the two men gripped each other in a firm embrace, broken as quickly as it had been made. Erik could not stop smiling at the joy of seeing his friend once more after nearly a year. Raoul stepped aside. His hand at Christine's elbow, he pressed her forward. Erik held his breath a second longer. For one moment, he wondered what was expected of him, what he desired, what Christine would permit. Then she placed her hand on his shoulder and guided him down. He bent and kissed her lightly on the lips. Raoul's hand clapped Erik on the back in a solid, familiar way, breaking the magic of the moment. Christine smiled, then laughed softly at the broad smile Erik could not disguise.

"Are we going to stand here all day?" Raoul's grin dispelled any hint of complaint his words might contain.

In the next few minutes, with less awkwardness, Erik greeted each of Christine's children. Then slowly they made their way to the carriages awaiting to take them to the Costanzi manor.

"So, how do you do this?" Raoul had reluctantly put on the leather headgear and gloves Erik had insisted were appropriate for this new sport to which he was about to be introduced.

"It's simple. You hit me if you can while I pummel you into submission."

"I can see why the sport appeals to you. Requires no skill whatsoever."

"Pure brute strength." Erik raised his fists up to the level of his chin, turned his body at an angle, and lightly bounced on the balls of his feet.

Raoul imitated Erik's position and movements, keeping at a safe distance from the reach of the man's hands.

"I do warn you that at university I did a bit of..."

Erik's fist shot out and clipped Raoul's chin in a glancing blow before he could finish his sentence.

"What were you saying?"

Raoul stood back a foot or two. The blow had stunned him more than anything. He stubbornly refused to let Erik know that the jab had rattled his teeth a bit.

"Very well," Raoul said, assuming the position again. "The Greeks had rules, you know."

Erik grinned, but he didn't take his eyes off the count.

Both men edged in, one's footing the mirror image of the other's, until they were in easy reach of each other. The blows came slowly at first as each judged his opponent's strengths and weaknesses. For several moments they circled and calculated. Then, as if a bell had sounded, the two men let loose a barrage of blows. A fist connected briefly with Erik's jaw. Another glanced sharply off a defending set of knuckles to bruise Raoul's upper lip. Raoul took a moment to wipe the blood from his mouth. Erik patiently waited, his defenses up just in case. Seeing that neither man was seriously injured, they continued to spar, delivering blows whose full effect was softened by friendly restraint.

At the end of a period of intense confrontation, Raoul and Erik intuitively relaxed. For the next hour they discussed and practiced defensive postures and commented on each other's reach, power, and versatility.

"What happened to your lip?" Christine put aside the book she was about to open and went to her husband. He took her hand before it reached his swollen lip and kissed it.

"Erik plays a bit rough." Raoul nodded toward Erik who had slipped into the room behind his guest.

"What's going on?" Christine asked, her question directed in equal measure to both men.

"A friendly match of fisticuffs. Nothing serious." Erik pointed to the darkened purple stain along his own jaw.

"I don't understand men. Why is it necessary to jab sharp things or to fling fists around at each other?" Christine looked back and forth between the two men.

"It's just a sport, Christine." Raoul examined a selection of whiskeys, gins, vodkas, and various wines in the cabinet Erik had pointed out to him.

"Try the Syrah," suggested Erik. "Marcelo had it sent from France."

"How's that tour of the continent coming along?" Raoul picked up the elegant bottle, studied the deep, dark color in the light of the lamp, and poured himself a drink.

"Madeleine and Marcelo may take another month or more and cross the channel. From their letters, it's clear that they're enjoying both the travel and the time together." Erik dropped his mask on the edge of a table near the door and crossed the room to the liquor cabinet.

Raoul sniffed at the glass of Syrah, took the smallest sip of the wine, and moved it about his palate before he swallowed. "Delicious. Anyone else?" He offered to pour a glass for the others.

Meg shook her head. She had come to examine Erik's bruises.

"I agree with Christine. Why do you have to choose such a violent sport?" she asked as she studied the bruise along the edge of Erik's jaw.

"Fencing is not without its dangers," Erik answered. He moved away, avoiding Meg's prodding fingers. No one but Meg seemed to notice.

"Yes," intervened Christine, "but you wear protective gear and accidents are infrequent in fencing."

"If you know what you're doing, your opponent is unlikely to do serious damage. That's true of any sport. Once Raoul learns to defend himself better, he'll have fewer busted lips."

Raoul raised both eyebrows and laughed. "I suppose that bruise is nothing? Were you as skilled as you suggest that I be, you'd not be turning a nice shade of purple now."

Erik accepted the glass and moved it in a soft circle to swirl the heavy liquid. He sniffed it appreciatively before taking a sip. As he raised the glass, his eyes met Meg's. For one moment, he thought perhaps she was disturbed. But even as he recognized concern in his wife's expression, she turned to speak with Christine, the former expression gone.

"Erik?" Raoul interrupted his reverie. "A game of cards? It's not as bloody, but I promise to make it as painful as I can."

"Careful, Raoul, my husband is a lucky man at cards."

"I should say he's lucky in many ways," said Raoul as he accepted a pack of cards Erik had taken from a drawer of the table where they would play. "And you, Meg, do you consider yourself lucky?"

When Meg did not answer, everyone's eyes went to her. She stood abruptly. Agitated, she seemed on the verge of tears. Raoul had only spoken in jest, but her silence had unnerved her guests. Raoul glanced Erik's way only to see him look away, similarly affected.

"Excuse me," Meg said. "I'm...I'm sorry." Without explanation, she rushed from the room.

Erik set his glass down on the edge of the table, careless that the contents sloshed over the rim and onto the varnished surface. He strode toward the door and would have followed after Meg, but Christine interposed herself between him and the doorway.

For one mad moment, Erik looked as if he would push her aside. But Christine placed her palms against his chest in a gesture that had only symbolic weight.

"Erik," she warned.

"Let me."

"No. Let her go."

"But…" He looked past Christine to the empty hallway. Meg had long disappeared up the stairs. "I should go after her."

"Just give her a moment. She's upset." Christine tried to make him look at her. But there was such longing in the green pools of his eyes that hers began to swim in tears for his pain. "Perhaps she was just overwhelmed."

Raoul stepped up beside Erik and put a firm hand on his shoulder.

"Sorry, Erik. I guess I should be more careful what I say. Come. Sit. Tell us what's going on."

Erik related what he could about the strange tensions that had grown between them since the previous summer. But so much was beyond his ability to put into words. When Raoul asked him for details and further explanation, Erik came back again and again to a 'feeling' he had.

"Well, one thing is clear. She's upset about her voice," said Christine.

"So am I, for Christ's sake."

"Perhaps that's part of the problem." Christine ignored the sulfurous look Erik gave her. "You're a hard man to say no to, Erik."

Raoul averted his eyes to hide his unexpected smile at Christine's understatement. Erik scowled but held his tongue.

"You laugh," she scolded Raoul who quickly drew a blank across his features. "And you," she said, addressing Erik, "you make your desires perfectly plain to anyone with eyes to see."

"Why shouldn't I?" Having lost what little patience he had had, Erik couldn't remain still. He paced back and forth, his eyes darting from his guests' faces to the half closed door. "Why shouldn't it bother me that Meg won't sing? Singing is her whole life."

"Her whole life? Are you listening to yourself?" Christine stepped into the path that Erik was making across the breadth of the room. Raoul moved to the edge of his chair, aware of the growing tension in the air.

Erik gritted his teeth, holding back the words he was about to say, and glared down at Christine.

"To whom is it more important that she sing?" she asked. "To her? Or is it really you who most wants…no…needs her to sing?"

Sensing his denial, Christine raised her voice, a note of disapproval making itself heard. "You're the one who wants her to return to the stage. Have you asked her if *she* wants to sing again?"

Erik bowed his head. His chest heaved from the exertion to control his frustration. Raoul came to Christine's side, prepared to lend support should it be necessary. Erik seemed on the verge of snapping in two.

"I...I...don't know." His words came in great bursts of air, addressed as much to himself as to anyone else. The former tension dissipated, and Erik slumped to the sofa, his face buried in his hands.

"Erik? She's in pain."

He looked up, his eyes greener than a field after a spring rain. "What can I do, Christine? How can I take it away from her?"

"We'll find a way," she said. "You'll see. It will be all right." Christine stopped just before she might have said, 'I promise.'

"Meg, you can't possibly doubt Erik loves you."

"I don't. Truly, Christine, I know he loves me. I know he loves me now."

"He'll always love you."

"You don't know that. Music is everything to him. If...if I don't...can't sing...?" Meg cupped her palm to her mouth. Her lips were trembling, and she could not finish her thought.

Christine almost had to look away. The intensity of Meg's fear went straight to her heart.

"But Meg, every singer must face the day when her career is no longer what it once was."

"That's so easy for you to say! You left in triumph. He'll always remember how you sang that night on the stage."

"Yes, the night that I betrayed him, Meg. He'll also remember that."

Both women regretted their sharp tongues the moment the silence fell between them. Christine was the first to reach out her hand. Meg grasped it hard.

123

"I'm sorry," Christine whispered.

"No, you were right to remind me. Besides, it was difficult for you to walk away from the stage. You could have had all Europe at your feet."

"I settled for one man on his knees." Christine smiled from ear to ear at the thought of Raoul prostrate begging her to come with him.

"You've been happy."

"Yes. And so have you."

"But it can't last."

"Would you ever stop loving Erik?"

Meg's eyes grew wide in amazement. "No!"

Christine said no more. There was no need. Meg took in the meaning of her own answer and understood.

Christine opened Meg's hand and traced the lines against her palm with the tip of her fingernail. In a heavy exotic accent, she lowered her voice and whispered, "I see your future. I see a tall, dark man. A tall, dark man with a bad temper and a loving heart…"

Meg giggled and tried to pull her hand away, but Christine was not finished. "My powers tell me that there is nothing but happiness for you, for you and your tall, dark man."

Meg leaned against Christine, their shoulders meeting, their heads nearly touching. Her eyes fixed on the palm nestled in Christine's open hand and examined the lines her friend had traced.

"Meg," Christine said in her natural voice, "you must realize that you are more than a tool, more than an instrument. I know he is a severe and demanding taskmaster. But he does not need you to sing his music. There is a whole company of artists who sing and play for him. Life is richer than he could ever have imagined it when he took me under his wing. You are so much more than I was ever meant to be."

"What are you afraid of?" Christine asked. She didn't hide her frustration. They had been in the music room for an hour. She had been urging Meg to accompany her at the piano.

"What if I sing and it's…it's…not the way it used to be?"

"Why would it be any different?"

"My voice has changed, Christine."

"The cold? But you sound fine to me, Meg. It's been months. You've fully recovered."

"I can hear it in the upper notes."

"So you have been singing?"

"Only bits and pieces, when I'm alone. I…I can't sustain the notes. My chest tightens. I can't breathe."

Christine wondered if the cold had truly damaged Meg's lungs or her vocal cords. Was it possible? Or was it fear and panic that took her breath away when she imagined that she would fail? Christine had been around the stage enough to know that nerves could wipe an actor's mind clean of the lyrics that he had spent weeks memorizing, that nerves could make a dancer's body tremble so fiercely that her mind could not tell her feet to move. Was it Meg's fear that was keeping her mute?

"With patience and practice, Meg."

"No, you aren't listening to me. I sing. But I can't be his songbird. Perhaps I could sing mezzo-soprano. But even that might be beyond my capacity." Meg waved her hand in the air in place of the words she could no longer say. Her eyes were shiny, and the tears crested and fell down her cheeks. "He will not love me." Her voice thinned and crashed into sobs.

Christine went to her. She wrapped Meg in her arms. Meg gave vent to all her fears and sadness and wept freely.

Erik had given Christine permission to browse through his personal archive of music. She had little idea of what she might discover in the bounded volumes stacked in floor-to-ceiling bookshelves lining two walls in Erik's music room. Besides holding the archive itself, the room was where Erik worked. Throughout the space were music stands, moveable chairs. An impressive number of instruments lined a portion of a third wall—mostly strings, violas and violins—almost as if they were ornamental, but one glance at them could tell the experienced eye that these were well-used instruments. Several were children's size, a row that ranged from the smallest through half to three-quarter sized violins, all roughened with use but recently polished to a high gloss and mounted for the next performance or practice. Not surprisingly, Christine noticed that the piano occupied a position of privilege in the room. It stood near the windows, far from the hearth to keep it away from the heat. It was well within the range of natural light that obliquely entered given the southwesterly exposure.

But Christine found herself irresistibly drawn to the archive. She barely glanced at the section devoted to music theory. Instead she passed directly to the heart of the collection, to stack upon stack of musical scores. All the most celebrated names in opera were represented. In a section on its own were symphonies, concertos, collections of music for strings, for quartets, for ensembles of all types—Classical, Baroque, Romantic. Excited she ran her eyes up and down rows and rows of music, amazed at the eclectic nature of Erik's tastes. Was he able to play these? Or was it solely his desire to possess all music for the sake of it?

Then she came upon the section of bound folios that she had been seeking.

Were all composers so productive? She thumbed her way along the rows of operas composed by Erik Costanzi, astounded by the man's fecundity. She counted the leather-bound folios, their names and dates embossed on the spines, impressed by the evidence of his steady production of original material until she came to a noticeable interruption in the dates. With a start, she recalled the moment when Raoul had told her of a fire and of Erik's death. The missing dates coincided with those lost months when Erik lived the invented life Lucianna had given him. A lone folio in deep red Cordovan leather stood as testament to those traumatic events. Christine ran her finger along its mottled skin. On the spine, she read the composer's name, Henri Fiortino, and the title, *The Stranger*. They had thought Erik dead, yet Christine had heard the Phantom in every note of the musical score. Now she experienced a brief shiver at the back of her neck almost as if the opera had indeed been pinned by a ghost.

On either side of this one bound opera, Erik had amassed

and catalogued an operatic biography that ranged from *Don Juan Triumphant* and *The Phoenix of the Opera* to his most recent work. Many of the works that he had written before the last days of the Opera Populaire had perished long ago. Only these two operas had survived.

How she wished she might have attended the performances of each and every one of his compositions. In spite of some losses, she was warmed to see so many bound volumes, such a rich treasure of music that might never have seen the light of day had circumstances been other than they were. Fate had rescued not only the man but his music as well.

At random Christine chose a volume toward the end of the lowest shelf, a recent work whose title, "The Fool," intrigued her.

"Let's see," she said as she flipped through the pages. Amazed and delighted, she realized that the story was a farce, not at all like Erik's usual work. She stopped and read the notes of one of the arias near the end. Christine hummed the notes, catching the thread after the first several measures, her eyes darting a half beat ahead as she anticipated the path of the music.

"It's an arpeggio, then a variation on a scale."

Christine jumped and slammed the tome shut, pinioning her thumb inside.

Meg apologized for having startled Christine and took the music from her. She opened to the same page and sang with a voice so sweet and so soft that Christine shuddered with joy.

"You see? It takes off at unexpected junctures. You think it will change here, but he always surprises you."

Meg looked away when she saw how Christine was looking at her.

"Why don't you sing it while I play?"

Before Meg could protest, Christine took the score to the piano and sat down. She set the score against the stand and within moments was playing the introductory measures.

"Sing with me," Christine urged when Meg came forward but stopped half way. "Please."

"I suppose I could sing softly."

"Oh, I'm sure you can. But you must help me if I get lost." Christine began again at the beginning.

Meg listened as Christine sang. As always her friend's voice tugged at something deep inside her. She could not always judge whether Christine's voice brought her joy or sadness. But its beauty was undeniable. At first Meg listened more than sang. She knew the piece as well as she knew her own name. She had performed the role of Galatea the season before she became ill. It was, after all, her last opera.

Like a ghost, her voice paralleled Christine's. She drew closer to watch Christine's eyes as they struggled to keep pace with the music. It had begun pianissimo and lento, the awakening of the creation, a creation of clay molded by Pygmalion, a creation that he had fashioned and then had loved. Through music, the lonely man had breathed life into the clay, and Galatea had awoken to his desire. As life infused her limbs, passion sparked. The music's tempo increased. As Christine began to falter, Meg urged her by singing the bridge to link her friend to the next measure. Her voice lifted to buoy Christine's so that they both sang the same song. Christine could not take her eyes from the score or she would become hopelessly lost, but she knew Meg would not abandon her.

As the song reached its culmination with a burst of notes that could only be called a cry of joy, Christine listened. Meg was singing, no hint of strain, no hint of constriction. She sang the final crescendo of notes, her arms raised, her eyes half closed as she recalled the notes, the swell of the orchestra and then the silence in which only her own voice rang. Meg sang the notes in which Galatea celebrated her life and demanded her independence from her creator.

Christine's fingers lingered over the keys, imagining the echo of the strings' vibrations. The last notes still hung in the air between them when Meg opened her eyes and met Christine's gaze.

"Meg, you sang."

Christine's words were met not with joy. Meg crumpled to the seat beside her.

"Don't tell Erik, Christine. Please. Don't tell him I can sing."

CHAPTER 2

Phantom Melodies

There is a tide in the affairs of men,
Which, taken at the flood, leads on to fortune;
Omitted, all the voyage of their life
Is bound in shallows and in miseries.

Julius Caesar, William Shakespeare

"Signorina Greco, we went over this section several times yesterday. Why is it that you insist on disregarding my instructions?"

Chiara Greco trembled, her face a brilliant red.

Erik had risen from the piano bench and stood, his arms braced, as if he were restraining his impulse to swoop down on her.

"My throat hurts," she said. "Your constant harping on a few notes that I've sung perfectly well has strained my vocal cords." Strained vocal cords not withstanding, Chiara spoke with more vehemence than usual to the artistic director.

Erik was somewhat surprised by her petulant response.

"Why didn't you say you were ill?" There was no hint of real concern in his question. Rather there was a distinct note of disdain.

"Not ill! Injured. Your endless badgering has damaged my voice!"

Impossible. Erik's jaw clenched tightly against an onslaught of invectives against her. She must have sensed his rising anger for she shrank away from him.

Perhaps he saw her defensive reaction. Perhaps he thought better of what he was doing. Had he exacted more of her than she was capable of giving? He could not accept her excuse. If her throat hurt, she was most likely ill. It had nothing to do with the exercises he had assigned.

He was not a man who was prone to explain himself—especially to a woman he barely knew.

"If your voice is strained, we will suspend the lessons for a few days." He sat again at the piano. He stacked the sheets of music and laid them to the side.

"I do not wish to continue."

Erik understood exactly what her intentions were, but he could not refrain from confronting her.

"You are unwilling to work? Are you leaving the company?"

Clearly Chiara Greco did not wish to lose the opportunity to perform at the Teatro dell'Opera.

"We have a contract, Sig. Costanzi."

"That works both ways, Signorina Greco." Erik couldn't keep the corner of his mouth from rising in a half smile. "There is a proviso in our contract, signorina, in case you've conveniently forgotten." Erik rose and faced his rebellious pupil. She stood her ground, although Erik could feel her anxiety. "Failure to perform to my satisfaction annuls our agreement. I will have a leading soprano who can rise to the occasion or I will cancel the season. Is that clear?"

Chiara Greco gulped and took a half step back. Her hand rested against her throat as if to protect it. The gesture stopped Erik cold. He could not remove his eyes from her hand. The floor tilted; a beam of sunlight sliced across the room wedging itself between them.

"Sig. Costanzi?"

Her voice had risen in urgency. Erik knew, even though he had not heard it, that she had already repeated his name several times.

"Excuse me." Erik raised his hand to wipe the sweat from his forehead only to find the mask in his way. Damned reminder! "You will finish the run."

From the corner of his eye, he saw her tentative movement. The hand that had protected her throat—against him!—had reached out toward him. He avoided the contact.

"Our agreement stands, signorina. Have Sig. Bianchi assign a pianist to accompany you in your rehearsal sessions."

"And the lessons?" she asked.

Erik sat behind his desk, his forehead resting against his palm as if he would study the ledger in front of him on the green blotter.

"The lessons are done, signorina. Please close the door on your way out."

She sang. This child—no, not a child but a young woman—this daughter of the one who had been his savior and protector sang with a voice that could not possibly be hers, could not possibly surge forth from the body of a dancer. Powerful, it filled the hollow vaults of this his tomb, rushed inside the gaping hole that once had been his heart. It made him tremble. Little Meg's voice resounded in the vault of his sanctuary, his cathedral, his stage and prison, his destined grave. Should he lie down and never rise again, this voice might ease his way toward oblivion. It would soothe his soul, whatever was left of it, as he waited for the final exhalation and then silence.

There was no such thing as true silence among the living. Only death could swallow all sound. He could not bear the thought. He would hold onto the slightest resonance of her voice, even though it was not the voice he had sought, the one his soul had cried out for and still remembered.

She sang. She stood, her feet turned out in separate directions, her arms slightly bowed at the elbows, the palms softly cupped as if to receive a gift. It struck him that the girl posed. She stood as a ballerina stood. At the ready, she held her body in place—a dancer in stasis—and let her voice spring forth in its stead.

He listened for the echo of another voice. The other one's sharp and clear as crystal, the voice of an angel, ethereal. This one's voice, throaty and rich, with filaments rooted in blood and viscera. Meg's voice was not as pure as her predecessor's, but still it moved him. She had been meant to dance, not to sing. And yet she sang. The knowledge frightened him, stirred him, and threatened to undermine his resolve.

What price would such a miracle demand?

Her voice grew in strength each day. He shut his eyes to concentrate on the phantom voice of the other as this one's swelled and swamped his mind, washing away his memory of other voices and filling the fissures of his loneliness.

And just as Meg's voice filled the caverns of his underworld, the child-girl-woman threatened to lodge in his heart, his poor, shattered heart. He could not hold her there. The pain was still too great, the heart too damaged to hold anything but a shadow. He understood he was in danger. He knew the woman who now sang in his sanctuary was stronger than he was. The only way he could save himself was to send her away. She had learned what he could teach her. It was over.

Meg was ready. He would have to let her go.

She let the last note fade, its wings fluttering against the stone walls. Seeking his approval, she smiled and waited for him to speak.

Instead he stared at her. His green eyes more a mask than the ivory one he wore to hide his ugliness, for he must not let her know what she had dared to make him feel. He could not let her see the naked wound she teased, the desperate ache that she had quickened, the fantasies that taunted him whenever she was not with him.

"What do you come for, Meg Giry?"

"To learn to sing," she answered. It was the standard response, the standard lie.

Had she not come to torment him? Had she not come to steal the treasure, the forbidden treasure that he protected but did not enjoy? The paltry remains of a soul that might have seen grandeur had been laid to waste in a futile search for love. Had this voluptuous temptress come to take even the shabby remains away from him? And what would she do with the shreds of his soul, his heart?

"What do you want, Meg Giry?"

She hesitated. She had already answered, had she not? He could see her confusion. But he was merciless. Hadn't they been merciless to him?

"What truth does a liar have, Meg Giry?"

"What do you mean?"

"What do you want?"

"I've told you. I want to learn to be a great singer."

"You are not meant to sing."

She blushed crimson. The color stirred him. He watched it rise as if it were his own hand gliding across her breasts, along her naked throat, to her cheeks, her lips. His mouth was awash in desire. He wanted to taste her, to know the soft hidden secrets of her flesh, to press against her the proof of his yearning. His body ached with the need she awoke in him.

Had he not buried hope? He would not endure it a second time.

"I don't understand how you can say something like that," she answered.

He heard the accusation. The challenge excited him.

"You came to steal Christine's place."

"No."

"You came to face the beast and shackle it with your golden chains."

"What are you trying to...?"

"You came for me, did you not?"

She looked away. The admission was clear. The confirmation shocked him.

"You want to whore yourself to a monster?" He could not resist drawing near her. He towered above her. She lowered her head and would not look up at him. It made him turgid with desire and power. "Do you want to lie with the beast, Meg?" He throbbed with need, afraid that she would not stop him and yet desperate to continue. "Do you want me to touch you?" He raised his hand and with the tips of his fingers touched her chin. She turned her face to look up at him. Her eyes glistened, but she was not crying.

He bent toward her, his eyes gliding over her features, drinking her in. In the back of his mind, a warning voice told him to be cruel.

"I've murdered, Meg. Blood drips from my hands. Dead souls stare out from these eyes. Would you lie with rotted corpses? Don't you taste their stench on my breath?" His fingers slipped from her chin to the soft, warm flesh of her throat where he caressed the smooth texture of her skin. Almost gentle, his hand encircled her throat, pressing against the throb of her pulse.

"Should I tell you what it felt like to choke my victims?" He had not done it with his bare hands. He had used a rope. But he would not use the rough weave of hemp on Meg's throat. He would use his hands on her if he were to strangle her.

In his palm, he held her beating heart.

"You wouldn't harm me," she said.

"Oh, wouldn't I?" he whispered, his face close to hers.

Her eyes—deep, dark, warm brown—fled from his and slid down the slope of his mask to the edge just above his mouth. There her gaze settled on his parted lips. Her mouth tilted towards his. He felt the groan before it emerged from his mouth. He released the pressure on her throat and walked away. He braced himself, his back to her, against the wall of the cavern. His body trembled. He wanted to rake his naked flesh against the jagged plains of the stone wall.

"Go." He waited to hear her leave. There was no sound. He knew she stood transfixed to the spot. "Go!" he shouted.

He heard her dancer's feet as they moved away from him. He fought the urge to call her back. The footsteps receded into silence.

Only then did the pain burst through the tattered walls of his heart.

Erik had asked Jacopo to watch out for Velia DeVita and to let him know her comings and goings. He was concerned that Mario's fascination with her might lead him to do something foolish. Until now, it had never occurred to him that his sons were on the verge of manhood. Such realization brought new worries. But it wasn't only Mario who weighed on his mind with respect to Velia. Her brother was trouble, and Erik had resolved to protect the young woman from his abuse if at all possible.

Jacopo had informed Erik that Velia left the Teatro each evening well after the performance. There was something furtive in the way she slipped out the back exit, silently on tiptoe, glancing about to see if anyone might spy her leave.

Was it a late night tryst? Erik did not watch his sons' comings and goings. He was fairly confident that François did not stray far or often from the mansion in the evenings. On occasion, he accompanied Mario. These forays were modest and often involved catching a play at one of several respectable theaters or perhaps a few hours strolling through the piazzas.

But Mario was another matter altogether. There were evenings when the young man set off alone to explore the city. Usually Mario would inform a servant or someone in the family of his departure and the approximate time he would return. The change in his sons' habits had, at first, disconcerted Erik. He had fought an almost instinctual impulse to keep his family within arm's reach, within the protective confines of the home and the theater. Fortunately reason had prevailed. He restrained his inclination in recognition that both François and Mario were approaching manhood. He would only push them away if he held onto them too fiercely. In particular it was inappropriate with Mario who had lived a good number of years on the street. Erik understood Mario's need to exercise his independence and knew that it would be a mistake to tether Mario to the Costanzi mansion.

Erik stood in the shadow of the wings, waiting. This was the hour when the young girls retired for the evening to the dormitories. They would be sleeping. This was also the hour when Velia would dress and sneak out.

As Jacopo had reported, at half past midnight, Erik noticed a figure make its way down the corridor from the dormitories and toward the back exit.

It was not a good idea for a young woman to be unaccompanied and on the street at such a late hour. Surely if she were out to meet Mario, he must be nearby. Erik waited a few seconds before he set out to follow the girl.

Velia rushed down the street, looking neither right nor left. She was definitely on her way to a rendezvous. Within moments, Erik realized that the purpose could not possibly be a tryst with his son. Mario would certainly have appeared by now. Instead Velia wove her way down the dark avenues, avoiding boisterous crowds of evening revelers, until she came to an intersection and turned onto a dark, narrow, dingy street that he recognized from one of his own late night walks. Taking a parallel path, Erik easily reached the Boar and Bow before Velia passed its threshold.

From the brightly lit interior came bursts of drunken laughter. An unfortunate man lay curled just outside the door, snoring a ragged and stuttering warning. Velia had barely glanced at the ragged heap. As several customers tottered out the doorway, Erik slipped inside, holding his cape high to shadow his mask. Keeping to the back wall, he avoided the attention of those present. He found a corner table just outside the glow of the many gas lamps suspended from the ceiling and sat down to wait.

It did not take long. A waiter had taken Erik's quiet order and had left a tankard of strong ale on the uneven wooden surface. Erik sipped at the sour brew, watching the customers at the nearby tables. One man glanced back over his shoulder at him, discomfited by his mask. Erik turned his chair at an angle so that he was closeted by the darkness that hung in the corners of the room. Those at his side spoke in whispers, but soon lost interest when they heard a piano begin to play the first notes of a boisterous drinking song.

Velia stepped out from a curtained doorway at the back of the establishment and took her place beside the man who played. She was not dressed like a snowflake or a wood nymph. Nor did she have on the modest dress that she normally wore at the theater when not in costume. Erik had perhaps misjudged her age. There was nothing childlike about the sleek lines of her body. The neckline and the lacy insert over her bodice revealed the upper swell of her bosom. The narrow straps of her gown fell low on her bare arms. She held her skirt hitched high on one side from which a naked leg visible from the knee down to her bare foot protruded saucily. She had darkened her eyes and her lips, making the full smile and arched eyebrows even more prominent than they might have been. Her hair was raised and pinned in what appeared a careless manner. The curls that hung loose and her bare leg and feet gave the impression that she had just come from her bed or was soon to lie down. The expectant silence carried more than interest. Desire perfumed the air.

Erik lowered the tankard that he had raised to his lips as Velia began to sing. It was not the usual drinking song that she had chosen. The arrangement was different, but Erik knew his own work well. The girl had adapted the melody and even changed some of the words. In spite of these modifications, Erik recognized the love song from a recent opera of his. Fascinated yet annoyed, he sat forward on the hard seat, aware that his right hand tended to fist. He considered interrupting the performance, but his ears betrayed him. He found himself anticipating each note, catching the minor shifts she had made in the original, taking note of flaws as well as several interesting turns that gave the piece a new and fresh dimension. At once pleased and disappointed, he listened to his music, which she now twisted and transformed into something else—catchy yet vulgar, sweet yet awkward.

In spite of her provocative costume and demeanor, no one bothered her. He had been prepared to intervene. It had not been necessary. Velia showed herself to be adept at placating or avoiding the few admirers who had approached her during and after her performance. Most were too deeply in their cups to be a serious threat. They cajoled her to sit with them—all bluster but basically inoffensive.

An hour later, he followed her back to the theater. At a safe distance, he watched until she slipped inside the theater via the same exit from which she had left.

Meg would wonder why he had not come home. It was nearly two in the morning. Thinking to hail a carriage, Erik searched the deserted streets. That's when he saw the man, on the opposite side of the street, across from the Teatro dell'Opera. He must have been hiding in the park, waiting for Erik to show up. Abnormally tall, as he stepped out of the shadows, he seemed to grow in the light of the lamppost.

Even at a distance, Erik recognized who he was. Erik bounded across the street, but there was no need to rush. The man waited for him.

"What do you want from me?" Erik asked. Unaccustomed to looking up at anyone, he did not like the sensation.

"It's been a long time. Are you well?"

Erik looked past the old man to the darkness of the park.

"I'm alone, Erik," said the man. "I mean you no harm."

"Why have you been spying on me?"

"I judged that you would prefer that no one see you with me. They might become curious."

The old man's name was Vosh, but Erik preferred not to remember it. It was easier to wipe the old man from his mind if he had no name, no past in common with Erik. Unfortunately, they did share a past. Vosh had worked the high wire in the fair, the fair where Erik, as a child, had been a prime attraction. Erik considered what Vosh had said. It eased his concern somewhat to think that Vosh was sensitive to Erik's position and wished him no ill.

"I can't live my life looking over my shoulder all the time. No one needs to know my business."

Both men understood that Erik was not only talking about his current acquaintances but of a certain woman they both knew in common.

"You've a new name."

"I've had many different names."

"She wants to see you."

Erik tensed. Warily he fixed the old man with his eyes.

"I've no overwhelming desire to see her," Erik replied.

The older man was silent for several moments. Then he nodded as if they had reached an understanding.

"I'll tell her you're not ready yet to meet with her."

"Tell her whatever you wish. But stop following me."

Erik didn't wait for the old man to respond. It was late, and he still had a long walk ahead of him.

Adamo had not noticed Erik Costanzi until Velia retired to the back to change her clothes. Once she was dressed in the modest dress that she wore at the Teatro dell'Opera, Velia took her leave of him and set off to walk back to the dormitories. Distracted, Adamo didn't give his sister his usual instructions. Perhaps they were no longer necessary. Erik Costanzi had stalked Velia to the inn and had sat in the shadows watching her perform. Adamo was pleased that he had insisted Velia dress like the siren that she could be. If she had had her way, she would have sung in her everyday clothes.

The plan was finally bearing fruit. The man lusted after her, had gone out of his way to place her among the chorines, and now stalked her through the dark streets. Adamo had watched Velia pick her way through the crowd of revelers and step out into the dark causeway beyond. Costanzi did not immediately rise from his table. Adamo was unconcerned. He, too, could be patient. When Costanzi rose from the table and left the inn, Adamo followed.

Velia did as she always did. She walked at a brisk pace, looking to neither side, taking the most direct path possible to the Teatro dell'Opera. As on other nights, Adamo shadowed her steps, unbeknownst to her, to make sure she arrived safely. Now he hung back, careful to leave a considerable distance between him and Costanzi, unconcerned that Velia was well beyond his range of vision. As long as he kept sight of Costanzi, he knew Costanzi would keep sight of Velia.

Adamo's mood darkened as it became clear that Costanzi would not approach the girl. When Costanzi reached the last leg of the walk, he did not increase his pace to catch up with Velia. He did not intend to address her. Like Adamo, he only followed. Within a block of the theater, both men lingered. Adamo estimated that his sister had easily gained the door and was now safely inside the theater. Costanzi did not enter. Instead he waited and then turned as if to leave again. But something stopped him. He faced the opposite side of the street.

Adamo looked toward the park and only saw darkness until movement brought his eye to a tall figure that stepped out into the glow of a nearby gas lamp. The man was thin as paper and tall as the grand doorway to the Teatro dell'Opera. Costanzi strode across the empty street. Face to face with the strange figure, Costanzi seemed dwarfed.

The unintelligible sounds of their conversation drifted Adamo's way. The young man strained to make sense of the brief exchange, but he could not come closer without giving his presence away. Even as he tried to think of a way to cross the street and perhaps approach the pair from the dark avenue of the park, the two separated. The tall man simply melted into the darkness, and Costanzi turned abruptly down the street in Adamo's direction. The young man pressed his body flat against the shallow depression of the doorway until he heard Costanzi's footsteps fade.

Once he saw Costanzi disappear down the street, Adamo set off for his own bed. He convinced himself that Costanzi's interest in his sister was a clear sign that the plan was working. Soon the man would want more than to hear Velia sing. Soon he would take her as a lover. Adamo would make sure Velia understood what had to be done. An unwise lover could easily be cast aside after the first urges of lust were placated. But a lover who knew how to barter her attractions could make a life for herself. He was determined his sister would perform her role with care. She was a clever girl. She'd handle Costanzi.

Once again alone in the back room of the Boar and Bow, Adamo stretched out on the narrow cot and drifted off to sleep. Just as he began to doze, he had one last fleeting thought.

It was a shame that Costanzi was married.

Ricci was tired of the smirks and snide remarks. He had just heard several allusions to his manhood from a host of rowdy performers at Il Café di Mondo. At first he had assumed it was simply the usual aspersions cast by the mediocre performers whose careers he had tarnished in his columns. At a nearby table sat several principals from the Teatro del Popolo, a company that was both amateurish and vulgar. Ricci had enjoyed composing a caustic and dismissive review of their rendition of *Hamlet*. One actor in particular he had recalled in a more than usually wooden performance of the prince. Ricci had dipped his pen in blood for that review.

But then Ricci had heard the name of Carlotta Venedetti in the mouths of several of the more vocal patrons of the café.

He finished his cognac, threw the coins on the table, and walked out of Il Café di Mondo. Behind him, the snickers and laughter increased in volume as if they had been meant to follow him even out into the street. Ricci hawked phlegm from the back of his throat and spit into the gutter.

Carlotta Venedetti would pay for her loose tongue.

"François, I want you to work with Signorina DeVita. Prepare her for the role of Yasmine." Erik laid his hand on François's shoulder and squeezed with affection.

The young man looked up from his scales. He had, as usual,

been immersed in his study and had not heard his father enter the small practice room where he spent several hours daily.

"But that's Signorina Greco's part, isn't it?"

"Yes. Velia will be her understudy. It will be good practice for the girl."

"You don't trust Chiara Greco."

François understood his father well. He was aware that the lessons with Chiara Greco had been suspended. She now rehearsed on her own schedule with one of the pianists from the orchestra.

Erik nodded. There was no need for delicacy with his son. François was more and more involved with the Teatro dell'Opera, and he needed to understand the way things worked.

"Do you think Signorina Greco might bow out of the performance?"

"No," said Erik.

"Then why does she need an understudy?"

Erik's lips curled up on one side. "She doesn't. But if she knows there is someone who could replace her..."

François smiled broadly and chuckled. "Oh, I see."

"Good."

"Sig. Ricci? Paolo Ricci?"

The journalist muttered an oath under his breath and turned to face the man who had called out to him. The stranger limped across the dark street. Ricci's natural caution eased somewhat as the man approached. Even so he was reassured by the weight of his cane. One had to be sharp on these streets to avoid being robbed or worse. From the shabby look of the man's clothes, he was common, probably looking for a handout. Ricci placed one hand over the bulge of his purse in his pocket.

"What business do you have with me?" Ricci rued that he'd not taken a carriage. He was already several minutes late for the performance at the Teatro Regio. The hackles on the back of his neck rose as he realized that the street was uncommonly quiet. He tightened his grip on the silver handle of his cane.

"Signore, you're the one who writes the reviews in the gazette."

The statement had only the hint of a question to it.

"What could my reviews have to do with the likes of you?"

The man's former smile slipped for a moment. His eyes went dead in the hazy light of the street lamp. Ricci took a half step back, considered retreating down the street in search of a carriage or familiar faces, but something about the young man made it hard to look away. As long as Ricci kept his eyes open, the man would not strike. He wondered if the limp had been faked. Was it a ploy to disarm a mark so that the thief could edge his way in, close to his victim, and then pull out a knife? Ricci noticed the arm pinioned to the man's side, the hand in a pocket of a frayed coat.

"You tell people what to like," the stranger said as he drew nearer to Ricci.

"In a matter of speaking." Ricci restrained the urge to step back.

"You don't like the director of the Teatro dell'Opera."

Ricci stiffened, anger making him forget his former suspicions. "Did Costanzi send you?"

"No."

Ricci scowled. He turned and started to walk away.

"There will be a new lead soprano." The stranger followed alongside the critic.

"Yes. I know all about Chiara Greco. She's got a nice voice, but there's nothing remarkable about her."

Ricci had attended several performances at her previous venue and had concluded that although the woman sang well, there was always something flat about her delivery—no life in it, no sparkle. Nothing to approach Meg Costanzi's performances.

"No, I'm not talking about Greco," said the man, slightly out of breath from the pace Ricci had established. "You must see my... you will be amazed by this new singer. She's talented, sings like an angel."

Ricci stopped and gave the man a reproving glance. Obviously he was in love with the woman in question. Probably doted on her like so many of those who hung about the backstage exit, hoping for a glimpse of their idol.

"As far as I know, Chiara Greco is the lead soprano this season."

Then it struck Ricci that perhaps the man had gotten wind of some news. Perhaps the lead was none other than Meg Costanzi, not an entirely new talent at all. The man may have no idea that Il canarino had been the reigning diva until just this past year.

In an entirely different tone of voice, Ricci asked, "Are you saying that Signora Costanzi is returning to the stage?"

"Costanzi? No. Someone better, younger, prettier, more talented than Costanzi's wife ever was."

Ricci made an unintelligible sound deep in his throat. Clearly the man had no experience in opera, he thought. He started to walk away without so much as a 'by your leave.'

"Velia DeVita," the man said. He gave a halting step forward directly into Ricci's path. His face glowed earnest, with a touch of madness in the artificial light of the lamp. "Mark my words, signore. You'll think you've never heard opera until you hear Velia DeVita sing."

The clatter of hooves and wheels along the cobblestone street announced the proximity of a carriage. Ricci's ears twitched and his eyes strained to see its approach. He walked toward the sound. Out of the corner of his eye he saw the young man follow, his body swaying choppily from side to side.

"Signore. Signore!" the lame man shouted after him. "You'll write a favorable review of Velia DeVita. You'll tell everyone to like her."

Ricci gained the side step of the carriage, barely waiting for the driver to rein in the horses. He shouted out his directions and urged the driver on. As they passed the young man on the street, Ricci tried not to look at him. There was something menacing about his request, his insistence, as if it held an unspoken threat.

CHAPTER 3

Oh, Terrible Love

her fingers unfurl and reach out even as her heart swells with the knowledge of her own strength, he will not vanquish her! he cannot destroy her love for him, she is terrible in her beauty, her love grows, unbending, unbroken, monstrous

The Phantom's Opera, Sadie Montgomery

Rome is blessed with culture. The gifts of antiquity are only rivaled by the glories of our contemporary artists. From the aqueducts to the Pantheon, our Rome is the envy of Europe. Who has not looked up in awe at the Sistine Chapel? Who does not marvel at the splendor of our piazzas, the grandeur of the Coliseum, the museums and the theaters that grace our city of eternal delights?

Grateful we should be indeed. The recent fall from glory of our masked genius of the opera and the fading brilliance of his kingdom at the Teatro dell'Opera would otherwise strike us as an overwhelming loss. How could we survive without the overblown drama of his characters' plights? Would we ever recover from the silence of his songbird? Alas it is a shame that mediocrity now sits where once the Muses held court. Yet let us not linger over the echo of past glories. Not in Rome. We have been blessed with treasures of much greater worth than the passing glitter of an Illusionist and his puppets. Paolo Ricci

"Why do you let him get by with it?" Carlotta threw the crumpled gazette on Erik's desk.

Without a glance at the contents, Erik picked it up and dropped it in the waste bin at his side. He resumed the work he had been doing when Carlotta had knocked sharply at his door and burst inside without awaiting his permission.

"Well?" she asked. She tapped her right foot in time to her rapid heartbeat. Each editorial by Ricci had been nothing more than an attack on Costanzi and the company. She hadn't minded it so terribly when the remarks had targeted Erik. Until recently the maggot Ricci had been careful to praise the performers, reserving his barbs for the 'masked genius of the opera.'

Erik glanced up at Carlotta and then continued to annotate, correct, and modify the score. When Carlotta did not take the hint, he said, "Ricci knows what readers want to read."

"But he is a critic. He is to review the art scene."

"Your point?"

"This…this…is all lies."

"I thought you didn't like 'la vacca-impertinente.' Didn't you say Chiara Greco was mediocre?"

"No, I said that she was…too…fat."

"And that her voice only appealed to dogs."

Carlotta's face blazed a pink to rival the deep reds in her hair.

"I do not like her voice."

"Why?"

Carlotta made several strange incoherent sounds deep in her throat and hugged her arms under her breasts.

"Ignore him, Carlotta. He thrives on attention. You know the type, don't you?"

Ignoring his allusion to herself, she answered, "But he is attacking us all. We will lose patrons."

"Will we?"

Carlotta pursed her lips shut at Costanzi's obtuseness.

"Our name is continually in his columns." Erik set aside the sheets and studied Carlotta. Since Rinaldo's departure, she had lost weight. Her current disdain for Ricci's reviews was also new. "His sarcasm sells the gazette. His readers expect him to find fault and to make it entertaining. If he can't find something salacious, he invents it. That's what Ricci does. But his reviews only excite the readers, encouraging them to come hear for themselves. It probably increases rather than decreases interest in our productions."

Carlotta let her arms drop limp to her side. "I don't like him."

"I doubt that it matters to Ricci."

The look that Carlotta gave Erik puzzled him.

"Ricci's insults would have mattered to the Phantom. *He* would have done something to silence…the maggot."

"Adamo, your girl has caught Rogelio Mazolo's eye."

Mid-morning at the Boar and Bow was normally a slow time. Constantino, a large and beefy man with broad square hands and short fingers, swiped at the crumbs and the residue of ale and wine on the rough wooden surface of the counter. He spread the gritty mess and spilled brew thinly enough so that to the naked eye the surface appeared cleaned.

Adamo squeezed the tankard in his fist. The coolness melted away, the heat from his hand seeping into the dark ale within. He watched Constantino's large, thick arm move in ever increasing spirals.

When Adamo didn't reply, Constantino continued, "Rogelio Mazolo. You know his shop. Down the block and to the left. Makes shoes, boots, belts—anything made of leather." Constantino leaned over the counter, his apron soaking up the remainder of soapy water and beer. "Has a unique collection in the back of specialty items— leather straps, whips—if you catch my drift." Adamo's eyes stared up into his, wide and unblinking. Taking the intensity of his look as a sign of interest, Constantino winked at the young man. "He let me see it one day. Rows and rows of straps, whips, collars with metal studs." He leaned in even closer and whispered in spite of the fact that they were the only two in the bar. "Didn't know what half of the stuff was for."

Adamo lowered his eyes, his brow heavy. He lifted the tankard of ale and swirled the dark liquid inside. "Why do you tell me this?"

Constantino was not the proprietor of the Boar and Bow. He paid a monthly fee to a wealthy man who owned many of the buildings in the area and who accepted a regular, set payment for the use of the space as well as a hefty percentage of the profits. Of course, only Constantino knew the amount of profit the inn made. He paid out as little as he could and never reported the actual earnings to the absentee landlord. But there were always new opportunities to increase the profits.

The barman dipped his dirty rag into the sudsy, lukewarm water and wrung it out before he went on to a nearby table. He regretted that the young man was not clever enough to pick up his meaning and make the suggestion himself.

"That girl of yours is fine. Her singing brings a few more in and makes the regulars stay on a bit longer. Perhaps they buy another drink, a bite to eat, while they listen. But it's nothing compared to the lira we could be making off her."

Adamo lifted the tankard. The sour smell wafted up his nostrils, filled his throat. A wave of nausea roiled up his gorge. Before the rim of the tankard touched his lips, he set it down again on the wet surface.

Constantino wasn't paying any attention to the young man. Instead he was calculating the percentage he would ask for the use of the back room. The cot the young man slept on was old and rickety. They would be best off to buy a good, strong frame and a thick, firm mattress. A modest investment now would soon pay off. Perhaps a bit of whitewash would brighten the room. Not that the men would be interested in the color of the walls once their eyes feasted on the creamy skin of the young girl's body.

"Mazolo is a richer man than you'd think. No telling how much he'd be willing to lay down for a piece of that ass."

The sound of running water made Constantino turn around. The crippled man stood on the other side of the bar, his one good arm raised high, the tankard of warm ale upended, the contents streaming down onto the surface of the counter. The ale splashed and spread across the wood, filling the air with its bitter fumes.

"What the hell did you do that for?" Constantino reached across the counter and ripped the empty container from Adamo's hand. He dropped the dry towel he carried over his shoulder onto the sodden mess to stanch the steady flow of ale as it spilled to the floor.

"Bastard!"

Adamo stood, impassive, until the man had wiped up the spilt ale.

"No one touches her," he said. "No one."

Constantino glared at the young fool.

Adamo's hand flicked forward within an inch of the barman's nose. In its grip, refracting the light from a nearby window as it bounced off rows of glasses, lay a blade, the sharpened edge paper-thin. Constantino held onto the edge of the counter, afraid to move.

"I may have only one good arm, but I handle a knife as well as the best of them. No one—do you hear me?—no one touches the girl."

Inside the practice room, someone was playing. Velia hesitated just outside, not wishing to interrupt the beautiful strains of a concerto. If Don Erik had not told her that he had assigned someone else to accompany her, she would have sworn that it was he who played.

"Don Erik said that I was to come here?" Velia peered through the narrowing opening of the door.

The sound stopped in mid-note. She stepped inside the room, but she pulled to an abrupt stop when she saw the young man rise from the bench and stand to the side of the piano.

"I'm sorry. I must have lost track of the time." The youth looked at a watch he pulled from his vest pocket. He bowed and gestured for her to approach.

"You must be..." she began to say, but then embarrassed she closed her mouth. How could she explain that the young man was darkly handsome and that she had at first been confused by his striking resemblance to the artistic director? After all, she had only imagined what Don Erik Costanzi looked like under the half mask he usually wore, for she had not seen him without it.

"François Costanzi, at your service, signorina. My father tells me that, in addition to some individual pieces he gave me, you are to learn the role of Yasmine." He gestured again for her to come closer to the piano. To the side was a stand upon which was the score she was to learn and to practice.

She took several tentative steps forward until the young man's smile gave her the confidence to close the gap between them. What was it about him that had made her think of his father? In her imagination, she thought of Don Erik's masked face. She imposed the son's features upon the hidden features of the father and produced a more mature version of the young man who stood before her. The shape of the face, the lips and eyes, the strong line of the jaw, were the same. Even the way the young man stood was the same as his father's.

"Signorina, do you want me to play through first?"

"No, I mean, yes, I would like to hear it." She had heard the music several times already during some of the preparation on stage. She had even listened outside another room where Chiara Greco rehearsed the score with a much less gifted pianist than either this young man or certainly his father. But she needed the time to catch her breath and to calm her heart. Her chest felt tight, and her breathing feathered, shallow and rapid. In this state, she could never hope to sing the opening aria.

François was happy to direct his attention to the score. The young lady's awkward approach and her obvious anxiety had infected him. He had seen her several times among the dancers, touched by her failure to follow the complex choreography. She was as beautiful as Mario had said she was. The thought of Mario sobered him. His brother had spoken of nothing else for days.

François assumed his place at the piano and played the intro. Even though he didn't need to read the score to play the piece, he trained his eyes on the black curls and lines, the staff leading him like a map deeper into the music. But he couldn't obliterate from his thoughts the first dizzying view of her face when she had walked into the room.

Unfortunately neither one of them felt any more relaxed when François came to the end of the score. He rubbed his hands against the fabric of his trousers and dared to look over at Signorina DeVita.

Yes, she was as beautiful as he had thought. He felt both elated and disappointed.

"Should we begin?" he asked. He stiffened his shoulders and took a deep breath.

His father had a way of looking as if he were made of granite, an impenetrability that François knew was a protection, a defense, and a challenge to whoever came within its range. Now François tried to imagine that he wore a mask like those his father wore. The illusion worked. He felt himself grow in stature and bulk. A calm determination infused his body. He glanced again at Velia DeVita, la bellísima donna, and saw that she, too, noted the change.

Just a step ahead of his body, his imagination soared. He almost rose from the piano. He saw himself slip his arms around the young woman's shoulders, her back, and then felt her fall into his embrace.

"So is this where you...?" Mario stopped in mid sentence.

François's mask fell. He shrank on the bench, and Velia escaped from his imagined embrace. The illusion had vanished. The moment was lost.

"Mario, this is our practice time," François managed to say. He kept his eyes trained on the music.

Mario licked his lips and swallowed as he took in the scene. François appeared to be focused on the music. Velia was nervous. But that made sense given her recent change of position at the theater. Even so, Mario dismissed with difficulty the peculiar impression he had gotten when he first saw Velia and François together. Ignoring the disquieting thought that he had interrupted more than their practice, he stepped forward into the room and grinned broadly at Velia.

"I heard rumors that you're being groomed for the part of Yasmine. Congratulations on your release from the ballet corps, signorina." Mario bowed with exaggerated aplomb.

Velia colored at Mario's teasing tone. She wasn't sure whether she felt slighted or pleased.

"It's just the part of understudy," she answered. She sensed tension between the two men and feared she knew the cause. Anxious, she could not think where to put her eyes. Both men were handsome in quite different ways. Mario's easy smile and teasing manner were not his only attractive features. He was not as tall as François, but his shoulders were broad, and his physique was powerful. She felt his eyes on her as if he knew what she was thinking and feeling. She had been attracted to him since the first time they had spoken.

But Velia hadn't been prepared for the effect François Costanzi had on her. He made her feel breathless. She found it difficult to look at him. His intense eyes, his silent strength, his tall and imposing physique pulled at her and frightened her in equal measure. She could not help but sense that he desired her, and the realization shocked and excited her.

"Don't be modest, signorina." Mario's initial hesitation had given way to his usual confidence. "Our father doesn't groom understudies just for the hell of it. He's chosen you for something significant."

François watched them from the corner of his eye. He marshaled his powers of restraint. The young woman warmed to Mario, and Mario was clearly fascinated by her. François schooled his expression into an impersonal smile.

"Mario, I'm afraid I have to ask you to leave. We don't have a lot of time to prepare Signorina DeVita." François congratulated himself on his professionalism, his apparent detachment.

"You're right, François. I just wanted to ask if you're going with me this afternoon."

François nodded.

"Good. Then, signorina, may I wish you the best of luck with your instructor? He can be deadly serious sometimes, but he's really quite sweet underneath the scowl. Keep that in mind if he begins to growl at you."

Mario stepped up to Velia DeVita, took her hand, and kissed it. François looked away to quell the sinking feeling in his chest. When he looked again, the girl's eyes were fixed on the empty space Mario had created upon his departure. François felt the cold lump settle somewhere near his heart.

"Signorina DeVita," he called to her. "Perhaps you would like to begin?"

Carlotta bit her finger and stomped her new shoe several times against the wooden floor just outside Costanzi's office. She was certain she had recognized the handwriting on the note. It was Rinaldo's! The address was somewhere in Milan. The silly boy had gone home to lick his wounds and to drive her crazy.

"Ouch!" She plucked her finger away from her incisors and waved it in the air to soothe the sting. She had bitten it to the quick until it had begun to bleed.

She must find a way to read that note. Erik had said nothing. He had certainly read it. She had intercepted the woman who cleaned his office and taken the waste bin from her hands to rifle through the contents. Nothing. So he must have left it somewhere on his desk in his office. All she had to do was slip inside and search for it among his papers. Surely it was there. Perhaps he would have put it aside on the surface or dropped it inside one of the drawers.

Jacopo was eyeing her from the other end of the corridor. A watchdog, he was! Nosy busybody, always looking out for the Phantom's interests. The Phantom's own personal Igor! Carlotta turned on her heel and marched off down the hallway until she was sure Jacopo would have stopped watching. She waited, casually licking the torn flesh along her nail where she had gnawed it. Then she doubled back via another passageway to come opposite Costanzi's office door.

She had seen Erik in deep consultation with Bianchi and Grimaldo not five minutes ago. She checked the corridor in both directions. His watchdog must have gone off to sniff at others' footsteps. The coast was clear. Determined to read Rinaldo's note, Carlotta darted across the narrow hallway and into the office. Quietly she closed the door behind her.

On the desk were sheets and sheets of music. She lifted and moved them aside, scattered the pile of receipts she found near the blotter. She paused to admire several charcoal sketches of scenes from the current opera they were preparing to premier at the end of the month. She hoped the costume she found on the fourth sheet was meant for her character. It was a confection of feathers and fabrics and would show off her best features. She absentmindedly adjusted her left breast as she studied the design of the costume. She couldn't help but look at the other sketches in the pile, admiring the vivid lines, the contours and depth. Erik Costanzi had more talent than a single man should be allowed! She was about to continue her search for Rinaldo's recent letter when she saw the corner of a drawing that was not among those she had been admiring. Instead it seemed as if it had been hidden away under several thick ledgers that she knew were related to the business of the opera house and which for this reason did not interest her in the least. Curious, she lifted the books and pulled at the sketch. For one moment she feared she would tear it before it came free.

It was a charcoal portrait of a dark-haired woman with large, black eyes. She was mature, attractive, with full lips and a broad mouth. There was something exotic about her. In her ears were long, golden hoops, around her neck a series of golden chains with bells dangling at different angles giving the impression of movement. She was no one Carlotta had ever seen, but the artist's hand was undeniably the Phantom's. Carlotta laid it on top of the ledgers as if to dismiss it, but the eyes followed her.

"I could play this woman!" she said as she imitated the sly look of the eyes, the tilt of the head. "Bah!" she said, shaking off the spell. She took one of the ledgers from underneath the charcoal sketch and laid it on top of the strange, dark woman's portrait. "Where is it?" she said as she continued her former search.

She was about to pull open the middle drawer when she saw the edge of the envelope peeking out from the pages of a book on classical architecture. She pulled it free before she could think to note the page where it had been placed, perhaps to mark the spot where Costanzi had left off reading. She studied the handwriting. It was indeed Rinaldo's. He was alive and well in Milan. He had written the Phantom but had not a word to spare for her! With nervous fingers, she opened the cover and drew out the single sheet.

She rushed through the first paragraph where Rinaldo apologized for having left in the middle of the season without a farewell, expressed concern over having abandoned il cuculo-vacca's training, and wished the Phantom success with the rest of the season. She scanned the entire note for her name.

Incredulous, she read the note from the beginning to the end more slowly and still did not find even a minor reference to herself.

"Humph," she said. Then it occurred to her. "Of course, he doesn't mention my name. Our love is too intimate. It does not concern Costanzi." She perused the note a third time. "Yes, he speaks only of the music. What interest does Costanzi have in our affair?"

So Rinaldo was composing. That was a good sign. He never had time to compose when the two of them were together. Surely that meant he had not replaced her. He was alone, definitely lonely, she told herself in spite of the tone of the note. Poor Rinaldo, no one to fill his time, forced to waste it on operas no one would likely perform. Her heart swelled. She would go to him. He was too ashamed to ask it of her, too afraid she was still angry with him.

"Carlotta."

"Ah!" she screamed, her hands flying up, the note sailing through the air to land at Erik's feet. "You scared me!"

"What are you doing?" he asked, stooping to pick up the sheet of paper.

Carlotta fanned her throat with her hand, exaggerating the fright that Erik had given her.

"I thought I heard someone in your office. I came in and... and...I noticed the window." She turned and pointed at the closed window behind the desk.

"The window?"

"Yes! That's it. I noticed that it was open."

Erik scowled. He knew he had not left it open.

"It was open," she went on to say when she saw his frown. "And the wind was blowing...and blowing." Carlotta waved her arms wildly above her head as if she were trapped in a storm at sea.

Erik knew the weather was calm.

"And it had blown your papers across the desk and onto the floor." She demonstrated by brushing a pile of sheets to the edge of the desk. She managed to stop them from pouring over the edge when she saw his sharp glare of disapproval. "I was just tidying up for you."

"I see." He didn't move. His eyes stared at her.

She moved away from the desk, but his green eyes followed her.

"All right! I wanted to read his letter." Her sore finger went to the corner of her mouth where her teeth tried to find purchase on the devastated and ragged tissue along the nail.

Erik sighed. He laid the sheet he had recovered from the floor onto the mess of papers on his desk.

"Does he miss me?" Carlotta asked, her voice small and plaintive.

Erik lowered his brow and considered.

"He is not an indiscreet man, Carlotta. He would never include something so personal in a letter to me."

"Yes," she said with a tad more confidence. "Yes, you are right. Of course he would want to be gallant. He would not refer to our..." She clamped her lips closed and glanced at Erik who stared at her curiously. They had never spoken of her relationship to Rinaldo. She didn't fool herself into thinking Costanzi didn't know what was going on when Rinaldo ushered her to and from the theater. But knowing and speaking of it were two different things. "Such a sweet boy. You are right, of course."

Erik hid his smile. She was willing to think that Rinaldo was lost without her.

"What did you do, Carlotta?" he asked.

"What? What do you mean?" She crossed her arms under her bosom in a defensive gesture.

Erik needed no other proof than her guarded expression to know that his assumption was correct.

"I...did nothing," she finally said to fill the silence. "He was foolish. He's young. He doesn't know what's important and what's *not* important. It's just a silly misunderstanding."

"I see," Erik said softly. It would take time for her to realize that she'd lost Rinaldo through her own foolish behavior. He was convinced the young man had had serious cause to abandon not only Carlotta Venedetti but his position at the Teatro dell'Opera and Rome itself. Nothing insignificant would have pushed the man to change his life so dramatically. Unfortunately Carlotta would be the last to see it that way.

"I will go now." Carlotta glanced sideways at the envelope that lay on Erik's desk—Rinaldo's new address prominently displayed on its surface—and went to the door. Before she closed it behind her, she said, "You should keep that window closed."

Erik wondered how she would deal with her loneliness and disappointment when she finally came to accept that Rinaldo was gone. He might never come back, not to Rome and not to Carlotta.

My Naldo,

You have had time to pout and think about your rash decision to quit Costanzi's employ. I'm sure that you have come to your senses. You have wounded me with your selfishness. I can barely sing.

I was silly to be angry with you that night you abandoned me to walk Greco home. So you have only yourself to blame that I did something that I should not have done. There, you see? I have apologized. I can be mature about this. Now that I have apologized, you will come home. I will make Costanzi take you back.

I have missed you. The rooms are too big without you. I have decided to give you a key to the apartments. That will make things more convenient. Come home, Naldito. All is forgiven.

Love, Carlotta

"Hey, you." Jacopo called out to the lame man who disappeared down the dark corridor. "Velpi, Nestor, go after that man. Make sure he states his business and then finds the door. Don Erik doesn't want him hanging around here."

"What man?" asked Velpi.

"Just round the corner. Limps. He won't have gone too far." Jacopo gave the man an encouraging pat on the shoulder. "He's up to no good, that one," he whispered under his breath on his way to Erik's office.

"Velia," Adamo whispered.

She stepped away from the stage and followed her brother down the wings to the back of the theater. She restrained the urge to warn him to watch for the cables that littered the floor, but she knew he would resent any suggestion that he was unable to maneuver through the debris.

"You must be more forward," said Adamo when they had found a dark, out-of-the-way corner. "There's not much time. The longer you're around, the more apt he is to take you for granted."

"What do you mean?"

"Costanzi." He took her by the arm and shook her.

Velia dug at his fingers to release her.

"Let me go, Adamo. You're hurting me."

Adamo loosened his grip but did not release her. Instead he edged in even closer.

"He wants you. I saw him watching you at the Boar and Bow."

Velia's eyes rounded in dread. Erik Costanzi had seen her perform at the inn? He had seen her in those clothes, barely clad, singing for the sad and drunken men that made the inn their home away from home? *Oh,* she thought, *I cannot bear it. What will he think of me?* But Adamo was still talking, insinuating, with his sly voice that she was practically already Costanzi's whore.

"No," she said as she tore her bruised arm from his grip. "I won't do it. I won't."

Adamo pressed his lips into a tight line. He ran his fingers through his dark hair and considered his sister. Her face was averted, but he thought he could see her tremble. Without thinking, he stretched out his hand and smoothed her dark blond hair. He stepped closer and pulled her back against him in an embrace.

"Velia, don't. It doesn't have to be like that."

His heart ached when she turned her face up to look at him.

Even in the dimly lit alcove, he could tell that her eyes were red and she was on the point of tears.

"I can't let him…"

"I know." He tried to soothe her. "But you could make him love you, Velia." She tried to pull away from him. He held onto her, his voice soft but earnest. "You don't understand men. If you make him need you, he'll believe it's love. He'll want to marry you." Adamo told himself that it was possible.

"But he's already married," she said. She pulled away from his embrace.

Adamo's hand stroked Velia's arm where he had left the smudged impression of his fingers.

"What if he weren't married?"

Velia stared at her brother. Before she could ask him what he meant, they both heard the approach of the sceneshifters.

"Find ways to be with him. If he wants you…." Seeing the return of fear to her eyes, Adamo continued, "Let him have a taste. You don't have to lie with him. Just…just…stoke the fire."

The voices were louder. The men would soon come upon them. Adamo kissed his sister on the forehead, turned, and scrambled into the darkness.

"Mix that with a pinch of bread dough and leave it in the corner of the cupboard. That will get rid of the pests for you. Just a few grains, mind you, is all you need. You don't have any children around, do you? 'Cause it will do them in for sure."

"Won't the taste put the rats off?" Adamo asked.

"Add a bit of sweet to the dough, the rats will eat it up and die with a smile on their faces."

"It's not painful, then?"

"Wouldn't say that. But who's going to cry over a few rats? If they eat enough of it, it goes quick."

The stout woman set the tray on the desk, took one cup and placed it near the far side where Erik usually sat.

"Move along now," she said to the younger woman who collected the trash from several waste bins, one by the desk, the other overflowing with torn or crinkled papers. "No, no, no, no. Leave that one be."

With a puzzled expression, the young girl pointed at the basket as if to make sure the older woman realized that it was trash.

"Don Erik sometimes changes his mind, he does." The stout woman wagged her finger toward the waste bin until the girl dropped the wadded sheets back where she had found them. "Then he goes tearing through that mess."

No longer paying attention to the girl, the older woman took the second cup from the tray and placed it in the nearest corner where she knew Meg would sit. "There now. I'll pour the tea." She cast a glance at the girl who lazily fluttered a long plumed duster over the surface of the piano. "Mind the papers, Luisa."

"Yes, signora." The girl redoubled her efforts under the scrutiny of the older woman. "Who's that?" she asked, pointing at the bust of Mozart that sat on the opposite corner of Don Erik's desk.

"Napoleon, I should think. One of them French kings they've had. They're from France, you know. You can hear it when the signora speaks. But he sounds like he was born here. As if he came into market in Spinaceto from the fields. But I've heard him and his signora speaking that Frenchman talk."

The older woman poured a stream of hot tea into the cup at the far side and then into the closer of the two. "Look lively. They'll be here any moment." Then she took a spoon and scooped out a thick dollop of honey. She stirred it into Don Erik's cup. Then with a cautious look at the door, which had been left open, she whispered to the girl, "Says the honey is good for her throat, he does. But she doesn't like her tea sweet. Says it tastes like medicine, she does. So I don't put the honey in hers. I just lay the spoon beside her cup so he thinks I have."

The young assistant held the feather duster over the lamp, listening.

"Don't dally, Luisa. Finish that up."

Within moments, the woman had finished tidying and picking up the tray. As they left, she cautioned the younger one in a whisper, "Remember. Not a word about the honey. What he doesn't know won't hurt him."

Outside the room, hidden in the recess of a nearby door, Adamo watched the cleaning women retreat down the hallway.

"Have you heard any further word from Rinaldo? Does anyone know if he's returned to Rome?" asked Meg. She toyed with the spoon resting on the saucer, smearing the sticky residue of honey on the porcelain.

Erik drained his cup of tea. "No. He's not written again."

"You still think Carlotta's to blame, don't you?"

Erik sighed. "Without a doubt."

"Did she tell you?"

"There was no need to. It was written all over her face."

"Shame. I had gotten used to thinking of them as a couple."

As Meg reached for her cup of tea, a knock sounded at the door.

"Come," Erik called out.

Christine stepped just inside the door. She was warmly dressed in her fall coat and made no move to remove it. Erik rose.

"Sit, please," she said. "I'm here to steal Meg. There are several shops that I'm dying to see, and she must come with me to be my glass. I hate shopping alone." Christine took Meg's hand and pulled her from her chair. "You can spare her, can't you, for an afternoon?"

"By all means. And please encourage her to pick out something for herself."

"I will. It's too depressing to be the only one making purchases. Besides there are so many lovely things that look better on you, Meg, than on me. It's great fun. We shall have to hire two carriages, I'm sure, for all the packages."

Meg barely had time to kiss Erik on the cheek before Christine pulled her from the room.

Erik distracted by the unexpected visit picked up his teacup. He brought it to his lips before he realized it was empty. He set it down. Meg's was untouched. He picked it up and sipped at the lukewarm liquid.

Bitter. He set it down and scowled. He had told the staff to put honey in Meg's tea. He was convinced that it had a soothing effect on the throat. Besides, Meg needed to gain back a few of the pounds she had lost last summer. Her thinness disturbed him. He would have to remind the staff.

Instead of sitting back down, he decided to go in search of Raoul. If the women were off shopping, it was a good opportunity for the men to get in a bit of fencing. Or perhaps he would take Raoul back to the club for a few rounds of fisticuffs. It was less elegant, but it was a more taxing sport on the body, and Erik was in the mood to push himself to the limit.

The rumble in his gut was louder than the hooves upon the cobblestone avenue. The twisting pain that such a sound announced was worsening with each breath he took. When the discomfort began, he abandoned his plan to spend the afternoon with Raoul. Instead he had made his way outside and given his driver instructions to take him home. By the time he stepped down from the carriage, he could feel the cold sweat inching its way down his face, making the mask float precariously over his flesh. He imagined his pallor.

The house weaved and bobbed at the end of the walkway. Teasing him, it receded as he forced his numb feet forward. He reached out his hand for the doorknob even though he knew it was miles from his grasp. In that moment the door opened, and Erik's eyes turned up inside his head. He didn't mind that he would land on the path just inside the gate. He didn't mind that the stones were rough and cold. He was glad that the twisting in his gut had dulled as had all the sights and sounds of the world around him.

Milky. Everything dripped in milk.

"Are you in there?"

That was Raoul's voice. A blob hovered over him. He smelled a cologne, something spicy that he thought was familiar. The blob coalesced, and Erik made out two blue eyes staring down at him. He saw the light curve of what had been an angry wound in the face that was gradually coming into focus. The face matched the voice.

"Erik?" The face dipped closer until Erik could see the fine stubble of a dark blond beard. "If you can speak, do so," Raoul whispered. "If not, blink your eyes."

Erik realized that his mask was gone. For a moment he enjoyed the feel of coolness on his skin. Then he wondered why he didn't speak. It was too difficult to speak. He fixed his eyes on Raoul's and blinked twice.

Raoul relaxed, moved back from Erik's face, and laughed. He looked over his shoulder to someone Erik couldn't see and spoke to that person.

"He's awake."

There was more than one person. Shadows flitted just out of range by the door. Servants were coming and going. But from behind Raoul two figures Erik recognized stepped out and drew near. Their features came into focus in wavering patterns of light and dark, one a petite woman with golden hair and fair skin, the other taller with a crown of dark locks.

Erik's lips tore apart, the skin so dry that his mouth had seemed pasted shut. He wet them with his tongue and groaned from the effort.

"The doctor thinks you ate something bad." As she came forward, the fair one took on the features of his wife. Meg's hands wrapped round his, her grip reassuringly fierce. Raoul stood and offered her his seat. Beside her stood Christine.

Erik shook his head. He couldn't remember anything.

"Do you want water?" asked Christine.

Meg answered for him. Raoul poured from a pitcher into a glass by the bedside and handed it to Meg. She wedged her fingers under his head and lifted him to the rim of the glass. The water was cool and refreshing.

"Just a few sips," she warned, but Erik wanted to gulp the entire contents of the glass and then empty the pitcher as well. His thirst seemed to permeate his body.

"What the devil did you eat?" asked Raoul who pushed Erik's legs over on the mattress so that he could sit on the edge of the bed. "You passed out on the walkway."

"How long?" Erik's voice was scratchy. He didn't recognize it.

"Nearly twenty-four hours."

"Erik," interrupted Christine, "are you feeling any better?"

"Better," he answered. In point of fact, he was much improved. The water had revived him. His eyes had cleared, and he was able to focus. "I didn't eat."

"Well, the important thing is that you're all right." Meg's fingers pressed into his. He returned the pressure.

At the back of his throat, he swallowed the memory of bitter tea.

Adamo kept watch outside the theater. The word should come soon. He waited for some sign of panic or grief. People came and went. Deliveries continued at the back of the theater. After several hours of waiting, Adamo eased his way inside through the large bay doors while the crew unloaded boxes of supplies. Inside everything continued as normal. As Jacopo approached the loading dock, Adamo scurried away. The dark interior was cool, yet his hand sweated. His heartbeat had accelerated as well.

He had killed a woman. The meaning of that fact escaped him. It was true, but he couldn't understand the full significance of it. He had done it for Velia. He repeated to himself several times that it had been necessary. Costanzi's wife was an obstacle that needed to be removed so that the path between his sister and the artistic director was clear.

Knowing that sooner or later Velia would pass this way, Adamo waited. From the darkness, behind a furled curtain, he watched dancers, chorines, sceneshifters, and musicians as they made their way through the backstage of the theater.

Perhaps the chemist had not sold him poison, but rather something harmless. To his surprise, the thought that his plan may have failed filled him with a giddy hope. Suddenly Adamo prayed that this be so—that the poison had been some benign substance and that Meg Costanzi had not died. *Oh, let it be true. Let her be alive.* Unable to bear the doubt any longer, he had to find out.

He nearly missed his sister when she passed. At the last moment, he lurched forward into her path, startling her.

"What are you doing in here, Adamo? You know Don Erik doesn't want you here."

He ignored her question. "Any news?" he whispered. His hand was like a vice on her arm. She tried to pry his fingers off. He shook her to get her attention. "Meg Costanzi. What have you heard?"

"About Donna Meg? Nothing. Just that she's home."

"She…she is…home?" His former hope turned to lead and fell to the pit of his stomach.

"Don Erik isn't feeling well. She sent word that they were going to rest for a few days."

Adamo's hand dropped. His mind raced over the words in an effort to make sense of what they could possibly mean.

"Oh no," he muttered, as his thoughts fell into place. He paced the floor, taking just a few halting steps in each direction. He ran his hand through his hair as if he might rip it out by the roots. "No. It can't be."

"Adamo, what is it? You're acting strange."

"Costanzi? You're sure?" He drew up within an inch of his sister's face and stared with such ferocity that Velia wanted to step back. Sensing he might strike her if she moved, she held her place.

"What?"

"That he's ill, not his wife? Damn it, pay attention."

"I'm sure. Don Erik is indisposed. They didn't say what he has."

Velia studied her brother. The announcement had made it sound like a minor complaint. But she had noticed how surprised Sig. Bianchi had been. Donna Carlotta had also seemed concerned.

"Damned luck," he said under to his breath. "To kill the golden goose."

"Adamo, you're frightening me."

"Frightening you?" Adamo's eyes were wild. "Never mind. What's done is done."

"Can I do anything?"

"Do anything? You? No. There's nothing...to be done." He paused. "Wait. Perhaps there's another way. The son. You said his son liked you?"

Velia blushed, but in the darkness Adamo could not see the rise in color in her cheeks. When she didn't respond, Adamo became agitated. "The son likes you. Encourage him. Let him know you're... willing."

Velia lowered her eyes.

"He could die. Do you hear me? Think. We have to think." He grabbed her chin and forced her face up.

Was he talking about Don Erik? she wondered. She felt her throat tighten. She jerked her chin away from his hand.

"You said yourself that you like the boy." Adamo's voice had calmed. He leaned down and whispered in her ear, "Just...let him know. Is that too much to ask?" Adamo raked her body with his eyes. "Just don't let him bed you."

Erik spent another day at home just to reassure Meg that he had recovered. As ill as he had been, once he awoke he got his strength back in short shrift. The doctor had left instructions to withhold food and to give water sparingly. Within an hour of waking, Erik had made such a racket that Meg gave up trying to enforce the physician's orders and sent a request to the kitchen for Cook to make up a tray of food for Erik.

He hadn't eaten in more than twenty-four hours, and he was famished.

His friends had sat watching him eat the fresh baked bread dipped in olive oil seasoned with rosemary, a handful of pitted olives, as well as a healthy serving of stewed apples with cinnamon, walnuts, and raisins. He asked for milk, but Meg insisted he drink only water. Although he grumbled about it, he was too content eating his meal to complain about the drink.

After the tray had been cleared away, the others waited for a violent relapse that didn't happen. Instead Erik burped discreetly into his napkin and asked them to leave so that he could dress.

That was when Meg became testy. She threatened to have his clothes removed if he dared rise from his sick bed until the next morning. Given that it was already late in the afternoon and that there was no evening performance to worry about, Erik indulged his wife and remained where he was.

The next morning he was up and dressed before Meg. He wasn't in the mood to be delayed. He was anxious to speak to the staff at the Teatro dell'Opera. Doubts circled in his mind. What if it had not been the tea? If he had caught something, it may well be making its way among the staff and performers. With the end of the week fast approaching, it would be disastrous if they were short-staffed or if roles had to be reassigned. Best that he anticipate problems and be on hand early.

As he was about to leave, Christine called to him to wait.

"Could you join me for a few moments in the parlor before you leave?" she asked.

He escorted her to one of the small parlor off the main hallway and closed the door behind them. He hoped that she had something to say about Meg. When he turned to face her, he was puzzled to see her take her time to arrange her skirts on the sofa. She kept her eyes averted, and he couldn't shake the feeling that she was hesitant to begin.

"What is it, Christine?" he asked.

Christine smoothed the top layer of her skirt and smiled up at him. "Sit here, please." She patted the chair placed at a right angle at the end of the sofa.

Erik sat where Christine had suggested. She was close enough that he might reach out and touch the lavender flounce on her skirt. She sat, her back erect, her hands anchored in her lap, fingers intertwined as if she were posing for a painting.

"Why are you uncomfortable? Do you want me to call for Raoul?"

"No," she hastened to say. "No, it's not that. I assure you, Erik, I'm not uncomfortable to be alone with you."

He felt the tension he hadn't recognized melt away. The moment she reassured him, the moment she smiled at him, it was as if they were back in the Chagnys' music room, rehearsing the arias from *The Phoenix of the Opera*. He leaned back in the chair at peace again.

"What did you want to say?" he asked.

"It's not as easy as I thought it would be." She bit her lip when she saw him scowl. "It's just that I've spoken with Meg on several occasions. She worries that she can't sing."

Erik rose, frustration latching onto him again. He already knew this. What good did it do him to learn the same things over and over again?

"You must control yourself."

"Control myself?" Only after he spoke did he hear the anger in his own voice. He softened it with difficulty. "I am in control, Christine. I know that she fears she can't sing."

"But it's more complicated than that."

"If only she would try," he said as if Christine hadn't spoken. "I would work with her. I know her lungs are fragile after the illness. I wouldn't push. I can be…patient. I can."

"Erik, it's that she doesn't want…"

"I know that I have been a stern teacher. I have been giving this a lot of thought. If she prefers, I could ask someone else to work with her."

"Erik, she…"

"She doesn't have to perform this season. There's always the next season."

"Stop!"

Christine bolted from the sofa and stood in Erik's path so that he would have to look at her. He was merely inches from Christine, and he stared at her with a mixture of confusion and anger. Before anger could win out, Christine placed her palm against his heart.

"Stop planning her life. She doesn't want to sing. She doesn't want to try."

The muscles in Erik's jaw tightened against the question that burned his throat. He took a step back, and Christine's hand fell from his chest. He dared not ask why. But Christine was determined to tell him.

"She's afraid that she can't live up to your desires."

Erik turned and walked to the window. His silence confirmed Christine's own fears.

"Erik, tell me she's wrong."

He bent his head. Summoning the courage, he asked, "Why?"

"Why?" Christine repeated, unsure what he was asking.

"Why is she afraid that I won't love her?"

Christine sighed. "She knows how important music is for you. She knows that you demand perfection of yourself as well as of others."

He turned to confront Christine, his resolve to remain calm forgotten.

"This is who I am, Christine. She knows that."

Christine ignored the irritation in his tone.

"Erik, this may be hard for you to hear, but I think I understand what's driving Meg. She worries that she cannot sing the way you would want her to sing. She fears her voice is damaged, that it won't heal. Not enough."

"Not enough?"

"She has begun to wonder if all these years singing your music she has been a substitute for what you really want and that she can no longer keep up the pretense."

Christine couldn't continue. His anger had receded, leaving in its wake an intimation of something neither one was prepared to face. Her words evoked a moment of splendor they had shared and lost—a moment of triumph and redemption. On the stage at the Opera Populaire, Christine had sung with the voice *he* had given her, accepting the admiration of all when only his mattered.

"Her voice is beautiful," he said.

"I know it is."

"I've never wanted her to be anyone but who she is."

"Yes, I know."

They both stared at each other for a long time, unspoken thoughts as clear as if they had been spoken.

"What does she want?" he asked, his voice straining for emotional control. "How can I prove to her that she is the one I want."

"And who is she, Erik?"

Christine went to him. She dared to touch him again, laying her hand on his sleeve. This time, he did not draw back.

"Is she your songbird? Is she the girl who dared you to make her into a diva? Is she the one who made your dreams soar again? Or is she a dancer who forgot her own dreams?"

Erik could not hide the shame Christine's words caused him. Had he been so blind?

"She thinks that she will disappoint you no matter what she does, Erik. She cannot be perfect. Someday she will fail. She lives in terror of that day."

The damp in the prison cell had soaked through his skin to his very bones. Those who enter here, abandon all hope. Wasn't that the warning burned into the gate of hell itself? It would have been apt for the Parisian cell that Erik now occupied. All hope had been abandoned. He could not remember when or where, but it had been long ago.

He was already dead. The pain was no longer significant. Only occasionally did a dull memory of aches wake him in the night. The trial had become an endless gauntlet that he was resigned to run. He had almost found peace in his torment.

And then they had awakened hope. Erik had listened as they detailed their plan to bring his bride to him. His bride! He had lain with her already. She vowed that she loved him. He wiped at his eyes, rubbed and scoured them with his knuckles to clear them of the indelible image of Christine.

When would her face fade so that he could see his bride's?

They had brought Meg dressed like a young monk. They had brought her to his cell and left them alone, knowing that she came to lie with him, knowing that she hungered for him, knowing that she would awaken him to life and desire. And that awakening would bring him pain, too.

Better the numb resignation. Better the death of sensation. For he was facing obliteration, the obliteration, the destruction of the body. He was to die. He had been sentenced. They would rip his soul from the flesh, and all he knew was the flesh. He knew that the sundering would be agony. But it was not only the flesh that would tear. It was also his heart. His poor heart. How could it stand more than it had already borne?

She came to him as she had before, so long ago now. No longer a child, she was a woman. Her body had been pledged to his. Her body had made him real, had brought him a peace he had not known. She had proven to him that he was not a monster. She came golden as if lit from inside by a thousand candles. As the footsteps receded down the dank hallway of the prison and they found themselves alone, she stepped out of her male weeds and stood naked.

He cried to see her so beautiful surrounded by so much ugliness. He wept to know that he would cover her. Her beauty would be eclipsed by his mangled flesh, dirty and beaten, his body doomed to rot. The stench, an unbearable omen. He saw her through tears, his tears glistening down her throat, down her breasts to drip from her dark nipples, down the slope of her belly, pooling between her legs, mixing with the cream of her swollen sex, dampening the inner flesh of her thighs where he would bury his face and lick, laving her until she smelled of him, until his stench covered her like a second skin.

Meg lay down on the soiled and tattered cover on his cot. She lifted her arms to him, and he felt ashamed of his ugliness. He wanted to save her from his corruption. He knew when he looked into her soft brown eyes that she loved him, and his heart ached to tell her of his love for her. But there would be no way to end the pain. She should not love him, not now. Once it might have been possible, but he had been blinded by a mirage, a phantom love, and had not understood. Now that he was condemned to die, the scales had fallen from his eyes. He could see what was but could no longer be.

End it. End the pain, he screamed inside his mind. He scratched at his eyes to blind them to her light, to her love. He bit the soft inside of his lip to taste the salt of blood, to remind himself, to no avail, that he was not yet a corpse.

The dead do not love the living. They hate the living. He would defile her. If he lay with her, he would destroy her.

"I dreamed last night," he had said to her.

"Of what did you dream?"

The question had been made so that he could answer it.

"I dreamed of my wedding night. I dreamed of my wedding night with Christine."

He had waited to see the light dim and go out. He watched her eyes to witness the severing of their ties. But she cried with her eyes open and fixed on his. The light flickered, but did not go out.

The violence he committed to save them both had not brought him oblivion or saved her from destruction. His pain had not eased. It had been a useless sacrifice. His body hungered no less for her, his heart throbbed as full of tenderness and pain as before, he would not save himself or her from their terrible love.

As his body sank between her thighs and against her breasts and in the hollow of her neck, the words bubbled like blood from his mouth, begging her forgiveness. To forgive him his cruelty and his cowardice, his attempt to deaden his body and soul to her desire, his fatal invitation to lie with him as his bride, his compulsion to drive Meg from his heart so that the ending would have already come before the ending had even begun.

"Donna Renata, may I have a word with you?"

"Of course, Don Erik."

As he escorted the tall, willowy ballet mistress into his office, Erik asked, "How is my wife's training progressing?"

Renata Cossa squared her shoulders and stuck out her chest. She was a tall, angular woman, impossibly thin yet one could see that she was not fragile. Her muscles were long and sinewy, strong and elastic.

"Training? Why, Don Erik, I've nothing to do with singing."

The blotchy red that marked her throat and blazoned across the hollows of her cheeks was sufficient proof of the lie.

"You know perfectly well to what I'm referring." Erik indicated the chair to the side of his desk. Renata perched on the very edge of the seat, her ankles crossed, her hands nested in her lap. Erik rested his hip on the corner of his desk, aware that in contrast to her studied pose, his seemed nonchalant, perhaps even rude.

"Don Erik, Signora Costanzi enjoys the exercise. Stretching is particularly good for the posture. There are Eastern philosophies that teach us that…"

"I'm sure there are, Donna Renata, but I want to speak of my wife."

Signora Cossa lowered her eyes and remained silent.

"She is…not attempting anything that might prove…harmful to her?"

"Sig. Costanzi, I am a professional."

"Forgive me. You're quite right to admonish me. But you must realize that I am…concerned."

His reticence gave Renata more confidence. She looked up to see his eyes fixed on her. An unsettled shiver returned to her spine. She forced herself not to let him see her reaction.

"Donna Meg is very careful, and I don't let her do anything that would be beyond her capability." She sustained his scrutiny for only a moment, but his gaze was so intense that she had to look away.

Erik left the corner of the desk and paced the room.

"Signora Cossa, I don't pretend to be an expert on ballet. But I would like to know more."

Renata Cossa stood, her hands flew out to her sides.

"You wish me to teach you to dance?"

Erik scowled. "Certainly not."

Renata took a deep breath and let it out in relief. She sat again, her hands obediently nestled again in the warm bed of her lap.

"I wish to understand it," Erik explained. He braced his hands on the wooden arms of her chair, leaned in close to her face. "How does it work with the music? How is it choreographed? What are the building blocks of the forms, the movements? Are there rules one is expected to follow? How does one write…compose…for a ballet as opposed to an opera?"

Renata had never been this close to the director. She had admired him. Certainly he was the type of man one had to admire, in spite of the mask. Anyone who worked with the body could not ignore the natural grace and proportion of a male figure as harmoniously composed as that of Erik Costanzi. Even his movements were pleasant. Nothing awkward about him, a perfect blend of mind and body. Except for the mask. The mask was the one thing that detracted from his classic beauty.

Erik stood back, expectant.

"Do not teach me how to dance. Teach me what I need to know so that I can write the music for a ballet."

"But you already do…"

"No," he interrupted. "I write interludes, set pieces that entertain, that serve as transitions in the story."

"But the opera about the dancer certainly…"

"Yes, you're right. But it was intuitive, and it was a theme, a part of the whole."

"You are considering writing a ballet instead of an opera?"

Erik paused. He resumed pacing. For several moments, he was silent. Renata wondered if she had been dismissed and should leave. Just as she began to rise, Erik stopped pacing.

"I want to compose a ballet as if it were an opera, an opera without words. Will you teach me what I need to know?"

Renata stammered, "I…I will…tell you, show you…what I can…"

Erik nodded. He stepped forward and took one of Renata Cossa's feathery hands and kissed it firmly.

"When?" he asked.

CHAPTER 4

The Scarlet Quill

"We are each our own devil, and we make this world our hell."
The Duchess of Padua, Oscar Wilde

"A lesson. You know what I mean? The point has to be made. But don't go too far, and don't get caught. You understand?"

The two men nodded as they accepted the coins.

"You'll get the rest when the job's done."

From his regular table near the entrance, Grimaldo could watch both the passersby on the street and the scenes unfolding inside the café among the various groups and couples. Most of these people he knew if not intimately by reputation and name. His location also guaranteed that he, too, would be seen. He was only half paying attention as the manager of the Teatro del Popolo plied him with flattery and wine. The man was urging the tenor to leave the employ of the Teatro dell'Opera and sing in his less well known but up-and-coming opera house. Grimaldo waited politely for the man to come to the end of a long list of attractions and then told the man that he had no desire to leave Sig. Costanzi's theater. As the man's chair grated across the wooden floor, Grimaldo wished him good luck. The manager grumbled as he shouldered his way toward the back of the café.

Don Erik and Grimaldo had an understanding. Grimaldo would continue as lead tenor for one more season. Then he would take a year off to explore the world and consider his options. He could always return and sing, but most likely in supporting roles. He could also take a position as docent and tutor the younger singers or work with Don Erik as an assistant. All in all Don Erik had been generous and thoughtful in preparing a transition that Grimaldo had been expecting for some time now. Once Don Erik and he had spoken, Grimaldo was relieved. Not only had a weight been lifted from his shoulders, but he found new joy in performing, knowing that soon it would be over. It gave him a new perspective on matters.

Carlotta Venedetti was clearly in her cups. She had already angered many of the women by flirting brazenly with their escorts and companions. Grimaldo nearly rose from his seat when he saw her tumble back and land in one man's lap, spilling her drink on the hem and shoes of the lady seated next to him. She kissed the man with drunken affection on the top of his bald pate, turning a tense moment into farce. Even the lady companion seemed appeased when Carlotta extricated herself and patted the man on the head to the laughs and cheers of those nearby.

Grimaldo put his coins down on the table, ready to leave, as Carlotta's face wavered between the color of unbaked bread dough and that of a recently sliced avocado. Brushing off the awkward attempt of a rogue's embrace, she stumbled toward the door. Grimaldo followed her out onto the sidewalk.

"Signorina Venedetti," he called to her. When she still swayed forward, he raised his voice and called, "Donna Carlotta."

She stopped and squinted at him.

"Grimaldo, is that you?" She smiled as he came forth and took her elbow.

"May I escort you home? It's not a good idea for you to be alone on these streets at night."

Carlotta smiled and stuck her finger into Grimaldo's chest. "You did forgive me, didn't you?"

Grimaldo had already told her on numerous occasions that he held no grudge for the night she had drugged him and Don Erik had had to step into his role and perform.

"I forgave you long ago," he said as he turned her toward a carriage.

"Oh Aldito, you are such a…such a…. You are, really. I would not lie to you." Carlotta's voice wavered, grew strained and high in her chest.

Grimaldo could not imagine a more beautiful woman. Until Jannicelli left the company, Grimaldo had been resigned to admire her from afar. He was not about to make a fool of himself. She clearly was enamored of Rinaldo. But the past months he had watched her mourn the loss of her young lover. He had almost regretted the man's departure. He did not relish seeing her so lost. Her grief kept Grimaldo at bay. He was a patient man.

"Carlotta," he said, enjoying the intimacy of her name, the way she clutched his hand in an effort to stand upright. Even the strong smell of drink on her breath excited him. "It's late. Let me see you to your door."

"Oh, Grimmy, you have a wonderful voice. It reminds me of… of…" She pulled away from him and stumbled toward a waiting carriage. "Enough! They're all alike. You open your heart to them, and they trample it. The least, tiniest, little problem and—poof!— like magicians they're gone. Gone, gone, gone. Their big hands, their big feet, their big…."

Grimaldo tried to steady her as she pulled herself up into the carriage. She held on with one hand and swayed back to look at him over her shoulder.

"No, no, no, no, no. You keep those big hands and feet away from Carlotta Venedetti. I'm done with men."

"Carlotta, let me…."

"Basta," she interrupted. Momentarily losing her balance, she tilted back. With one hand, she held on to the carriage. Her other hand swung back and hit Grimaldo across the chest. Unaware, she pulled herself back to the carriage steps and lurched forward. As she landed with a dull thud on the seat, she pounded with her flat palm on the roof and told the driver to go.

Grimaldo stood, arms empty, staring after the carriage as it wound its way down the empty street.

Grimaldo reminded her of Piangi. He looked nothing like him, but his voice played tricks on her. At times she would hear the familiar strains of Piangi's voice, the voice he had had when he was young and virile and would have laid his life down for her slightest whim. Piangi, Piangi, Piangi. They had spent a lifetime together. She had given him her best years. But he had changed. *Men. Inconstant. Fickle.* When she had most needed Piangi, he had left her. And after all she had done for him. Even now he was in Milan. Milan. Where Rinaldo had gone to punish her.

Carlotta let the tears run down her face. She licked the salty stream as it collected at the corners of her mouth. She gave in to the painful sobs that racked her chest.

The driver tapped with his whip on the window of the carriage to alert her to their arrival.

She sniffed to clear her nose and wiped at her face. At the bottom of the carriage steps, she fumbled with her purse and managed to drop only one or two coins in the road as she paid the driver.

As the carriage made its way down the street, Carlotta bent in a half-hearted effort to locate the fallen coins. Dizziness dissuaded her from insisting. She had just managed to regain her balance when a pair of large hands grasped her from behind, pulling her arms back. The light shifted. A huge dark mass blotted out the dim light from the street. Carlotta felt the pain burst across her cheekbone; a white light exploded in her eye. She sagged, yet the vice on her arms kept her from falling.

"Signorina Venedetti sent this." Jacopo handed Erik the folded sheet of pink paper.

Erik lifted the mask from his face and wiped his brow. Jacopo was used to Erik's face and stood silently awaiting instructions. Erik took the sheet and held it as if it dripped with poison. He had been fuming for an hour or more over Carlotta's failure to show up. He unfolded it and read.

"We'll see about that," he muttered as he crumpled the note and stuffed it into the pocket of his coat.

Two days later, Carlotta Venedetti returned to rehearsals. She stole in without anyone noticing and went straight to her dressing room. More than an hour passed before she came out. Erik had not sent one but two notes reminding her of her duties and obligations and insisting that she cut her "rest" short.

A hush settled on those who watched Carlotta pass on her way to the stage. Whispers rushed from mouth to mouth, group to group, in her wake. Her steps quickened and brought her dead center just an arm's length from Erik who stood, slack-jawed, his conversation with Grimaldo suspended in mid-sentence, gaping at her.

"What?" she asked, her voice too loud, her head raised so high it must have hurt her neck.

"Your face, Dio mio!" exclaimed Grimaldo. "Who did this to you?"

"What? It's just a little white foundation. To make the character more dramatic." Carlotta shifted from foot to foot, looking from one man to the next. "It...it...is like...a...mask."

"Carlotta," Erik said, his voice not above a whisper. "It doesn't hide the bruising."

Grimaldo stood speechless and watched as Carlotta's hand went to her cheek.

"Who did this? Who struck you?" Erik asked.

Carlotta's lips began to tremble. In a thin voice, she said, "There were...two of them. They said my mouth...was...too big. They called me a...."

Erik took Carlotta by the elbow and brought her in against his chest, unconcerned that the heavy white layer of make-up would stain his dark vest. As Erik led Carlotta off stage, Grimaldo stepped aside, arms lax, a look of woeful impotence on his face.

On the way to his private rooms, Erik caught Meg's eye. She followed.

"What did she say?" Erik asked Meg.

He had left Carlotta alone with Meg, sensing that Carlotta would more likely speak in confidence with another woman—even if it were Meg—than with him.

"She was attacked just outside her apartment."

Erik listened. He could not tell if Carlotta had held back information or if Meg were doing so. But something was not being said.

"How many?"

"Two men, she thinks. She didn't know them. She can't describe them. It was over almost as soon as it began."

"Did they take anything?"

"Yes, they stole her purse."

Erik relaxed only slightly.

"What about jewelry?"

Meg lifted an eyebrow in surprise.

"She didn't mention it. She's still wearing her diamond and ruby."

Robbery would have been a likely explanation. But why not take her jewelry? If they were looking for easy money, why such brutality?

"You said they were outside her apartment? Were they waiting there for her?"

"She said," Meg paused, trying to recall Carlotta's words, "She said they stepped out from the shadows just as the carriage pulled away. One grabbed her from behind before she could call for help."

Erik scowled. He imagined the building, two men hidden in one of the dark recesses, Carlotta oblivious to their presence or their purpose. They had not followed her to her rooms. They had already been in place. It might have been happenstance that she was their victim, but it didn't make sense to take her purse and leave her jewels.

"You think they were after *her*, don't you?" Meg interrupted his thoughts.

"There's no way to tell unless Carlotta is willing to speak with the police."

"She doesn't want to talk about it," Meg rushed to say. "I did mention it. She became rather upset and made me promise not to tell anyone."

Erik expected as much. He sighed and said, with a touch of sarcasm, "As if the whole staff didn't know already. How is she?"

"She insists she's fine."

Erik raised a brow in question. "You don't believe her."

"I wish she would confide in me. If only Rinaldo were here."

"If Rinaldo had been here, she wouldn't have been alone on that street."

Meg ignored Erik's tone. She knew his irritation was a mask for his concern.

"She's lost without him."

"She has only herself to blame."

"You don't know that."

"I can guess."

"Yes, I suppose you're right," Meg admitted. "Have you heard anything more from him?"

"Only odd bits of information."

"Will he come back?"

Erik studied Meg. He could hear the hope in her voice. She could not bear to see a love affair end badly. She wanted Carlotta and Rinaldo to make amends and be together again. She wanted the whole world to be in love. But Erik knew life wasn't like that.

"I don't know, Meg." He cupped her face in the palm of his hand. So soft, her skin was warm and smooth to the touch. The need to know that she was and always would be safe from all harm was so sharp it felt like a blade lodged in his heart. "Sometimes life doesn't work the way we want it to."

"It works, as you put it, if the two people who love each other make it work." Her voice was stern, her eyes unflinching.

Erik smiled. "Mais, oui, ma petite. But they must understand what it is that they want."

She lowered her eyes.

"Do we know what we want?" she asked in a whisper.

Erik forced her to look up at him. He brushed aside a stray lock of hair that teased her eyebrow, allowing his fingers to linger by her ear. He bent and kissed her on the cheek. "I know, Meg. I know."

"But..."

He stopped her words with a touch of a finger upon her lips.

"I know, Meg. And if I have to, I'll do the work of two, ten, or a thousand."

He saw her eyes shine. Her lips curled into a hesitant smile.

"I know," he said gruffly, his voice a husky whisper as it grazed her mouth. "I know what I want," he said as his lips molded to hers, the tip of his tongue tentative and gentle. "I know because I want whatever you want, Meg," he breathed, his parted lips hovering over hers, moist and open. Then he kissed her again before she could answer, lest the answer be a protest.

Meg lay exhausted, her head on Erik's shoulder, her body cuddled close to his, her thigh draped over his groin. Erik cradled her in his left arm. He slept, his breathing deep and sonorous. As the last tingling sensations of their lovemaking faded, she couldn't keep the thoughts from her mind.

He had told her that he wanted only what she wanted. But when he had asked her what she wanted, she hadn't been able to say. Instead, her mind had wandered to the past, to the heady days when he taught her to sing, to the plans they had made when they left Pianosa and came to Rome, to the life Marcelo's protection had made possible. In Rome, they had rebuilt their lives, together, in a world that was sanctuary to him and home to her. Opera was what had saved him. It was everything to him. If she retired from the stage, she would no longer be a part of the world in which he lived.

Meg tilted her chin up and studied her sleeping husband. She kissed the underside of his chin and caressed the right side of his face, the side that was so strange and haunting. In sleep, Erik turned towards her. She could feel the warmth of his breath flutter across her face as he hugged her into his sheltering body.

She had to find a way for them, for herself.

He had told her that he knew what he wanted—her. But what did she want? She thought perhaps she had an idea. There was a risk. But, for the first time, she felt excited. He had vowed his love to her, no matter what she wanted to do with the rest of her life. It was time for her to make a commitment, too—one that would strengthen, not weaken their ties.

My dearest, sweetest Naldo,

> *I have written you several times, and you have not responded even to one of my letters. I have been thinking. I know that you would tease me and say that when I think I get into trouble. But the hours are long, and I have gotten better at thinking than I might have been. My thoughts do not make me happy. It is sad that a woman of my age has only recently begun to know herself. I was wrong to do what I did, Rinaldo. I won't lie. I knew it was wrong at the time. Perhaps it will help you to know that it brought me no pleasure? I have little or no excuse except to say that I was a fool and that I was mad with jealousy.*

> *You say that it doesn't matter that you are younger than I. It does matter. It fills me with doubts and fears that I have not been able to ignore. Chiara Greco is a beautiful, young woman—she's even a little talented. When you walked away from me that night, Greco's arm in yours, I couldn't help but realize that the two of you looked as if you belonged together. The thought blinded me to everything, to your words of love, to your promises, to your character and nobility.*

> *I allowed myself to be used, and I broke our trust. Can you forgive me, Naldo?*

If I could bear to cut myself, I would use my own blood to write 'I love you' in this letter and to seal it. If there is a chance that we might mend this wound between us, please let us find it together. I know that someday you might want things that I cannot give you. That day I will kiss your brow and wish you happiness. But until then, let me share your life. I promise that I will be less selfish and more thoughtful.

I beg you respond to this letter. I can't bear your silence.

Love, Carlotta

Grimaldo combed his hair and smoothed it down. He examined himself in the mirror. He was not a bad looking man. He still had his hair. The silver at his temple gave him a distinguished and serious touch. He was of moderate height, slight of build, but he was not a weak man. He kept himself fit. His eyes were a light brown with golden specks. His face was a bit round, but he had good teeth and a warm smile.

His wife's death more than fifteen years ago had driven him into his work. It had not been a conscious decision. It had simply happened. He had found peace and comfort in the constant presence of people and in the music. He drowned himself in his roles, living the parts in his lonely rooms as well as on the stage. He socialized infrequently because he wasn't quite sure who he was during those relaxed moments with his co-workers and fellow performers. So he smiled good-naturedly and laughed at the jokes. He was glad when the evening was over and he could return to his rooms alone. Eventually he found that the others left him alone. He would take the musical score or a book with him and sit for hours at the café content to be surrounded by the sounds of others. It was enough. Until recently.

Carlotta had swept away everyone in her path. She had silenced the others' voices, and everyone's eyes had watched her for months in her cat-and-mouse game with Don Erik. No one ever quite understood what had been afoot between those two. Then, one day, inexplicably, the disguised patroness, Signorina Venedetti, cast off her veil, stepped onto the stage, and revealed her identity as the renowned opera diva, Carlotta Giudicelli. Within the week, she had been incorporated into the company under the name of Venedetti.

Even before the enigmatic diva had abandoned her disguise, Grimaldo had felt his heart scrabble like a trapped animal in his chest. He had loved her from the beginning—her voice, the way she moved as if she were the axis around which the world turned, the arrogant wave of her hand. When he awoke under a doctor's care and realized that Carlotta had drugged him, causing him to miss the premiere of *La canzone di cuore*, and that Don Erik had performed in his stead, he had been foolishly content to have been of service to her. Nothing irreparable had happened. Standing in for Grimaldo, Don Erik had received several standing ovations, but the artistic director had made it clear that he had no intention of performing in public again. Grimaldo could only remember the joy he had felt when he learned that Carlotta Venedetti was to continue as a member of the company at the Teatro.

Each day had been a pleasure. It had dampened his spirits to learn that the young Rinaldo had besotted the beautiful Carlotta. But Grimaldo had assumed such a strange affair would not last long. Unfortunately, he had been wrong. Even as time passed, it had not cooled. Grimaldo had contented himself, as best he could, by finding excuses to be in Donna Carlotta's company. He had given in to the fantasy of being lover to her characters in the operas. The stage kisses he gave to Donna Meg were, in his mind, amorous exchanges with Carlotta.

Now that Rinaldo was gone, Grimaldo had decided that he would love in secret no more. The recent attack on Carlotta's person had occurred only because she was a woman alone and unprotected. He would not let that happen again.

He gave himself one more cursory glance in the mirror, straightened the edge of his vest, and left his dressing room.

As he came out of the wings to the stage, he heard the rumble of voices. One look toward the center of the stage and he saw the reason.

Not two feet from Carlotta Venedetti stood Rinaldo Jannicelli.

Grimaldo held his breath and blinked several times. Then he turned on his heel to rush back to his dressing room.

Word of Rinaldo Jannicelli's return was on everyone's lips in the opera house. The pianist assigned to work with Chiara Greco announced it even as he arranged the score they were to rehearse. Chiara could not contain her excitement. She excused herself, leaving the young pianist in the middle of his warm-up, and went in search of Sig. Jannicelli.

"Where is Sig. Jannicelli?" she asked several chorines huddled together on the staircase. They were speaking in excited whispers. One rubbed her toes while others sat and stretched out their tired muscles along the bottom several steps of the narrow, winding stairs.

The one who rubbed her toes said that she had seen Don Erik lead Jannicelli to his office.

Chiara was about to set off in that direction when she overheard the young girls mention the name of Signorina Venedetti.

"What were you saying about Carlotta?" Chiara interrupted.

The chorines hesitated, casting guilty looks among them, perhaps afraid that the new soprano would chide them for their loose tongues. But when they saw how avidly Greco hung on their silence, they gestured for her to come nearer so that they would not have to raise their voices.

"Well, he just appeared, you see."

"Yes, no one was paying any attention, when…"

"No, I saw him. He came in from the auditorium, up the stairs, stage right. And then he…"

"When I saw him, he was already dead center stage. It was eerie as if he were about to perform the…"

"Carlotta Venedetti nearly threw herself into…"

"But he didn't move, not a hair."

"She came to a dead halt."

"He just stared at her."

"I got a shiver up my spine."

"It was so tense because he…"

"…wasn't interested in whatever Carlotta had to offer."

Several of the girls giggled maliciously, but one spoke up. "I felt sort of bad for her especially after…"

"You can still see the bruises just under the foundation she wears." The girls seemed to have forgotten Chiara's question or even that she was still there, huddled among them.

"Do you think they did anything else to her?"

"I thought of that, too."

"Don't know. If they did, she's not telling."

Chiara was losing patience with their wild speculation. Although she sympathized with the older woman's pain, she was only interested in Jannicelli. "So what did he do?" she asked.

"There was more than one of them," answered the chorine to her right, mistaking her question.

"I didn't mean Venedetti's attackers. I meant Sig. Jannicelli. What did *he* do?" said Chiara.

"Nothing," answered the same young girl. "He stood there like granite. I swear it was as if they were speaking without words. Then he nodded. Like this." The girl imitated Rinaldo. She stood, shoulders back, looked down as if she towered over them, and brought her chin down in one curt nod of the head. "Then he turned to greet Don Erik."

Chiara didn't listen to the rest of their prattle. She was thrilled to know Rinaldo Jannicelli had returned. She far preferred working with him to her current accompanist.

She was about to leave the girls when something tugged at the corners of her mind.

"Excuse me," she said to get their attention once more. "Did Signorina Venedetti accompany Sig. Jannicelli? To Don Erik's office, that is?"

The same girl who had spoken directly to her before answered. "No, she just stood there in the middle of the stage when the two men walked away. It was rather sad really."

The mood among them had shifted. Though they had enjoyed recounting the dramatic arrival of the assistant, the farce had turned to tragedy. Now they spoke as if moved by Carlotta Venedetti's part in it.

"She didn't stand there for long."

"Long enough that everyone started to whisper about whether or not she was going to have a fit or faint or something."

"I think she was rather dignified as she left the stage."

"She was crying, you know."

All the girls turned to listen, their mouths open in a silent 'oh' and their eyes wide with sympathy.

"That's what Sophia said. Carlotta walked right past her, and Sophia could see her wiping at her make-up. She was all smudged."

Chiara felt a burst of sadness for the older woman. So Rinaldo had come back, but not to Carlotta Venedetti.

Rinaldo laid the folio on the desk. Erik picked it up and examined the first several pages. Aware that his former assistant watched him, he flipped forward, pausing at each major break to get the gist of the story and a feel for the music.

"You've been busy," Erik said.

"I value your opinion," Rinaldo answered Erik's neutral response.

Erik looked again at several sections, lingering over the music. Rinaldo studiously avoided showing signs of impatience. Even so, Erik could sense from the man's unnatural stillness that he was tense and anxious for Erik to speak.

"It's good."

Rinaldo's face muscles relaxed as he gave into a soft smile of relief. He leaned back in the chair against the firm cushion and stretched out his right leg.

Erik hid his own smile at Rinaldo's self-satisfaction.

"The role of Katerina is meant for an older woman, I see."

Rinaldo rubbed the edge of his hand across the moustache he had allowed to grow, his eyes roving to the piano at the far end of the room. He glanced back at Erik. His lopsided smile said it all.

Erik found himself unable to disguise his own. Both men chuckled.

"Will you tell her?" asked Erik.

"Not yet."

Erik nodded.

"I'm still not sure," Rinaldo said, his smile drooping. "We'll have to see."

"Do you have a backer in Milan?"

"I thought I'd give you the first shot at it."

"Confident, aren't you?"

"You've taught me the value of determination."

Erik opened the folio once more and studied the opening measures. "It's not a particularly original story."

"I know. But it's never been done quite like this."

Erik considered Rinaldo, waiting for him to make his intentions clear.

The younger man leaned forward, his elbows resting on the edge of the desk.

"Don Erik, I'm not just asking you to produce and stage this opera. I would like to come back and work as artistic director."

Erik scowled. "There's a difference between confidence and arrogance."

"I'm sorry, but you never actually taught me to distinguish the difference."

"In case you've forgotten, I'm the artistic director of the Teatro dell'Opera. You can assist me on the piece."

"But this is my work, my opera," Rinaldo said. "The position you're offering me is basically the same one I left."

"No, that's where you're wrong. Before, you were my personal assistant. In the position that I'm offering, you are the assistant director for the show itself. Your focus will be on the staging of the opera."

"Will I have full autonomy over the production?"

"As long as we agree on the overarching concepts, you'll have a certain amount of autonomy."

"I'm not sure that I'm satisfied with those arrangements."

"Is this not my theater?"

"Yes, but..."

"I don't share my power easily, Rinaldo." Erik recognized the struggle in the grim set to the young man's jaw. He was pleased by Rinaldo's return. Moderating his tone, he added, "I'm willing to step back, although it's not in my nature. I can offer you the assistant artistic directorship. As such you will be in charge of the piece."

Rinaldo considered for a moment, then held out his hand to Erik. "Agreed."

Erik accepted Rinaldo's gesture. Before the young man could rise to go, he motioned him to stay.

"By the way, Rinaldo, what brought you back at this particular moment." When Rinaldo seemed about to answer, Erik added, "Besides the opera."

Rinaldo shrugged and leaned back in his chair. "I secured a modest position at Teatro degli Angeli."

"I know. In part that's why I ask."

"All I had to do is mention your name."

Erik tamped down the fluttering sensation in his gut. He told himself that there was no danger in Rinaldo's using his name. After all, Costanzi was only the last in a series of names and identities. At this point it was as removed from his past as he was.

"They know your work," added Rinaldo. "The position was similar to the one I held here, but..."

When Rinaldo hesitated, Erik offered the most obvious answer. "They didn't pay as well."

"True, but it wasn't the money. It was just...not as lively...not as stimulating an environment. It was more like a business than... than... I can't think how to explain it. But here, with you, with Donna Meg and...the others...it was always about the music, the art."

Erik, for once, was glad he had not yet removed his mask. It took several attempts before Erik could swallow the lump in his throat.

"I'm glad you finally came to your senses."

The knock was barely a rap of knuckles at the door. Both men wondered if they'd been mistaken and heard wrong until they heard the voice—also quiet.

"Greco?" Erik muttered under his breath. He looked beyond

Rinaldo at the door and called out in a voice from which he studiously culled the note of irritation. "Come."

The door moved as if the air, instead of Chiara's hand, were perhaps pushing it. Chiara Greco stood in the doorway, waiting.

Erik clenched his teeth against his exasperation and beckoned her forward.

Rinaldo rose to greet her.

Once the formalities had been completed, Erik asked, "Signorina, may I help you?"

"Don Erik, yes, please. I thought perhaps, now that Sig. Jannicelli has returned, he might resume my practice."

Rinaldo was about to answer, but Erik spoke first. "Impossible."

Still unaccustomed to Erik's curt manners, Chiara stood with her mouth partially agape, waiting.

Erik saw Rinaldo's embarrassed glance at Chiara Greco and realized some explanation was expected.

"Sig. Jannicelli will have more important matters to tend to, signorina. Are you unsatisfied with your accompanist?" Before she could agree, Erik offered her the alternative, which he knew would be less to her liking. "I will resume our lessons if you are discontent with the present arrangement."

Chiara's mouth opened and closed several times before a sound came clear. "No, Sig. Costanzi, the current arrangement is adequate. If Sig. Jannicelli's duties are so important that he cannot tutor me, then I expect it would be a particularly difficult matter for the artistic director to find time for me." With that, Chiara Greco curtsied in a most aggressive fashion and took her leave.

After several moments, Rinaldo said, "I take it she did not enjoy having you as a taskmaster?"

Erik waved a hand in dismissal of the sarcasm. "Let's say that we had artistic differences and leave it at that."

Rinaldo chuckled as he took his leave. But just as he was about to close the door behind him, he remembered something he had meant to say earlier. "Don Erik, I was commended by one the owners of the opera house to give you his regards."

"Yes?"

"He said he knew you back in the days of the Opera Populaire."

Erik's hand fisted, but he remained silent.

"He prefers your more recent works, he told me to tell you, and congratulates you on your success."

Erik kept his eyes focused on the smooth surface of the desk.

"Who is the owner?" he asked. "What is his name?"

"Piangi, Ubaldo Piangi. I think he was once a lead tenor."

"Yes," whispered Erik, as he heard Rinaldo pull the door closed. "He was."

Carlotta's hand shook as she dabbed at the tracks the tears had made in her make-up. She studied her face in the mirror ravaged by the sleepless nights and regret. She was still a woman in her prime, she told herself. She took the dampened cloth and wiped a broad swath across her face. The pull distorted her features for a moment. Underneath the heavy foundation were still darkened reminders of the cruel attack she had suffered. No longer tender, they disguised the fact that she still cringed from the fear that they might return one night and find her alone and unprotected.

Alone and unprotected. She thought of Rinaldo. He had come back.

The moment she had seen him climb the steps to the stage and advance, she had lurched forward. But his lack of response, when he must have seen her, had fixed her to the spot. Her first burst of joy had turned to dread. When he came to a full stop, still at several removes from her reach, Carlotta knew he'd come no closer. It had been worse than if he had not returned at all.

Carlotta clamped her hand over the stretched opening of her mouth to still the staccato sounds of her sobs. She leaned forward so that she could not see her pathetic display in the mirror. Her tears were hot. They dripped into the oily paste that she had prepared to smooth over her face—to hide the lingering trace of bruised flesh and heart.

Oh, she had been such a fool.

"Carlotta," he said.

She had not heard Rinaldo enter. He stood behind her. She grabbed at the nearby towel and buried her face in it.

"What?" came her muffled voice.

"Are you all right?" he asked. His voice was so sweet. She felt her body respond to it as it once had.

How could she answer him? If only he'd give her a few moments to collect herself. She was a mess, worse than a mess. How could anyone look at her now and feel anything but pity or revulsion. She would not have him pity her.

"We have to talk."

"Talk, talk, talk. That's all you men know how to do. There are too many words in the world."

"Turn around and look at me, Carlotta."

Reluctantly, Carlotta turned sideways in her seat and looked up at the young man. He was dark and stern, and she searched his face for some sign of the desire he used to have for her. She had once played with his heart as if it were putty in her hands, a mere bauble. Did he still yearn for her? Or had he finally opened his eyes? It could not have lasted, she reminded herself.

"What is that?" Rinaldo asked. His fingers reached out and grazed the darkened area under her left eye. "That's a bruise. What happened? Who did this to you?"

She squeezed her mouth shut and shook her head against the sorrow of past and future pains. The bruise was nothing. It would go away.

Rinaldo bent on his knee beside her chair. His arms folded around her, and she slipped forward onto his knee, her face buried against his neck.

"Tell me."

Carlotta managed to tell him between sniffles and hiccups that she had been assaulted and robbed. When he pressed her for details, she insisted that she had told him everything she knew.

As Rinaldo held Carlotta, he tried to understand the feelings roiling inside his gut. When he had taken her in his arms, an emptiness that had plagued him since he left Rome was suddenly filled. He should be angry at her. He was. He should know that she was self-centered, selfish, and foolish and that she could easily break his heart again. And he did. But though he could think of no course of action involving Carlotta Venedetti that didn't lead to disaster, he was relieved and happy to have returned and to have found her inconsolable without him.

"Did you get my letters?" she asked between sniffles.

"Yes," he said. But he didn't look her straight in the eye.

"Did you read them?"

He hesitated, then answered, "Not at first."

"When?"

"I read all of them, together, the afternoon before I left to come back here."

"Oh, Naldito, mio amore," she said as she threw her arms around his neck.

He didn't particularly like her nickname for him, but he smiled and held onto her for several moments.

"Carlotta, should we go home now?"

Grimaldo shouldn't drink. He couldn't hold his liquor. Yet he held his finger up when the waiter glanced his way and beckoned for him to pour one more whisky. He had been so close. He would have been good for Carlotta. Rinaldo was a young man, too young for Carlotta Venedetti. Eventually he would tire of her. At some point a younger woman, one who could grow old with him and give him a handful of children, was bound to catch his eye. No one could blame a man like Rinaldo for wanting what most men wanted. Carlotta was not a woman. She was a lifetime commitment. She would consume Jannicelli's whole life, taking, taking, and taking until there was nothing left for her to take.

Grimaldo was willing to give everything. He had nothing else to live for. Gladly would he devote himself to the fiery diva. His career was coming to an end, but he would watch over Carlotta Venedetti and her career as if it were his own. He would, if he were given the chance. But Rinaldo Jannicelli had returned and stolen this one opportunity—the first time that Grimaldo had managed to find the courage to lay his heart at the amazon's feet.

"Another," he muttered as he downed the contents of his glass.

The waiter seemed reluctant. But Grimaldo was a regular customer, so the man poured another shot of whisky. Around Grimaldo the sounds of various different conversations were nothing but jostled notes, incomprehensible. He paid no attention except to mark that he was perhaps the only person who sat drinking alone. Taking his glass, he stumbled to his usual table and decided to sit back and watch the general hubbub around him, hoping that the distraction would take his mind off his own sadness. It was the usual crowd, he noticed.

At the other end of the room sat the musical director and several principals from the Teatro Regio. Among them, at the same table, was Sig. Bianchi. Grimaldo observed them, intrigued by Sig. Bianchi's relaxed and affable manner. He wondered if Bianchi was smiling more at the beautiful blond cantante at his side or, across the table, at the musical director, Sig. Testa. Testa was a virile and passionate conductor, reportedly a scourge to the performers at the Teatro Regio.

Grimaldo lifted his glass to his lips and barely realized that it was empty, for something caught his eye that immediately dispelled the alcoholic haze that had blurred his vision. Two large men, common in their attire, were just getting up from a table off to one side of the bar. The dumb show played itself out before Grimaldo with all the clarity of Punch and Judy. There was no doubt that the man at the table, Paolo Ricci, had hired the two men. In plain view—although Grimaldo was the only one interested in the spectacle—Ricci slipped the money to the men. The latter seemed reluctant to leave until another dip under the table brought out a few more coins that Ricci slid, with little grace, across to them.

Oh, he would have to be an idiot not to understand the meaning of this. Grimaldo knew it deep in his bones as if Ricci himself had stood in front of them all and boasted of having paid Carlotta Venedetti back for her public taunts. Grimaldo had cringed to know that Carlotta had bedded the journalist. Was everyone but him to taste her pleasures? When she had made jokes with no thought to veiling her failed lover's identity, Grimaldo had worried that she might suffer the consequences.

Paolo Ricci should not get away with this. Someone had to do something. Someone had to make Paolo Ricci pay for what he had done to Carlotta.

Meg wiped the dry rag across the back of her neck, along the slope of her breasts, over her face. She took several deep cleansing breaths and closed her eyes to enjoy the calm that seeped from the center of her chest and out along her limbs. She felt incredible, as if she might float to the ceiling.

She should be tired, but she wasn't.

A second film of sweat rose from her skin as her body tried to throw off the internal heat stoked by the recent practice. She folded the cloth and pressed it to her brow. This time she did a more thorough job of wiping down the soft curves of her arms and then down the long expanse of her thighs and calves.

Renata Cossa had been pleased, but no more so than Meg herself. Signorina Cossa had been trained in classic ballet. She had had hopes of performing, but an unfortunate fall from the stage had permanently weakened her back, making the demands of nightly performances increasingly painful. After weeks of demanding more than her body could handle, Renata Cossa had awakened one morning unable to stand. Her back twisted in agony, she was forced to keep to her bed for weeks. When she was once more able to walk, she learned the limits of her body, the warning signs when she was pushing beyond these. She accepted that her performing days were behind her. For Renata Cossa, the opportunity to work at the Teatro dell'Opera had been a godsend. Not only was she able to maintain contact with the profession she loved, but she had been given unrestricted license to choreograph the dance scenes.

Meg eased her feet out of the ballet slippers and wiggled her toes. Renata had just the right balance of criticism and praise. As the ballet mistress led her through the complicated exercises and the movements of the dance itself, Meg had found a new grace and versatility in her body. She bent and massaged the ball of one foot, worked the toes, and then gave equal attention to the other.

She didn't hear Carlotta enter until the older woman spoke.

"What is it that you are doing?"

Startled Meg twisted to see Carlotta Venedetti fill the doorway. Although it was Monday and there was no performance this evening, Carlotta had lingered at the theater.

"Carlotta, I thought you'd gone hours ago. Everyone else has gone already."

"Ah, everyone but him. He paces in his office. He waits for you to finish whatever it is that you do here." Carlotta stepped inside the brightly lit room. The bank of mirrors on either side reflected an infinite series of Carlottas. As if Meg were not in the same room, Carlotta checked the line of her gown, smoothed the material across her bosom, and smiled contentedly at her figure. For a moment, her smile fell as she glanced at her face. The make-up disguised most of the faded bruises her attackers had left her. Remembering that she had a witness, the older diva pulled her eyes away from her own reflection and examined the younger woman.

"What does a prima donna do in a dance room?" Carlotta asked.

Meg considered ignoring the accusation in her question. A rush of memories came crowding into her mind. *Carlotta scolding M. Reyer because the tempo was too fast or too slow, Carlotta stomping on a costume and complaining that the fabric scratched her sensitive skin, Carlotta laughing at the missteps she and Christine, young dancers at the Opera Populaire, made as they rehearsed the dance routine.* Carlotta had treated her mother with disdain, had told the manager that the ballet corps was amateurish and that they had too many scenes in the productions. She had never taken the time to learn the young girls' names. The calm Meg had felt slipped away. Annoyed, she prepared to go to the dressing room to change.

"It's late," she said as she gathered her things.

"I thought you knew him." Carlotta's voice taunted Meg.

Dressing would have to wait.

"Are you referring to my husband?" said Meg.

Carlotta smiled, satisfied that once more she had Meg's attention.

"You waste your time. The Phantom…"

"Signorina Venedetti, you forget yourself," Meg warned.

Carlotta waved her hand in front of her face as if to shoo away a fly.

"Yes, yes, yes, but we are alone. We know who he is." Carlotta dared Meg to disagree.

"You think you know him?" Meg took several steps towards Carlotta, her feet skimming smoothly, silently across the glossy waxed boards. "Do you know what it was like for him?"

"Bah! That's old news." Whether she felt intimidated by Meg's obvious irritation or not, Carlotta walked over to the bank of mirrors and pretended to inspect something on her cheek. Meg could see the telltale smudge of the bruise on Carlotta's cheekbone where the powder had faded.

"Don't act as if you can lecture me on who Erik Costanzi is." Meg turned her back to go, her steps less fluid, hard and quick across the wooden floor.

"I know one thing, Meg Giry, that you have forgotten," Carlotta called after the retreating figure. "I know that he hates a coward."

Meg stopped in her tracks, but did not turn.

"Ah, you understand," said Carlotta. She barely hid the note of triumph in her tone. "The Phantom rejected me. Why? He plagued me because I had stopped trying. Your husband has not changed in this. You think he is not the Phantom? I see the Phantom when I look into those green eyes. The Phantom does not respect the artist who doesn't work for the art." Carlotta waited for Meg to answer.

"And what does 'the Phantom' think of the artist who can no longer meet his standards?" The voice was small.

Carlotta scowled. She pursed her lips, considered as if she were reluctant to go on. "Do you think that I sing as well as I once did?"

Meg relented and looked at the older woman.

"Do you think my voice would bring the house down now?" Carlotta continued. When Meg was silent, Carlotta approached. "I know what I can do, Giry. I know that my voice is not what it should be. But...but Costanzi has pushed me as far as I can go. You think that he doesn't hear the difference? Is my voice the one he wants to hear, the one he imagines in his mind for his music?"

"Carlotta, your voice is beautiful." The anger had drifted away.

"No, you are not fooled. You are being kind." For one moment the two women stood facing each other, aware that they shared something fragile and intimate. Carlotta continued, "I know that I fall short of what he imagines. So why does he not dismiss me? Why does he not tell me to leave?"

"He knows how much work you've…"

"Yes, yes, yes! That is my point, you silly woman." The intimacy of the moment was broken. As if exasperated with a recalcitrant servant, Carlotta raised her arms and gesticulated at Meg. "You don't even try. You are breaking his heart."

"What?"

"You must try. That is all he wants. If you try and cannot do it, then he will be resigned. He will be proud of you. There are many singers. That vacca can serve his purposes. Or he will pick another young thing from among the chorines. But you, you, you spend your time dancing. You dance—you do not sing—but you are a singer. You are his songbird. So why do you not sing?"

"Meg." The deep voice from the far side of the room interrupted them. Both women turned their gaze to the doorway. Framed by the darkness in the corridor behind him stood Erik Costanzi. "It's time to go," he said. He lifted his hand, his palm up, for Meg to take. "Come."

As Meg went to Erik, Carlotta whispered, "Think."

Raoul had been trying to pry Erik out of the theater for the past hour. Meg had asked him to occupy Erik for a few hours each afternoon, and Raoul had found that the best way to do so was to offer to spar or to fence with him.

Now as they were about to make it to the front doors, Erik pulled to a stop and looked out toward the stage. Chiara Greco sat to the side, waiting for Grimaldo to reach her cue. Beyond them, taking up a good portion of the stage, were the dancers.

"Erik, we are leaving the theater. Now." Raoul was about to take hold of Erik's sleeve and pull him to the door. The carriage had been waiting for more than an hour.

Erik's green eyes flashed for one moment, irritated that Raoul had interrupted his train of thought.

"Look at them."

"The Greco woman and Grimaldo?" asked Raoul, innocently.

"No, no, no. The dancers."

Raoul arched a curious eyebrow, but Erik was unaware. He would not take his eyes off the dancers.

"Is there a reason that we're watching Signorina Cossa instructing the dancers?"

"Look, man. Look at the formation."

Raoul stared intensely at the figures that from this distance appeared to him like ants swarming on an anthill.

"Something's off," Erik said.

"Well, I'm sure Cossa will have them ready by the time the opera opens."

"No, you're not looking carefully enough. The dancers are doing exactly what she has told them to do. I've been watching for an entire week. It's the same routine, over and over again. But they're dancing…around something…that isn't there. See how they raise their arms toward the center?"

Raoul squinted and watched as several rows of ants circled, creating in their absence an obvious vacant spot.

"Perhaps Carlotta is supposed to be in the center?"

"There is no center. That is to say, the center, the empty space, continually shifts, as if it were moving, too. Carlotta will not be moving about on the stage as she sings her aria. She'd be a laughing stock."

"I see what you mean. Can we go now?"

Erik's jaw clenched as if he were worrying the inside of his mouth. "There must be an explanation."

"Well, if you don't find out in the next day or so, I'm sure you'll find out on opening night. Why don't you ask Cossa?"

"No," Erik said, his tone a bit sullen. "I trust Donna Renata. It just struck me as bizarre."

"Modern times, Erik. Things are changing." Raoul patted Erik on the shoulder. "Come on before everything disappears on us and we find ourselves in the land of Jules Verne."

Erik relented, and the two men left the theater.

"Who are you looking for?" François asked.

Velia stumbled and nearly fell first down the marble stairs. François reached out and stopped her. His arm wrapped round her narrow waist and yanked her back to the landing. He was too aware of her body, slight and trembling, and his own suddenly grew in strength and assurance. He held her for a heartbeat too long for it to seem insignificant.

"Are you all right?" he asked as he released her.

"I have two left feet." She smiled up at him.

François stared at her, at her hazel eyes, at her parted lips—one lip thin, the other swollen and red—at her nose that turned up slightly, and at her hair. It was golden, like wheat in sunlight.

"I was just trying to catch Don Erik before he left," she said. She pointed toward the massive front doors through which Don Erik and his friend, the French count, had left.

"I see," François said, unable to let the moment slip away.

"I guess he's gone for the day?"

Why would she need to speak with his father? His father had placed her in his charge. Unless perhaps she was unhappy with his instruction and wished to complain or to be reassigned to someone else? It unsettled him to know that it mattered so much to him.

"Are you not happy with our arrangement?" he asked. He was unable to mask a hint of irritation. One look at her face told him that she had not expected such a question. "Never mind. It's none of my business."

He was nearly halfway up the flight of stairs when she called out to him.

"What makes you think that I'm not happy?" She climbed several steps.

He stopped and stepped down to meet her.

"I thought…I mean to say…I wondered if you…wanted to tell my father that…"

"No," she said.

François was relieved and concerned at the same time. Her answer had pleased him, but she had blushed and seemed upset.

"Please, don't mention it to your father."

"But why…?"

"I don't need to see him. Not really. It was a question I had about…something entirely different. I've forgotten it already, you see?"

François stepped closer, trying to understand why she was so agitated. His closeness must have disturbed her, for she bolted down the steps and out into the main hallway. He was about to follow when he saw Mario come in from the street. François gripped the banister, fixed to his place on the staircase, as he watched Mario take Velia by the arm. Before he might see anything else between the two of them, François bounded up the stairs to disappear among the upper corridors of the theater.

A few days later, Renata Cossa approached Erik.

"Don Erik, may I have a word," she asked.

"Yes?"

"I've been working on a piece that I would like to add to the scene just before the intermission."

"You mean to extend the dance between scenes?"

"Not exactly. I'm referring to the final scene of the act before the intermission. The dance would not be so much an entr'acte as part of the scene itself."

"I've seen you working on something lately. Is that it?" He did not add that the choreography was not up to her usual standard. Perhaps all the pieces had not yet come together.

"It's part of the dance. There's more to it."

Erik waited for Renata to explain why this would be wise.

"I've spoken with Donna Carlotta. She understands how it will work," she said instead.

"The act needs a big finish, Donna Renata. I'd prefer that the audience focus on Carlotta's aria." It was, after all, the moment when her character, an aging and betrayed Queen, was to declare her intention to avenge herself on Yasmine, a slave girl whose beauty had captured the eye of the King.

"I understand completely. I think the dance will enhance, not detract, from the moment. You'll be pleased."

Erik couldn't help but think that Renata Cossa was not telling him everything. She clutched her hands so tightly that the fingers were white.

"I've always given you free rein with the dancers."

Meg's mother, Madeleine, had been mistress of the ballet at the Opera Populaire. When she married Don Marcelo, Madeleine had chosen to step down as mistress of the corps de ballet at the Teatro dell'Opera. She had wanted to devote herself to her marriage, tour the continent, watch her grandchildren grow. She encouraged Erik to hire Renata Cossa and advised him to allow Signorina Cossa to handle both the dancers and the choreography. Madeleine's advice had proven wise. Erik rarely intruded on Renata Cossa's direction, and the results had always been impeccable.

Still there was something unsettling about Renata Cossa's request. Her nervous smile did not ease his doubts.

"You've worked this out with Sig. Bianchi, I assume?"

"Oh, yes. Everything is prepared."

"Then, I'll leave it to you, Donna Renata."

CHAPTER 5

A Stunning Performance

"Hell is empty and all the devils are here."

The Tempest, William Shakespeare

Christine slipped inside Meg's dressing room.

Meg swiveled in her seat toward Christine. "Oh, it's you," she said in relief.

"Are you nervous?"

Meg smiled and patted the edge of a nearby chair for Christine to come sit.

"No, I'm excited. I do wish Maman were here." Meg tightened her lips and applied the bright red lipstick.

"She would be thrilled to see you tonight. But there will be other opportunities for her to see you perform."

"If all goes well." Meg crossed her fingers and kissed them for good luck.

"What's that?"

"What? Oh you mean the charm? Erik taught it to me."

"Really?"

"Yes, I think it's something old he learned. I think it's Romany."

Christine crossed her own fingers and kissed them, too, after a moment's silence. "There. It can't hurt."

Meg picked up a half mask studded with silver and gold flecks. Along the top ridge was a row of feathers—each a different color.

"What's that?" Christine asked.

Meg held it up in front of her eyes. It was beautiful. The cut of the mask accentuated her eyes. The feathers gave her a magical look, as if she were fairy and maiden.

"Just in case," Meg said.

"You can't think to fool Erik with this."

"No. No, I'm sure he'll recognize me—with or without the mask. But the audience doesn't have to know who I am."

"It will be a tremendous success, Meg."

Meg squeezed Christine's hand in appreciation.

"Did you have any trouble with Erik?"

They had devised a plan to explain Meg's absence.

"Not really. At first I thought he'd insist on staying at home with you. He was upset that you were indisposed."

"What did you say?"

"I had to suggest it was something related to your monthly courses. That kept him from asking for details. I think he was uncomfortable that I mentioned such an intimate detail."

Meg blushed. It was unlikely that Erik believed Christine's last minute explanation. But it was even more unlikely that he would have had the nerve to tell Christine that Meg's courses were not due for another week.

"Poor Erik." Meg screwed up her face in a parody of grief. Both women burst out laughing.

"You were right to wait until the last minute. If he had had time to reconsider, I don't know that we would have gotten him into the carriage."

"He's never missed an opening," said Meg.

"This is one he'll always remember."

Ricci sat back in his box seat and studied the audience. Their enthusiastic attention to the stage told him, if nothing else did, that they were enchanted. Another success for Costanzi. Act III was about to begin. Ricci knew that, just before intermission, Carlotta's big scene would bring the act to a close. He scanned the auditorium until he found the men he had planted. There were only three, situated in different zones of the auditorium. The hard-to-get seats had cost Ricci more than the amount he had paid the men to carry out his instructions. It was simple—all they had to do was disrupt the scene.

He chuckled with glee to imagine the opening lines of his review tomorrow.

From his box seat, Erik listened and watched. In the back of his mind, he thought of Meg. The excuse she had given for missing the performance was too flimsy to be credited. Christine had alluded to Meg's courses. He knew, for a fact, that the timing was off, but the intimacy of the excuse had kept him from questioning Christine further. Something was afoot, and Christine was apparently complicit in the matter.

As he watched the performance, his mind was drawn back to Renata Cossa's strange choreography. Over the past several weeks, he often found Meg in the company of Renata and the ballet troupe. He knew that she spent hours in the dance room, practicing her jetés and pirouettes, sometimes alone and sometimes with the young dancers. She had always done so, but never with such intensity as in the past several weeks. Ever since Renata Cossa had broached the subject of extending one of the dance scenes, an inkling of a suspicion had begun to tease him. Now, as the final scene of the act drew near, he leaned forward in his seat, anticipating and hoping that his intuition was correct.

Carlotta wandered out onto the stage, her character beset by jealousy and black thoughts of revenge. This was her scene—Carlotta's best and most dramatic moment in the opera. She was in fine tune this evening, hitting her mark and sustaining the notes with strength and accuracy. Her performance seemed without effort, and Erik was pleased. As the first notes of the aria were played, the dancers had filed out onto the stage somewhat behind and to the side of Carlotta who occupied the area close to the pit, just left of center. Erik continued to listen to Carlotta, following the score in his mind's eye, even as he watched the dancers. They fell into a bizarre pattern, creating that same emptiness that had disturbed him during rehearsals. Distracted from Carlotta's performance, he noted the lone figure who stepped out from among the back tier of dancers and into that vacant area. She was not one of the usual young girls.

The dancer wore a mask, but the moment she began to move, Erik knew who it was.

"It's Meg," he blurted out to Raoul, who sat beside him. Erik could tell Raoul was not surprised. Seated just beyond her husband, Christine smiled and nodded enthusiastically. She, too, had known.

Erik's momentary irritation could not compete with his excitement. Meg was dancing. Her steps were a pantomime of Carlotta's desire and plans. Like a dumb show, the story in verse was repeated in Meg's graceful movements.

"Give it a rest, love."

The harsh voice rang out below, somewhere in the mid section of the audience on the main floor. Erik's attention was torn from the stage in search of the anonymous voice. Before he could fasten onto the location, another jeering outburst—equally coarse and biting— sounded at the opposite end.

"Yeah. My ears hurt."

"Can't someone shut the cunt up?"

"Are you tone deaf, you great sow?"

The insults seemed to come from various locations in the auditorium.

Raoul and Erik rose as one and scanned the audience. Several more insults competed with the music. Then something shot across the expanse between the front left bank of seats and landed on the stage, just feet from Carlotta. The pulp of the tomato scattered across the stage floor. Carlotta shrank back, but her singing didn't flag. If anything, it grew in strength and vigor, straining the limits of her vocal range. Sig. Bianchi encouraged the orchestra to pick up the tempo and volume to compete with an ever-increasing rumble of agitated voices among the audience. Another volley of tomatoes exploded onto the stage, accompanied by insults and obscenities.

Erik had disappeared down the gallery before Raoul reached the door.

Meg heard the knock at the door. She had not yet changed. The bodice and leggings of her costume left little to the imagination, clinging to every curve of her body. The sparkles in her make-up gave her a whimsical look in spite of her worried expression. The feathered mask lay on the vanity as if to watch her undress. She opened the door just enough to see Erik on the other side. He slipped in and shut the door behind him. Before she could speak, Erik lifted her into an embrace that left her feet dangling in mid-air.

"Are you all right?" he whispered against her cheek.

"Yes, I'm all right." As he relaxed his hold on her, she slid down his body to rest her toes on the floor. "You knew it was me, didn't you?"

"How could I not know you?" he whispered still.

"The jeers, they weren't for me, were they?"

Erik shook his head. "They were meant for Carlotta." He couldn't be sure until he spoke with the heckler. But the content of the insults was directed at the singing, not the dancing.

"I thought so. She's with Rinaldo. She's angry."

"Good. Anger is good. Will she be able to complete the opera?"

Intermission had been extended to allow the performers time to recover from the mêlée. Erik should be in the wings, supervising preparations for Act IV, instead of in Meg's dressing room.

"Did you catch the men?"

Erik had appeared, as if by magic, in the central corridor of the auditorium even as the hecklers continued to hurl their insults at the stage. Meg saw him drag one from the third seat in the sixth row center. A host of cheers sounded throughout the auditorium. An elderly couple, seated between Erik and his target, were outraged by their neighbor's uncouth manners and his vulgar insults. They barely felt the man's body as it scraped across their laps. The woman lashed out with her beaded reticule at the miscreant before Erik pulled him clear. When the man's accomplices saw Erik shake his prey like a rag doll, they panicked and scurried, of their own accord, bolting from their seats for the exits. While the audience voiced its encouragement, Erik's staff gave pursuit. Between Raoul and Erik, the first man was hauled to a side door and taken from the audience to the general applause of the spectators.

"No. The ones that ran got away."

"What about the other one? The one you caught?"

"Don't be concerned. I have him in a safe place."

"What are you going to do with him, Erik?"

"Just ask a few questions."

He was not going to share his plans with her. Meg scowled.

Erik smiled, one edge of his mouth slightly higher than the other. "You were incredible, you know." Erik's eyes traveled warmly over her face.

Joy suffused every inch of her body.

"You used to say that my true talent was in dance. Do you remember?"

"That was true, but it was not always meant kindly."

"I know."

"I tried so many times to dissuade you from putting your hopes on a phantom lover."

Meg chuckled and leaned in against her husband's body.

"Monsieur, you are no phantom. You are very real to me."

"So my songbird is now my dancer?"

"Perhaps." A cautious look stole into Meg's eyes.

"Are there any other surprises in store for me tonight?"

"No," she laughed. "It was difficult enough to keep this one to ourselves."

With great reluctance, Erik stepped away from Meg and went to the door.

"After the final curtain, go home. Christine will go with you."

Before she could protest, he had slipped outside and was gone.

"Who put you up to it?" Erik's spit landed on the man's face. His hands were wrapped round his victim's throat, cutting off all but a wheeze of air.

Raoul grabbed Erik's arm, ready to pull him off his captive.

"Talk, you piece of shit. Who paid you? Who bought your ticket?

Who told you to hiss and boo and shout your filth? Who told you when to start?" Erik shook the man as if he were a rag doll. His fingers tightened on the man's throat.

"Erik, you can't strangle it out of him. He…can't…breathe!" Raoul pulled at Erik's arms. The force of his efforts kept Erik from crushing the man's windpipe. Just as Raoul thought he might have to take something and pummel Erik into unconsciousness, Erik released his grip on the man's throat. The man collapsed to his knees, coughing and sputtering.

Erik ripped off his mask and threw it on the ground in front of the man so that he could see it. Without thinking, the captive glanced up. At the sight of the disfigured maniac hovering over him, he scurried backwards, pushing with his feet, to get away from the horrid face twisted with anger.

Erik wiped his hand across his mouth. He was deathly pale, almost as pale as the man he'd nearly killed. Both gasped for air.

"Well, that was close." Raoul sighed in relief to see the temporary abatement of violence. Unfortunately he relaxed too soon, for Erik stalked over to his victim, leaned down, took hold of the man's stained jacket, and yanked him to his feet.

Raoul stood at the ready, but didn't interfere.

Erik's face was intimately close to that of the frightened man.

"Do you know how I got this face?"

The man's wheeze was all the sound in the room. He shook his head when Erik tightened his grip on the jacket and pulled him in closer to his face.

"There are things I could do to you that would make *this* look pleasant. I have an unusual skill at carving, a true sculptor's talent at the blade."

The man's bowels relaxed. The air was putrid with the odor.

"Raoul, open the drawer to my desk."

Raoul hesitated only a moment. Then he walked to the other side of Erik's desk and opened the middle drawer. Inside were staff paper, a tuning fork, violin strings wrapped in ever tightening spirals and tied in place with a string. He looked up at Erik, but Erik's eyes were fixed on his victim's.

"Should I ask him for my chisel or for something more delicate?" Erik watched the man's eyes flare in panic.

"Oh God, oh merciful God, dio mio, no. No, no, no, no."

"Names."

"I don't know…"

"Not acceptable." Erik's nose came within a feather's width of his victim's.

"I…I…"

"Who?"

"Ri…Ricci…Pietro…no, Paolo Ricci. I swear I'm telling the truth. He…he's the man who writes things. Says his name's Ricci."

Ricci? Was that it? Carlotta's strident voice cursing Ricci, calling him a maggot, forcing him to the very edge of the stage. It had nothing to do with Meg. Only a privileged few knew she was to perform. A disruption timed, planned to coincide with Carlotta's aria. 'Can't someone shut the cunt up?' Bruises hidden under a thick layer of white makeup, dusted with rice powder. Other wounds? Others that no one would see? A woman, alone and unprotected, attacked on a dark street by two faceless men, men paid to teach her a lesson in humiliation, a lesson meant to teach her to keep her mouth shut.

Erik gritted his teeth. The growl began in his chest and surged up his throat and burst through clenched teeth. It rose to an ear-shattering pitch as he hurled the man across the room.

The man bounced against the wall to the floor. He scrambled to his feet, his hand rubbing at the bruises, ran to the door, and flung it open. Outside the office, a crowd had gathered. The man pushed his way free and fled down the corridor. No one pursued him. Nor did anyone step over the threshold into Erik Costanzi's office.

Raoul knew better than to lay a hand on Erik. Let the storm spend its force.

"I'll kill the bastard. I'll kill him." Erik paced the room, heedless of those just outside who watched. "I'll kill him with my bare hands. I'll rip his face off and make him eat it."

Raoul glanced over to the stunned faces of those standing in the hallway. Among them he noticed Jacopo whom he indicated should draw near.

"Have him followed. Be sure we know how to find him again.

Get these people out of here," he whispered in Jacopo's ear. Jacopo nodded, took hold of the knob, and drew the door closed behind him.

Raoul went to Erik who now leaned against his desk, his fists clenched on the smooth wooden surface. He laid one hand on Erik's shoulder, the other on his left arm. Erik tensed but did not move.

"I'm so glad you didn't ask me to bring you the tuning fork. It gives me shivers to think what use you might have put it to."

Against his will, Erik let loose a snort of laughter. Raoul sighed in relief to recognize his friend once again.

The moment did not last.

"He has to pay," Erik said, the laughter in his eyes dying.

"It's a matter for the law," Raoul reminded Erik, but he knew that Erik could not present a demand at the police station. It was a recourse that might put him into harm's way.

"I have to go," Erik said.

"Where?"

"To find Meg."

"Christine took her home. We both know that's not where you're headed." Raoul positioned himself between Erik and the door.

"Get out of my way." Erik's voice was low and ominous.

"I don't think that would be a wise thing to do."

"Imminently wiser than standing in my way."

Erik lunged forward into a solid wall. Raoul repelled him.

"Listen to reason, Erik."

"I think not."

Erik surged forward again, angling his shoulder into Raoul's chest. Raoul grunted from the impact, found himself pinioned against the very door Erik was attempting to reach.

"Get. Out. Of. My. Way." Erik growled each word as he tried to shift Raoul to the side, away from the door.

"Think, damn it! You *are* capable of thinking, aren't you? What do you think you'll do?"

Suddenly Erik pulled back, chest heaving. But Raoul could see that his purpose had not changed.

"He can write all the filth he wants. But there are limits. He's not going to get away with it."

"What are you planning to do? Arrive at his doorstep and drag him from his bed?"

Erik seethed. "Step aside, Raoul, before I hurt you," he said through clenched teeth.

"You think it would be so easy?" The challenge was inevitable between them.

"I don't want to hurt you."

"How kind." Raoul laughed, but it was a mirthless sound.

Erik charged forward, but Raoul was ready. He jabbed Erik in the jaw with an undercut from his right.

Erik was pushed back a couple of steps by the impact of the blow. He hadn't anticipated Raoul's agility. He felt his teeth rattle.

"You've improved, I see."

"Sorry," Raoul said. But he didn't move away from the door. Instead he assumed the position, fists raised, left leading the right, his body squeezed in upon itself to take the brunt of Erik's attack.

Erik fumed. He glared at Raoul. He paced back and forth like a caged leopard, his eyes never leaving the obstacle that lay between him and his desire.

"You know you have to wait," said Raoul, his eyes never leaving Erik. "At least until the morning."

"I'll find him," Erik said. His left fist feinted a blow, which Raoul shifted to ward off. Instead Erik's right caught Raoul in the gut. Raoul doubled over, clutching his lower body, expelling a gasp of lost air. He pitched forward to his knees. Braced against the floor, his left hand kept him from falling prone. Erik stepped over him. He had only managed to crack the door open when Raoul lunged at his legs and dragged him down. The rug muffled the sound of his collapse. Each struggled—Erik to free himself, Raoul to hold on to his prey.

Neither could tell how much time elapsed. Muscles contorted and strained. Each took any chance he could to get in a punch—most were ineffectual, glancing off hard bone or missing altogether. Eventually they lay—like lovers—exhausted in each other's embrace. They rolled apart, gasping for air. Neither could speak for several moments.

"Rest," Raoul panted. "Time…tomorrow."

"Tomorrow," gasped Erik in turn.

When Raoul awoke the next morning, he was still lying on the floor of Erik's office. He ached all over. He glanced around.

"Damn," he cursed. Erik had already gone.

Just outside the four-story brick building where the offices of the gazette were located, Erik waited. At some point, Ricci would have to show up. Raoul had been right. It would have been a waste of time for Erik to go out in the early hours of the morning looking for the journalist. Il Café di Mondo had long closed, and Erik had no idea where Ricci lived.

Raoul and Erik had fallen into an exhausted sleep after their futile struggle. When Raoul had begun to snore, Erik had awakened and slipped out. He knew Raoul would only try to interfere.

When Erik saw Ricci descend from the carriage outside the building, Erik headed across the street. Ricci disappeared inside. Erik followed.

The assistant had barely waited for Ricci to take off his coat before he handed the notes to the journalist. Ricci slapped the back of his knuckles across the crisp sheets of paper.

"Josefi, this is good work. Very nice indeed."

That Erik Costanzi frequented establishments such as the Boar and Bow would not shock anyone, but the thought that he recruited his elegant and refined divas from among the gaudy and hapless denizens of that world would certainly undermine the prestige and sophistication of the Teatro dell'Opera. Patrons who brushed elbows with the theater crowds fed the illusion that the talented men and women who performed the works of Bellini, Verdi, Wagner, and Mozart were of a special station. They did not like knowing that those who sat at their table, drank their wine, accepted their homage had been born in the gutter or were as common as the faceless poor that they ignored on their way to galas and exhibitions.

Ricci sat at his desk, his fingers perpetually stained with ink, and spread the sheets out before him.

"Let me see what I can do with this."

Raoul was too late. He had followed his intuition and gone directly to Paolo Ricci's offices. But before he could reach the third floor, he heard the unmistakable sounds of a fight emanating from the far end of the hall. Erik had already arrived.

Just inside the anteroom, in a narrow doorway that must open into Ricci's office, a crowd had formed. Those behind craned over the shoulders of those who had managed to find a place inside. Raoul wedged his way through to the front.

It was easy to pick Erik out among the knot of arms and legs. His mask had fallen or been ripped off in the struggle. The anger Raoul had seen the night before had turned to rage. Two of the men were trying to restrain Erik, one on either side of him, but neither had succeeded in dislodging his hold on the journalist's throat. Ugly grating sounds were coming from Ricci's mouth.

Raoul pulled one man, then another back from the pile until he could gain purchase on Erik. Ricci's face had gone from red to purple, the veins along his temples bulging as if on the point of bursting, his eyes wide and unfocused.

"Erik, listen to me," Raoul urged just inches from the deformed side of Erik's face. "Stop. Stop before you kill him."

"I want my face to be the last thing this bastard sees." Erik's voice was barely more than a rasp, but Raoul could tell that, on some level, Ricci had heard it. Ricci's eyes were wide as saucers. His strength was dissipating; his grip on Erik's hands had gone limp. The air forced through constricted airways made a strained, wet hissing sound.

"Erik, you want to go to prison? You want Meg and your children to see you hang?" Raoul let go of Erik's arm. He grabbed his face and turned it so that the two men saw eye to eye. "You want to go back to the madness?"

Erik's features fell into a smooth mask. His hands loosened, but did not release Ricci's throat. Instead, Erik pushed Ricci so hard that the journalist stumbled over his chair and crashed to the floor. Raoul bent and picked up Erik's mask. He handed it to Erik who took it but did not put it on. Instead, Erik let the mask dangle at his side as he turned to leave. The crowd retreated to either side of the doorway to let the men pass. In the hallway, Raoul fell into step beside Erik. Neither spoke until they reached the street.

"Let me do the talking," Raoul whispered out of the corner of his mouth. "Keep your hands in your pockets." He nodded his chin at the scratches on the back of Erik's hands.

They opened the doors to the small parlor where they knew they'd find Christine and Meg and stepped inside.

"Thank God," said Christine.

"Where have you been?" asked Meg.

Raoul was prepared to explain when Erik spoke first.

"I almost strangled Ricci. Raoul stopped me." Erik made his way to the opposite side of the room, to a bank of windows that opened onto the garden.

Raoul sighed.

The women stared at them. Both men were bruised and disheveled. Their clothes were dusty and wrinkled as if they had slept in them.

Meg was the first to gather her wits about her. "Is Ricci alive?"

"Yes," Raoul said. "He got a bit of a scare, that's all."

Erik glared at Raoul. Raoul cleared his throat and gestured with a frown in the direction of the two women. Erik remained silent.

"We were worried," Christine said as she rose and came to inspect Raoul. "Who did this to you?" She touched the beginnings of a purple mark on the edge of his jaw.

"We fought," Erik said.

Meg dropped the book to the floor. It landed with a loud thud that made Erik turn in her direction. Their eyes met.

"Don't, Meg," he warned.

"Christine, perhaps you and I should take a walk." Raoul led his wife to the doors that opened onto the garden. He closed them from the other side and urged his wife farther along the path.

"I'm glad they're gone," Meg said. "I don't think I want them to hear our conversation."

"There's no conversation. There's nothing to say."

"I beg to differ," said Meg. "I think this is something that needs discussing."

"I don't."

"Well, I do."

Both glared with fierce determination. Erik was the first to look away.

"Erik, you can't force the world to conform to your will."

"He paid those men to..."

"To throw a few tomatoes and shout nonsense. He's a bastard. You've always known it."

"But he went too far this time." Erik had narrowed the gulf between them. He bent and spoke down to her, his face taut with building anger. "I couldn't let him get away with it."

"So you were willing to murder him?"

Erik's eyes darted away from Meg. He stepped back. "Things got out of hand," he admitted. "He taunted me." He would not repeat the vile things Ricci had said, not just about Erik's work but about those with whom he worked, about Carlotta, and even about Meg. When Ricci had begun to speak of Meg, Erik had not been able to check his anger.

"So you would risk destroying our life together to defend the opera? To defend it from some bad reviews?"

Erik felt stung by Meg's sarcasm. How could she think he'd be so petty?

"I won't let him…" He clenched his teeth hard, biting back the words. *What else had those men done on that dark street? What besides the livid bruises did Carlotta hide? What if it had been Meg?* "There are lines that…must not…ever…be crossed."

Her brows knit in concern, Meg studied the man that stood in front of her. She had seen him in rage and in despair. She knew when there was something that he was not saying. Not only did his eyes avoid hers, but his fists were closed and braced against his body. Every muscle in his body was tense, as if ready for battle. What line had Ricci crossed?

"Erik?" Thoughts too appalling to put into words came to mind. "There's something else, isn't there?" Meg could see his defenses begin to relax. She kept her voice soft and soothing, knowing that he was on the verge of opening up to her.

"There's no proof."

Meg brought the flat of her hand to cover her mouth, pressing hard against her lips. After a moment, when she thought her voice would not crack, she asked, "Carlotta? You think Ricci paid the men to do more than disrupt the performance."

"She won't talk about it."

"No. She insists that she's put it behind her." Meg knew Erik suspected as much as she did that Carlotta had suffered more than a few vicious blows.

"The man has no shame."

Meg stepped up to Erik and grazed his cheek with the back of her hand. Then she took his hands in hers and kissed the wounds that marked his knuckles.

"This, too, shall pass," she said.

"Don't be angry with me, Meg," he whispered. He bent until his forehead rested on her blond hair.

"How could I be angry with you, my love?" She kissed his hand again and placed it over her heart.

Victor and Mario careened into each other while François beckoned them to pick up the pace. Mario gave Victor a mock jab to the ribs, which Victor easily avoided. François laughed at the two of them. Mario was shorter than the Frenchman, but he was solidly built and had a powerful punch. Victor and François were closer in build and height, but Victor had begun to fill out and looked older than either François or Mario.

"Hey, hold on. This looks like a good place." Mario pointed to a boisterous tavern where several customers were pummeling away at each other even as the boys strode by.

Victor laughed and pulled Mario by the lapel down the street and away from the brawl.

"Your father will be very upset if we come back bruised and bloodied," said the Frenchman. "I thought you were showing me the ancient splendors of Rome."

"The ancient splendors have been around for a long time. Don't worry. They'll still be here tomorrow."

"François, Mario is going to get us all into trouble. You and I may have to drag him home."

François's lips curled in a sarcastic grin. Victor had already insisted on having drinks at several small taverns along the way. At the last one, François and Mario had had to slip him out the back way to avoid a nasty encounter with a jealous bricklayer whose companion had sparked to Victor's beautiful French accent. While the bricklayer was in the privy, Victor had sidled up to the young woman and was chanting a list of naughty words in her ear. François translated those that he heard, under his breath, for Mario's French was not nearly as fluent as François's. The young woman, probably five or more years older than they, didn't understand a word of French, but Victor's meaning was clear in the bulge in his trousers and the gravel of his voice. The bricklayer, a man with huge beefy arms and fists the size of melons, was buttoning his fly when he saw Victor's hand disappear under his woman's skirts. He didn't like foreigners in general, but he liked Victor even less.

"Where are we going?" groaned Mario, who was perhaps tipsier than any of them had thought. "I need a drink."

François and Victor burst out laughing.

"What?" Mario stopped in the middle of the street they were crossing and stiffened his back, obviously offended by their laughter.

The absurdity of his wounded dignity set Victor and François off on a new burst of laughter until they heard the sounds of an approaching carriage. They grabbed Mario and forced him to pick up his pace and reach the safety at the side of the road before the carriage came rushing by.

François wiped the tears from his eyes. The lightness of the moment faded. In its stead fell a dull heaviness over the young man, a heaviness that he couldn't shake. His father had told him to ignore the rumors. But he could tell his parents were tense. Someone had planted hecklers in the audience to disrupt the performance. His father had dragged one of the miscreants from the auditorium bodily while Sig. Bianchi played the overture in the middle of the mêlée. The accomplices had bolted from the auditorium, and the performance had proceeded without mishap from that point on. Mario and he weren't supposed to know, but of course they did. There was no way for their father to silence all the talk that was making the rounds at the theater and even in the household. When François had heard about the incident, his first concern had been his mother. He knew she had performed in the scene. But she acted as if nothing had happened. Then he had thought of Velia. The disruption had occurred during Carlotta's aria, so Velia had not been subjected to the insults. Even so François had rankled at the fact that he hadn't been able to see Velia—their usual practice time had been suspended along with everything else for a few days.

Since the adults insisted on treating them like children, excluding them from their hushed conversations, Mario and François suggested that they get out of the house. They needed to slough off the tension, find something to do with their pent-up energy. They needed an adventure.

What were they looking for? It occurred to François that there was nothing innocent about the jaunt they were taking through the city. He couldn't dispel the thought that they were after more than a few beers and a few laughs. When Victor flirted shamelessly with the young woman at the last tavern where they'd stopped, François choked back a strange mix of emotions including envy. With his lips pressed to the woman's ear and his hand edging up her leg, Victor had seemed years, not months, older than Mario and he.

How experienced was Victor? François was aware that Victor was handsome. He took after his father but had his mother's dark hair. He had an easy manner about him as well that suggested he was open to new ideas and acquaintances. François had seen on more than one occasion how the women admired Victor, were drawn to his friendly banter, and glowed in his presence. Like Mario, Victor had an easy smile and glib tongue that attracted women. François imagined that Victor's confidence came from some experience.

Mario also had a gift with women. François knew that his brother had had at least one encounter. Just months ago, a married woman at a particularly lively soirée had seduced him. François had run into Mario shortly after it had happened. In the exuberance of the moment Mario had told François how the woman had led him out into the night air to a gazebo. They did not undress, but she let him feel her through the layers of satin and lace. Barely had he realized what was about to happen when she raised her skirts, hoisted herself onto the edge of a wrought-iron table, and guided him inside her. François had listened in silence, knowing even as Mario was compelled to tell him the details that, in the light of the next morning, Mario would regret having betrayed his lover's confidence.

François himself was still inexperienced. He imagined he might remain so until marriage unless something unexpected happened. Unlike Victor and Mario, François's dark looks attracted women initially but his intensity sent them scurrying for shelter as if it would burn them. He couldn't seem to avoid it. If a woman approached him, he met her desire with a silent stare, dumbfounded by her beauty. Words failed him, and he found it impossible to explain. For he found all women beautiful, whether they were plump or skinny, dark or fair. Even peculiar features, such as a long nose or lopsided grin, intrigued him and made him want to reach out and touch her. In fear that he might someday act upon his impulse, he kept his hands down, rigid by his side. But he could not control his eyes.

Of course there were women at the opera house that would raise their skirts for a few coins. Given who he was, they'd do it for nothing, assuming future advantages from the son of the great Erik Costanzi. If it hadn't been for his father's frank talk the summer before with both Mario and him, François would have been tempted to satisfy his curiosity and to seek relief from the desires that were now a constant distraction. But it wasn't only the fact that his father had warned them not to dally with the company. François understood that those women would be faceless—bodies and nothing more. The experience would diminish him, reduce him to his bodily needs. His desire was too intimate, too powerful to slake in such a fashion. His desire went beyond the promise of momentary relief.

But seeing Victor caress that unknown woman with words and touch had stirred François beyond the usual limits of his desire. He tried to dispel the image of Velia.

"Wait." Mario's voice—urgent and strained—broke into François thoughts.

François turned to see that Victor was holding Mario by the shoulders. Mario was bent, one arm braced against the lamppost to keep from tumbling forward into the street. The sounds of retching were unmistakable. François hung back until Mario groaned in relief and wiped his mouth with his sleeve. Then he stepped up, careful to avoid looking at the sodden mess his brother had spewed onto the walk.

"Now all you need is a good beer," Victor teased.

Mario waved his hand as if he wanted Victor to move away from him.

"I think we should cut the tour a bit short and head home," said François.

Victor winked at him. "Yes, I think we've found Mario's limit."

"No," protested the young man. Mario still bent slightly at the waist, the flat of his hand on his gut. "I think it was that meat pie."

François and Victor looked at each other and shivered dramatically.

"We told you," they said with one voice.

"Avoid eating the last slice of any pie that they drag out from the back of the shelf," said Victor.

"Don't eat anything that's moving," added François.

Mario groaned and expelled the final contents of his stomach narrowly missing Victor's and François's shoes. Both young men jumped back several steps, cursing Mario.

"Ah, that's better," said Mario, breathless but content.

The other two waited until they were sure that Mario was recovered and was unlikely to puke again.

"Should we hail a carriage?"

"Do you have any money left?"

They all examined their pockets.

Victor shook his head. "Not enough for the fare."

"Neither do we."

"That settles it. We walk."

"This way?" asked Victor, pointing over his shoulder the way they had come.

"No. We'll go back the short way." François set off in another direction.

Moments later they came round a corner. Just ahead was Il Café di Mondo.

"Help is on its way," said François at he pointed out the establishment.

François could borrow a modest sum from any of a number of acquaintances and friends from the Teatro dell'Opera who were surely still carousing even at this late hour of the night. He'd repay them the following day.

"Wait, François. Is that Ricci?" Mario pointed at one of two men half in shadow a few feet from Il Café di Mondo. Neither Mario nor François could make out the identity of the second man in the shadows. Although from the boys' vantage point, the men's conversation was incomprehensible, it was clear that they were arguing. Ricci raised his arms, pointing his cane in a threatening gesture, and the other man withdrew further into the shadows, apparently disappearing down the side street.

"Ricci? Isn't he the one who's always writing such sarcastic reviews of your father's shows?" Victor asked.

"The man's tone deaf," muttered François under his breath.

"A fool," added his brother.

Victor wondered if this had anything to do with the recent events at the Teatro, not to mention the row Don Erik had had at the journalist's office. He had overheard his mother and father talking about it and had shared what he knew with Mario and François.

Seeing Ricci lingering in the semi-gloom of the café's lights, Mario pulled the waist of his trousers up an inch and nodded to François.

"Let's have a bit of fun," he said, but his eyes were cold and his expression grim.

Victor considered that perhaps this was not a wise course of action. But he was a guest, and one look at his friends' faces told him his advice would be ignored.

Across the street from the Teatro dell'Opera, the tall figure of a man was silhouetted by the flickering light from passing carriages. Stretched thin, he stood, like a spectral guide, at the entrance to the park.

Before Meg could question him, Erik closed the carriage door and beat twice on the wooden panel.

"Go ahead," he told the driver.

As the carriage sped down the street, Erik waited for it to pass. There beyond, Vosh waited.

"I told you to stop following me," Erik said as he approached the man.

"Sabia wants to see you."

Erik tensed. The darkness spiraled and coalesced around him. The whites of Erik's eyes shimmered as if he were lit from within by strong emotion.

"I have no desire to see *her*."

"She's dying."

Vosh waited to see recognition in the younger man's eyes. There was no change, no visible sign that his words had been heard, their understanding accepted. He waited. Erik did not speak.

"She wants to see you. Before she dies, she wants to speak with you."

Erik glanced away. His gaze seemed fixed on some point beyond the old man, lost in the darkness, lost perhaps in his own dark thoughts.

"Take me to her. I'll follow."

*   *   *

"They've found a body."

"Down the street in an alleyway."

"Dead?"

"What else?"

"Who is it?"

"They don't know. Face was caved in, mangled beyond recognition. Not a bum either. You could see that from the clothes."

PART III

CHAPTER 1

Dead Men Tell No Tales

Tomorrow, and tomorrow, and tomorrow,
Creeps in this petty pace from day to day,
To the last syllable of recorded time;
And all our yesterdays have lighted fools
The way to dusty death.

Macbeth, William Shakespeare

A dead body.
Face mangled.

It couldn't be Erik. Raoul pushed his way through the crowds. Nothing seemed to move until he wedged himself into the mass. Several men jostled back, muttering oaths under their breath. Once they saw the fine cut of his coat, they grudgingly stepped aside. The smells were acrid, even at this hour in the morning. Voices rolled like thunder over the crowd. Ahead, at the mouth of the alley, there were signs of a commotion.

Erik had not returned last night. Meg was concerned.

Raoul had thought of a hundred reasons for Erik's absence, the most likely of which was that he had lingered at the Teatro dell'Opera and fallen asleep. Knowing she was worried, he had offered to accompany Meg at first light to the theater. He had convinced Christine to remain at the estate should Erik arrive before they returned. However, when they searched the theater, they had not found Erik. He had not fallen asleep in the small private room off the side of the office nor was he anywhere else in the building.

That was when one of the staff rushed in to share the news he had heard on his way to the theater that very morning. *A dead body. Face mangled.* Even Raoul had been unsettled by the thought that it might be Erik.

The crowd was thickest at the edge. Those who had managed to get to the front protected their position with elbows and sneers. Raoul forced his way between two stalwart men. They were short and stocky, with the large muscles of physical laborers. There was a dust upon their clothing that suggested masonry work.

Using his best Italian, he spoke to one of them.

"I heard someone's been killed. Does anyone know who he is?"

The man shrugged his shoulders, looked Raoul up and down, and nodded toward the area cordoned off by the officers just feet away. "A swell like you."

Raoul felt the temperature in his body plummet, but he kept a tight rein on his imagination.

"Officer," he shouted at one of the men whose uniform boasted the emblems of rank.

When the officer in question turned, Raoul stepped forward. Several of the policemen approached to hold Raoul back, but a nod from the officer granted him permission.

Raoul introduced himself briefly. The officer gave his name, Sig. Verduce, and explained that he was in charge of the investigation. His blank features showed no curiosity as to the reason a Frenchman would be roaming the streets and asking about dead bodies. But then again this dead body was not that of the usual sort of victim the police found in a dark alley.

"May I see the body?" Raoul asked.

Sig. Verduce raised a skeptical eyebrow, then narrowed his eyes and considered the count. "Do you think, Sig. Conte, that the man is an acquaintance of yours?"

Raoul swallowed hard. "Yes. It's possible."

"Mi dispiace," he apologized. "We just had the body removed to the morgue. If you wish to accompany me, I would like you to make the identification."

Raoul's mouth was too dry to speak, so he nodded.

"You will wait?" the officer asked. "I have a few matters yet to do here. Then we should go, no?"

"Yes."

Verduce had been notified shortly after two in the morning. He had given instructions that an officer be posted to keep the curious away until dawn, at which time Verduce and his officers arrived to inspect the body and the area.

Verduce scowled down at the puddle of blood. It had coagulated but was still sticky to the touch. A small group of street urchins had alerted the patrolling officer to the presence of a body. The policeman had gone to check out their story. In the dark, he had slipped and fallen in the puddle of the dead man's blood. It had still been fresh, which indicated that the murder had occurred not long before the body was discovered.

There were several bloody footprints, one belonging to the officer that had found the corpse, but there were also others belonging to officers and the curious. How many times had he told them to stand clear of the area until he could inspect it? Nevertheless, Verduce took out his notebook and sketched the tracks, knowing that they more than likely belonged to his own men. He indicated to one of his officers, who leaned against the nearby building, that he approach.

"Measure these footprints. This is number one, that one number two, three, four, and five." In each case, Verduce followed the sketch in his notebook and pointed to the footsteps. "Pay attention. In that order. You understand?"

The officer nodded.

"Bene. Measure them. I want the size and width. See what you can find out about them." He patted the young man on the shoulder in encouragement.

Then he beckoned his assistant, Cortale Paccara, to approach. Both squatted and studied the red imprint on the ground.

"This one," he said.

Paccara studied what looked like a partial print. "What is it? It's not a shoe or boot."

"No," said Verduce. "It's not. It might be a hand. See?" he said, holding out his hand palm down and pointing toward the smudge. "It could be the flat of the palm and just a hint of the fingers."

"The police officer who found the body slipped and fell in the blood," Cortale reminded his superior officer.

"That was a foot or so over in that direction," muttered Verduce. He rose and nodded to his assistant. "Get one of those students from the art academy to come and draw it. I want it to scale. You understand?"

"Yes, Tenente," the young officer said, using Verduce's recently acquired title as Lieutenant.

"Sig. Verduce," the older man corrected. It was not that he was humble or an anarchist. He had learned that his title sometimes made witnesses nervous. He got more information when they thought him just a simple police officer.

For a third time, Verduce walked the circumference of the alleyway, narrowing in on the spot where the victim had fallen. Reluctantly he had allowed the body to be removed to the morgue. He would have liked more time with it in its original location, but the crowd was growing and the officers were anxious to dispose of the corpse. He had given instructions that nothing—including the man's clothes—was to be disturbed until he had had the opportunity to examine the body at the morgue.

Now that the victim was out of the way, the investigator could examine the scene from all angles. Unfortunately there was little to note—a coin, a small notebook, and torn bits of paper scattered about. He had these collected and placed in bags upon which information regarding their specific location was written. He would examine them later. As much of the original crime scene as possible was to be recorded and saved.

Satisfied that he had taken note of the area and original position of the body, he was about to instruct the officers to disperse the crowd and return to headquarters when the French count called out to him.

They spoke briefly. The Frenchman was curious to see the body. Verduce decided that such curiosity should be rewarded. But first he had his own questions to ask.

Sig. Verduce glanced at his notes. The body was that of a male of medium height and build. He had been found, apparently bludgeoned to death, the face unrecognizable, in the vicinity of the Piazza Beniamino and the Teatro dell'Opera, just off Via del Viminale.

No more than a hundred meters from the Teatro dell'Opera, he thought. The Frenchman had mentioned that he was a guest of Sig. Costanzi, the artistic director of the Teatro dell'Opera.

When Verduce had asked the foreigner why he was interested in the corpse, the Frenchman had been evasive. Sensing that he was hiding something, Verduce was tempted to disregard the fact that the man was a titled gentleman and treat him as a suspect. But that was probably not the best course to follow in this case. Sometimes cross-examination only alerted a criminal to be on his guard. Sometimes it was best to be patient and silent. Inadvertently a suspect would give away more information to a silent officer than to one who asked a long list of direct questions. One had to know what tack to take and when.

Verduce had left the French count in a small, empty room. It was bare except for three straight-back chairs and a simple mahogany table. The one window in the room was high and barred. It allowed some natural light to filter into the room. It was a large room, but the ventilation provided by the window was poor. There was an undefined smell that hung in the air. The door was usually locked.

While the count waited in the room, Verduce visited the morgue just down the hall to be sure the cadaver and its effects were intact. He waited a few extra minutes before returning to the interrogation room, judging that the time would unsettle the man and make the interrogation go more smoothly.

"Sig. Chagny, you are enjoying your stay in our lovely country?"

asked Verduce as he pulled his chair up to the opposite side of the small table.

Raoul sighed. He was not fooled by the Italian officer's pleasant tone. "Yes, it's beautiful. Sig. Verduce, may I see the body now? I've waited now for…"

"You must be patient. What is the expression? Ah, yes. 'Rome wasn't built in a day.'"

Raoul ground his teeth in an effort to remain calm. His answers had been brief and cautious. The officer was obviously suspicious as to why Raoul would assume that he knew the dead man.

"Tenente Verduce, may I speak frankly?"

Verduce nodded.

"I must satisfy my curiosity."

"Curiosity? Are you one of those people who enjoy…?"

"No," interrupted Raoul, catching the direction of the other man's question. "Good God, no. I fear that the victim may be a friend of mine."

"What makes you think so? Is your friend missing?"

Raoul hesitated. "Something about the description."

"What description? The face is unrecognizable."

"Was the man disfigured?"

Verduce scowled, genuinely puzzled. "Disfigured? The face was bashed in, the nose was pushed into the skull, and the face is pulp. Is that clear?"

Raoul sat back in the chair in thought. "My friend didn't come home last night. His wife is worried."

"Is this unusual for him?"

Raoul considered. Meg had mentioned several occasions when Erik had arrived late. But since the destruction of the subterranean rooms of the Teatro dell'Opera, he no longer stayed away for days at a time as he once had. "No, it's not usual that he stay away all night."

"Perhaps there is a lover? Perhaps the wife doesn't know."

Raoul frowned. "No, my friend does not have a mistress."

Verduce considered the stranger. Something in his frank expression convinced the officer that he was not lying.

"What connection would this friend have to this corpse?

Unfortunately there were three other murders last night in Rome. Why have you not inquired about them?"

"This one is near the Teatro dell'Opera."

"And your friend is…?"

"He…works at the Teatro dell'Opera."

"Works? In what capacity? The victim's clothes suggest that he was not a simple workman, signore."

"My friend is the artistic director of the Teatro dell'Opera, Sig. Erik Costanzi."

The officer studied the count. Verduce prided himself on being able to judge a man's character. The Frenchman struck him as an honest man. Perhaps it was simply personal concern that had brought the count to the murder site. "Wait here, Sig. Chagny. I will call you back soon to see if our victim is your friend. Let us hope that he is not."

Romulo Verduce rubbed the thick salve under his nose and into his gray mustache to cover the smell of dried blood and putrefaction. Only those who worked with the sick, the dying, and the dead knew that blood itself had an odor. Verduce was used to the smell of blood. But as blood dried and as flesh turned livid and filled with gases, a corpse expelled a stench that could sicken the hardiest of men. The salve itself had a strong odor of vinegar and masked the offensive smell.

The stenographer had taken notes as Cortale Paccara inspected the body, pointing out to his chief officer what he could glean from its condition. Paccara had studied medicine, but he couldn't stomach inflicting pain on the innocent. When Verduce had read his file, he had requested that Paccara be assigned to work with him. The knowledge the young man had was invaluable.

In this case, Paccara had been able to deduce from the condition of the cadaver that the victim had been a man in his early forties, in reasonably good health. The obvious cause of death was a crushed skull. The wound could not have been caused by anything except a series of blows to the face and head with a blunt instrument. There were no fragments of a weapon in the wound. The face was battered so mercilessly that it was impossible to decide the thickness of the weapon. The young officer ventured to suggest that the blows could have been made with a club, stick, or cane, something made of hard wood or metal. Verduce was satisfied with the information and thought the young man had finished when Paccara pointed out that there were bruises around the throat and a knot on the back of the victim's head.

"So someone strangled him? Or was he bludgeoned to death?"

"Usually in strangulation the cartilage in the neck is broken, the windpipe is crushed. That isn't the case."

"Were the bruises made at the same time?"

Paccara shook his head. "I couldn't say, Tenente."

"Let's look at what else was found. First the contents of his clothes."

Verduce and Paccara examined the meager contents of the victim's pockets. There was a watch, on the back of which were engraved the initials "C. R." Several folded bank notes were hidden away inside his vest. One pocket of his trousers held loose change. The other was torn an inch along the seam and was empty. From the inside pocket of his coat, they had collected the remains of a ticket for a performance at the Teatro dell'Opera and of another for a recent night at the Teatro Regio. There was nothing to identify the man. Next Verduce picked up the notebook that the officers had found a foot from the body. It was similar to the one that Verduce used. Pages had been torn from the book, leaving the rest blank except for a bloody print along the margin. Verduce showed the print to Paccara. He lifted an eyebrow as if to question the young assistant.

"Thumb, I should say. It's from the left hand." Paccara mimicked holding a book with the thumbs to keep the pages open.

Verduce nodded in appreciation. On the outside cover of the notebook were other bloody smudges. The officer returned the notebook to the side table next to the articles removed from the clothing. He glanced at the torn bits of paper and noted their color was consistent with the paper inside the notebook.

"What kind of man is this?" Verduce muttered half to himself, half to his assistant.

"He has a fine coat," said Paccara.

"Hmmm. Let's see." Verduce lifted the coat, ran his finger along the edge. "Look." He held the coat up to the light to reveal the glossy sheen on the surface of the weave. "It was certainly expensive when he bought it. No label. Handmade. Good material. But it's worn. Look at the thread on these buttons." Verduce showed the young man the small circular stitches that held the buttons in place—black and compactly sewn. Then he drew the man's eye down to a third button. The thread in this case was thicker, coarser, a dull black, almost gray. "Let's look at his hands, shall we?" Paccara and he returned to the cadaver.

The assistant lifted the left hand. "He didn't fight his attacker. The nails are clean. Perhaps he was taken by surprise and struck down before he could react."

"Or he knew his murderer and was unsuspecting until it was too late. Good work, Cortale." Verduce turned to the stenographer who was slumped in his seat, watching a fly buzzing round the table. "Are you taking notes of this?"

"Si, signore." The man sat up stiff in his chair and wrote furiously.

Verduce examined the left hand, then raised the right hand, too. "His right hand is more developed than his left."

"He's right-handed."

"Yes, but he also uses his hands a good deal, the right one more than the left." Verduce felt the man's arms. "He's not a laborer. The skin on his hands is too tender, and his muscles are not strong enough for physical labor." He picked up the right hand again and looked at the fingers. "Here, feel this." He ran his own finger along the inside of the middle finger to the first joint. Paccara felt the flat callus. "Huh?" He invited Paccara to deduce the facts.

"I don't…"

"What built that callus up between the index and middle finger?" The investigator took a swab of alcohol and wiped the tip of the index finger. "Look." The corpse's fingers were nearly blue, which was to be expected. But it was a blue that did not rub off. On the swab was a dark indigo smudge. "Ink."

"Someone who writes for a living," said Paccara.

Verduce smiled at his earnest assistant.

"Yet he has a notebook with nothing in it. The pages have been torn out. Perhaps someone didn't want us to read what was in that notebook?" Verduce patted his assistant on the back. "I think it's time to have our Frenchman come in and take a look at the victim, don't you?"

Raoul held his breath and swallowed the urge to vomit. The minute he walked into the room, he could tell that it was not Erik. The man was too short. Unless his limbs had been sawed and his feet removed, the corpse belonged to someone of only medium height at best.

He was about to explain this to the officer when the man pulled him forward, refusing to listen to him, and lowered the cover from the corpse. There was a mass of dead tissue. He blanched and stepped back.

"No, no, it's not Sig. Costanzi," said the count.

"Do you recognize him?" asked Verduce, as if the man's features had not been blasted.

"No, I have no idea who this is."

"Perhaps you might recognize something else? His coat, for example?" The officer held up a dark coat in one hand, a watch in another. Raoul barely glanced at them.

"Monsieur, I mean, signore, this is useless. I'm a foreigner. My circle is quite small."

"Well, at least we can rest easy knowing that it is not the masked genius of the opera."

The phrase made Raoul look up at the officer. Verduce looked at him with kind eyes. There seemed to be no malice whatsoever in his use of Ricci's favorite term for Erik. At that moment, an involuntary movement on the table caught Raoul's attention. The dead man's arm had slid free of the cover, the hand dangled over the side.

Recognition burned in Raoul's mind. His eyes glanced at the place where the man's face should have been. The hair was matted with dried blood, but Raoul noticed the way it was cut. Then the side of the man's neck—a neck that was thick and short—was ringed by the marks of a large hand. Raoul doubled over and held his stomach.

"Sig. Chagny, are you going to be ill?"

"I think the smell…may be…getting to me." Raoul allowed the young assistant to help him to the door. "I'm sorry, Lieutenant Verduce, that I couldn't be of more help."

"Not at all, Sig. Chagny. You've been most helpful. I hope your friend comes home soon."

Verduce watched the count step out into the hallway. He had no doubt that the man felt ill. But he could not erase the feeling that the foreigner had more information than he was telling.

CHAPTER 2

The Gift

"We know what we are, but know not what we may be."

Hamlet, William Shakespeare

"So you've come."

Erik could barely make out the figure of the woman amid the blankets in the dark corner of the tent. But he recognized her voice, low and smoky. The smell of incense did not disguise the smell of death in the tent.

"The old man says that you want to see me," he said. He had stepped just far enough inside that he would not have to bend his head to stand.

"Come closer. I don't see as well as I used to."

Erik scowled. He did not want to be close to the woman. She had turned what few peaceful memories he had had of his childhood into something tawdry. She had stripped him of the illusion of a beautiful trapeze artist who had brought him the sound of a thousand chimes.

"What? Are you still afraid of me, boy?" She chuckled deep in her chest. The sound was swallowed by a raspy fit of coughing.

Erik did not answer her taunt. He knew it was only to goad him into action. He gritted his teeth and approached her bed. There he saw the spiraling smoke of the incense stick and a charm bracelet of copper and brass bells on a small table next to her. He looked about and found a chair, which he drew near to the head of the bed, and there he sat.

"I had not expected to see you again," he said.

"Not this side of the river," she added when the coughing eased.

"What do you want, Sabia?"

"Impatient. Your emotions are always just under the surface, aren't they?"

Erik shifted uneasily in his chair. For a moment, he thought perhaps she had fallen asleep and he would be able to leave. It had been a mistake to come.

"You were such a dark and intense creature." Her voice was smooth like honey but with a sting that Erik could feel even after all these years.

"And you? What were you, Belle?" he taunted.

"Ah, yes. I remember how you called to me. I've not been Belle for many a year."

"You were never Belle. That was a dream."

Sabia's dark eyes flashed in the semi-gloom.

"And you were a hideous little monster."

Erik's lips turned up slightly in one corner.

"I'm dying," she said, and this time her voice had no guile in it. "They've all gone. All except Vosh. He has always been loyal." She seemed lost in thought for a moment. Then she resumed, her tone more purposeful. "I am uneasy. It's not a good thing to know that you are dying and to feel…uneasy."

Erik bowed his head. He had faced death too many times to act as if he didn't understand. "What is it that makes you fear death?"

"I didn't say that I feared death." The woman pulled herself up onto her elbows and in that moment her face came out from the gloom into the dim light of the lamp that hung from the pole in the center of the tent.

The face sent a shiver through Erik's gut. She had not aged. It was as if he were seeing the same woman who had enslaved him so many years ago. The illusion lasted only a moment. Then Erik saw her as she truly was—older, stricken with constant pain that had twisted her features. Yet her eyes were the same, bright and cold and piercing, as if she had seen things no mortal had the right to see.

"I should go," he said.

The Medusa laugh turned his feet to stone.

"Now who's afraid?" she said. "You have been running from me your whole life."

"No. Not from you."

She stared at him for several seconds. Then as if the effort had wasted what little energy that remained to her, she sank back down into the blankets and let out a deep sigh.

"Perhaps you still think that I stand outside that cage of yours. But you're wrong, Erik. None of us stands outside that cage."

"I am tired of your riddles. Why did you send for me? Is it money? Is that what you want from me?"

"Yes and no. Look around you, Erik. Vosh tells me about your palace. He has described the fine clothes you wear, the jewels around the blond woman's throat, the fine carriages and horses, the theater where you now perform. He says that Midas would envy you."

"I will leave a sum of money that will…ease your way. In exchange, I want you to leave me alone. Don't send for me. I don't wish to know anything more about you."

He was about to rise, but her hand struck out and grasped his wrist. More a claw than a hand, the bones of her fingers dug into his flesh and held him with a preternatural strength.

"You will not leave me so unsatisfied, my little monkey. You will regret it, if you do."

"Don't threaten me, Sabia."

The anger in his eyes flared green and cold. Sabia released him.

"I know what you're capable of." Her eyes stared at the scratches Ricci had left on Erik's hand. "I understand the threat in your voice. You do fear me, don't you? And when you fear, you are cruel and evil."

"Don't," he whispered. Pain replaced anger.

"I once read your future. Do you remember?"

Erik felt his limbs grow numb with a cold dread. He had banished that memory long ago to some dark corner of his mind. He had tried to discount it. It was the mumblings of a charlatan, an act. The girl had chosen the name Sabia for the performance. It meant 'wise.' But she was not a sage but a gifted actress, no more a witch than he a phantom.

Yet he could not block the memory of those words.

"'You were born in darkness and in darkness you will end.' I can see that you do remember."

"You also told me that you saw a crossroad, a light that...could lead me." He forced his voice to remain even and calm.

"Ah, yes. I did mention a flickering light somewhere along the path your life would take. A light that would burn...for a time."

Erik's chest tightened. He could not listen to her tell him of catastrophes to come. He had to get out. Again the bony fingers pressed into his wrist. He could not shake her off.

"Listen to me. Open your hand."

Two obsidian stones for eyes—what could possibly be the substance of her soul? Yet he found his fist unfurling. As if it did not belong to him, his palm lay exposed, cupped in her hand, drawn in close to her breast. She smoothed it flat, then drew the finger of her other hand along the creases. Her yellowed and thickened nail scoured the line.

"Here," she pointed, her nail gouging the soft center of his palm. "This is the heart." She glanced up at him to find his eyes riveted to his palm. "Yes, you do have a heart." His eyes flicked to hers for a brief moment then returned to the path she had marked. "Here, too, is the light."

She dropped his hand. He crushed his heart, squeezing his fingers tight, against his chest.

"And the darkness?" he asked, incapable of restraint.

"What darkness?" she asked. She lay back upon the pillow. Her lids were partially drawn over the agate stones of her eyes.

"You had said..."

"I read your palm. It's not always an act. Sometimes the sight comes upon me. Sometimes...well...sometimes there is an advantage to telling someone his future. Sometimes one can bend another's will by suggestion."

"You admit that you lied?"

"I don't always know the difference between prophecy and lies. Do you believe there is one?"

"What you told me then is not what my fate will be?"

"I'm dying, Erik. That is the only prophecy that I can make with any degree of certainty. You, too, will die someday. There. That is my last prophecy for you. The rest is just words." Her voice caught in her throat. A series of deep, dry coughs shook her.

Erik waited, unable to stop his mind from spinning in all directions. He waited until her spasm quieted, until she lay back again and rested.

"Tell me," he demanded.

"I will tell you. Then I will no longer feel this uneasiness. I told you what I wanted you to hear. I saw no light. I saw no darkness."

"Then you can't know my fate."

"No, you're wrong. I can read your fate as easily as I can read the sunshine or the clouds on the horizon and know the weather. All I have to do is read your eyes. Your fate has always been there." She stared up at him. "My gift to you is a truth that is inside you. You have always struggled against a darkness that was not yours. Your light is not outside you. It's there." She pointed toward his eyes, then to his chest. "The light is inside you. Your fate is whatever you decide it will be."

Erik buried his face in the thick nap of the lamb's wool blanket that covered her bed. He swallowed against the rising emotion that he could not bear. A frail hand lay soft upon his hair.

"Poor little monkey," she crooned.

As Belle caressed his hair and spoke to him, he could not stay the tears.

"I will give you a gift," Sabia, who had once been Belle, said as she stroked Erik. "I will give you the gift of memories, memories that you've cast aside or buried in the darkness with the bars of that cage, your cradle and cross."

He scratched at his calf. The irritation went from pleasure to pain as his ragged nails raked across the skin, leaving in their wake a gloss of red blood. He willed himself to stop. He knew that the itch would flee, just out of reach, until he tore at his skin on both legs then his arms and chest. Hopeless to stop the waves of sensation, he would have to rub his back against the roughened surface of the bars. He remembered from experience how he would regret afterwards the open sores. Better to withstand the itch than to scratch away at his body.

He licked his dirty fingers, wet his fingertips, and rubbed with them along the open sore he had just opened. The pressure allayed the desire to do further damage and diluted the bloody path he had left.

"Listen to me, you dirty thing." The girl's voice was without cruelty.

He looked up and through the bars as if they were not bisecting the young girl's body. She smiled when she caught his attention. Dangling from her upraised arm was a golden bracelet with evenly spaced tiny cymbals interspersed by bells the color of wheat.

He had seen wheat late in the summer as they traveled the countryside. It had soothed him to glimpse through the ragged drape the man kept closed around the cage patches of blue sky and green grasses. The burst of reddish-gold wheat shimmering in the gentle breeze, like a sea of color, had quickened his breath and made his eyes strain to capture its texture, its movement along the landscape of their route. His ears had caught even the sizzle of summer wheat, sifting it from the crack and groan of wood and wheel. It was as if he could see sound and feel the colors and taste the air filtered through the fields. The chimes the girl wore around one wrist and another caught his eye and made him recall those quiet moments alone in the cage as the caravan approached each new town.

He reached out his hand, the nails blackened with skin and blood.

"No," she scolded. He lowered his hand to his lap, wrapped the fingers into a fist, and squeezed hard against the desire to grab at the shiny metal charms. "You're dirty. I don't want you to touch my bracelet. You'll smudge the bells."

He turned his back on the girl. She came to visit him often. She came and held out her hand or tossed her night-black hair until it brushed the bars of his cage and, when he was very close and holding the bars, the knuckles of his hand. But she told him he must not touch, that he was dirty, that he was an animal and didn't know anything about beautiful things like her, like her naked arms, like the beautiful and shiny things she wore on her wrists, ankles, and the soft lobes of her ears.

She would say 'no' until frustrated he would shake the bars of the cage, which had a curious effect on her. Her eyes would grow wide and flash with a strange light. Her mouth would lie open. She would step away from the cage and then step even closer. That was when she would sometimes let him reach out and touch.

"Listen. I know you can listen." She raised her wrist again and shook her hand. The bells struck against each other and emitted a burst of sounds that were only the sum of the tiniest of notes.

He could feel himself smile. The tightness in his chest melted, and he took in a deep breath. His body felt light.

"Make it again," he whispered. He must keep his voice down. The man could return at any moment.

The girl smiled at him and cocked her head to the side. She shook her wrist again and watched him react. She raised the other and shook it. Then she twirled on one foot, both arms bent at the elbow, hands at the level of her face, wrists twisting in syncopation with her body. Notes flew from her to the darkened corners of the tent. He felt his own body moving to the ebb and flow of her dance. His ears twitched with the yearning to capture each of the sounds that her movements produced.

She stopped, teetered one way and then the other, laughed, her head thrown back. The boy watched her throat as the happy sounds burst forth as if escaping.

"More!" he demanded.

"No, silly monkey. I'm dizzy." She laughed quietly, her hands on her hips. "Listen."

She came very near to the bars and motioned for him to come near, too. He held his breath, knowing that this was the moment when she might let him touch the slick, cool surface of the bells or the warm, soft skin of her arm. Either would be pleasure. Either would keep the tightness in his chest at bay, for a while, perhaps until the man came again.

When he reached out his hand in anticipation, she shooed him back. He felt his brow lower over his eyes, his mouth tense. He waited for his opportunity.

"Put the bag on," she demanded.

The boy glanced at the back corner of the cage. The rag was crumpled in the dirty straw. He did not want to put the bag on. Its fabric made him itch. The holes were difficult to line up so that he could see through them. It smelled. It was hot. He had trouble breathing when he wore it.

"No," he said.

"Then I won't show you," she said and made as if she would leave.

The boy slid on his knees through the shallow straw to the back corner and picked up the burlap sack. He shook out the straw and the bugs that had nested in it overnight and found the holes for his eyes and the slit for his mouth. He looked over at the girl to see that she was waiting for him to put it on. When she just stared at him, he knew that she would not stay if he didn't do as she said. He kept his eyes on her as he brought the rough burlap over his head and down across his face. The world became a narrow tunnel, and at its end stood the girl.

"Now, come closer," she said. "Listen." She selected one lone brass bell. She flicked her nail across it. The sound was soft and brief, almost gone before he could catch it. Then she took another and flicked it twice, a third one she flicked once, the fourth one she flicked quickly and then more deliberately. "Now," she said and nodded at the boy.

The air in the bag was already warm and stale. He breathed in and sang the sounds that she had just made as if he were the keeper of the bells and this was the language in which they spoke.

The girl smiled, her broad mouth stretched wide, her teeth white and even. He made the sounds again because he liked to see her smile.

"Louder this time. Now listen, little monkey." This time she went quickly through the bells; each note was higher or lower than the last one, the pattern complex.

The boy easily recalled the sounds as if they were still repeating in his ear. He sang the notes. Then he took the same notes and sang them backward. She laughed. Her eyebrows rose high on her forehead. She laughed again.

"What was that?" she asked.

The boy sang the first string of notes she had played, then the second and longer one. He finished with the chain in reverse. But no matter how much she insisted, he kept his voice low and quiet.

He knew better than to make noise. The man did not want him to make noise. The sounds reminded the man of something that he did not want to remember anymore.

As if the boy's thoughts had conjured him, the curtain swished aside and the tall, dark man stumbled in. His stringy hair grew past his shoulders and shadowed his sunken cheeks. The green of his eyes, the only color in his face, the man blinked and strained to focus in the gloomy light of the tent.

The girl stepped well away from the bars of the cage.

"You! What the devil are you doing here?" The man couldn't stand without weaving back and forth. It was as if a strong wind buffeted him from all directions.

The boy took refuge in the corner, where the light from the one lamp did not easily reach him. He shoved his knees into his chest and brought his elbows and neck deep into his body, his chin rested against the thumbs of his hands that were braced against his legs. He could see the man as he approached the girl. She easily sidestepped him and stood just outside the range of his long, sinewy arms.

"Hold still, you bitch," the man said. The words were slurred and hazy.

"The monkey can sing, you fool," she taunted the man.

He lunged for her, but she again eluded him.

"Sing, boy!" she commanded.

The man turned and stared at the child in the cage. The tightness in the boy's chest came back as if the man had reached inside and was squeezing his heart in his black fist. The boy tried to disappear. He shut his eyes, letting the burlap sack dip, the slits moving away from his eyes. Darkness surrounded him, but the man's voice would not let him slip into it.

"What have you been doing?" The man would not say the boy's name. He only said it when they were alone, and then the lash of the whip usually accompanied it. "Have you been playing with this girl? Has she let you touch her, boy?"

"I wouldn't let a dirty monkey touch me!" The girl's voice was shrill. The boy could hear the anger in it. He knew the anger was directed at the man, not at him. But her words were still sharp and flinty. "Why won't you let him talk? Why can't he sing? Why do you keep him…?"

The sound of flesh slapping against flesh followed by the high note of a cry of pain brought the boy to his feet. He ripped the bag from his head and saw the girl on the ground, her hand raised to protect her against the next blow. The tiny bells cried notes of panic. The boy wedged his body hard against the bars, his shoulder just small enough to jut out between, his arm extended outside the cage. The man's back was to him. Just barely within reach were the long, dark tangles of the man's hair. The boy's fingers stretched to their fullest length and dipped inside the dark curtain, curled, and pulled at the mess of hair.

The man cried as his head jerked back. His hand flew to the boy's and twisted it hard. The boy swallowed the pain that rose from his throat, one eye on the girl as she scurried to her feet and ran from the tent.

Later, as the man whipped the leather belt across the boy's back, the boy ran over and over again the notes the bells had given him. He restrung them and sang them inside his head again and again until the pain became a memory and the man's hoarse curses drifted away into darkness.

Erik opened his eyes to the semi-glow of dawn. The silk against his skin was hot and sticky. As he lifted his cheek, then pushed with both palms against the firm cushion of the mat, he felt his skin rip away from the tiny threads that had burrowed into his flesh. The silk floated back like the forlorn caress of an unwanted lover. Just beyond his reach, Belle reclined against mountains of pillows, her feverish body sheltered by the ivory lambs' wool blankets. Vosh was nowhere to be seen.

His clothes wrinkled and sweaty, Erik rose from the low bed, disoriented and unsettled. The dream—was that what echoed in his mind?—its images fanned before him. A young girl, the silhouette of Belle, lay across the dying woman's body. Erik swallowed against the pull of sorrow. A gift of memories she had given him, a last show of compassion, a deathbed ploy to ease her journey to the afterlife, but a gift nonetheless.

He laid the money on the table by her elbow. Beside the stack of bank notes rested, silent and dreaming, a charm bracelet laced with tiny copper and brass cymbals. As he picked it up, it chimed a cascade of sweet notes. He hesitated only a moment. Then, he put the bracelet inside his pocket. He tried to discern again the young girl in the dying woman's face. It shimmered for an instant and was gone.

Outside it was dawn. Vosh leaned against the trunk of an oak, staring out into the eastern sky.

"Let me know if she needs me," Erik said to the old man before he turned and walked away.

Erik stopped at home. The staff informed him that Meg and the count had already departed for the theater.

"The countess?" he asked.

"She's still in her chambers. Should we wake her?"

"No, let her sleep," Erik said. He was somewhat curious as to why Meg and Raoul had left so early. It was barely seven o'clock.

After he bathed and changed, he went down to the servant's hall. He knew it would be quicker if he ate below in the kitchen. He passed various rooms where the staff was busy in a number of daily tasks—from ironing linens to polishing silver. Signora Bruno must have heard him approach. She stepped just outside her office and greeted him. He wondered at the funny look she gave him. But he was anxious to get to the theater, so he didn't stop. Inside the kitchen the warm smell of baked bread made his mouth water and his stomach churn. He was famished. He sat at the solid oak table and asked Cook for some bread and cheese. As he ate in silence, Cook slipped a plate of sliced apples onto the table for him. He nodded his appreciation.

Signora Bruno came and stood beside the table. The sound she made distracted Erik from the wedge of buttered bread he had stuffed rather too quickly into his mouth.

"Donna Meg was up early this morning," she said. Her look suggested that the words were only a screen for her real meaning. "She looked haggard."

Erik chewed and swallowed while considering his reply. He had not meant to stay out all night. Matters at Sabia's had gotten out of hand. He had let time slip away. When he awoke and realized that morning had come, he had had no choice but to deal with things as they stood.

"I was detained," he said.

Signora Bruno made her disapproval evident without words. After a tense pause, she took leave of him. Cook hovered nearby.

There was nothing wrong with her hearing. But she kept her reaction to herself, removing the empty plates as Erik finished his breakfast.

He rose from the table, thanking Cook for the meal, and left for the Teatro as expeditiously as he could.

Within minutes he had arrived. He decided to enter through the main doors. When a young man only vaguely familiar to him ran as if the devil were on his heels, Erik checked his mask to make sure it was in place. As he came into the auditorium, Erik saw a scene that could only be called chaotic. Everyone was talking at once and running around the set as if they'd lost their minds.

All hell had broken loose. Then in the middle of the chaos one figure stood stark still against the backdrop of a palatial ballroom. It didn't matter that it was small. Erik recognized Meg from across the room. She stepped forward, one foot at a time until she began to run. He found himself drawn forward to meet her somewhere in the middle of the auditorium where she threw herself into his arms. Out of the corner of his eye he saw the others slow and stop in their frenzied dance.

"I thought it was you!" she cried, her cheek next to his ear. "I thought it was you they'd found dead!"

"What are you talking about?" Erik asked. He had taken Meg by the elbow to his office. She had collapsed onto the sofa. Now concerned by her strange words, the pale smoothness of her skin, the terror barely controlled in her wide-eyed stare, he knelt on one knee before her.

"They found a body," she managed to say. Her cheeks were wet, but Erik could not remember having seen her cry.

"Where's Raoul?" he asked.

Raoul would have calmed everyone. If Raoul were present, there would not have been such a mêlée. If Raoul were not here, it was because he was involved in putting things in order somewhere else.

"He went to speak with the police."

Dread settled like an undigested piece of beef in his gut.

"Who died?"

Meg's lips began to tremble. "We don't know. I thought...I thought...." She began to cry again, her mouth buried in her wet palm.

"Meg, calm down. Why would you think such a thing?"

"Where were you?" she accused, fear turning to anger.

"It doesn't matter. I'll tell you later." Erik watched as a tempest of doubts assailed Meg. "I'm all right. There's nothing to worry about." He pulled her down into the cradle of his arms. Erik felt her slide inside his caress and lean in against him. He held her, forgetting time, forgetting everything but the need to console her. He tilted her face upwards and settled his lips on hers. Meg sank more deeply into his embrace.

She was still his, he thought. She had thought him dead. She had cried for him. Even now he could feel her tremble. How could he have believed she was slipping away from him?

Her hand brushed against his chest and stopped.

"What's that?" she asked.

He clasped his hand over hers. Inside the pocket, their sharp edges softened by several layers of fabric, lay silent the tinkling charms of Belle's bracelet.

"A gift," he whispered near her mouth.

"For me?" she asked softly.

"If you like," he said. He leaned back from her kisses and delved inside the pocket of his vest. He brought out the bracelet. In the light of Meg's dressing room the cymbals and bells had lost their sheen. Tarnished, they revealed themselves to be of little material value.

"What is this?" she laughed as she took the bracelet from Erik's hand. "It looks as if it already has had an owner."

He flicked his finger across the tiny charms.

"Ah," she exclaimed in innocent pleasure at the sound. Erik chuckled at her unguarded reaction.

"Once upon a time these were the only instruments I knew. Theirs, the only melody."

In her eyes, he saw the softening sadness. Before it took up permanent residence there, he smiled and took the bracelet from her.

"Give me your hand," he said as he worked at the clasp. Meg held out her wrist, and Erik fastened the bracelet around it. "There. Now you will have music wherever you are."

"I don't know what I would have done," she said as her arms entwined his body, and her mouth bruised his.

From somewhere deep inside the two lovers came the muffled vibrations of a moan. They broke the kiss reluctantly, their lips hovering one inside the other, the barest breach between them for their sigh. Her hand went to his mask. She angled her thumb under its edge and pushed it aside. Metallic notes danced between them. She cupped his face in her palms. Her eyes glossy held him in place.

For one moment, Erik wondered if they had locked the door behind them. But as Meg pulled him down with her to the floor, he forgot caution.

CHAPTER 3

The Sword of Damocles

I am tied to the stake, and I must stand the course.

King Lear, William Shakespeare

"Erik, why didn't you come home last night?" Meg turned so that Erik could button her gown.

"I went to see an old friend."

"You have no 'old friends' in Italy."

Erik didn't reply. He concentrated on the delicate buttons and loops that began at Meg's neck and didn't stop until they reached her waist.

Meg jerked away so she was able to face him. "Don't shut me out."

"I don't mean to, Meg. I don't want to worry you. Let's go home. They can do without us today."

"Tell me."

Erik sighed. "Sabia. I went to see Sabia."

Meg's eyes darted to the bracelet that even now served as their chorus. She recognized Sabia's name from the stories Erik had told her of his childhood, his captivity in the cage at the fair, before her mother had brought him to the Opera Populaire. Sabia had been a trapeze artist and acrobat in the same fair. She knew who Erik was. Many years later, Erik had once more come face to face with

Sabia. He had happened upon her among a caravan of circus acts traversing the Italian countryside. Sabia was the sword of Damocles hanging over her husband's head. "Is that where this comes from?" she asked, holding up the chimes.

"It was a gift." Erik could feel her eyes on him. "Turn around so I can finish fastening your gown."

Reluctantly, she gave him her back again. "You were there all night?"

Erik frowned. "You've nothing to fear."

Meg gnawed at the tender flesh of her bottom lip.

Having finished the last button, Erik bent and kissed her on the side of her neck. "No fears, no doubts." He turned her in place so that she was facing him, and he kissed her in the soft spot at the bridge of her nose, between her brown eyes.

She leaned her forehead against his lips and whispered, "No doubts. But it's hard sometimes not to be afraid." She moved back and stared up into his eyes. They were watching her closely. "She knows where we are?"

"It doesn't matter, Meg. She's dying."

Meg studied Erik in an effort to understand what he might be feeling.

Avoiding further questions, Erik made sure Meg was not visible from the doorway. He opened it and beckoned to someone down the hall. After a few brief words with the workman, Erik closed the door and returned to Meg who was pulling on her stockings.

"Raoul still hasn't returned," he said to Meg as she fastened the garter high on her thigh.

"That's strange. I would have thought he'd have gotten back by now. Obviously the poor man they found isn't you."

"Perhaps I should go and see what's keeping him."

"If you like. I can't think what would have detained Raoul. He knew I was anxious."

"Why would you assume the worst?"

"Something about the cut of the clothes. They said he was someone important."

"No one is missing? Rinaldo and Bianchi...?"

"Everyone was accounted for, except you."

"I'll take a look down the road. Maybe I'll come across Raoul on his way back."

Erik didn't find Raoul at the scene of the murder. The police officer stationed at the mouth of the alleyway told him to move along. The fuss was over, he said to encourage him and a few passersby to continue on their way. But Erik was not easily dismissed. He glanced over the shoulder of the police officer to the dim recess of the alleyway. Although the body had already been removed, he smelled the acrid taint of blood, feces, and urine in the air. Along with the odors was a strain of tension. Erik tried to dispel the sensation.

"Did you notice a foreigner? A Frenchman, about my height, dark blond hair, a gentleman?"

"Oh that one. Yes, he wanted to get a look at the body. He went to the police station with Tenente Verduce."

The officer had not said that Raoul had gone to the morgue but rather to the police station. Raoul had gone with the lieutenant, not on his own. This had not been a natural death. The smell of death spoke more eloquently than any words. The tension Erik had sensed was the residue of violence. The investigator in charge had assigned this policeman to watch the area because someone had been murdered here.

He nodded. Just as the police officer was about to shoo away three young boys who were edging round the corner to get a glimpse of the blood, Erik asked, "How did he die?"

"Looked to me like he had his skull bashed in with a club."

Erik reminded himself that as unfortunate as the incident was it had nothing to do with him. Everyone he cared about was safe and accounted for. The streets were dangerous at times. The victim had probably been attacked by thieves. More interested in his money than his life, the foolish man must have put up a fight and lost. Erik pushed the uneasiness aside, thanked the officer for his help, and headed back toward the theater. Raoul would soon realize that the dead man wasn't Erik.

Meg saw Carlotta coming their way well before anyone else did. Erik had returned, saying that Raoul had gone to identify the body and would likely meet them later at home. He was giving some instructions to Sig. Bianchi and Rinaldo as Carlotta approached. A carriage waited to take Erik and Meg to the estate. After the harrowing events of the past twenty-four hours, the last thing they needed was to deal with Carlotta Venedetti. Meg was tempted to grab Erik by the hand and pull him away from the other men. Perhaps there was still time if they made a wild dash for the door. She reached for Erik's sleeve.

Too late.

"I told them. I told them, eh? You are not so easy to kill."

Erik studied Carlotta. Rinaldo's return had restored the woman's energy and confidence. Nudging Meg aside, the diva wedged her way inside the small group. Erik's eyes hardened into green stones. She nodded at Bianchi and Rinaldo and turned her back to them so that she faced only Erik.

Rinaldo was on the verge of saying something, but Erik shot him a warning glance.

"Carlotta, don't you have some special practices to attend?" asked Erik.

Meg had listened to Erik play through Rinaldo's opera. Carlotta had obviously been the inspiration. The music played to her strengths, and the story of the willful Queen suited her temperament perfectly.

"Yes, yes, yes. But they were all talk, talk, talk. You would think they were glad to think you dead so that they could gasp and shriek and talk, talk, talk."

Meg covered her smile with her hand. She could tell Erik had no idea how he was supposed to react to what Carlotta had said. Rinaldo must have realized how unintentionally offensive was Carlotta's account, for he interrupted her.

"We were all concerned."

"Meg and the count were looking for you," Carlotta went on to say, undaunted by Rinaldo's remark. "You had disappeared, been abducted. But I said," and she looked meaningfully at Meg, "…I said 'that one, he is only found when he wants to be found.' I told them. He's that way. We artists are sensitive. Sometimes we need our solitude. Then the boy comes in raving about a dead body with no face. I know your body, it was not yours."

Sig. Bianchi turned a deep crimson while Meg and Rinaldo tried to make sense of what Carlotta meant. Erik tilted his head slightly to the right as if to examine a curious painting. He seemed about to say something but shook his head instead, exhaling deeply.

"I knew," she reiterated.

"Carlotta, you're…"

"I knew you weren't dead."

"Yes, I'm…"

"You have more lives than a cat."

"I wouldn't say…"

"A dead body. I would have to see that body before anyone could convince me that it was the Phan…"

"Carlotta!" Meg and Erik spoke as one.

Carlotta slapped the palm of her hand across her open mouth.

Meg took Erik's arm in a clear sign that they should go.

"Carlotta, shouldn't you and Grimaldo be practicing your duets?" she suggested.

"He is not here," Carlotta said. All her previous energy focused on this recent irritation.

"He sent word early this morning that he needed the day for personal business," Rinaldo explained.

"Then you have all the time you want to work on Rinaldo's opera." Erik nodded and made as if to leave.

Carlotta beamed with pride. "It's good, isn't it?"

Erik nodded again and turned Meg toward the passageway that led to the front hallway of the grand entrance. Over her shoulder Meg watched Carlotta as she addressed Sig. Bianchi and several of the stagehands that happened to be nearby.

"Naldo's opera is going to be the success of the season. You wait and see. Just like I knew Erik would not walk in dead. My Naldo's opera will be sung on everyone's lips."

Rinaldo whispered in Carlotta's ear.

Erik pressed his hand firmly on Meg's back to hurry her along. As they slipped away, heading for the door, they could still hear Carlotta's piercing tones.

"Don't be silly. I never call you 'Naldo' when we are here at work. You're hearing things. I said 'Rinaldo.' You are so difficult sometimes, Naldo. Really you must listen more carefully."

"She seems to have recovered," said Erik as he handed Meg up into the carriage.

"Reminds me of someone I know," answered Meg.

Erik scowled.

"What? Don't like the comparison?" Meg restrained her desire to laugh.

No sooner had Erik removed his mask inside the doorway than Christine approached and said, "Thank goodness you're here. They're fighting." She turned, expecting Erik and Meg to follow. "I heard shouting. I was about to call for the servants."

Past the rose garden, on the lawn that ran the length of the property between a high brick wall and a copse of trees, they found the children. Only the twins and the Chagnys' youngest were not among those who now occupied the 'stage.' For Meg and Erik could not believe that what they were seeing was in earnest. Audience to the performance in the center of the grassy clearing were Laurette and Elise. They stood dumb, looks of amazement and concern on their faces.

Erik sensed Christine's fear and Meg's incomprehension. The two women fell behind as he rushed forward.

Mario and François circled each other. Their mouths were bloodied. Their clothes were soiled from grass and dirt and torn where they had yanked at each other in an effort to get an advantage. On the side, uninvolved in the fray, stood Victor. Upon seeing Erik approach, his grim face relaxed in relief.

Erik stepped between both his sons as they lunged for each other. Instead of reaching their goal, they found themselves on either side of a brick wall. Erik fisted wads of material under each of the boys' chins and pulled them even closer to his side only to propel them backwards, releasing them so that they tumbled to the ground.

"What is going on?" Neither boy was deceived by his calm tone.

"Papa, they were shouting names at each other," said Laurette. "They've been acting like idiots all morning."

Meg went to her and put a comforting arm around her shoulder. Only then did she recognize that Laurette was not so much afraid as irritated by her brothers' confrontation. Laurette whispered to Meg who listened quietly.

"Uncle Erik," said Victor. "They were arguing over…" He ground to a halt when Mario gave him a warning glance.

"Nothing," said Mario, his eyes fixed on François.

Victor took his cue and shut his mouth. When Elise seemed as if she might speak, her brother shook his head. She, too, kept her tongue. Victor marched off in the direction of the house.

"François, what is this all about?" Erik asked the only one who had attempted to remain unresponsive. François's gaze was fixed on Mario. Erik's stomach lurched. The anger in François's eyes recalled his own. He knew that look. He understood the danger of such intense emotion.

"Right. Ask him. After all, he is your 'real' son."

Erik's head swung back to Mario who had gotten up from the ground. Erik reached out to him, but Mario turned on his heels and ran to the house.

"Meg, Christine, take the girls inside. I need some time with François."

François didn't move. He seemed determined to stay, morose and silent, on the ground until judgment day. Erik crouched a few feet away. He picked at the blades of grass. The afternoon sunlight shimmered, broken by the intermittent passage of clouds overhead. The breeze was gentle. Erik could hear the sizzle of crickets in the copse of trees on the edge of the property. It was a peaceful moment except for the sound of his son's ragged breathing.

"I love all my children," Erik said. He examined the blade of grass he had plucked. When he looked up, he saw François wipe at his face with a dirty sleeve. Erik dropped the blade of grass, stood and stretched in the warmth of the sunlight, and offered François his hand. The boy hesitated, stared up at his father, took the hand, and allowed himself to be pulled to his feet. Erik didn't let go once François stood. Instead he drew him into his arms and gave him a fierce hug that made his son grunt from the violent pressure. "What happened here, François?"

The boy pushed away so he could face his father.

"It's between Mario and me."

"You were both angry—angrier than I've ever seen you."

François lowered his head, kicked at the grass with the toe of his shoe.

"I won't ask," said Erik as he braced his hands on François's shoulders, wanting his son to meet his gaze. "But you must promise me that you won't forget that you are my sons."

François glanced up at his father but was silent.

"Listen to me, François. Last night I learned that my fate is my own. I decide if I walk on this path in the light or on the other in the dark." Erik bent and whispered to his son, "You are my son. It gives me great joy, but it also…frightens me."

François wrenched away, but Erik held onto him, keeping him close.

"There is such an intensity in you. I recognize that intensity. You must use it for beauty. Don't let it overwhelm you. Don't let it lead you to anger or hatred."

"Is that what happened to you?"

Erik heard no recrimination in his son's question. But a swatch of blood crossed his mind's eye. His memory brought him back to the vaults of Paris, his son chained, a demented parody of the law hovering in the darkness.

"You're my son. But you're also your mother's child. And…you have been loved…all your life."

"But not Mario. That's why you love him, isn't it? That's why you took him in."

"At first, perhaps. But I love Mario for who he is, not for what he suffered as a child. Mario already knows what I've taken a lifetime to understand. We hold our destiny in our hands."

"Papa, I…" François squeezed his eyes shut. "It just seems easy for Mario."

"What is easy for Mario?"

François sighed. "No, it's not Mario. It's…me."

"Talk to me."

"I can't talk about it."

Erik frowned. He studied the boy. Almost a man. Intuition told Erik that the tension between his sons might be a rivalry for a different kind of love—not a fight for Erik's attention but for someone else's. He had spoken frankly with his sons about desire and about responsibility. But words were a weak defense against passion.

"Who is she?" he asked.

François's startled reaction was all the confirmation Erik needed. He rested his hand on his son's shoulder, pressing his fingers into the softness and kneading the flesh as if to soothe an aching muscle. His mouth turned up in a twisted smile as he remembered.

"François, the solution is simple."

His son waited, hope in his eyes.

"You let her decide. That's all you can do. Anything else…," Erik paused to let the tightness in his chest ease, "…is madness."

Meg followed Mario. She called to him just before he reached the top of the stairs. She could tell from his stance he did not want to obey her. His back was an impervious wall. He didn't move. She had to climb the stairs so that she could confront him. When she did come up alongside Mario, she couldn't read the emotions—they were too many and too confusing—in the firm set of his brow and the grim line of his mouth that distorted what was usually a pleasant face.

She took his hand and led him, as if he were a child again, to a small room off the master bedroom. Inside it was cozy in spite of the lack of a fire in the hearth. The furnishings were simple—a sofa with deep cushions, two over-stuffed wing chairs with ottomans to match, and an escritoire by the window where she wrote her correspondence. Along either side of the fireplace were built-in bookshelves filled with treatises on dance, biographies of great women in history, and a number of novels. The floor was carpeted in a rich, thick pile that gave the room a soft, quiet ambiance. Meg didn't release Mario's hand until he sat beside her.

She could tell from his stiff posture that Mario was going to be difficult. Where had the easygoing child gone? Mario had never given them any cause for worry. His even temper, positive outlook, and openly affectionate manner had often restored peace among them in times of strife. The "peacemaker" Madeleine had dubbed him on one occasion when Erik and François had been arguing nonsensically for hours over something she could no longer remember. It had been Mario who had pointed out to each of them that they had migrated so far down the path that there was no hope of finding their way back again to the original disagreement.

The person seated beside her was no longer a child. Meg fought a stab of regret. They had shared so little of Mario's childhood. But even though Mario had been with them less than half his lifetime, he had long been grafted to her heart. He could not doubt Erik's love or hers. Nevertheless the child had given way to the young man, and his parents' influence was perhaps waning. He was already moving out into the world—and Meg feared—away from them.

They sat silent for several moments. Meg held his hand, hoping to convey her love and concern. Just as she was about to broach the subject of his fight with François, he spoke.

"I'm sorry, Mama."

Meg's eyes watered to hear him speak her name in his native Italian. The other children, and usually Mario followed their example, called her by the French, "Maman." But sometimes Mario would slip back into his Italian and call her "Mama." Meg sensed the deeper connection the word had for Mario's growing acceptance of Meg as his mother.

"I lost my temper," he added.

"What were you fighting about?" she asked.

Mario slipped his hand away. He straightened his trouser leg to disguise the withdrawal from her contact.

"Just things."

"I see."

Mario heard the disappointment in her tone. But instead of

making him want to confide in his mother, it made him angry again.

"It's between François and me. I can't explain." He regretted the sharpness of his response the moment he saw its effect on Meg. "I'm sorry," he repeated. His shoulders sagged, and he let out a deep sigh as he collapsed against the back of the sofa. "It's Velia."

It took Meg only a few seconds to place the name and to dredge up a face to go with it. Velia DeVita was the dancer turned chorine that Erik had singled out for great things. Meg recalled Mario having spoken of the young girl at length one afternoon. His infatuation had been clear.

Meg listened as Mario described his feelings for Velia DeVita. He told Meg how he had met Velia and how he had confided to François his attraction to the young woman. Then he went on to accuse François of stabbing him in the back. François planned to take Velia away from him. Mario had seen her first. François had no right.

Meg didn't doubt that Mario found Velia DeVita attractive. Nor did she think his irritation with François was completely without foundation. But behind the words, Meg heard the anxiety, the latent rivalry between the boys, the subtle tug-of-war that they had always waged for their position in the family. Mario was the older of the boys. François was Erik's and Meg's first born. The clash was inevitable.

"Do you love this girl?"

Mario blushed. "Love? Well, isn't that what I've been saying?"

His response made Meg smile. In fact he had spoken more of his irritation with François than of his affection for the girl. Was he truly in love? Or did he resent competing with his brother on yet another level—for the affection of Velia DeVita?

"Does François say he loves her?"

"He's besotted. But how was I supposed to know?" Mario rose and paced in front of the sofa. He wavered between anger and frustration. "He accompanies Velia on the piano during her practices. That's the extent of their contact. How was I to guess that he was falling in love with her? Here I was going on and on, telling him what we talked about, describing each and every encounter with her.

And he just listens. He never says a word. Not until today. What the hell was I supposed to do? Read his mind?"

Meg ignored the rude language.

"So your brother finally gets up the courage to open his heart to you and to confess that, without meaning to, he is falling in love with the same girl that you obviously find…irresistible. Is that how it is?"

Mario stared at Meg. Her words put all the pieces into order, but it created a picture that he'd not seen before. His brow furrowed in deep reflection. He focused on the nap of the carpet, digging in with the toe of his shoe as he took in what Meg wanted him to understand.

"I hadn't thought of it from that angle. But, still, it would have helped to know. That is to say, if he'd just said something, maybe all this…wouldn't have happened."

Meg stood and wrapped her arms around her son's waist. He was too big to cuddle, but she hugged him anyway.

"Did you say anything that can't be taken back?" she asked.

"What do you mean?"

"Well, sometimes words can do a lot of damage. They can't always be unsaid. Did you hurt each other too much to mend the breach?"

Mario thought a moment, then shook his head. "We've said worse. But…"

"What were you about to say?"

"This felt different."

"It's because you're no longer children. When men fight, more than toys get broken. Can you make it up?"

Mario smiled down at Meg, his characteristic good humor restored. He straightened up and held her in position. With his palm flattened against the crown of his mother's head, Mario brought the edge of his hand in a straight line across until it rested just under his nose.

"Look," he said. "I've grown again. I'm much taller than you."

All anger had disappeared in the delight of the evidence of his recent growth. Meg laughed. There was still a bit of the child in Mario. She hoped that in all her children there would always be a glimmer of the child.

"Don't worry," he said, as if he could read her thoughts. "François can't stay mad at me forever. I'm just too irresistible."

The investigator seemed a competent man, but he had made Raoul nervous. He had questioned and examined him as if he were a suspect, keeping him well into the afternoon. Had the dead man nothing to do with him or Erik, Raoul would not have felt uneasy. But once he had recognized that Ricci was the victim, he found it impossible to distance himself from the crime. He became acutely aware of the bruises on his own face, the ones Erik had given him when they struggled the night of the hecklers. He was convinced the inspector had noticed them, too. Although he knew it was irrational, a vague feeling of guilt hovered over him. At the same time, Erik's absence took on a sinister aspect that Raoul was loath to admit.

By the time Raoul left the police station, it was early afternoon. He had not been allowed to send a message to the theater or to the Costanzi estate. For a moment he stood indecisive. Should he return to the theater or go directly to the estate? The estate was closer. He'd pass by the estate. If there was no word and Meg had not returned home, he would set off for the Teatro dell'Opera.

He prayed Erik had returned. He had to be warned. Once Lieutenant Verduce found out the identity of the corpse, Erik would be a prime suspect.

Raoul waited until the servant left. Christine, Meg, and Erik had joined him in the drawing room, anxious to hear what had kept him away well into the afternoon.

"Where the deuce were you?" Raoul asked Erik. All his anxiety rose to the surface as anger. Irrationally it was all focused on one person—Erik. Had he come home last night, Raoul would not have hesitated to cooperate with the authorities and would have identified the victim as Ricci.

Erik ignored Raoul's tone. "I'm touched by your concern."

"You know damn well I'm more than concerned. I could care less if you stay out all night. But last night was an unfortunate night to disappear like the Phantom."

The reference to the Phantom put Erik on his guard. Aware of the tension between the two men, Christine and Meg remained watchful but silent.

Exasperated by Erik's silence, Raoul explained, "I just spent all morning and half the afternoon in a police station. Did you know someone was murdered just feet away from the theater?"

Meg interrupted, "Erik arrived shortly after you left."

Raoul saw that the women were obviously confused by his agitation. It dawned on him that once Erik had returned, they were no longer worried. The murder had no apparent connection to them. If anything, they were curious but not alarmed.

That is until now.

"Raoul, what happened at the station? What's wrong?" asked Christine.

Raoul steadied himself. He kept his eyes on his wife and took several deep breaths. Perhaps he was overreacting. Erik was safe. At least for the moment. It was evident that he was also unaware that a storm was gathering on the horizon.

"Sorry," Raoul said to everyone present. "Looking at a man who's been bludgeoned to death is not pleasant. It's even more upsetting when you know the man."

Erik's guarded manner slipped, and he took a step forward.

"Who?"

Meg and Christine were equally puzzled. Meg went over again and again the possibilities. No one came to mind. The only possible victim stood in the room with them. She couldn't imagine who the dead man might have been.

"Ricci."

A perfect silence fell over the room.

"How horrible," said Christine. "He was a despicable person, but no one deserves to be bludgeoned to death."

Erik and Raoul exchanged somber glances. Meg was the first to draw the conclusion and say it out loud.

"They'll think Erik did it."

Christine stared wide-eyed at Raoul as if she expected him to argue with Meg. When she saw that his eyes were unwavering and fixed on Erik, she realized that her husband had already come to the same conclusion.

"But he didn't. He wouldn't," Christine said.

"This is what we should do." Raoul rubbed his hand over his face to gain time to think.

"They know it's Ricci?" Erik interrupted.

"No. I…only recognized him at the last minute. I wanted to give us time to think this through."

"To think what through?" Erik lowered his voice in an effort to mask a rising tide of anger.

"To protect you, you great…" Raoul broke off before he called Erik something he might later regret. Now was the time for cool heads, he told himself. "Look," he began.

"To protect him from what?" Meg asked. She stood and glared at Raoul. "He's done nothing wrong."

"If he hadn't been out all night, we might be able to persuade the police of that fact. But since he was not…"

"This is absurd," said Erik.

"Where were you?" asked Raoul.

"It's none of your business." Erik's answer had a warning edge to it. "Where do you think I was? With a mistress? Or do you think that I killed Ricci and walked the streets until morning, came home, changed out of my bloody clothes, and had breakfast?"

"No. Don't waste your anger on me. I'm not the enemy."

"No, perhaps not. But it did cross your mind, didn't it? You thought I killed him."

Losing his precarious control over the irrational anger that had gnawed at him the entire day, Raoul shouted at Erik. "Yes, I admit it. For one moment, it did occur to me that the Phantom would do exactly *that*."

"Did you forget my preferred way of killing my victims?" Erik's tone was laced with venom.

Raoul's breath shuddered as he fought to calm himself. "No,

I didn't." He quieted his voice before he continued. "I said that it occurred to me."

Erik held his tongue and waited.

"I'm sorry," said Raoul, regretting his own irrational display. "I dismissed the thought the very moment it occurred to me."

Gradually Erik's expression lost its ferocity, his breathing calmed, the obvious tension in his shoulders and fists relaxed.

Raoul wiped his hand across his face as if with the gesture he could wipe away the past few moments. In an effort to bring home to everyone present the gravity of the situation, he tried to explain, "Once they know that the victim is Paolo Ricci, you are going to be the prime suspect in this case. That's inevitable."

Meg smoothed away nonexistent wrinkles in Erik's sleeve.

"I'm innocent," Erik said.

Raoul whispered, "I know. But you *look* guilty."

"What were you going to suggest, Raoul?" Christine encouraged her husband. From the moment Raoul had entered the house, telling them that he needed to speak with them, she had understood that he must have a plan. "What should Erik do? What can he do?"

"Leave Rome."

Stunned Erik glared at him. "Leave? No. I'm not leaving Rome. I'm not running. I'm innocent. I didn't do anything wrong."

"You threatened to kill Ricci. How many times was it? At least twice that I know of. Once the evening of the hecklers and again the next morning when you practically strangled him to death in his office."

"I won't run," Erik said again. "My fate is my own. I won't run again."

Raoul considered Erik. Misgivings sounded in the back of his mind. Even so he had no doubt that Erik would stand by his decision. On some level, he even understood Erik's refusal to become a fugitive. But he didn't like it. He was too aware of the risks and the consequences should things go badly.

"Well, it's going to be difficult. But you won't be alone." Raoul stepped forward and offered Erik his hand.

Erik clasped it and held on tightly. "I have to go." He relaxed his grip and released his friend's hand.

"Where?" asked both Christine and Raoul at the same time.

Erik barely acknowledged their question. He was on his way to the door when Meg's voice made him stop.

"Tell me you're not going to do what I think you're going to do."

Over his shoulder, as if it meant nothing, he answered his wife.

"Ricci. I have to identify the body."

"You can't be serious." Meg rushed to step between her husband and the door. "Raoul, tell him." She leaned to the side and looked past Erik toward Raoul.

"Do you think that's the wisest course of action?" he asked.

"Listen to reason, Erik," Meg said.

Erik considered Raoul and Meg. Then he looked over at Christine. She alone seemed to understand. She alone would not try to stop him.

"Give the dead their due," he said, his eyes on Christine. "He had a name. No one knows who he is."

When he moved Meg away from the door, she held onto his sleeve.

"All right. I understand, but it's late. Let it wait until the morning." Her eyes pleaded with him.

"She's right, Erik." There was such tenderness in Christine's voice.

Raoul shook his head, raised his hands up in a sign of defeat, and added, "I know it's useless to argue with you. I would think the last place you would want to be is a police station."

Erik took Meg by the hand and led her to a seat. He pushed her down onto the cushion, turned, and addressed them all. "Is it so irrational? Would my silence make me less suspicious?"

"Well, I suppose Lieutenant Verduce would not expect the murderer to come forth to identify the victim," Raoul admitted. "But Meg's right. Let it wait until the morning."

Erik felt Meg's hand slip into his. He squeezed it.

"Fine. I'll go first thing in the morning."

"Why didn't you try to stop him?" Raoul slipped under the bedcovers and stretched out against the coolness of the sheets.

"I did. I agreed that he wait until tomorrow." Christine brushed her dark brown hair, pulling the waves out only to see them bounce back into place.

"I saw you, Christine. Meg was terrified. I was taken by surprise myself. But not you. Why?"

Christine laid her brush on the table and came to the side of the bed. She removed her robe, extinguished the one light in the room, and got into bed with her husband. The light from the open window reached only the edges of things, making the hard corners of the wardrobe opposite the bed stand out ominously.

"I remembered our first-born," she said.

Raoul slipped his arm under Christine's shoulders and brought her closer. She leaned into him. "What does this have to do with our son?" The child had drowned. Christine's grief had been so deep that she had withdrawn from everything. Raoul had thought she might never recover.

"When Erik abducted me, he took me to our child's grave. He threatened to open the grave and make me look at him. I couldn't. I couldn't allow him to do that to our child. He knew that it would shock me. He made me face the fact that little Raoul was gone."

"I don't understand, Christine. I don't see how this relates to what happened in the drawing room."

"Even though our son was dead, I was still his mother. I couldn't bear that Erik would disturb him in his grave. It became clear to me that the Phantom had lived all those years in communion with the dead. He sees in them his own mortality."

"So even though he doesn't—didn't—particularly care for Ricci…"

"Give the dead their due. Our son was loved. We did for him all that we could. I had to let him rest." Christine was quiet for a moment, her thoughts consumed by the past. "When the Phantom was executed, his body was to be buried in an anonymous plot. I think that was the final indignity. It was as if he weren't human."

Raoul shivered as he remembered Leroux's corpse. Erik had washed his enemy and laid him out in a primitive funereal ceremony. If he could do that with Leroux—a man who had nearly destroyed him—then what honors would he accord Ricci?

"It's about human dignity," said Raoul.

"He imagines his own body laid out on a table under strangers' eyes and no one to grieve for him."

Raoul lifted her chin and kissed her on the lips. She smiled up at him.

"It's simple," she said.

Raoul stared out into the darkness. In his experience there was nothing simple in the motivation and behavior of the Phantom. At times like these, he suspected the same could be said of Erik.

"Papa?" François stepped inside the music room.

Erik had wanted a few minutes alone. As he often did, he had gone to the music room. Distracted by the recent events, he had not been able to lose himself in the music, as he was wont to do. Instead he found himself playing the same lyrical passage over and over again, varying it as he did so. The rhythmic repetition had begun to soothe him. Then he had heard the faint knock on the door and looked up to see his son standing in the doorway.

"What's wrong?" he asked. François held himself stiffly, as if he expected to be chided for having interrupted. "Don't just stand there. Come in."

François approached the piano, drew up one of the nearby chairs, and sat down. Erik waited, sensing that his son was having difficulty summoning the words he needed.

"I overheard you."

Erik studied his son. *Did he believe him guilty?*

"You were eavesdropping?"

"I heard the voices."

"And stopped to listen in the hallway."

François shrugged his shoulders.

"I would have told you in the morning," Erik said.

"Is Uncle Raoul certain that it's Ricci?"

"I'm afraid so."

Again his son hesitated. "I need to tell you something."

Careful to contain his impulse to berate his son for his foolishness and to swear him to secrecy, Erik listened as François told him of the night Victor, Mario, and he had slipped out and made the rounds of the inns and taverns. His disappointment in his sons' behavior could not compete with his stronger desire to protect them from harm. Under the circumstances, it was simply unfortunate that the three boys had run into Ricci. It was disturbing that they had harassed the man. It was damned bad luck that the largely harmless encounter had occurred the night Ricci was murdered.

When François finished unburdening himself, Erik rubbed his hand across his forehead. "Let's keep this to ourselves, François."

"Yes, Papa. I just thought I should tell you about it."

"You did the right thing in telling me."

Exhausted, Meg had fallen asleep. They had made love. The first time had been tender. Erik had allowed Meg to set the pace. But afterwards—even though they were sated—Erik had roused Meg again and brought her to climax once, twice. He had buried himself deep inside her body, hovering over her and staring down at her to watch the play of pleasure across her face. It was as if he never wanted their lovemaking to end. He held back. Several times she thought he'd come, felt him resist, pull back, gather renewed strength and purpose. She reached out to him with her heart and mind, wanting to soothe him, to take the desperation out of his possession of her. But her body betrayed her time and time again, obeying his touch and his demand, forgetful of his pleasure, as she shuddered in ecstasy, the onslaught of sensation too powerful for her to resist. Yet she understood that this was what he wanted. He stared down at her and drank in her pleasure, watched as her features twisted and her hands clawed at him. She lost herself in the passion he brought her until she lay limp in his arms. When she feared she could no longer breathe and that pleasure would turn to pain, she heard the groan escape his lips. A groan, a gasp, a sob, its sound was so fierce she held Erik as if he might break apart. She met the grinding force as he flexed and stilled inside her. She caressed the back of his nape as he buried his face against her damp hair. Content to feel him welded to her flesh, warmed by his solid presence, she held him. Even as he pinned her to the mattress, invaded her, anchored her in place, she was filled with the knowledge of her own power. She nuzzled the side of his face, feeling the uneven texture of the disfigurement. His surrender was so complete that she knew he needed her tenderness, knew how utterly vulnerable he was as he sagged against her.

She didn't remember him leaving her, slipping away. She had fallen asleep, loose-limbed and content. Only when she woke—just hours before dawn—did she sense he'd left her. She reached out to find he was not beside her. She called out to him.

"Here," came his voice, the sound low and rich, like darkness itself, the promise of such beauty, a beauty only discerned by the heart.

The breeze told her the window was open. She lifted herself to her elbows and in the soft moonlight made out the silhouette of her husband. He sat in a chair drawn up to the open window. His long legs were stretched out and resting on the sill of the casement.

"Come back to bed," she whispered.

"Can't sleep."

She scooted to the edge of the bed, found her robe, and slipped it on.

"It must be near morning," she said.

Erik didn't reply right away. She made her way round the bed to his chair. She saw movement but didn't recognize his gesture until his hand came to rest on the side of her hip.

"You're not as bony as you were," he said as he stroked the slope of her hip down to her thigh and back up to her waist. Her muscles were taut, the flesh compact and pleasing to the touch.

"I was never bony," she said, pretending that his remark had offended her.

"Come here," he whispered.

He drew her down to sit upon his lap. He was naked. Meg giggled as she slid across his thighs, her hand flattening against the soft curls of his chest hair. She rubbed her fingers lazily over the nipples, traced the contours of his muscles with her nail.

"I thought I had worn you out. You should be asleep," he said.

She leaned in and smiled against his throat. She teased and licked the salty flesh. He jerked slightly from the sensation.

"It will take more than that to wear me out," she lied.

He stroked her hair away from his mouth and chuckled. "You're a vixen, ma petite."

Meg's eyes had adjusted to the low light. She looked out the window to see what her husband had been observing. Although the moon was waning, there was enough light to make out varying shades of gray. At first she only discerned the difference between the lighter patches of lawn and the deeper hues of the trees beyond. Then she noticed movement.

"What's that?" She pointed at something flitting across the grounds from the far copse of trees.

"Our fox. Rénard chases the rodents, mostly rabbits and field mice. He manages the grounds for us."

"Rénard?" she repeated. "So is our fox as crafty as the one in the medieval tales?"

"Of course. You didn't even know he lived with us, did you?"

"True. Are you and he on good terms? After all he's poaching on our land, isn't he?"

"He hardly makes a dent in the rodent population. And he's great entertainment. There," he said, sitting up straight and pointing at the fox who sprinted across the lawn on the trail of some prey.

Meg pushed slightly away from Erik's embrace so that she could follow the fox's mad dash.

"Oh, poor bunny," she said when Rénard pounced on something small and dark.

"How do you know it was a bunny?"

"I don't." She leaned back against her husband's chest. "I just imagined it."

"Could have been a field mouse."

"Well, I suppose it's the nature of things."

"Don't worry. I'm sure the mouse didn't suffer long. Rénard is an efficient hunter."

Meg turned her cheek and pressed it over his heart. She listened to the thrum of its beat. Her breathing fell into step with the comforting sound. She almost drifted off to sleep again, but she knew sunrise was not too far off and wanted to watch with Erik as it spread across the sky. That thought led to others. Once the sun rose, the day would begin.

"Couldn't Raoul go and identify the body?" she asked.

"No. It would look suspicious. Raoul missed the chance to identify the body yesterday. If he returned now, the police would wonder why he had hesitated. It's best that I go."

"Are you worried?"

"Perhaps. Just a bit."

She felt him swallow. She pushed her arms between the cushioned back of the chair and around his torso as far as she could and squeezed him with all her strength.

"It's all right, Meg," he whispered. "What Sabia told me last night lifted a weight I didn't even know I carried." Erik had told Meg that Sabia was dying and had asked to see him. Vosh had led him to what was left of Sabia's traveling carnival. They had pitched camp just outside of the city. Erik had also explained that Sabia and he had come to terms and made peace with one another. "At the fair, years ago, she lied to me. She read my fortune. She said that I was born in darkness, but there was also a light." He tilted her face up and kissed her. "That light was you." He hesitated before he went on. "But…she also said that I would end in darkness."

"That was a terrible thing to say. But you knew it was an act, didn't you?"

"Even so I wasn't able to forget what she had said. In some part of my mind, I believed her. It was always there—a sense of doom—hanging over my head."

"Did she tell you something different this time?"

"Last night I sat with a dying woman. She needed to tell me the truth. She told me that the fortune she had read in my palm was a lie and that my destiny was my own. The future is not written. You can't see it in the tealeaves at the bottom of a cup. Nor can you read it in the lines of the palm of your hand. The only certainty is that someday we all will die. There's no darkness in me. The darkness is what men do. I can make my own destiny. It's my right to determine my own fate."

"Erik?"

"Yes, ma petite?"

"I understand you don't want to run from this, but…"

"I won't start over, Meg. I won't lose the world you and I have built together. All of this is much more than I ever had or lost at the Opera Populaire. This is real, solid. It's my life with you. It's my work. It's Marcelo and Madeleine. Our children are here. I won't drag you and the children into hiding. My destiny is in my hands. My life is here."

"But what if they accuse you of killing Ricci?"

"I won't let that happen. I'll make them see that I'm innocent."

Meg smoothed her hand across his face, first on one side, then on the other. "You need to sleep, my love. You have a long day ahead." She kissed his lips. They were soft and yielding.

What could she do for him? How could she soothe him? She sat up on his lap and took a deep breath. She held his hand to her breast.

She began to sing.

CHAPTER 4

Give the Dead Their Due

"An honest tale speeds best being plainly told."

Richard III, William Shakespeare

Verduce was only mildly surprised when Erik Costanzi was announced. After all, the corpse was a well-to-do individual and was found not far from the Teatro dell'Opera. He might have been an accountant, a writer, or a copyist. Perhaps he even worked at the theater. The Frenchman's interest in the deceased, as well as his association with the artistic director, was another indication that the incident involved the bohemian art scene, perhaps even the Teatro dell'Opera itself. Verduce had put his right-hand man Cortale Paccara in charge of assembling a number of officers to follow possible leads. Several were making the rounds among the establishments frequented by the theater crowds. One way or another Verduce was convinced that an identification of the victim would soon be made. Once they knew who the victim was, the investigation would proceed with a clearer focus.

The lieutenant had not expected Costanzi to be such an imposing man. He must measure more than six feet. The officer had read about the enigmatic artistic director and knew he wore a mask. He expected him to be foppish and vain. "The masked genius of the opera" was none of these things. Austere, even menacing, Costanzi was a striking figure of a man in his prime.

"Sig. Costanzi, I see you're safely returned?"

Erik nodded and took the seat opposite Verduce.

"Your friend, the Count de Chagny, was concerned enough to assume perhaps our murder victim was you. Do your friends often assume you to be the victim of foul play?"

The corner of Erik's mouth twitched. Verduce watched his visitor's eyes. He saw the flash of humor as Costanzi considered his answer.

"My friends have vivid imaginations. Tenente Verduce…"

"Please call me Sig. Verduce or just Verduce. I'm still not comfortable with my promotion."

Erik studied the man. Perhaps in his fifties, Verduce had light brown eyes, brown hair streaked with gray, and a steel-gray mustache. His face was pleasant but not handsome. He appeared fit, but not athletic in build. As he leaned back in his chair, the beginnings of a paunch were evident. But his expression was kind. His eyes, intelligent and perceptive. So different from Leroux. The differences made Erik want to relax, but he knew it would be a mistake to let his guard down. This man had the gift to see beyond the mask.

"Sig. Verduce, I've come to see if I can identify the corpse."

"Why?"

"The proximity of his death to my theater." Erik might have said that certain elements in Raoul's description were familiar, but he didn't want the officer to suspect that Raoul had indeed recognized the victim and had withheld the information.

"I see." Instead of moving, Verduce continued to study Erik. It was an effective ploy meant to unsettle an opponent. Sometimes the strategy led to a garrulous and nervous attempt to fill the silence. Costanzi was apparently immune to such ploys. He met Verduce's gaze with his own intense inspection, silence with silence. "Follow me," said Verduce after a few uncomfortable moments.

They found themselves in a subterranean room. The stench of death seeped from the walls. The inspector offered Erik the salve, but he declined.

"You're used to the smell of dead men?"

Erik held his tongue. Before the assistant could beckon for him to approach, Erik went directly to the slab upon which lay the corpse. Instead of waiting for the officers, Erik pulled the covering back and stared at the devastated face of Paolo Ricci. He felt Verduce watching him. Erik avoided the face and took in the entire body at a glance. He stopped and examined the hands. If he had had any doubt, it would have been removed by one look at the cadaver's hands. Hands had as much character as faces, and Erik could identify many people he knew simply by the length of the digits, the bend of the knuckles, or the shape of the thumb.

"The clothes are on the side table." The assistant pointed to the far wall.

Erik took note of the clothes. Empty and crumpled, the various articles of clothing, more than the corpse itself, suggested the absolute loss of life.

"Why do you undress them?" he asked.

Momentarily Verduce was taken aback by the question.

"I assure you, signore, that it's only in order to collect information regarding the murder and the identity of the victim. Sometimes a loved one will recognize a birthmark or a scar otherwise hidden under the clothing. A knife wound or signs of a struggle may be obscured. Violation in the case of a woman, if not immediately obvious, can only be confirmed by removal of the garments.

Erik nodded, as if he found the explanation reasonable.

"Paolo Ricci. The dead man's Paolo Ricci, a journalist."

"You're positive?"

"Yes." Erik headed for the door, his task completed.

"I would like to ask you a few more questions, Sig. Costanzi. Do you have the time?"

To gain a few moments to compose himself, Erik took out his pocket watch as if to inspect the hour. "Yes, of course."

Behind Erik sat the stenographer who was taking notes. In the right-hand corner of the room, facing Erik was the lieutenant's assistant, Cortale Paccara. The assistant had a large tablet on his lap and several charcoal pencils in his pocket. The movements of his hand as he sketched were fluid. Erik knew he was drawing him, not once but several times. Verduce had apologized by explaining that modern crime detection required the meticulous accumulation of facts. Facts and information were the cornerstones of any investigation.

Erik had not objected.

"Ricci. This is most helpful, Sig. Costanzi. Now a few more questions. In what capacity did you know the deceased?"

"He wrote reviews of our productions. He was a regular patron of all the major opera companies in the city, as well as the Teatro dell'Opera."

"Were you friends?"

"I wouldn't say that."

"What kind of reviews did he write?"

Erik paused. He would not point out that they would already know this information if they had any interest at all in the arts.

"Sarcastic ones," he answered.

Verduce smiled. "Did this anger you?"

"Sometimes."

"Would you say it angered you enough to consider Sig. Ricci an enemy?"

"I'm an artistic director of an important opera company. When a performer doesn't learn his part, I warn him. If he continues to fail in his duties, I dismiss him. When a young girl auditions for the chorus and has no talent, I'm the one to destroy her illusions. I don't need to choose enemies. There are many people who don't consider me a friend."

"You are being evasive, aren't you?"

"Yes."

Verduce raised an eyebrow and presented his conclusion. "So I can take it that you and Ricci were not on the best of terms."

"Yes, you may."

"Did you often disagree and argue?"

"We always disagreed and sometimes argued."

"Did you ever fight? Come to blows?"

Erik's eyes flared. He held himself in check.

"Yes."

Verduce seemed surprised at Erik's candor.

"When was the last time you saw the victim?"

"The morning I tried to kill him in his office."

The sharp tap of the pencil as it hit the wooden floor distracted Verduce for only a moment. The stenographer leaned over and picked it up, resuming his notes.

"You meant to kill him?"

"I was angry."

"Do you often feel like killing people when you get angry?"

"..."

"I'm sorry. That was an inappropriate question. What had angered you so much that you would try to kill this...art critic?"

"He had placed hecklers in the audience and paid them to disrupt a performance."

"So you..."

"I went to his office two days before his death and tried to reason with him. He was not cooperative. I wanted to make my position clear."

"How?"

"I wrapped my fingers around his throat and squeezed."

Verduce looked at the stenographer to make sure he had gotten this down.

"What stopped you?"

Erik looked away for a second. When his eyes again engaged the lieutenant's, they were blank.

"My friend, the Count de Chagny, stopped me."

"How? Did he reason with you?"

"He tried to pull me off. But that would not have worked. He... convinced me that I did not wish to go to jail."

Verduce steepled his hands in front of his face and leaned in closer to the witness. "You must realize that what you've been saying amounts to a confession of motive?"

"Yes, I have what the police would assume a sufficient motive. But there were others who had motives as strong or stronger than mine. Someone acted on his motive. I did not."

"But you said..."

"I went to his office in broad daylight. I wanted to kill him, but I did not."

"Perhaps you only wanted to wait for an opportunity to kill him without witnesses so that you would not have to go to jail."

"So I killed him practically on my doorstep and left him there for the police to find? Surely you know I'm not a stupid man."

Verduce considered the grim-faced man opposite him and smiled.

"People are complex. Intelligent people perhaps are even more so. Passion sometimes leads an intelligent person down a fool's path."

Erik was silent.

"Where were you, the night before last? Your friend has already told us that you did not come home."

"I was visiting an old friend."

"All night?"

"Yes. I returned early yesterday morning. I went directly home. My wife and the count had already left for the theater. I learned of the crime some time later."

"Will your friend vouch for your whereabouts the night of the murder?"

Erik hesitated. "Yes. Is that all, Sig. Verduce?"

"You've been most cooperative. Just a few more formalities."

Erik had risen. Reluctantly he took his seat again.

"A bit of personal history. Where were you born?"

Verduce scowled at the man's silence. The eyes shifted. Costanzi was obviously uncomfortable with the question.

"I don't know where I was born. I was orphaned at a young age. Before Rome, we lived in Pianosa. My children were all born in Italy."

"You grew up in France, did you not?"

"Yes."

"What was your last place of residence in France?"

"I can't see what this has to do with..."

"Is there any reason that I should not know this information?"

Erik swallowed. The portion of his face that the mask didn't cover had darkened.

"Paris. Opera Populaire. Rue des artistes."

Verduce nodded to the stenographer. Erik remained rigid in his chair, his eyes fixed on the lieutenant.

"One last question, Sig. Costanzi. The mask."

As the assistant turned to a fresh sheet of paper in his tablet, Erik's eyes slid to Paccara. The assistant sat, hand poised over the blank surface, his attention riveted on him.

"Is it an affectation, Sig. Costanzi?" asked Verduce, suddenly unsure of his original intention.

"No."

Verduce studied the masked man. He could see how attractive he was. The mask added an allure of mystery.

"It hides…?"

"A deformity."

Verduce nodded. He could not read the expression in Costanzi's eyes. The memory of the man's question came back to him. *Why do you take off their clothes?* The sensation of an invasion of privacy, a stripping away of dignity reverberated in the words, the tone. He lowered his eyes to the blotter on the surface of his desk. "I think that will be all for the moment." The officer stood. Costanzi's knuckles were white as his hands gripped the side arms of the chair and he hoisted himself to his feet. Verduce gestured toward the doorway. Composed once more, Costanzi nodded and took his leave.

Outside the police station, Erik did not get into the carriage parked outside the door. Instead he walked, careless of direction, down the broad avenue. Blindly he walked.

Someone at his side put his hand firmly on Erik's elbow—Raoul. Erik stumbled. His friend kept him from falling.

"Let's get you home," Raoul said.

CHAPTER 5

The Worm Turns

...The worst is not
So long as we can say, 'This is the worst.'

King Lear, William Shakespeare

"Ricci?" Carlotta shook her hands as if she'd touched something disgusting that clung to her fingers. "Ricci?" she said again.

Word had traveled like wildfire throughout the opera house. The chorine that had stopped to tell Carlotta, Grimaldo, and Sig. Bianchi had tried to wear the appropriate expression of shock and regret, but her wide eyes glistened from the macabre delight of delivering the news before anyone else.

"How do you know?" asked Sig. Bianchi. He grimaced at the girl for making such an outrageous claim.

"My friend works at the gazette. They're going to run the story today. She was there this morning when the policemen came. They asked everyone all sorts of questions. My friend said that Ricci was murdered. They called it a 'crime of passion.' Said most likely someone who knew him clubbed him to death."

Carlotta had shrieked. Before she let the girl slip away to carry the news, Carlotta had made her repeat the information more than once.

"Grimmy." Carlotta grabbed Grimaldo's arm and shook him.

"The maggot's dead. Someone killed the worm. They'll think it was me."

Sig. Bianchi snorted in disgust, but the blood in Grimaldo's face drained to his toes.

Carlotta didn't notice how pale Grimaldo was.

"It's a sign of the dangerous times in which we're living. Mark my words," said Sig. Bianchi. "They'll find that a gang of shiftless hooligans cornered him on the street and beat him to death with their bare hands for the fun of it." Sig. Bianchi strode off to the pit.

"No, no, no. They'll ask their questions, and they'll find out that I tried to kill him once before and think I did it again."

"Carlotta." Although his hands were unsteady, Grimaldo recovered sufficiently to try to reason with her. "What are you saying? You've never raised a finger to harm anyone."

"With this finger." Carlotta held up her right index finger and pointed it into the air just inches away from Grimaldo's nose. "I poked the maggot, and he somersaulted through the air and down those stairs." She indicated the staircase that led from stage left down into the auditorium. Grimaldo had forgotten about the day that Ricci had backed away from Carlotta. At the edge of the stage, he had tumbled down the steps in an effort to avoid her insults. "He nearly broke his neck." She put the index finger in her mouth and chewed at the nail. "There were hundreds of witnesses to testify against me. Oh, Grimmy, I can't go to jail. I don't like rats. Bread is too fattening. I won't survive a day if they lock me in a cold, dark cell. Oh dio mio, my voice! I can't stand the damp. I'll lose my voice."

"No one, do you hear me? No one will harm you." Grimaldo spoke with a vehemence Carlotta had only seen him display when in character. She slipped her finger from her mouth and touched his nose briefly with its wet tip. The man's color had gone from white to crimson. "I won't let any harm come to you." He seemed about to say something else. He inched closer to Carlotta. But Rinaldo drew up behind him.

"What's going on?" he asked. "Someone said Ricci was murdered. Is it true?"

Grimaldo shrank back, his words silenced. Rinaldo's voice

and demeanor were stern, but his attention was focused solely on Carlotta.

Carlotta collapsed against Rinaldo's chest, buried her face in his waistcoat, and moaned. "Dead, dead, dead. The maggot's dead."

Grimaldo slipped quietly away. He stuck his hands in his pockets so that no one would notice their trembling.

When her rehearsals with the young Costanzi were canceled, Velia had almost been relieved. She saw it as a reprieve. She hadn't seen either Mario or François for days. If Adamo accused her of not carrying out his instructions, she would simply tell him that she had lacked opportunity to press on with her seduction. Her brother would have to believe her. But she had also not seen Adamo for several days. What if something had happened to him?

Velpi, who worked on the riggings for Jacopo, told her that an old drunk was asking for her outside the side entrance. Her former uneasiness mushroomed into dread. Adamo dealt with their father, keeping him away from the Teatro dell'Opera. Her father's appearance outside the building could mean only one thing. Adamo had not given him his usual allowance for drink, food, and shelter.

To tell the truth, Velia had missed her father. Even though Jacopo frowned upon his visits to the Teatro, she was relieved to know that no harm had befallen him. He would sometimes wander into the Boar and Bow when she was performing. For such occasions, Velia had gotten in the habit of setting aside, unbeknownst to her brother, a small portion of her wages. She would press the coins into her father's dirty, callused hand. Or if he were already befuddled by drink, she'd put them in his pocket, urging him to go to his room and sleep.

Velia slipped out the side exit and into the alley where her father awaited her. His voice was hoarse, his color sickly. He coughed so fiercely that Velia was amazed that he hadn't drawn blood.

"Papa, where's Adamo?" she asked.

The old man scowled. He hawked up a thick wad of green phlegm and spit. "Don't know. Haven't seen him."

Between coughs Velia managed to understand that her father's landlord was threatening to throw him out onto the street. Her heart ached to know that her father's only concern was that Adamo was late in paying the owner of the building where not only her father but a host of unemployed and broken men made their meager homes.

"Papa, take this. It might be enough to keep him from throwing you out. Tell him there will be more later." Velia laid the coins in the cupped palm her father held out. Instead of pocketing the money, he fingered each coin and muttered under his breath.

"The money for the room," he repeated. He dropped the pitiable tone and spoke with severity. "Where you hiding it from your papa?"

Velia lowered her eyes in shame. She had nothing more to spare. The old man grumbled but leaned forward and kissed her on the top of her head. She nearly gagged from the combination of strong liquor and days of sweat and dirty clothing.

She watched until the old man staggered out to the street and disappeared, becoming one of the anonymous passersby again. Then, her heart a leaden weight in her chest, she made her way back inside.

The news of the murder was sufficient excuse for a disruption in the routine among the performers. Renata Cossa had insisted on running the dancers through their paces, but Sig. Bianchi seemed only marginally interested in rehearsal. Velia felt at odds with her own body, unable to decide what to do with herself. Just off stage from the wings she watched Renata Cossa direct her dancers. In a vague imitation of the precise and complex movements performed on the stage, Velia swayed, lifted her arms, and bent in time with the music.

"I thought you weren't a dancer."

Velia jumped and swung around to find Mario Costanzi studying her.

"Sorry," he said as he reached out to steady her. "I didn't mean to startle you."

"I...I..." She released an irritated sigh.

Mario's usual smile was gone. He stared at her, and Velia felt that she couldn't breathe. She recalled exactly what Adamo had demanded that she do. It would be so easy. Mario brought out strange feelings in her, a desire to be touched, to be engulfed and swept far away. She leaned forward, but her feet stubbornly refused to follow. She took a breath, determined to make her offer plain. But before she could speak, Mario interrupted her again.

"Velia, are you all right?"

She groaned, closed her eyes, and turned her back to Mario. His hands rested upon her upper arms close to her shoulders. A face flashed across her mind's eye, but it wasn't Mario's. Her lips trembled as she felt Mario solid behind her. One tear slipped down her cheek.

Their father had told Mario and him that they were to go to the teatro and carry on with their routines as if everything were normal. But everything was not normal. François had listened as his father explained the crisis. He took both his older sons into his confidence. He made it clear that he would be a likely suspect in the case of Ricci's murder. Laurette was given a somewhat milder version of the events. Only to his sons had their father revealed the details so that they could appreciate the gravity of the situation. In return for his trust, their father had asked only one thing of Mario and François. To allay suspicion and gossip, it was important that the boys act as if nothing were wrong. Their father and mother would also return to reassure the company.

François's gut twisted. He had not been able to eat. The few bites of food had stuck in his throat, threatening to choke him. Although his father's predicament was uppermost in his mind, he couldn't imagine anyone believing that his father had murdered the critic. Ricci had been an irritant, not a serious threat to his father or even to the theater. François knew his father was capable of violence. After all, he had seen him kill. But only because François's own life had been at stake. No one could seriously believe that he would murder someone like Ricci. Even so, François was on edge and found it difficult to go through the paces of his day as if nothing had happened. Besides, the recent fight between Mario and him still nagged at François, making things even worse. On their parents' suggestion, the two boys had agreed to a fragile truce. François had accepted his father's counsel. Velia DeVita would have to choose. Whatever she decided, both brothers promised to abide by the outcome and hold no grudge against the more fortunate of the two.

Seeing no one in the practice room, François asked after Velia. He was anxious to resume their practice sessions. They had made a good deal of progress. Not only had Velia memorized the small part she had in the current opera, but she had also nearly perfected the role of Yasmine. François was sure that his father would be amazed to hear her progress. François felt giddy in anticipation of hearing her sing Yasmine's aria to the dawn. But it was more than professional interest. He couldn't fool himself. His one advantage over Mario was that he had an excuse to see Velia nearly every day, and he was determined to make the most of it.

After asking among the chorines to no avail, François ran into Velpi and asked if he had seen Signorina DeVita.

"At the side entrance. That drunk came looking for her again."

François recalled hearing about Velia's father. When he got to the side entrance, it was clear she was no longer there. He walked along the back corridors, asking as he went. Someone mentioned having seen her in the wings. Approaching the stage from the back of the theater, François glimpsed a solitary figure silhouetted in the relative darkness at the edge of the stage. He recognized the figure as Mario. In no mood to ask his brother the whereabouts of Velia, François was about to retreat when Mario moved to the side. There stood Velia. Mario's body had shielded her. François couldn't take it all in. He blinked, pressed his palms to his eyes, thinking to clear the image from his retina. But when he opened his eyes again the result was worse. Velia's head tilted up to receive Mario's kiss.

François lurched back into the shadows, buried himself in the plush folds of a curtain. She had made her choice. *Had it been so easy?* Only when he was sure he'd mastered his emotions, François made his way to the practice room, taking a wide path around his brother and Velia. Just outside the door to the small room, he found one of the chorines and sent her to find Velia.

"Tell her that I'm waiting to begin our session."

"It's around here somewhere," Renata Cossa muttered *sotto voce* as she rummaged through stacks of dusty props made of balsa wood. Using only the tips of her fingers, she picked up a crescent moon painted to a silver gloss. She set it aside with the five or six stars that she had already found. A flash of movement across the room caught her eye. She held her breath and stared out into the darkness. Her eyes were wide as if they could hear what her ears might miss.

A rat, she told herself silently. *It could be a rat more afraid of you than you are of it. Not likely*, she answered herself. Gathering her strength she raised the lantern high above her head so that its outer edge drenched the interior of the storage room. She cursed that she hadn't asked one of the prop men to do this errand for her. "Is anybody there?" she asked, her voice too high to sound familiar to her. The light did not quite reach the far wall. Yet among all the hard angles and straight lines of box upon box, her eye lit on a dark and irregular shape ensconced in the corner. *It moved.* Her heartbeat accelerated from a trot to a wild staccato gallop. Whatever it was, it was alive and far larger than a mouse. She gasped and lowered the lantern. She was on the verge of either screaming or flying up the stairs when she heard the voice.

The words—if they had been words—were unintelligible. But the movement now was clear. There was no mistaking the unfurling blanket with the scamper of a rodent. The entire bulk shifted and grew before her startled eyes. Had she been placed under a spell she could not have been so fixed to the spot, incapable of flight, incapable of speech.

Her panic lessened only slightly when she saw that it was a man. Again she raised the lantern. The light shimmered and fluttered in her unsure grasp. The face was familiar. Dark eyes and dark unkempt hair, several lazy curls graced his forehead.

"Don't," he said.

This time Renata understood the word. His voice was low and gruff. *Was he whispering? Of course he was. He was hiding in the storage room. He had no business down here among the props.*

"I'm going upstairs now. You should gather your things and get out." Renata judged the distance to the steps and the speed with which she could take them. She made it to the second step before she heard the man groan and a loud thud behind her. She swiveled and peered over in the direction of the bulk. It had shrunk. But she could see a face. The man had slid to the floor and was resting his head against the wall. She could see that his breathing was labored.

Against her better instincts, she backed down one step and called out to the intruder, "Hey, you there. Are you all right?" Getting no response, Renata backed down to the level of the floor. Fear still teased at the fringes of her imagination. She almost wished he'd move again for the anticipation that he might suddenly jump out at her was almost unbearable. "Are you hurt?"

As she came nearer, the man opened his eyes and looked up at her. She hesitated. But when he didn't move to attack, she edged closer. What had seemed dark hair from the distance now came into sharp focus. On one side of his head the hair was matted down with dried blood, a dark brown in the dull light of the lantern.

"You *are* injured. Wait here. I'll call for help."

"No," he said. The word was followed by a broken cry of pain as he tried to lift his arm. He squeezed his eyes shut.

Renata put the lantern down on one of the nearby boxes and stooped to inspect him. "Let me see," she demanded with her instructor's voice. "Is it your head or your arm?"

"Both," he said through clenched teeth.

The arm was pinioned to his side to relieve the pain of having lifted it. Now that she was close to the man, she could see a trail of blood down his jacket. "This might hurt." She rubbed her hands together and flexed her fingers. Then gently she felt the shoulder through the material of his coat.

He bit back a scream.

Startled Renata's hands jerked back to her chest. She took a deep breath to steady her nerves. "It's dislocated. I know it's painful. I can put it back in place if you let me, but it's going to hurt like the devil."

There was a question in her statement, and she studied him to read his answer.

He nodded only slightly.

"This would all be easier if I could call for help," she suggested.

"No," he whispered. He sounded exhausted.

Indeed Renata knew that pain alone could drain a person of his strength. By the look of the man's injuries, she judged that he had been lying there in the storage room for a long while. The blood was caked and dried. She fought back a slight twinge of nausea at the sight and smell of it.

"First you tell me why you're here. I know you, don't I?"

His lungs tugged at the air. He looked out at her from the corner of his eye.

"You're Velia DeVita's brother, aren't you?" she said. "I've seen you hanging about."

She saw she was right. His nod was almost imperceptible. She felt her chest tighten. At first she hadn't noticed his limp or the unnatural way he held his left arm as if it were fastened to his side. It was his right arm, the good one that was dislocated. She couldn't imagine how he had managed to stand. He could barely use the limb.

"What happened to you?" she asked.

"You have to help me," he said. "You can't tell anyone I'm here."

"Why?" But something told her that she might know the answer. "Does this have anything to do with the murder?"

He pushed his back against the wall as if to rise. His face was a mask of horror. "Dead? I didn't mean to kill him."

She scooted away from him, still braced in a squat. The arm that was nearly useless from the injury jerked forward—to plead or to threaten?—but the pain brought it back to rest by his side. Her good sense screamed at her to run for help. The murderer everyone was looking for was inches from her.

"No, no, don't go. I promise," he said. Fighting the pain, he took several deep breaths. "I didn't mean to. I swear. Oh my God, I swear."

Renata didn't know what to do. The man leaned back again, turning his face toward the wall. Great voiceless sobs racked his body.

She could hear the air dragging in and stuttering out. She wished, for his sake, that he could scream. The sound trapped inside seemed almost as painful as his wounds. She waited until the violence of his sorrow abated.

"I really should tell someone," she said. But her resolve was weak.

Had he protested, she might have gathered her purpose and gone for help. But he lay there, propped up against the wall, like a broken doll. Resigned to the pain, he didn't plead or complain.

"When was the last time you had something to drink or eat?"

He shook his head.

"Can't remember?" she asked, in encouragement.

Even though he didn't move, she sensed his answer.

"I'll set that arm for you. Then I'll go find some water. You'll need something on your stomach. But it's best to wait until after I set the arm or you'll probably throw it all up."

Renata stood up and planted her feet wide apart. Before she took hold of his arm, she found, in a nearby box, a relatively clean piece of cloth and wadded it into a tight band. She helped him place it between his teeth. "There. Now brace yourself. This is going to hurt."

When Erik stepped outside the police station, he didn't even notice that they were waiting for him. Instead he set off down the road. More than once, he reached out to steady himself against the wall of a nearby building. Raoul bolted from the carriage and went after him. Meg waited inside and watched Raoul as he escorted her husband to the carriage. His skin was ashen.

Within moments of taking his place next to Meg, Erik's color returned. He shook off the last of the residue of shock. Meg urged Erik to allow them to take him home. Erik insisted that the carriage take him to the theater instead of the estate. Seeing him recovered and knowing in the set of his jaw that he would not be dissuaded, Raoul and Meg had no choice but to keep their misgivings to themselves.

As the carriage pulled up in front of the theater, Meg rose as if to follow Erik to the grand entrance.

"No, I want you to go home," Erik said. He stood, arms braced on either side of the doorway to the carriage, preventing Meg's descent. "I'll check in on the boys and be home early."

That morning, before departing for the station, Erik had told François and Mario to report to the theater. They were to act as if nothing were wrong. The sooner they reestablished business as usual, the sooner rumors would die down.

Meg wanted to argue, but Erik insisted that he preferred to be on his own. He would stay just long enough to make an appearance and to reassure everyone that all was well. Then he would come home.

Reluctantly, Meg complied.

Once inside the Teatro dell'Opera, Erik asked Jacopo to recommend a couple of trustworthy men for a special assignment. Jacopo had several young men who were eager to please—Calvino and Raphael.

Erik had to think. *What would Verduce do next?* It was easy to imagine himself in the lieutenant's shoes. The most logical step was to question those with whom Ricci worked, track down anyone who had a grudge against the journalist, follow the man's routine. He called the young men over and gave them their instructions. They were to wait outside the lieutenant's office, follow him and his assistant, and send word to Erik the moment they knew where they were going.

Forewarned is forearmed. Erik would know what evidence the inspector was collecting against him and find a way to undermine it. Until the actual murderer could be found, Erik would have to derail the inspector's case against him.

CHAPTER 6

Observation and Inference

> *But it is in matters beyond the limits of mere rule that the skill of the analyst is evinced. He makes, in silence, a host of observations and inferences. So, perhaps, do his companions; and the difference in the extent of the information obtained, lies not so much in the validity of the inference as in the quality of the observation.*
>
> *"The Murders of the Rue Morgue," Edgar Allen Poe*

"Cortale, in most cases we despair for lack of information." Verduce collapsed onto his chair. It groaned under the impact. "Oh, my feet are burning." He kicked off his shoes and raised his feet to the surface of his desk.

Cortale avoided smiling at the worn sock on his superior's left foot. The nail of the big toe threatened at any moment to pierce the thinning fabric. The assistant pulled one of the chairs to the side of the desk and sat. He took out his notebook and flipped through several pages of dense notes.

"Where to begin, Cortale. I went to Ricci's office expecting to gather sufficient cause to indict a murderer. If all had gone the way I imagined it, we would be closing this file and moving on to the next case."

The assistant read from the notes. "Let's see. Yes, here it is. 'Costanzi grappled with the victim in an attempt to strangle the life out of him.' Several affirm that he threatened Ricci. Even if Costanzi hadn't meant to kill Ricci there and then, this shows that he hated the man. There's no doubt that there's been a long-running feud between them. We have motive. Isn't this damning evidence?"

Verduce sighed and leaned back in the chair, his arms folded behind his head. "Had Sig. Costanzi not shown up and asked his questions, I might have been content with such obvious proof of motivation and intention."

Cortale nodded.

Verduce and his assistant had spoken to the reporters in the small offices of the Gazette. The basic facts had confirmed what Erik Costanzi had already confessed. He had entered the offices, spoken for a few moments with Ricci. No one had paid attention to the conversation, so no one could report what the two men had discussed. Only when Costanzi reached over the surface of the desk and grabbed Ricci by the throat had the journalist's co-workers dropped their own business and paid attention. Verduce had scowled at the lot of them. He had dragged from them the admission that only a couple of them had tried to intercede physically to stop Costanzi from strangling Ricci. The others had excused themselves by painting Costanzi in the most gruesome and wild terms possible. He was a maniac. They feared for their own lives. Verduce suspected that they were all cowards. They had little personal regard for Ricci and were loath to risk their own safety to save him from a man who appeared to be rich and powerful.

Verduce had more or less sifted through the information in the desk, collecting all the notes and papers that Ricci had left on the surface and in the drawers. Cortale Paccara had taken some of the workers aside and spoken to them about the character of the victim, his habits, his friends and enemies. Verduce had decided to depart for the station with their evidence when Erik Costanzi entered the room.

"Sig. Costanzi, your presence here is unexpected," Verduce had said.

"I imagine so. May I ask what the witnesses have told you about my meeting with Ricci?"

"That's confidential, signore," Verduce had replied. However he was puzzled that Costanzi would appear at the scene of their violent encounter and that he would pretend to question his investigation.

From the day Costanzi presented himself at the station and identified the deceased, the man had intrigued Verduce. There was nothing so confounding as a suspect who told the truth. Erik Costanzi had spoken frankly about his relationship with the victim, making no attempt to hide incriminating information. It had to be the truth because it did not protect the suspect. In spite of his attempt to remain distant, Verduce admired Costanzi. He was either innocent or the most confident and egotistical of murderers. Verduce wanted to believe the former. Yet all the evidence pointed in Costanzi's direction.

"May I ask a few of my own questions?" the tall, enigmatic man had asked.

Verduce had sensed the cautious regard of the journalists in the office. They stared at Costanzi. Actually Verduce recalled that they stared mostly at Costanzi's mask. *What harm could it do?* he had thought. Verduce gave his consent. "But, Sig. Costanzi, I must ask you to refrain from intimidating the witnesses."

Erik bowed in sign that he would comply. "Did I have my hands on Ricci's throat?"

"Yes," they said, one encouraging the other to voice their agreement.

"Let's simplify this, shall we?" Verduce interrupted Erik and beckoned to the witness who had furnished the most complete picture of the encounter. "Sig. Napoli, could you answer Sig. Costanzi's questions? I don't think everyone has to answer. Do you agree, Sig. Costanzi?"

Both men had given their agreement.

"How long did I have my fingers around his neck?"

Verduce scowled, as did Sig. Napoli. No one had asked that particular question. It's relevance seemed nil.

"I...I...think...it was...a few minutes." Napoli looked to his left and to his right for confirmation. The others mumbled various lengths of time ranging from two minutes to five or more.

"Sig. Verduce, did your medical examiner check the throat?"

Verduce had not expected to be included as one of those

interrogated. He refrained from snapping at Costanzi and replied, "Yes, of course. There were bruises around the throat consistent with evidence of strangulation."

"Was he strangled?"

"No." Everyone turned to Cortale Paccara who was at the far end of the room taking notes. Cortale seemed a bit abashed by the attention of so many eyes. He stared down at his notebook as if to read the answer there. "The throat was not crushed. The pressure was enough to cause bruising, but ..."

"Can anyone tell me what names Ricci called me?" All eyes swiveled back to Costanzi.

"Bastard was one," quipped a man from the back of the room.

"I heard worse than that," added another. Several of the men laughed nervously.

"When the other gentleman came in and tried to stop me, did he pull me off?" Costanzi continued.

Verduce smiled against his own will. The man had ice water in his veins.

"He tried."

"Did he?" asked Erik, sounding puzzled. "Did he strike me?"

Several voices muttered disagreement.

"Did he grab me around the waist and pull me off?"

More disagreement.

"Actually the best way to pull a man off another is to wrap one's arm around his throat and pull with one's weight until the man, choking and sputtering, has to release the other one. Don't you agree?"

The men quieted as they tried to imagine the picture Costanzi had drawn.

"Did the other gentleman take his arm and put it around my neck in an effort to pull me back?"

The sound of the negation was uniform.

"No," said Napoli. "He didn't pull at you at all. He just stood there with his hand on your arm, talking at you real quiet."

"So he did not pull me off. I did not strangle Ricci. I released him of my own accord. Had I meant to strangle him to death, he would have died in a minute, perhaps two, either from lack of oxygen or from drowning in his own blood from a crushed larynx. Nor would he have been able to call me such choice names as he did. One cannot speak if one cannot breathe. In this case, the opposite also holds true." Erik nodded to the assembly of witnesses and to Verduce. "I think that's all. Thank you, Tenente Verduce, for letting me speak with the witnesses."

Then Costanzi had turned and walked out of the office.

Now that Verduce and Paccara had returned to the station, Verduce went over and over the information they had gathered at Ricci's office. Putting aside the evidence against Costanzi, a disturbing picture of the victim was emerging. Instead of narrowing down the circle of possibilities, their evidence had brought to light a number of people who had possible motives to attack Ricci. Apparently the man had more enemies than friends.

"Cortale, I'm glad you're a young man," said Verduce. He wiggled his toes and flexed his foot to get the kinks out.

"Why is that, Tenente?"

"Because you have young feet. You're going to need them. We're going to draft a list of suspects. You're going to be doing a lot of walking."

"Could you see who they were?" Verduce leaned back in his chair as if he were simply passing the time. A few paces away, another officer took notes.

The waiter wasn't fooled. Of course he knew who the young men were—at least two of them. But he was weighing the danger of identifying Sig. Costanzi's young sons to the officer investigating a recent murder.

"It was dark, you see."

The officer nodded. He laced his fingers together and waited.

"They had these scarves or handkerchiefs tied around their faces." The waiter mimicked the act of covering the lower part of his face with a cloth that he fastened behind his head. "And hats," he said, in an afterthought, as if that piece of information were a true godsend. How could the officer expect him to know that two of the rogues were François and Mario Costanzi? Just a little innocent fun, that was all it was. It was only significant because the man they had decided to torment ended up dead, his face caved in, in an alleyway in the vicinity of their father's opera house.

"What exactly did these young men say to Sig. Ricci?"

"Just…insults, vulgarities." He hoped this would suffice, but the officer listened as if there must be more. "They…they called him names, told him that he should leave town, that he should use his column to wipe his…bottom."

"Bottom?" The officer's lip curled up in the corner, and he chuckled. "His column, did you say?"

"Yes, they called him an envious sod who wrote reviews to make himself look clever."

"So these young men knew that they were baiting Paolo Ricci, the journalist and theater critic."

The waiter felt the blood rise in his face.

The officer's assistant jotted in his notebook for several seconds.

"These men jostled the victim, did they not?"

"Well, I wouldn't say that they…"

"Did Ricci fight back against his attackers?"

The waiter was no longer hot. He shivered. The scene the officer was painting was not the scene he had meant to describe.

"I have to protest, Sig. Verduce."

"Oh, have I misunderstood something?"

"The boys were just having fun."

"They jostled Sig. Ricci. Is that not so?"

The waiter didn't protest.

"He didn't fight back?" Verduce continued.

"Well, he waved his arms around a few times."

"Didn't you say there were three of them—three young men? They surrounded him, did they not?"

"Young men? Just boys, really."

"What is the difference between three older boys and three young men? I'm confused."

The waiter wiped his mouth with the back of his hand. His forehead was glossy in the hot light of the room. "Look, Tenente

Verduce, I could tell they were just boys. They were just playing around with him. You know how it is. You were young once."

"My wife would beg to differ. Please, let's return to the facts. The young men attacked the victim?"

"They pushed him a few times, but nothing meant to…"

"Did they threaten Sig. Ricci?"

"Threaten?"

"Did they tell him to leave town?"

"They may have warned…"

"Warned him to do what?"

"They didn't mean to.…"

"You knew what they meant to do?"

"Yes, it was clear that they…"

"How did you know they meant Sig. Ricci no harm?"

"Because their father would have had their hides had he…" The waiter slammed his mouth closed, but the words had already escaped.

"Their father? So you know who their father is? And I would assume that this must mean that you know who the boys are?"

The waiter looked frantically about him in the hopes of a catastrophe to save him from the next few minutes.

"Sig. Lambre, failure to cooperate with the authorities is in itself a crime. Did you not know that?" Sig. Verduce's tone was patient, as if he were schooling a young child in a complex subject.

The waiter lowered his gaze to his lap. He could only hope that what he was about to say would not reach Sig. Costanzi's ears. He almost thought prison might be preferable to Sig. Erik Costanzi's anger.

"Look, Sig. Verduce," he said. "Let me start over. I know the boys. They're good boys."

"Go on."

"Ricci is…well…there are a lot of people who don't like him."

"I think 'didn't like him' would be more appropriate, don't you? Why is it that he was disliked by so many?"

"He is…was…a sarcastic bastard. No one was good enough to lick his boots. He wrote about the cultural scene, in particular the opera season."

"Did he write about young boys having fun?"

"No, of course not. He wrote reviews about the Teatro dell'Opera."

"And these boys are?"

"Two of them I did recognize," the waiter confessed.

"In spite of the scarves and hats?" The officer smiled.

"Don Erik Costanzi's two oldest sons, François and Mario."

"What do they have against Sig. Ricci?"

"Ricci has been attacking their father in his column for years. He's always been known for his sarcasm, but lately he's been vicious."

"These sons of Costanzi are big boys, are they not?"

"They're just boys."

"Yes. Just boys. You keep reminding me of that." The officer paused and studied the waiter. "They were out on the streets of Rome well past a boy's bedtime, weren't they?"

The waiter didn't have to answer.

"These boys had been drinking. These boys were drunk. Weren't they?"

"Sig. Verduce, how would I know that?" The waiter shrugged his shoulders and attempted a weak imitation of a laugh.

"You work in a café. You serve the crowds until the early hours of the morning. My officers have often been called to your neighborhood to deal with disturbances. You know when someone has been drinking." The former easy manner of the officer disappeared. "Were the young men drunk when they accosted Sig. Ricci, the victim?"

The waiter hung his head. From the window of the café he had seen the boys harassing Ricci. He had come out with the thick club he used to break up fights and pulled one of the boys to the side. He remembered the smell of strong drink in the air.

"Perhaps."

"Perhaps?"

"Yes, they were a bit tipsy," he answered.

"Thank you, Sig. Lambre, for your cooperation."

"Carlotta? Is that you?" Meg bent to look inside the wardrobe.

"Shhhh," Carlotta whispered. She squatted on the floor at the back of the deep wardrobe closet between two pairs of satin slippers and a pair of walking boots.

"What on earth are you doing in my wardrobe, Carlotta?" Meg stood and folded her arms under her breasts, waiting for Carlotta to crawl out from among her costumes.

"I'm hiding," she said, making no move to unfold herself and depart from the wardrobe.

"From whom?"

"You don't know? The policeman, the one who is investigating Ricci's murder, is in the auditorium. He's come to ask questions."

Meg's arms loosened and fell to her sides. She blanched. Feeling lightheaded, she sat down on her chair beside the vanity.

"Ah hah! You see? I can draw my feet in. You can sit over there." Carlotta crammed her feet in as far as she could toward her body and invited Meg to join her inside the hiding place.

In spite of the momentary panic Meg had felt, she couldn't help smiling at the older woman. "It's disturbing, I admit. But there's no use hiding in there."

"I don't want them to question me."

"Why not?"

"They think the Phantom murdered the maggot."

Meg fought the chill that tugged at her limbs.

"You must stop thinking of Erik in those terms," she warned. But her thoughts were only half on Carlotta. Erik took every opportunity to reassure her that the circumstantial evidence was damning but that the lieutenant was a fair and an intelligent man. He would see through to the truth.

Carlotta waved her hand at Meg in exasperation. "Here, with you, I don't mince words. He's the Phantom and will always be the Phantom. How do we know that he wasn't up to his old tricks?"

"Carlotta, my husband did not kill Ricci."

Carlotta huffed. She shook her head as if annoyed. Then she met Meg's disapproving gaze. "I know, I know, I know. The Phantom did not kill him. But the police suspect him. They are going to throw him in jail."

"God help us if they do." Meg folded her arms on the vanity and buried her head against them. The thought of Erik wasting away in a prison cell was more than she could bear. If Erik were locked away, as he had been years ago in Paris, it would kill him.

"That's why," said Carlotta, grunting as she stuck her feet outside the wardrobe, grabbed the edge of the door, and pulled herself free. She battled for a moment with the clothing, but emerged largely unscathed into Meg's dressing room. "That's why...," she repeated now that the clothes weren't muffling her voice, "...I can't be questioned."

Meg tilted her face and looked at the bizarre woman with her right eye. Carlotta's dress was twisted and her hair had fallen from its complicated chignon. She looked entirely lopsided, and Meg thought for one moment that this was the true Carlotta.

"Why?"

"Because they will ask me about your husband and in my mind I will be thinking, 'the Phantom, the Phantom, the Phantom.' What if I say it out loud? What if I say something stupid like, 'He didn't kill *this* one'? What if they make me tell them who Erik Costanzi really is?"

"Was," groaned Meg. "When are you going to accept that he's not the Phantom?" Her voice had risen in her exasperation.

"Shhhhh, you silly girl." Carlotta screwed up her face and placed her index finger before her lips and shushed Meg several times. Then she mouthed the words, 'They're going to hear you.'

"I thought you were afraid that they thought you were the murderer."

Carlotta raised her hands up in a gesture to indicate that what Meg had said was irrelevant. "Naldo, I mean Rinaldo, explained it to me. I have a...what they call a...it's a legal term for.... I was somewhere else when the maggot died."

"An alibi?"

"Yes, that's what I have. And besides Naldo said no one would believe that I could be vicious enough to beat a man to death. And besides that, he reminded me that I don't like blood."

"Oh I see. Clearly you're safe."

"Si. I am not in danger, but the Phantom…Erik…is. We have to protect him."

"How do you suggest we do that, Carlotta?"

"Come. We hide in the wardrobe until Verde goes."

Meg smiled at Carlotta. She didn't bother to correct her on the lieutenant's name. She just sat back and watched the woman crawl back inside the wardrobe. Once Carlotta was inside, instead of joining her, Meg said as she closed the door without latching it, "I may join you later. But first I think I need to be with Erik."

Meg had arrived too late. Tenente Verduce and his officers had set up their interrogation in an upper salon reserved for modest parties of thirty to forty guests. The room was sufficiently large for a buffet and even a quartet. The middle of the room could accommodate a small dance. Chairs lined the walls, awaiting the next occasion for their use. The police had arranged a few around a service table in the center of the room. The sounds of men's voices rumbled, reverberating off the high ceilings and rebounding in the vacuous interior.

The inspector hesitated when he saw Costanzi's wife standing in the doorway. She looked for a moment like an oil painting, beautiful except for the obvious signs of worry on her face.

She did not wait for permission to enter. One of the police rose as if to stop her, but Verduce raised a hand and the officer assumed his position once more near the door.

"Signora Costanzi, you are welcome, but I warn you that you must not speak."

Meg glanced at her husband whose eyes stubbornly refused to look her way. She nodded and accepted a chair a young man offered her. He was, like the lieutenant, dressed in a modest suit, not in a uniform similar to the other officers in the room. He sat down again near the table at an angle so that he could see Erik's face. Across the way from her, to the left and slightly behind her husband, Meg noticed another man. He sat, his hand poised and intent, over an official notebook. He was evidently charged with transcribing the interrogation.

"You're correct, Sig. Costanzi. The deceased had many enemies. But only a handful had ever threatened his life." As the lieutenant spoke, the man positioned behind her husband took notes with amazing dexterity.

Not far from Meg's side, the man who had offered her a chair took out a small tablet and flipped the pages until he came to the place he wanted. He jotted a few words, and then fixed his attention on her husband. He studied Erik as if he could pick up clues by the subtle tilt of the head or the stray movements of a hand. Meg found herself examining Erik's body, trying to guess what the man at her side was assuming from her husband's stiff posture, the folded hands in his lap, the unconscious clench of his jaw when he wasn't speaking.

She told herself that only she knew Erik's body well enough to read the signs. He was tense, but he was in control. He was wary and being cautious, listening intently for more than the surface meaning of the inspector's questions and statements.

"I didn't realize that it was the law that a murderer had to announce his intention to kill before he acted upon it."

Verduce's lip curled for a second. "I assure you we are investigating even the least likely suspects."

"Am I to consider myself one of the latter?"

Verduce leaned forward. He planted his elbows on the table and folded his hands in front of his chin. When the lieutenant glanced her way, Meg felt dizzy. She saw a flicker of Erik's eye, too.

"Sig. Costanzi, I regret that I will need you to tell us where you were the night of the murder."

Erik hesitated. He seemed to be considering whether or not to answer. "I was with a dying friend."

"I see, Sig. Costanzi." The lieutenant's face was drawn, without a hint of a smile. In a serious tone, he added, "Let's hope for your sake that your friend has recovered somewhat and can vouch for your whereabouts."

Erik was silent.

"You will give the particulars to my assistant, Sig. Paccara."

"That's impossible."

Verduce was genuinely shocked. He recovered himself quickly. "Are you refusing to cooperate?"

"No, not at all. I simply can't give you an address or clear directions. I will have to take you there." Erik pulled his watch from his pocket.

It had been a gift from Marcelo. Meg wished with all her heart that her father-in-law and her mother were back from their travels.

"I am free at the moment if that would suit you, Sig. Verduce." Erik placed the watch back inside his vest pocket and rose from the chair.

Verduce rose a second later and motioned to his officers. "Show us the way, Sig. Costanzi."

"Why didn't you ask to speak with the sons?" Cortale Paccara whispered to Verduce as they sat back in the carriage.

"The suspect is in the other carriage, Cortale. I don't think you have to whisper." Verduce smiled and accommodated himself more comfortably on the cushioned seat. The carriage had been offered by Sig. Costanzi and was upholstered in a lush velvet fabric. Verduce settled back to enjoy the ride.

Mildly put out by Verduce's reminder that the suspect, the French count, and several officers were riding in a separate conveyance, Cortale cleared his throat. "I assumed we were going to interrogate Costanzi's sons."

"Ah, don't forget that one of them was probably the count's son. Didn't you find out that the Chagnys have a son about the same age as Costanzi's boys?"

Cortale nodded. "Maybe that's why the Frenchman is always hovering about. He's protecting his son," he suggested.

"Bah. Lambre insisted that they were harmless. He confirmed that he sent them on their way. Ricci had already set off in the opposite direction."

"He didn't see them get into a carriage," Cortale said.

"No, he didn't. But I spoke with my wife about this. Concetta says the boys are innocent."

Cortale was accustomed to Verduce's references to his wife of thirty-five years. In matters of interpretation, he often bowed to her wisdom. Still Cortale couldn't stop himself from arguing. "Perhaps the fact that they are boys influenced her?"

"Of course it did. That and the fact that there were three of them, and the fact that they were outside a café where many of the customers and the waiters know them and at least one of the fathers. Not to mention the fact that they jostled Ricci and called him names."

When Verduce saw his assistant's frown, he decided a clearer explanation was necessary. "It's possible that the young men circled round and followed Ricci. It's also possible that they stoked their anger again and pummeled him to death."

Cortale relaxed against his seat.

"It's possible," repeated Verduce. Then he looked out the window and observed the landscape for a while. "But it's not likely. They spent their anger, were caught by someone who could get word back to Costanzi, and were told to go home. They are young, not children, but not men either. Yet I agree that they probably scared themselves and went home." Seeing that Cortale was still not convinced, Verduce folded his arms across his chest and continued, "Something more tangible is what you want? Bene. Fine. Consider this. Three young men—strong men—a bit drunk and very angry follow this man. This is closer to your reconstruction of the events, no? How far is the Café from the Teatro dell'Opera?"

Cortale calculated. "About ten minutes."

"Ten minutes by carriage. Walking it would be more like twenty minutes or a half hour. Do you agree?"

"Yes, depending on the speed and the stride."

"Of course. Let's accept twenty minutes because they're young and they're excited."

Cortale nodded with caution, sensing something he hadn't expected was coming his way.

"Why? Why do these excited, angry young men wait for twenty minutes? They walk and they walk—for twenty minutes, mind you—and then not a street away from the Teatro dell'Opera they ambush and murder him. Is that more likely than my version?"

Cortale blushed.

"Another point to consider. There are three of them. They are angry and drunk. They lash out at Ricci. There are multiple blows. Their anger won't leave them until they destroy their victim. They kill him with a club or a stick. Yet nearly all their blows strike the victim on the face alone. How can three young men—drunk and enraged—beat up this man and hit him only on the face? Does that make sense?"

"Is that what Donna Concetta said?"

"Well, no. Nonetheless what she did say made sense. Concetta knows boys. We had seven, you know."

Indeed Cortale did know. Romulo Verduce's sons were grown, married, with children of their own. Cortale had met them all on several occasions when Verduce invited him to dinner on Sundays.

"Then why did you act as if the testimony concerning the boys was something that we could use?"

"We can. Trust me, Cortale. It will serve a purpose. But only if we need it."

Erik was glad to have Raoul's company. Two of the officers sat inside the carriage with Erik and Raoul while at least two others were seated at the foot of the carriage and next to the driver. Erik would have liked some privacy. As it was, he didn't feel comfortable speaking with his friend. Never able to hide his thoughts, Raoul worried his bottom lip with the edge of his hand and kept his eyes on the landscape passing by the window. He was concerned. Not an unreasonable reaction to the recent events. Erik, too, was on edge.

Once he established his alibi beyond suspicion, Erik would no longer be the insect under the lieutenant's magnifying glass. He would be able to get back to running the opera house. The current production was winding down, and Rinaldo's opera was not yet ready. Then there was the piece on which Renata Cossa and he were working. Nothing significant could be accomplished as long as a shadow of suspicion lingered over him or his theater.

Erik had hoped that it wouldn't come to this. It was foolish to think that Verduce would not demand proof of his alibi. The danger was that Erik didn't know what might happen when he brought Verduce to Sabia. Erik had made peace with her. But once the police officer explained that Erik was suspected of murder, would Sabia regret her pact of silence? Everything about his past could come tumbling out. He had murdered before.

He could even imagine hearing Sabia's voice, the deep resonance of which would seal his fate as if judgment had been handed down from Jehovah himself. *Though shalt not kill.* The commandment was clear. It did not come with provisos. *Thou shalt honor thy father and thy mother.* Guilty again. Sabia knew his secrets. She might save him from one murder to convict him for another.

Raoul strained outside the small window to see up the road. "Over the crest of this next hill, did you say?"

Erik looked out the side window. "Yes," he said. The officers called out the instructions to the driver. The carriage slowed.

Outside Erik's window, the vineyard stretched for miles. The plants, green and heavy with purple grapes, lined the rolling hills. Vosh had taken him beyond the limits of Rome, out into the countryside, past vineyards and olive groves, to a clearing, a fallow field, where the modest caravan had pitched its tents. Even in the darkness, with a dull diffused light trapped by a low layer of clouds, Erik had watched the route, taken note of landmarks along the road so that he might find his way back. Over the crest of the hill, a meager caravan of rickety wagons had dotted the clearing. So few were they that, from the distance, they had looked like a pack of wild dogs huddled together for warmth around a campfire.

The carriage reached the top of the hill and began its descent. Raoul craned his neck, his head outside the carriage window, searching the side of the road.

"It's on this side," Erik said, working from memory. Raoul settled back against the seat and looked past Erik through the opposite window. They could see the last row of the vineyard give way, then a small copse of trees. Dread and anticipation warred in equal measures in Erik's mind as the carriage slowed and came to a halt.

Before anyone could know what was happening, Erik bounded from the carriage. Raoul stumbled after him, but he held onto the carriage and looked out across the open field for a moment to steady his nerves. The second carriage, bearing the lieutenant and his assistant, pulled up and stopped.

Erik was unaware of the men rushing up from behind him. He searched the horizon. He sank to his knees. The field was an unbroken expanse of mottled green.

They had gone.

Someone squatted beside him.

"Erik." It was a voice he recognized. It was soothing. But Erik couldn't wrench his eyes away from the emptiness.

"They were here," he muttered.

At his side, Raoul urged him to stand. Erik let his friend help him to his feet.

"Vosh brought me," Erik insisted as if Raoul had argued with him. "Sabia's tent was over this way." Erik took several steps forward, then stopped. *What use was it?* They had gone.

On the wind the police officers' voices carried.

"I thought we'd see the other freaks."

"Except for this one, there weren't no fucking freaks."

Erik hurled himself at the voice. Raoul grabbed him under his arms, locking his fists against Erik's breastbone. One of the officers who had spoken had raised his firearm and now leveled it at Erik's mask.

Verduce struck the barrel of the firearm, forcing the man to aim at the ground.

Erik strained to break Raoul's hold, but he couldn't think straight. In the officers' expression, he saw the same disgust, the same fascination. He had seen this face peering in at him, a child raised to be a monster, from the other side of the bars. This face had been among the mob with their torches as they searched the vaults and among the witnesses that had anticipated his last breath on the scaffold in the public square. Freak, that's what they had said. Freak was what they had thought and what they still thought. The mask didn't change the facts. It was merely the curtain behind which the freak show played.

Sabia, Vosh, Erik—they all belonged in those shabby wagons, were part of that mawkish caravan that stole across the back roads on the fringes of civilization and pitched their tents, sang their heathen songs, practiced their strange *danse macabre*. Again and again, the freak performed his parody of humanity.

Look, come see the bizarre story of the disobedient son who killed his father, not his brother, and was marked with the sign of Cain. Watch him as he pretends to walk on two legs like a man. Watch while he pretends he has a right to seek peace, if not happiness, forgiveness, if not love.

Sabia, Vosh, all those poor creatures banded together not by love but by the common disgust of those who shunned them. And he stood somewhere between, not part of either world.

"Let me go," he insisted. His voice, husky and low, sounded exhausted.

Raoul's hold loosened, and Erik broke away from him, staggering, his chest heaving.

They had gone. They had abandoned him—lost somewhere between one world and another.

The officer Erik had meant to attack stared at him belligerently, the muzzle of his firearm resting across his forearm. Cortale Paccara drew up beside Raoul. Erik could tell the two men were talking about him. A wave of nausea overtook him, but he swallowed it, forced his gorge to settle.

"I can hear you," Erik said.

The voices behind him quieted.

Verduce was walking out toward the center of the field, kicking at the scrubby ground cover, inspecting as he went, his eyes cast down in search of something. Erik strode out past Verduce. He didn't stop until he came to the place where the caravan had staked their tents. Verduce came up alongside him. On the ground the lieutenant could just make out the holes—too cylindrical to have been made by an animal—where the stakes had been pounded into the soft dirt.

"Here. This is where her tent was."

Verduce raised an eyebrow. Until this moment, Costanzi had not revealed the sex of his friend. But the lieutenant asked no questions, sensing it was better to let Costanzi talk. Verduce stooped and feathered his fingers through the grass. The plants were already springing back after having been crushed under the weight of wagons, animals, and people. The outline of the fair had left its ghost-like imprint, and Verduce could almost imagine what Costanzi had seen—a circle of wagons and inside the circle the tents.

"Do you see it?" asked Erik.

Verduce stood and brushed his hands on his trousers. "Yes, I see it. They must have left a few days ago."

Erik smirked. It hadn't occurred to him until this moment. Sabia had waited just long enough for him to visit her. They must have left that very day, shortly after he woke and made his way back into the city.

"Tenente Verduce." One of the officers called out to the lieutenant. In tow, the officer led two field hands from the nearby vineyard.

Erik watched from a distance as Verduce spoke with the men. Raoul glanced nervously his way. Erik turned his back to the men so that he would not have to see them.

The day was warm. The wind gusted and blew his hair loose about his face, but he could only feel it tease at the line of his jaw, the lower part of his face that wasn't hidden under his mask. He breathed deeply the smells of grass, wood, and manure. He closed his eyes and tilted his face toward the sun. But the darkness made him dizzy. He opened his eyes and looked out across the field, toward the distant hills, toward the horizon, out into infinity.

Later, in the carriage, as they returned to Rome, Raoul told him what the field hands had said. One of the foreigners—for those who called the caravan their home were always foreign—had died. They had left late that night, stealing away in the darkness as if they were afraid of pursuit.

"Where did they bury her?" asked Erik.

"They didn't know. They didn't even know it was a woman. One of them thought perhaps they buried her out there somewhere in the field."

Erik was grateful that the lieutenant had allowed Erik and Raoul to journey back alone. One of the officers road with the driver, but otherwise they were unattended. Nor had Verduce interrogated him, as Erik assumed he would. Raoul must have been thinking along the same lines, for when he spoke that was what he asked.

"Why didn't Verduce arrest you?"

Erik shook his head. "I can't say. Perhaps he's waiting for me to confess."

Raoul rested for a few moments. Erik stared blindly out the window.

"What concrete evidence does he have?" asked Raoul. "He knows you hated each other. He knows you threatened Ricci—more than once. But he has no witness to the murder. He has no murder weapon."

"He knows that I was out all night. I've no alibi."

"But he saw the proof that the fair had been in the clearing."

"I could have known that without having spent the entire night out there. I could have gone there before. The field hands didn't recognize me. Why would they? The only people to see me there are gone."

"What about the driver?"

"It was one of their own wagons. They took me out and brought me back."

"Did anyone see you arrive at the estate?"

"No. I took them by surprise. I slipped in before they knew I was back. The wagon had already left."

Raoul leaned forward and let his head sag between his arms for a few moments. "It's your word against theirs, I guess."

"If they find nothing to exonerate me and no evidence to shift blame to someone else, their suspicions are probably enough to put me away in prison for the rest of my life or to have me executed. I'm having great difficulty deciding which option I prefer."

CHAPTER 7

A Tangled Web

Oh, what a tangled web we weave,
When first we practice to deceive.

Marmion, Sir Walter Scott

"Cortale, stop pouting. I've explained why I haven't arrested Sig. Costanzi. It's premature."

"But he has no alibi," said Cortale. "He's by far the most likely suspect we have."

"So rash. You would like to look at what is possible and what is likely and be done with it. This case is not an easy one. There are many things that puzzle me. Sig. Costanzi won't escape. If he is the man we want, we will have him."

"Motive and opportunity. Didn't you tell me that those are powerful proofs?"

"Yes, Cortale. But if you were going to murder someone, would you go about the city a few days beforehand announcing it to everyone?"

"He's irrational. It was a crime of passion."

"Perhaps. But it strikes me as not our suspect's style."

"Style?"

Verduce could hear the sarcasm in his assistant's voice. "I know that it's not rational, but it doesn't fit. The crime does not fit this man. Now, let's go over the information we've collected so far."

"Sig. Costanzi…"

"Not about Sig. Costanzi. What else have we found out?"

"There are rumors that Ricci hired two men to rough up one of the performers at the Teatro dell'Opera."

"Really? Did anyone make a report of an assault?"

"No. No record."

"Who was it that was supposed to have been 'roughed up' as you put it?"

"Signorina Venedetti."

Verduce leaned forward, his brow furrowed. "A woman? Venedetti, Venedetti, is that the new one?"

"No, it's the older woman, red hair."

"Ah, yes, I know which one she is. She's a very…shapely woman." When Verduce saw Cortale looking at him strangely, he added, "Just an observation. Concetta doesn't need to hear it, does she?"

"Of course not." Cortale hid his smile and acted as if he were searching his notes. "Oh, by the way, I forgot to mention that I pieced together the scraps of paper we found at the scene. It appears to be a review of some sort."

"Good. Let me see it."

Cortale went to the cabinet next to the door. He pulled out a large envelope and opened it over Verduce's desk. Out slid a flat sheet upon which scraps of dirtied and wrinkled paper had been glued. The original text was nearly complete, missing only a few words in a couple of places. Verduce took his magnifying glass from the drawer and inspected the evidence.

"Yes, it is a review. Was it published?" Verduce asked.

"No, I checked it against the gazette reviews by Ricci. It hasn't been published."

"It's not a particularly nice review, but then again Ricci had a nasty streak." Verduce laid the magnifying glass on the table and asked, "Do we know who this Velia DeVita is?"

"I spoke with several of the girls working at the theater. She started as a dancer and then was handpicked by Costanzi to take a small role in the current opera."

"Is it possible that he's having an affair with the girl?"

"Well, there were a few rumors, but it sounded like sour grapes to me. There is something mysterious about her comings and goings. I had Gregorio check her out. He followed her to an inn, the Boar and Bow. She's singing on the side."

"Needs the money?"

"A drunk for a father and a brother who's unfit for work."

"Unfit?"

"He was injured on a frigate. Got a bad limp. Looks like he lives off his sister. I spoke about the girl with one of the staff that works the flies. He mentioned the brother comes and harasses her for money."

"Sad." Verduce was trying to recall something Lambre at Il Café di Mondo had said. "I think I want to talk with Sig. Lambre again. Bring your notebook."

"Always," said Cortale. "Oh, by the way, I also heard that one of Costanzi's boys fancies her."

Verduce smiled over his shoulder at his young assistant. "Pretty, is she?"

Cortale pulled up short. His face turned a soft pink. "Yes, I suppose you could say she's attractive."

"Well, it's no crime to fancy a pretty young girl, Cortale. If it were, our prison cells would be stuffed to the brim with the guilty. Let's go. It might be time to speak to the young Costanzi brothers. But first let's have a drink at Il Café di Mondo."

Verduce read the reconstructed review again. Someone had torn it into pieces. Velia DeVita's name was prominent in the text. Through unsavory innuendo, the review suggested that the young girl was little better than a prostitute.

From Ricci's work habits, Verduce knew it was unlikely that Ricci himself would tear up a complete draft of a review and toss the pieces to the ground. In the journalist's desk drawers, Verduce had found copy after copy of various articles that Ricci had apparently meant to keep. Either he liked his own work to the point that he wouldn't part with even an imperfect version of an article or he feared someone might come upon discarded fragments of his work and plagiarize them in another newspaper or journal.

It was rather careless of the murderer to leave the fragments next to the body. Too careless.

Chiara Greco had been watching Renata Cossa go back and forth all day between the downstairs storage rooms and various places in the theater. Something in the furtive way the dance instructor waited before she descended the stairs put Chiara on the alert. Everyone was nervous these days in the Teatro dell'Opera. Chiara had made up her mind to resign several times only to change it back again at the last moment. She did not like the way Sig. Costanzi manipulated her. Putting the new girl with his own son and encouraging them to practice *her* role was obvious, albeit effective, in pushing Chiara to prove to the artistic director what a fine singer she could be. She had sung better the last several weeks than she ever had at her previous venue. If Costanzi weren't so distracted by all the brouhaha surrounding that dead man, she was sure he'd regret having treated her so insolently.

Unable to resist her curiosity another minute, Chiara Greco snuck as quietly as she could to the head of the stairs. The soft whispers echoed up the stairwell, the words too imprecise to make out, but one thing was clear. Renata Cossa was not alone. She was with a man. Chiara leaned forward but when she saw a shadow darken the wall at the bottom of the stairs, she pulled back and looked for some place to hide.

Renata climbed the steps, carrying a tray with an empty bottle and plate.

Was it possible? Renata Cossa was hiding someone in the storage room. Who could it be? A lover? Why? Chiara Greco could only accept one possibility. Nothing else made sense. Renata Cossa was hiding the murderer.

François knew the music by heart. Yet he kept his eyes fixed on the black curls, dots, and lines of the score. With a life of their own, his fingers raced across the keys. Velia's voice strained to match the tempo at which François played. Suddenly it stuttered and stopped.

François risked a glance in her direction. She was panting, her hand rubbing at a charm that dangled from her necklace. He felt a curious sensation—an electric current surged through him. As if she were rubbing him instead of the charm, he became aroused.

To divert his and her attention from his discomfort, he asked her why she had stopped in the middle of the aria. His question was rational, devoid of emotion, devoid of criticism. Her reply caught him off guard. She was angry.

"The pace is too fast. We've never practiced it at that tempo." She pointed to the notations in the margin of her copy. "It does not say 'presto' in my notes."

"I'm sorry. You're right. But it is to be sung 'espressivo.'"

"I thought I was singing with expression."

"Let's try again. This time I'll be careful to watch the tempo." François shifted on the bench, placed his fingers on the keys, played the introduction. When they were discussing the tempo, Velia had drawn near the piano bench. She had not stepped back to her usual position to the side, a few feet away from François. Instead, she was practically at François's shoulder.

Mario and he had not spoken of their mutual attraction to Velia. Since the day he saw them kissing in the wings, François had given up any attempt to deepen his relationship with Velia DeVita. He focused on the music, treating Velia with the utmost respect and professional decorum. He congratulated himself that he was able to control his wayward heart. The first couple of sessions had gone well, but today his hands had begun to sweat the moment Velia entered the room. François couldn't understand why she would have such an effect on him in this instance and not before. Was it the perfume she was wearing or the fact that the pale chiffon gown matched her eyes or the way she had pinned her hair lazily in a chignon from which dark, honey blond curls escaped? His eye returned again and again to one such curl as it grazed the pale skin of her collarbone.

His fingers slipped off a key, hitting a discordant note. He jerked away from the piano as if he had broken it.

"I'm sorry," he said again. His fingers hovered over the keys. Turning on the bench, he looked up at her. "Could you resume your normal place, signorina?"

Velia raised her eyebrows. Without a word, she moved to the side of the piano. François thought perhaps it had been a mistake to ask her to move. From where she stood, she had a direct view of his face. If he raised his chin, even a fraction of an inch, he could look straight into her hazel eyes, watch her mouth make the sounds, see her breasts lift as she took in the air she needed.

He concentrated on the sheet of music in front of him as if he needed to remind himself of which piece they were rehearsing. He began to play. She began to sing.

The velvet strains of her voice lulled him. He wanted to imagine that she sang to him the words of love in the aria. But there was no emotion in the sounds she made. She sang, but it lacked fire. Angry he reasoned that it was because she sang to him that there was no passion. If only he could hear desire in her notes, if he could then pretend that she sang the love song to him, it would soothe the emptiness that had plagued him since the day she chose Mario.

"Signorina, you're supposed to be in love." Still playing, he darted a look in her direction. He raised his voice so that his words were audible over the music. "Listen to the words. Sing as if you meant them. Imagine his face. Imagine looking into the face of the man you love. See him. Sing to him. Do you see him?"

Her voice took on an emotional weight it hadn't carried before. François's gaze drifted up to see Velia looking down at him. Her eyes glistened. Her cheeks were red, her lips swollen. When he saw her eyes fill with tears, he stopped. Velia didn't. She continued to sing the final verse a capella. She sang it to François who sat mute and dumb. As the final note echoed between them, Velia stepped forward.

François had seen her kiss Mario. She had already chosen. But she laid her hand on his shoulder. Confused he rose from the bench and walked to the other side of the room.

"That was...was...much better, signorina," he said, his heart bursting in his chest. "I didn't realize what a good actress you were."

Before Velia could reply, Renata Cossa knocked sharply on the door even as she opened it. "Velia, I've been looking for you everywhere. I need to speak with you."

François returned to the piano and gathered the sheet music. "That's fine. Signorina DeVita and I are finished. I'll see you tomorrow, signorina. Ciao, Signorina Cossa."

As the carriage entered the crowded streets of the city, Raoul stared out the window at the rush of pedestrians. Beside him, Erik had withdrawn into his own thoughts. Both men were silent, for there were no facile words that could set Erik's mind at rest.

Barraged by images of a cold, dank cell, Erik leaned back upon the squabs of the carriage and closed his eyes.

Was it so difficult to choose between death and confinement? Erik pondered the question. Wouldn't anyone prefer life over certain death? Few had come as close to the hangman's noose as the Phantom had and lived to tell the tale. The terror of execution on climbing the steps to the gibbet had been allayed by the assurance that it was a sham. Erik had not really faced execution, had he? And even so he had quaked in his boots that morning. He had strained to keep from resisting the guards as they led him to the top of the platform. He had nearly shat his trousers, like a mewling infant, when they put the noose around his neck. He had not trusted that the Count de Chagny would willingly break the law and arrange for a rescue of the Phantom of the Opera. And yet Raoul had kept his word. He had dug him free from his grave even as Erik had blacked out from panic and lack of air.

His knowledge of execution might be flawed, but he knew well the agony of confinement.

He recalled the thin, dirty cot. He remembered shivering so violently that he could not sleep. He had walked the few feet up and down between the stone wall and the iron bars to keep his blood from freezing in his veins. He had forced himself to breathe through his mouth to avoid the most pungent of the odors that inhabited the cell like despised partners in crime. The smell of his own body at first made eating the meager, greasy porridge they fed him twice daily, impossible to stomach. Only when hunger dug at his gut with the force of a dull blade did Erik quell his nausea and eat with his fingers, his dirty fingers, the sloppy gruel. For a moment he would know peace until the churning in his gut would send him to the open bucket to relieve the hot, burning waste of his bowels. Weak and disgusted with his own animal existence, he would pull the thin mattress from the cot, using it as a barrier and blanket, and hunker down in a corner. Eventually the heat from his own breath and body would warm the small sanctuary so that he could close his eyes and sleep and dream of the safety of the vaults below the opera house. As sleep deepened, his hold on the thin mattress would give way. If he was fortunate it would simply rest against him, but most often it would fall away and leave him exposed to the icy air of the night and early morning. His breath would rise like tiny white clouds as his teeth chattered and his hands turned blue.

He had sung. It was his only music, his voice, his only instrument. It helped to silence the scream building up inside him. It helped to fill the empty painful hours, the unrelenting loneliness. The guards had been kind to let him sing, but when it was late at night, they would eventually strike the bars with their clubs and in a voice that was not kind or cruel tell him to pipe down and let the others sleep. But he sang anyway, in a soft and quiet voice only he could hear. He mistakenly thought that the music would save him. But it did not always work its magic.

After several weeks as a prisoner, new torments assailed him. He had grown accustomed to the filth, to the stench, to the cold, to the pain in his fingers that the inspector had cruelly twisted and broken. But he could not become accustomed to the humiliation and he could not, in the end, withstand the loneliness. The whippings continued sporadically, the taunting from Leroux and his handpicked guards punctuated his days.

Erik had thought his body would surrender and waste away. He expected illness to ravage it. In this hope he saw the end of suffering, a modest victory. He waited for his lungs to congest, for a fever to sap his energy, for a gangrenous rot to burrow into his wounds. But below the *layer of dirt, below the bruises and lacerations, Erik touched firm, vibrant, healthy, rebellious flesh. His body became his master. It forced him to eat the food even when the meat tasted rancid. It forced him to squat over the stinking bucket as the hot contents of his gut gushed and spilled over the rim and onto the floor, spewing its stink into the air. And then it forced him, in his loneliness and despair, to touch himself, in spite of the fear that the guards would come upon him in the act or hear his shuddering groans upon release. He and his body became not one but two separate entities. In its desperate search for satisfaction of all the baser needs, his body protested its right to exist, to go on living, its refusal to die.*

Prison had taken him back to the cage of his childhood. It had ripped away all the beauty he had ever possessed. Had Inspector Leroux not been his jailor, had the conditions been more humane than they were, Erik would still have wished for death.

Upon arriving at the estate, Raoul had retreated almost immediately. Erik assumed he was informing Christine of the fiasco. Alone with Meg, Erik made short shrift of the journey out to the site of the fair, relaying the facts as if he read from Cortale Paccara's notes. Dissatisfied, Meg had not rested until she pulled each and every detail from him. His coolness maddened her. But no matter how much she ranted and raved about the unfairness of it all and the need to do something to stave off disaster, Erik had flatly refused to consider flight.

"The lieutenant might have arrested me on the spot, but he didn't." Erik offered Meg his only evidence for hope.

"Maybe he's playing with us, like a fat and vicious cat with a mouse," she argued.

"I prefer not to see myself in the role of a mouse."

Against her will, Meg smiled. Erik's heart lightened for one moment to see her sadness abate. But in a blink of an eye her smile fell into a frown that could not hold back her sobs. Erik let her cry until she exhausted herself. Desperate to restore a frayed connection between himself and his own life, he suggested they have a late afternoon meal. Erik took out a handkerchief and wiped at Meg's swollen eyes.

Raoul tapped at the door and peeked his head in.

"Erik, the lieutenant sent a note." Raoul took in the scene in a glance. Reluctantly he went on. "I took the liberty of reading it. He wants everyone at the theater this evening at seven o'clock."

"Sig. Lambre, did you know that Carlotta Venedetti was assaulted?"

The waiter wiped his chapped hands on the soiled towel and laid it on the counter top. There were only a handful of customers at this time of day. No one seemed that interested in the fact that the officers were interrogating him.

"Why didn't you call me into the station?" he asked.

"I thought it would be more comfortable for you here. Perhaps being in the surroundings would trigger memories. You can more effectively explain to us what happened." Verduce smiled, but Lambre was not fooled.

"I knew," the waiter admitted. "There was talk when she didn't show up for several nights."

"Talk?"

"She was a regular, you see. Even more so when Jannicelli left for Milan."

"Her lover," Verduce said. The waiter was a bit taken aback either by the officer's frankness or the fact that he knew such a detail.

"Well, she made a scene or two. Jannicelli was able to handle her. With him gone, she was…a bit…wild."

"Did Signorina Venedetti know Ricci well?"

"Everyone knew Ricci."

"Did she socialize with him?"

Lambre scowled. He took the towel and wiped the surface of the counter in steady circles, going over the same area again and again. "I don't like spreading gossip."

"Do you prefer spending time in a jail cell?"

Lambre blanched. His hand stilled on the surface of the counter.

"I don't want any trouble, Tenente Verduce. I just don't know that I should tell what goes on in my customers' personal lives."

"There is no personal life when you're suspected of murder."

"Donna Carlotta? She's loud and irritating, but she's no murderer."

"Her relationship with the deceased?"

"Well they didn't have much to do with each other until one night when she was making a spectacle of herself. Then I saw Ricci go over to her table. They started talking and carrying on, you know, in an intimate kind of way."

"She was flirting with him?"

"Yes, you could call it that. Anyway, they left together. Saw them get into the same carriage."

"Were they having an affair?"

"Affair? Those two?" Lambre let out a loud guffaw. "Just the opposite. After that night, they sat on opposite sides of the room, throwing daggers at each other with their eyes."

"So they had a falling out."

Clearly nervous again, Lambre twisted the towel in his hand. He leaned in a little closer and whispered, "There was talk that..."

"Go on. This is just between you and me—for the moment."

Lambre scowled, but he continued, "Donna Carlotta let the word out that Ricci was not a very good lover. That kind of remark gets around."

"Ricci must have heard it?"

"Oh, I'm sure. The point is that when she finally turned up again here at the café she had some bruises on her face. A few of the men said she got what was coming to her for being a loud mouth bitch."

"Do you think Ricci assaulted her?"

"Ricci? Have you seen the guy?" Lambre's eyes shifted. He cleared his throat to hide his embarrassment. "Of course you have. He wasn't the physical kind. He was more the kind that would hire someone else to do his dirty work." Lambre stretched up and looked out toward the doors. Two large men entered, found their way to a back table, and sat down.

"Someone to do his dirty work?" Verduce asked as his eye followed Lambre's.

"You didn't hear that from me," the barman whispered. "I'd rather be in jail and alive than dead."

"Cortale, I think we should buy those two men a drink in a few minutes." Turning to Lambre again, Verduce asked, "There was something you said when we spoke last about the boys."

Lambre groaned. "I told you all I knew."

"We were wondering if you could go over a few details."

"Look, I told you. Ricci went outside, and then a few minutes later I see the boys come over."

"A few minutes later? It wasn't immediate?"

"Well, no." Lambre pulled at the collar of his shirt. "Ricci had left with this fellow."

Verduce scowled. "You never mentioned that he was with someone when he left."

"I forgot."

"This other man?"

"I don't know him. He wasn't one of the usual crowd. Looked seedy. I might have thrown him out except that he went over to Ricci's table."

"Did Ricci know him?"

"Couldn't tell. I got busy. Next thing I know they're walking out the door. I suppose they were talking outside."

"Why do you suppose?"

"They walked off a bit to the side. From here, it was hard to see them. But now that I think of it, that's what caught my eye. I had thought Ricci long gone, but then I saw him through the corner of the window, over there." Lambre pointed toward the large plate glass window at the front of the café. "For a moment he just stood there. I thought he was going to step back inside, but then that's when he must have seen the boys coming. They kind of corralled him away from the front of the café."

"You didn't think there was a problem?"

"Not until Ricci started waving that cane of his around."

"Cane?" Verduce looked at Cortale who scanned through his notes. "You didn't mention a cane before."

"I didn't?"

"No, you said he waved his arms about."

"Oh, I thought I'd mentioned it. He sometimes liked to use it for show. Is that important?"

Verduce didn't answer his question. "The man who was with him. Let's get a description of him."

"Medium build, dark hair on the long side, a bit scruffy looking. He had a limp, favored his right leg. Didn't seem able to bend his left one too well."

"A limp, you say?"

Lambre nodded. "Yes, and he held his left arm in a weird way. Like an old man who's suffered from the palsy or something."

"Was he still there when the boys showed up?"

"Can't say. Didn't notice."

"You talk to the men over there. It may not be that relevant, but let's be sure to have our facts." Verduce looked at his watch.

"The cane could be the murder weapon, couldn't it?" Cortale said.

"Yes, I think that's likely, especially given that we didn't find it at the murder site."

"The man with a limp has to be Adamo DeVita, don't you think?"

"Likely. Send one of the men to track him down. Find out his whereabouts." Before Cortale set off to carry out instructions, Verduce said, "I think this evening at the Teatro dell'Opera will be interesting. We'll have some of these people in the same room and see what happens."

"Tenente Verduce, may I have a word with you?" The waiter had approached the two officers.

Verduce was surprised that Lambre would want to say anything more to him on the subject of the night in question. "Of course, Sig. Lambre."

"Since you want all the details of that night, something else occurred to me. I don't think it's important, but I don't want to make any mistakes like the one about the cane."

"Go on."

"There was another person who seemed awfully interested in Ricci that night. He watched from the front window over there. That's where he usually sits. He got up when Ricci looked like he was leaving. But when the man with the limp went out with Ricci, he changed his mind and sat back down. Then when I came back in, after dealing with the boys and seeing Ricci off, this man practically ran me over trying to get out the door."

"And he set off in the same direction as Ricci?"

"Yes, even though he usually goes the opposite way."

"His name?"

"Grimaldo Tessari. He's the lead tenor at the Teatro dell'Opera."

Verduce thanked Lambre. When the waiter returned to his place behind the counter, Verduce whispered to Cortale. "Too many suspects. Mark my words. It's a regular vegetable soup we have here."

The Chagnys and the Costanzis arrived at the theater well before seven o'clock. Erik excused himself almost immediately, pleading the need to make arrangements. Meg decided to spend some time in the exercise room, burning off her anxiety through physical exertion. Raoul and Christine mingled with the performers, counting the minutes before the police would occupy the auditorium and stage. Mario, François, and Victor wandered the backstage, unable to think of anything but the fact that the police were perhaps on the verge of making an arrest. Erik explained to Rinaldo that the police had requested that the entire company be present and asked him to supervise the gathering. Then he sequestered himself in his office in order to think his way out of the nightmare that grew around him and his loved ones.

Since the arrival of Verduce's summons, Erik had gone over and over the sparse information he had gathered about Ricci's death. Most of the evidence pointed to him. He had not been overly concerned about his own standing in the investigation until he stood on that barren field and realized that he had no way to confirm his whereabouts the night Ricci was murdered. Without an alibi, his situation looked dire. It was nigh on impossible to prove that he wasn't the murderer. The only recourse he had was to find the real culprit. Only that would exonerate him from suspicion.

Calvino and Raphael had reported back to Erik that the police had shown great interest in Il Café di Mondo. Ricci had evidently been there the evening he was murdered. Unbidden the memory of François's confession came to mind. The boys had harassed Ricci, in plain view, outside the café. Verduce would surely hear an account of the incident. Icy dread made it impossible for Erik to think. Who else? Who else would have been glad to see Ricci dead? Carlotta certainly had not mourned Ricci's death, but she was not a murderer. Rinaldo? Erik discarded the thought the moment it occurred to him. Rinaldo was not a murderer, either.

Among all those he knew, he was the only one who had killed. And not once but several times.

At that precise moment, Chiara Greco knocked on his open door to get his attention. The vague residue of past wrongs held him even as he tried to shake free of it. He mustered his resolve to cling to the fact that in this case he was not guilty. He was innocent. He would not let past crimes determine his fate now.

Chiara Greco stood on the threshold of his office, her face whiter than the ivory of her dress.

"Sig. Costanzi?" she whispered.

"Yes?"

"I've found the murderer."

Carlotta couldn't help but peek inside the small opening of the door to Grimaldo's dressing room. The light was burning, and she could see movement inside. Her own anxiety about the police officers' summons that the company be present at seven o'clock on the stage, which was the only place large enough for all of them, had not been quelled by Rinaldo's assurances. She was beside herself with fear.

She pushed the door open and was about to speak when Grimaldo turned to her with such a look of panic that she screeched.

"You frightened me," she said. She fluttered her hand in front of her face.

"I…I'm busy, Carlotta," Grimaldo said.

It was so unlike Grimmy. He had been following her around like a puppy dog for weeks. He always warmed to her attentions. She had long imagined that he was a little in love with her.

"What's that behind you?" asked Carlotta.

Grimaldo's eyes widened, his mouth opened, but no sound came out. Instead he stepped forward and shut the door in Carlotta's face.

Velia knelt beside her brother. They spoke in whispers that Renata couldn't make out. Wiping her eyes, Velia stood and went to Renata.

"We have to get him out of here," she said. "The police are coming. They'll search the theater."

At the far end of the room, Erik descended the staircase. Halfway down, he paused to take in the scene. Behind him, a curious Chiara Greco craned her neck around Erik's shoulder, in an effort to see.

"I think the police might be interested in talking with your brother, Signorina DeVita."

Renata Cossa and Velia DeVita were clearly startled. When the two women began to talk at once, Erik strode across the room to find Adamo DeVita propped up against the wall. Erik waited for the women to quiet. Then he told them to leave. DeVita and he needed to talk.

Reluctantly, they complied. At the top of the stairs, they strained to hear what the men were saying. Renata tried to calm Velia. Chiara Greco stood, leaning over the stairwell, so as to better hear the voices below. On occasion, she'd call out a word or two that she gleaned from the conversation between the two men. After several minutes had stretched into nearly an hour, Chiara stood back from the stairs, whispered to the other two women, "He's coming," and then ran to join them a few feet off to the side.

At the top of the stairs, Erik saw the three women waiting. He hesitated.

"It's late. The officers will be arriving soon."

Stepping into his path, Velia pleaded, "Don't tell them my brother's hiding."

Erik considered the girl, his green eyes cold. He moved as if to shake off her hand from his sleeve, but she held on fast.

"Please," she begged.

"How can you plead for him? The things he was willing to do, to have you do?"

Velia's face reddened, and Erik knew that she understood to what he was alluding.

"He didn't murder that man," she said, weakly.

Erik's cold gaze wavered. He studied the girl before him, a girl determined to save her brother. In a voice that sought a deeper truth, he asked, "How do you know?"

"I just do."

In the girl's simple response, Erik heard more than just the words.

It would be so easy to cast blame on the young man. Adamo had as much as confessed that he had murdered Ricci. But as Adamo DeVita described the night and what had transpired between Ricci and him, Erik knew the facts did not match the evidence.

"The police will be waiting, Signorina DeVita. There's less than an hour. Hardly time to do much of anything." He looked meaningfully at the girl. "Be sure you're back and on stage at seven."

CHAPTER 8

All the World's a Stage

"Perhaps the mystery is a little too plain," said Dupin.
"Oh, good heavens! who ever heard of such an idea?"

"The Purloined Letter," Edgar Allen Poe

"Rinaldo, tell him. Go on." Carlotta was leaning against Rinaldo, pushing him forward across the stage. Erik watched them from the center near the pit. Rinaldo stopped several times and spoke with the woman, but Erik could tell, even from this distance, that Carlotta Venedetti was an immovable obstruction.

Rinaldo's arms dropped limply to his side, and Erik knew Carlotta had won the battle. His assistant artistic director—Erik and Rinaldo had eventually agreed upon the title for the new position Rinaldo occupied—drew up, Carlotta positioned behind just in case he lost his nerve at the last moment.

"Go on," she whispered.

Erik was puzzled. Why wouldn't Carlotta tell him herself? She was just inches away.

"Rinaldo, there's not a lot of time," Erik said, drawing out his watch and checking it again. "The police should be here any moment."

Carlotta was making hissing noises. She clung to Rinaldo's coat as if she were hiding.

"Carlotta's upset," the young man began.

"I can see that," said Erik without a drop of sarcasm. Indeed Carlotta was making him nervous. He was tense enough with the knowledge that Verduce was drawing near to a point where he'd have to take action.

"She wants me to tell you that you should run."

"Tell him that he needs to disappear. That was what I had told you, Naldo. The Phan...Costanzi should do one of his tricks and disappear, like the...a...ghost."

"Carlotta, for God's sake. I can hear you. I'm right here."

Carlotta released the tails of Rinaldo's coat and stepped between the two men. "I thought that if Naldo told you that you would listen. A man listens to a man. You don't listen to me. You think that I'm senseless."

Erik considered denying the charge, but it was too close to the truth. "I'm not disappearing. I'm the artistic director of this company. The Teatro dell'Opera—or a good percentage of it—is mine. I've nothing to run from."

Carlotta's lower lip began to tremble. Her eyes filled with tears. Erik's mouth sprang open, and he cast around for somewhere to put his eyes. Her obvious concern for him moved him more than he could have expected.

"You're a stubborn man, a mule, a donkey, an ass. It always has to be your way."

"Carlotta," warned Rinaldo.

Erik stared down at the toes of his shoes, waiting for the storm to pass.

"There's one other thing. Two... No, three. No, two things. I did not kill the maggot. You have to tell the police that I did not kill Ricci."

"No one in his right mind would think you had, Carlotta." Erik's mouth turned up in a slight smile. "What were the other two things?"

"No, you aren't paying attention. There is one thing more." Carlotta pushed Rinaldo slightly back and came so close to Erik that he could not avoid gazing at her considerable décolletage. When he realized that his eyes had indeed dipped to admire her bosom, he stepped back. She followed. "It's Grimmy."

"Grimaldo?"

"He's acting strange. You know he's a bit in love with me." Evidently Carlotta was concerned that Rinaldo might be upset. Even though she whispered, Rinaldo could hear every word she was saying. Erik noticed that the young man seemed only mildly intrigued.

"What's Grimaldo done?" asked Erik.

"He's been gloomy and nervous. I think he's been sleeping in his dressing room. He's hiding something. I'm worried about him."

Erik could see that on this one point Rinaldo did not think she was overreacting. "Rinaldo?"

"He's been depressed, withdrawn. The other day he wouldn't let the cleaning women in his dressing room. He yelled at them not to come into his room. And Jacopo said that he put a lock on the door."

"The door has a lock."

"This is one that only he has a key to."

"I see." Erik heard the far doors of the auditorium open. "We'll talk later," he said to Rinaldo and Carlotta. Verduce and his men had arrived.

Erik scanned the stage to find that Meg was standing off to the side, by François and Mario. She had wanted to be with Erik when he met the police officers, but he had convinced her to let him face them alone. Not part of the company, Raoul, Christine, and their son had been ordered to remain off the stage and out of the officers' way.

Glancing around those assembled, he saw Renata Cossa and Velia DeVita step out from the wings. They seemed frazzled. But he could not find Grimaldo.

"Sig. Costanzi," Verduce greeted Erik as he came up the steps to the stage. He stopped and looked out on the auditorium. "Uff. Exhilarating. Is this what it feels like to be up here during a performance?"

Erik smiled. "One gets used to it."

"I don't think I would." Verduce indicated to his assistant to go round and take down the names of those present. "Thank you for assembling your company. I hope we won't take too much of your valuable time. By the way, Sig. Costanzi, my men are taking the liberty of searching the backstage rooms, including your office."

Erik grimaced but knew there was nothing he could do to stop them.

"We've been able to piece together much of what happened the night Paolo Ricci was murdered. I thought perhaps it might be more efficient to go over the events with everyone present so that any flaws or gaps can be adjusted or filled." The lieutenant smiled at the company.

"I take it that there are details that are missing?" asked Erik.

"Oh, odds and ends really."

"Do you know who the murderer is?"

Verduce pursed his lips as if considering the question carefully. "You'll have to be patient, Sig. Costanzi. Before we make our arrest, we want to ask a few more questions."

Erik glanced at Meg before he could stop himself. She was worried for him. "What can I help you with, Tenente Verduce?"

"Oh, I don't think our initial questions are for you, Sig. Costanzi. We need to speak with the younger Costanzis, your sons François and Mario."

The general reaction among the company was one of surprise.

"I can't allow that," Erik said without hesitation.

"I'm afraid that you can't stop me." Verduce's men drew near when Erik took several steps in Verduce's direction. "I wouldn't do anything foolish, Sig. Costanzi. So far you've been more than cooperative. I hope that you'll continue to show good judgment. After all, young people today need us to set good examples."

"Leave my sons out of this, Verduce."

"I'm truly sorry, but that's not possible." The lieutenant nodded to the boys.

Mario and François had to pry their mother's hands from their sleeves. When they stepped forward to answer the police officer's questions, Meg rushed to Erik's side. He wrapped his arm around her. Never taking his eyes off the lieutenant, Erik held Meg tightly to steady himself and her.

"We've had several interesting talks with witnesses who saw you two and a friend surround and harass the victim the night he was killed. That would have been between midnight and one o'clock outside Il Café di Mondo. Do you deny this?"

Mario spoke first. "No," he gave a short laugh, "we don't deny that we jostled him a bit."

"Did you threaten him?"

Mario was about to speak again, but François said, "Yes, we told him to get out of town. Of course, we knew he wasn't likely to take us seriously."

"Really? And why wouldn't he take three young men pushing him about and calling him names seriously?"

A young man with dark blond hair strode up the stairs to the stage. "Because we were drunk and just giving him a scare."

"And you are?" asked Verduce.

"Victor, the Count de Chagny's son. I was with François and Mario."

"You're aware that the man was bludgeoned to death just shortly after you attacked him on the street?"

"Attack is a bit strong a word. We didn't harm him," said Mario.

"We took a carriage and went home. That was the last we saw of Ricci," said Victor.

"Any witnesses?"

The three boys looked at each other sheepishly. Mario spoke for all three of them. "We didn't want anyone to know we'd been out drinking. We snuck back in. I don't think anyone heard us."

"Do you have any witness that says that they followed Ricci?" Erik asked.

Ignoring his question, Verduce addressed François and asked, "Did Ricci wave a cane about as if to keep you at bay?"

"Yes."

"Was Ricci alone when you first came up to him?"

François brushed against Mario's arm. The gesture was not lost on the police officer.

"The witness said that there was another man who accompanied Ricci when he left. Who was the man?" Verduce looked at each of the young men in turn.

A crash from the floor of the auditorium startled the company. The door of a side entrance banged against the wall as officers dragged someone inside the auditorium. Erik recognized the man as Adamo DeVita.

"He turned up at the Boar and Bow, just like you said he would, Tenente," said one of the men as he yanked Adamo DeVita forward to the stage.

"Was this the man who was with Ricci?" Verduce asked the three boys.

François and Mario saw Velia lurch forward as if she intended to run to the man. The women near her held her back.

Before anyone noticed her, Chiara Greco stepped forward.

"He...," she began to say.

Erik's voice interrupted Chiara's.

"He is the brother of one of my performers. Isn't that what you were going to say, Signorina Greco?"

Chiara Greco evidently had learned her lesson. She nodded and said that that was what she had meant to say. Verduce scowled at Erik and turned back to Costanzi's sons and their friend.

"As I was saying, did you see this man with Ricci the night you accosted him?"

François glanced Mario's way and then stared down at the ground. Mario fixed his attention on the back of the amphitheater as if waiting for someone to arrive. Puzzled, Victor looked at his friends. Hesitantly, he answered, "I think so. He had a limp."

"I did it," said Adamo.

Everyone's attention shifted to Adamo DeVita. The man was stretched like a rag doll between the two officers. His head hung low.

Verduce asked him to repeat what he had said.

"I saw the boys. I pretended to leave, but I hid nearby in a dark entryway. They pushed Ricci around for a few minutes until someone from the café came out and told them to leave."

"Why were you waiting for Ricci?"

"We had argued." Adamo lifted his eyes to face the officer and then tried to plant his feet more firmly beneath his weight.

Verduce indicated that the officers could release him.

Once Adamo had regained his balance, he continued his confession.

"He was going to publish a review of my sister's opening. She has a part in the opera. He might have made her reputation. But what he wrote was filth. He...read it to me. He took this notebook out and read to me a review that had nothing to do with the quality of my sister's performance. He painted her as little more than a...." Adamo's eyes scanned the back of the stage. He swallowed and remained silent.

"When did he read this to you?"

"In Il Café di Mondo. I ripped it out of his notebook."

"You must have been angry. What did you do with the pieces?"

"What do you mean?"

"What did you do with the review, Sig. DeVita?"

"I took it like this." Adamo raised his fist as if he still held the crumpled sheet of paper in it. "I tossed it on the table. Ricci stormed out. I followed. He raised that cane of his and warned me to stay back. That's when they came up." Verduce followed Adamo's gaze to the three young men.

"After the boys left, you followed Ricci?"

"I followed him. When I saw we were close to the theater, I grabbed his shoulder and asked why he was headed for the Teatro dell'Opera. He said...he said...he was going to talk with my sister. He said that perhaps she could persuade him to write a nice review of her performance. If she was...nice, he might..."

"Pig! Maggot!" Carlotta's voice rang out over the entire company. Then there were several muffled sounds as someone quieted her.

"So you were angry." Verduce encouraged Adamo to continue.

"I pulled at him, to stop him, but he hit me. With that cane. He hit me on my arm several times and once on my head. I went down. He came and bent over me like he was going to hit me again. I raised my foot and kicked him backwards. I just wanted him to stop. He slammed against the wall. I heard...I heard the sound his head made when it hit the brick. Then he slid to the ground."

"And the cane?"

"I don't remember. I think he dropped it when I kicked him."

"You didn't pick it up?"

Adamo looked up at Verduce, puzzled. "No. I just wanted to get as far away as possible."

"You did not pick up the cane and strike him repeatedly in the face?"

"What?" said Adamo, shocked by the gruesome question.

"Inspector Verduce, may I say something?" Renata Cossa stepped forward. She ignored Erik's warning glance. "I found Sig. DeVita in the storage room a few days ago, just after the murder. He was in a lamentable state. He was delirious with the pain. I thought he had been assaulted. What with the recent murder and an attack on one of our performers a few weeks back, I thought perhaps this man had been waylaid by the same hooligans. I can attest to the fact that in his condition this man would not have been able to beat Ricci in the face or body with a cane. His shoulder was dislocated, bruised and swollen. He couldn't even lift a cane much less use it to harm anyone."

"Is this true?" Verduce asked DeVita.

"I didn't touch his cane. I swear."

"But you confessed to having killed the victim."

"I thought…that he was dead."

"Arrest this man," Verduce said. When the officers started to put the cuffs on Adamo, Verduce said, "Not him. This man. Sig. Erik Costanzi."

"No!" Meg placed herself between Verduce and Erik as if she could keep back the officers. François and Mario took their place on either side of their father.

"I'm sorry, but it's clear to me that Erik Costanzi heard the commotion. He often wanders about at night through the city. Seeing this young man scuffle with Ricci, he waited. When DeVita ran off—thinking that he'd killed Ricci—Costanzi saw his opportunity to do away with an enemy that had been a thorn in his side for years."

Verduce ignored the angry mutterings that fanned through the company. He had to raise his voice to make himself heard over the general din. Erik's hands squeezed Meg's shoulders to keep her from hurling herself at the lieutenant.

"He found the cane a few feet from the body and beat the man in the face," continued Verduce. "Clearly he had some personal reasons for focusing on the face, perhaps the fact that he himself wears a mask, a mask that Ricci often made the centerpiece of his reviews."

Reluctantly banished to the first row of the auditorium, Raoul and Christine had been observing the proceedings with growing concern. When Victor climbed the stairs to the stage, Christine had lurched forward as if to stop him. Raoul had placed a protective arm around his wife's shoulders as much to keep her from running after Victor as to comfort her. When guilt was shifted away from the boys to Adamo DeVita, the Chagnys were momentarily relieved. However, as Verduce focused his attention on Erik and described the case against him, Christine could bear it no longer. She grasped the sleeve of Raoul's coat, twisting it in her fist. Although her face had gone as white as Erik's half mask, Raoul was unaware, his attention drawn to the drama unfolding before their eyes. He pried Christine's fingers from his sleeve, giving her only the slightest glance of reassurance, and made his way to the stage.

"Then he must have been curious." Verduce directed his version of the events to the huddled people on the stage, scanning their faces for a reaction. "Costanzi searched the reporter's pockets, knowing that Ricci, like all those who live by their words, had to have a notebook on his person. He rifled through the pages where Ricci wrote his barbs against the Teatro dell'Opera. He ripped the pages out of the notebook, leaving only the blank pages intact. No doubt my men will find the stolen pages and the murder weapon somewhere on the premises."

Erik waited until he was certain that Verduce had finished. Then he gently pushed Meg into François's arms. "You can't seriously believe what you're saying."

Verduce sighed. He nodded to the officers who advanced, cuffs ready. Erik glanced in Raoul's direction. He shook his head so slightly that it was barely noticeable. Raoul drew himself up short, a quizzical look on his face. Erik lifted his hands, palms up, and offered his wrists for the handcuffs. Meg slumped in François's arms when she heard the mechanism click into place. Erik lowered his arms and waited for Verduce's next move.

"Speak of the devil. Here they come, and it appears they've found something," said Verduce as several policemen came out onto the stage from the wings. One of the men carried a long wooden cane with a silver handle in the shape of an eagle.

"We didn't find them in the main office, Tenente. It was in one of the dressing rooms. We had to break the door down. None of the keys worked."

The general uproar was silenced by a voice that fell from the sky. Someone was singing. Everyone searched the flies above the stage. On one of the catwalks, several stories above them, stood Grimaldo Tessari. His voice, a pure tenor, rang out over the assembly with the clarity of a bell. The short cavatina was one of Grimaldo's favorites. Its merit was its brevity and simplicity. It was a melody that Erik had often heard the tenor hum.

Erik held his hands out to the officers. "Get these off me," he demanded.

Verduce didn't hesitate. He took the key himself from the policeman and unlatched the cuffs. The moment he was unshackled, Erik ran to the back of the stage. Jacopo and several of his men were already climbing to the flies. Erik grabbed the nearest rope ladder and hoisted himself up. He climbed with the elegance and speed of one who worked above as well as on the stage. At the top, he stepped out onto a perpendicular catwalk that intersected with the one where Grimaldo now stood looking down upon the assembly.

"Grimaldo, what are you doing?" Erik asked.

"I'm sorry, Don Erik. You must believe me. I wouldn't have let it go any further. I wouldn't have let them take you or François or Mario off to jail." Grimaldo wobbled giddily. He clutched at the vertical ropes that suspended the narrow wooden slats above the abyss. He looked down on the people below. "It's very high."

"Yes, it is. I'll come brace you so that you don't fall." Erik took a step toward Grimaldo.

"No, you mustn't come any closer, Don Erik. Please." Erik stopped. "It was supposed to be DeVita. I saw him skulking around. He's no good. He torments his sister. I heard some of the things that he told her to do. He wanted Donna Meg out of the way."

Erik didn't want to take his eyes off Grimaldo, but he found himself searching among the crowd on the stage until he saw his wife, safe in his son's arms.

"He was here the day you…" Startled by the sudden lurch of the suspended bridge, Grimaldo gasped and clutched at the rope. The catwalk swayed under the men's weight.

"Grimaldo, you don't have to say anything. Just reach out and give me your hand."

"I thought they'd blame DeVita." Grimaldo clutched at the rope. He spoke as if he were in a trance. "Ricci deserved to die. I saw him pay the men, the men that…beat…Carlotta. It was after the deed had been done." The trance ended. Anger distorted Grimaldo's features. "He was celebrating at Il Café. He sat there, drinking his wine and laughing. I…I wanted to kill him then." He could not sustain the violence of the emotion. "But I knew I couldn't."

A policeman had managed to climb to a parallel bridge over the stage. Grimaldo caught sight of his movement from the corner of his eye.

"Tell them to stay back," Grimaldo insisted. His hand had gone white as it gripped the rope.

Erik signaled for the officer to stop where he was. The distraction had unnerved Grimaldo, and Erik felt him tremble through the riggings of the catwalk. The poor man could easily lose his footing and tumble headlong onto the stage below.

"Grimaldo, give me your hand. Now."

"No, Don Erik, you can't stop me."

Grimaldo took a deep breath and shook off whatever emotions had assailed him. He steadied himself on the boards. He raised his voice, and Erik had the sickening realization that Grimaldo meant for everyone to hear his next words.

"I've been thinking for the past week, watching what I did unravel the lives of people…people that I love. I know what you're trying to do. You want to save me, but it won't work. I killed him. I killed Paolo Ricci. They heard me, didn't they?" Leaning precariously over the top transverse rope, Grimaldo called out to those below. "Sig. Verduce, did you hear me?"

"Yes, Don Grimaldo. But it would be easier if you came down to the station."

"No. I won't be going to the station."

Erik took a small step toward Grimaldo. The tenor raised one leg, swinging it over the thick guide rope to the other side. He straddled the rope in such a way that he was half on and half off the suspended walkway. One false move and he'd fall. Erik stilled.

"That night, at Il Café di Mondo, I heard DeVita and Ricci arguing. Ricci read a review he had written, saying you scoured the gutters for your talent. He implied things, distasteful and cruel things, all lies. He called us mediocre and our work a travesty of art. DeVita grabbed the sheet away from Ricci and crumpled it. After they left, I picked it up and read it. I tore it up and stuffed the pieces into my pocket. I followed them. DeVita pushed Ricci into the alleyway. I waited. I heard them fighting. Then I saw DeVita come stumbling out. When I found Ricci, he was still breathing. It all fell into place. I found his cane. I hit him with it for what he had done to Carlotta and what he had said about her, about you, about all of us. I didn't mean to strike him more than the one time. He kept making this strange gurgling sound. It frightened me, and I hit him again and again to stop that ugly sound. I smashed the cane across his face until his horrible mouth was gone. Later, after the sound stopped and I knew he was dead, I searched for the notebook. I didn't want anyone to read his filth. I tore out the pages he had written. As I put them in my pocket, I felt the torn pieces of the other sheet of paper. I tossed them on the ground, thinking that they would lead the police to DeVita."

"The cane, Grimaldo? Why didn't you get rid of it?"

"I didn't realize I still had it until later. I locked myself in my dressing room. I didn't think I could make it home. I was bloody. I washed, changed. That's when I noticed the cane leaning against the door. I didn't remember putting it there. I washed the blood and the…. I washed it and stuck it in the back of my closet. I didn't know what else to do with it. I burned the pages that I tore from his notebook."

Grimaldo was silent. Erik slowly slid his feet down the passageway toward Grimaldo. "I think I've said everything that has to be said. Don Erik, it's been a privilege to know you. Promise me one thing. Promise that you will take care of Carlotta. No matter what."

"Don't, Grimaldo. Don't do anything. You have to take care of Carlotta. She expects it. You know that she's more than any one of us can handle."

Grimaldo smiled and chuckled. "You are the only man I know, Erik Costanzi, who could fall from the flies and walk away unscathed. God must be watching over you. But don't risk it a second time." Grimaldo stepped over the rope, leaned back, hands folded over his chest, and fell.

Erik reached out and clutched at the empty air.

CHAPTER 9

Dearly Beloved

Men must endure
Their going hence, even as their coming hither;
Ripeness is all.

King Lear, William Shakespeare

The sun didn't shine that day. The mourners assembled pulled their collars high and held their black umbrellas low and tilted into the cold wind and rain that slashed the gray sky. An entourage of performers, musicians, composers, technicians, and staff had undulated, a black serpent, along the route from the Church to the cemetery. With heavy hearts, each said farewell to the deceased. As the priest ended his prayer, Erik Costanzi led his wife and Christine, the Countess de Chagny, to the head of the grave. In a deep, resonant voice, Erik began to sing. Those present would remember for some time the strength and beauty of that voice. Joining the baritone, the two women on either side added their voices like two limpid pools, notes that could only be called angelic.

No one, except those closest to Erik Costanzi, knew how Grimaldo Tessari had earned a dispensation that allowed him to be buried in the Catholic cemetery. The priest could not budge Costanzi from his story. When the priest had said that suicides could not be buried in hallowed ground, Costanzi had insisted that Grimaldo had accidentally fallen from the flies. Skeptical, the priest reluctantly accepted Costanzi's story that Grimaldo Tessari had slipped and fallen, that Costanzi had been unprepared to catch him. Even when the priest lectured Costanzi that his false report would jeopardize his own salvation, Costanzi had calmly insisted that Grimaldo's death had been accidental and that the deceased had a right to be buried in the same cemetery where two days before the victim Paolo Ricci had been laid to rest.

Although Costanzi managed to have the onus of suicide lifted from Grimaldo, he could not dispute the priest's complaint that the man had murdered and died unshriven. But he did argue that Grimaldo's accidental death had made confession impossible. Surely something could be done. Costanzi intimated that Grimaldo had expressed repentance just moments before the tragic fall. Worn down by Costanzi's calm resolve and insistence that Grimaldo had a right to the rituals and ceremonies of his religion, the priest agreed to say the mass and to accompany the deceased on his journey to the graveyard.

As the mourners filed past the grave, they whispered their farewells. Some gathered a bit of wet earth and let it fall, along with the raindrops, with a dull thud on the lid of the coffin. Much more affected by Grimaldo's tragic end than anyone could have expected, Carlotta Venedetti refused to allow Rinaldo Jannicelli to usher her away from the graveside. Rinaldo stood back among the tombstones and waited while Carlotta scattered her bouquet of flowers on the open grave. Erik Costanzi lingered, too, watching pink petals, dark green stalks, purple, lavender, and red blossoms, float down in the rain.

"I'm cold," she said.

Erik stepped forward and put his arm around her waist.

"He was such a sweet man, Erik."

Erik nodded.

"He might have been a little angry with me when I drugged him, but he forgave me." Carlotta turned and looked up into his eyes. "Erik, I never wanted this. It's not my fault, is it?"

"No, Carlotta. He wanted to protect us all."

Erik took Carlotta by the elbow, his black glove on her black lace. "Come. Rinaldo's waiting for you."

He led her to the carriage where Rinaldo, his hand on the carriage door, stood. Then Erik joined his family and friends for the long ride back to the estate.

More than a month had passed since Grimaldo's funeral. Erik had reopened the theater. Rinaldo Jannicelli had resumed rehearsals for his opera, *An Affair with a Madwoman*. From what Erik had seen, it would be enormously popular. It was both ribald and naughty. Carlotta was never more vivacious or commanding as the willful and outrageous widow in search of an affair with a handsome youth. Grimaldo Tessari's understudy, Enzo Marino, a young man who was both delighted and cowed to be playing opposite Carlotta Venedetti, was doing a reputable job playing the role of a gigolo in search of a fortune.

Taking a bit of license with *The Taming of the Shrew*, Rinaldo turned the tables nicely on his characters. Guido, the young gigolo, falls for Francesca, the extravagant widow, and sets out to bend her to his will. During a drunken party, he convinces her that they are married. The widow finds that she has more than she bargains for when Guido begins to treat her as his wife, expecting love and obedience. Neither ends up victor over the other. Both are vanquished instead by love.

While Jannicelli occupied the stage mostly in the afternoons, Erik hid away with Renata Cossa working on his most recent work. He had scheduled more than enough time to prepare the piece, but their lack of progress had already forced him to readjust his calendar and to postpone the premiere twice.

He still had some time before Renata would be ready to meet him in the practice room. Sitting in his office, he glowered at his notes and flung them aside. Before him on the desk he spread out the score of the ballet. He flipped through the pages, pausing now and again and humming through a couple of bars. The music was perfect. It was everything else that was wrong. He was so engrossed in the details of the entr'acte that he was startled by a knock.

"Sig. Costanzi?" Romulo Verduce stood just outside the office, looking in through the open doorway. The past several days had been warm, and the air inside the office had seemed stale. Erik had opened the windows behind him and the door as well.

"Sig. Verduce." Erik rose to greet the officer. In his right hand, he clutched a sheet of paper. He felt it wrinkle and forced his grip to relax.

"I apologize for intruding, but I thought perhaps you would want something that we found during the investigation. May I?" he asked, indicating the chair near Erik's desk.

Erik nodded. He waited for the lieutenant to sit before he sat down opposite him.

"It was a rather incriminating piece, but it pointed as much to DeVita as to you." Verduce pulled out a folded sheet from an inside pocket of his vest. "My assistant Cortale Paccara managed to reconstruct the complete text of Ricci's review. This is what Sig. Grimaldo Tessari tore up and left at the scene of the murder."

Verduce held out the sheet to Erik, who took it and began to read.

Such beautiful women, such remarkable men. Our theaters abound with talent. Where do they come from, one might ask. Look around you, dear signori, at the common man. Listen to the vendor as he hawks his wares on the street, watch the scrubwomen cart their dripping baskets up and down the hills. Surely not among them. The soprano and the tenor, the dazzling dancers and chorines are as distinct from these poor figures as silk is from burlap.

Who would imagine that an artistic director would scour the streets and inns, the brothels and jails, to find his performers. How desperate then must our masked genius of the opera be to have taken a girl who sang for coins in

*the common houses and assume that by dressing her up as
a princess he could fool his public?*

*Well desperate he must be. He has lost his songbird. Il
canarino remains silent. First Costanzi steals from a
rival company a lead soprano who is competent, but
without fire. Next he combs the streets and alleyways
and foists an untried barmaid in an important, even
if secondary, part. Obviously he intends to groom
this common woman, Velia DeVita, to perform in Il
canarino's roles.*

*Is our masked genius so desperate that a girl who sings
for her supper is the best he can offer his adoring and
indulgent audience? Of course, he would not be the first
man to be seduced by common pleasures. For shame, Sig.
Costanzi. The star of the Teatro dell'Opera is forever
dulled. It will not shine when you promise silk and
deliver burlap. Paolo Ricci*

Erik clenched his jaw against the irritation that Ricci's words could still cause. When he finished, he glanced up at the police officer and smiled a half smile. "Damn sarcastic bastard knew how to twist the knife." He tossed the review on the desktop.

"Unfortunately once we eliminated DeVita, you looked like our most likely suspect."

Erik raised an eyebrow, but the officer could not see his expression. With the door open, Erik had not taken off his mask.

"I'm curious, Tenente Verduce. How did you know DeVita wasn't guilty? He was ready to confess to the murder."

"The victim certainly had a bad knot on the back of his head. I suppose we might have taken DeVita in for assault. But from his story it was arguably a case of self defense. Returning to the point of your question, we had certain physical evidence that placed someone else at the scene, someone who had the use of his left, as well as his right, hand. There were smudges of fingerprints inside the notebook. DeVita had crumpled the review in his one hand and tossed it on the table. Someone with two good hands tore up that review and conveniently left it by the dead body for us to find."

"So DeVita was never really in danger of arrest?"

"No. Although if Ricci had been poisoned, DeVita would have been our prime suspect."

"Poisoned?"

"He bought a rather large dose of poison. We found a half-emptied bottle in the back room of the Boar and Bow, where DeVita was living. From the look of the rodents, I don't think he used it to keep down the rat population."

Erik recalled Grimaldo's words on the catwalk, something about DeVita wanting Meg out of the way. A bitter taste rose in the back of his mouth. He fought to push it down.

"Nor were your sons likely culprits." The police lieutenant was still speaking. "In part I've come to apologize for using them to rout the actual murderer."

Erik pushed the thought of DeVita to a corner of his mind. Verduce's reference to his sons brought back the emotions of that moment when he feared they would be accused of the crime. Incapable of dissimulating his residual anger, he averted his gaze, knowing that his eyes flashed cold and fierce.

"You threatened my sons, used them." He kept a tight rein on his tone.

"Yes. It was a ploy. A less conscientious officer might have been happy to blame them, but it was a weak case. I gambled that putting your sons on the chopping block might unsettle you enough that you would let something slip. When that failed, I decided to accuse you."

Although a part of Erik was still furious with the police officer's methods, he accepted that the man had never meant to put the boys in danger.

"I assumed it would stir things up, which it did," continued Verduce, his voice calm and reasonable. "Even if Sig. Tessari hadn't come forward, we found the murder weapon and other evidence in his room. It was just a matter of time."

"My arrest was meant to draw him out?" Erik risked looking up at the officer.

"I wish I could say that I had figured it all out by that time, but I hadn't quite. There were still a few loose ends. Lucky for you, Sig. Tessari was not an evil man. I think he was genuinely haunted by his crime." Verduce studied Erik's mask for a brief moment before he looked him in the eye. "He didn't want you to be accused of murder. Admirable, really. It takes a great deal of courage to accept the consequences of one's actions. Then again, the truth has a way of coming out."

Phantom fingers stroked the back of Erik's neck. He looked away. "Is that all, Sig. Verduce?"

"Nearly so. In our investigation, we found some interesting information regarding your friend, the Count de Chagny."

Erik's gaze returned to the lieutenant's face. He waited.

"He was a patron at the Opera Populaire. That's the address you gave me as your last residence in Paris, was it not?"

Erik gave a slight nod.

"The count met his wife at the Opera Populaire."

"Is there a point?"

"Your wife's maiden name is Giry, is it not?"

"Yes." Erik's throat tightened. He could see the path the questions were taking. He could see the tunnel narrowing to a black pit.

"Is that also where you met your wife? I mean, in Paris? She got her start in Paris, did she not?"

Erik cleared his throat. His mouth was dry. "Yes."

"Amazing," Verduce said as he examined Erik, his attention mostly on his mask. "They have no record of anyone there by the name of Costanzi."

"There was a fire."

Verduce smiled broadly. "Why yes, that's true. The records. Why hadn't I thought of that? They must have been destroyed. Were you perhaps caught in that fire?" Verduce eyes would not leave the mask.

To still his hands, Erik folded one inside the other and leaned forward to meet the inspector's gaze. "I have matters to attend to, Sig. Verduce."

"I'll be brief. Tell me, Sig. Costanzi, would you have been tempted to kill Ricci had Tessari not beaten you to it?"

Erik's lips were a thin, tense line.

"No matter," Verduce said, as if his remark had been a mistake. "You didn't murder him. That's all that concerns the law." Verduce stood up. "Oh, before I go, just one more question. My wife Concetta is a remarkable judge of character. I confide all my cases to her. She thinks rather highly of you, Sig. Costanzi. Would you mind setting our minds at rest on one particular point?"

Erik wondered if Verduce could hear his heart racing. Not trusting his voice, he nodded.

"Ricci was mistaken when he implied that you were having an affair with the lovely Velia DeVita, was he not?"

The corners of Erik's mouth twitched. He let out a deep breath and answered, "Have you seen my wife, Sig. Verduce?"

Verduce chuckled, his smile broad and friendly under his steel-gray mustache. "Touché, signore. You would have to be mad."

"More to the point, I love my wife." Unbidden he recalled the image of a tray with two teacups.

Verduce bowed. It was a strangely elegant gesture. "Good. That's exactly what Concetta said." The lieutenant walked to the doorway where he paused and turned once more to address Erik Costanzi. "I'll leave you to your work, signore. I don't expect that I'll be bothering you again."

As the police officer disappeared through the doorway, Erik reached up and ran his fingers along the edges of his mask. It was firmly in place. Yet he sensed that Verduce had seen through it to the very heart of his secrets. If the lieutenant had seen the Phantom, he had chosen to disregard his discovery. He had simply looked the other way.

Erik leaned back in his chair. He told himself that he should feel relieved. The case was closed. The Phantom was safe. The police lieutenant would keep his secrets.

But Erik still tasted the bitter dregs of tea on his palate, the lingering memory of having sipped at Meg's cup, the nausea and dizziness, the twisting pain in his gut. One sip had laid him out for a couple of days. What would have happened had Meg not been interrupted and stolen away by Christine? What if Meg had stayed and drunk that cup of tea?

Grimaldo had known. It struck Erik that Grimaldo had warned him. He had alluded to DeVita stalking the theater, to the unsavory tasks that he had set his sister. DeVita had wanted Meg out of the way. Before he died, Grimaldo Tessari had wanted Erik to know to be on guard.

"Thanks, old friend," Erik whispered.

Adamo DeVita made his way down the street from the Teatro dell'Opera. Instructions had been left with Jacopo and the others not to admit him. Renata Cossa would think he had decided not to come, but he had no choice. He wouldn't stand outside, waiting for Costanzi to find him.

"DeVita."

Adamo heard the voice before the hand grabbed him by the throat. He pulled at the wrist, but the fingers of the hand had latched on and wouldn't budge. He felt his throat close. His heart nearly stopped when Erik Costanzi's unmasked face, one side handsome and the other a nightmarish parody of a face, came out from the shadows.

"That's right. Take a good look, DeVita."

Erik Costanzi was so close that Adamo felt the warmth of his breath fan across his face, leaving behind a strange and exotic scent of mint and fennel. He reached out with his good hand to claw at the hideous face that was bearing down on him. Costanzi caught it easily in his other hand and twisted it back at a sharp angle. Adamo cried out in pain, the sounds thin but audible.

"You see? You can still breathe. Enjoy it, DeVita. It won't last long."

Adamo could feel the pressure mounting as his blood pounded at his temples.

"I could break this hand. Then you'd have nothing. I could crush your windpipe." Costanzi squeezed, then eased the vice-like grip he had on Adamo's throat. Suddenly, the hand released its hold. But Costanzi still held Adamo's hand, the wrist twisted almost backwards.

Adamo might have pleaded for his life, but he couldn't speak. A series of coughs doubled him over.

"Tell me why I shouldn't kill you."

Adamo sank to his knees. Only Erik Costanzi's hold on his hand kept him from falling face down onto the cobblestone.

"One chance. I'll give you one chance, DeVita. Tell me why you tried to kill my wife. Make me understand why I shouldn't rip your throat out."

If Adamo had been afraid before at the sight of Erik Costanzi's twisted face, it was nothing compared to the panic that now gripped him.

He tried to check the reflex to gag and sputter as he spoke. "I…I'm sorry. I wasn't thinking."

"I find that peculiarly dissatisfying. It verges on inanity." Erik's grimace flashed white in the shadows. "Try harder."

"I wanted…I thought you'd warm to Velia if…"

Erik scowled at the man at his feet. "You meant to kill her. How?"

"Poison. It was supposed to be fast."

"Oh, I see. You were being merciful." Erik's hand lurched forward and trapped Adamo's throat again. "You missed your mark and got me instead. I can tell you from experience that there's no such thing as a merciful murder. But you'll find that out for yourself—very soon."

"Adamo?" someone called out.

The voice belonged to a woman, but it was not Velia's. The pressure from Erik's hand stifled any response the younger man might make. The voice called out again for Adamo, concern bordering on urgency in its tone. Erik searched Adamo's panicked eyes. They both recognized the voice. Renata Cossa. Erik squeezed Adamo's throat, watched the man's eyes widen in terror.

"Adamo?" Renata called again, this time louder, sharper.

Was there a bit of desperation in the sound?

For a moment, Erik stood, indecisive, and then he withdrew his hand from Adamo's throat. Leaning in to whisper, his face was only inches from his victim's.

"You wouldn't be the first man to be saved by a woman's love." He released Adamo's wrist and stepped back into the shadows.

When Renata Cossa called out again, Adamo DeVita struggled to his feet. But it took several more minutes for him to find his voice and to stop the shaking of his limbs.

Erik stood outside his sons' room, listening to Meg sing to the twins. He waited until she had finished and the noises of splashing water drowned out everything except his sons' laughter. Then he quietly opened the door and stepped inside.

"Where have you been?" Meg asked as she lifted little Raoul naked from the bath, wrapped him in one of two matching towels, and set him down beside Étienne.

Erik ruffled his sons' hair.

"Which one are you?" he asked each of the boys.

"I'm François," said Étienne, all giggles.

"I'm Mario," said Raoul.

Erik grabbed both, one under each arm, holding them upside down.

"Careful," said Meg, half in earnest as she watched Erik drop each of the boys onto the mattress of the large bed in which they slept. He growled at the boys who scampered, still naked, from the bed and ran around the room, trying to escape their father's grasp. When they ran behind Meg, lifted her skirt, and disappeared underneath, their father roared in mock frustration. Then with a deep, raspy voice he said, "I will have to settle for gobbling up your mother, the Queen of Bath." Meg screamed as Erik hoisted her over his shoulder. He turned toward the bed, but he made slow progress. Sitting on the top of Erik's boots, each boy had latched onto a leg. At the edge of the bed, Erik dropped Meg. She bounced on the mattress. She was laughing so hard that she couldn't speak. Then he bent and pulled one boy, then the other, from their perch and threw them on the bed next to their mother. He was about to step back when Meg grabbed him by the hand and yanked him down. He nearly landed on them.

"I…I…give up," Erik cried out as Étienne crawled over his head to join his brother Raoul who sat on his back. "Enough. The monster's dead. Get these monkeys off me."

"OK. You've killed your father, I mean the Monster of Grim. Time for bed. Put your night shirts on."

Erik helped her get the twins into bed. No sooner would they get one under the covers than the other would slip out again. Finally Erik had them both in bed. He pulled the blankets tight and anchored his sons firmly underneath, knowing that it would take the boys a few minutes to pull the covers out again. By that time, they would be drowsy.

He bent and kissed little Raoul. "Goodnight, Hector." Then he kissed Étienne. "Goodnight, Achilles."

"Goodnight, Marcus Aurelius," they chimed back.

"Now if you're quiet, I'll sing," he said. He sat on the edge of the bed and kissed them again. This time he gave them their proper names.

As he sang, Meg came up behind him and placed her hands on his shoulders. She squeezed and kneaded the muscles. Softly she joined her voice to his until the two blended and ushered their children safely into their dreams.

The cold woke him. He lay, his bare legs tangled in the sheet, his arm draped over emptiness. His skin shivered as the breeze wafted over him. It stole the warmth. Unwilling to rouse from his dream— soft and rolling visions of contentment—he gathered his elbows in close to his body to trap his heat against the mattress. Again he shivered, the lick of wind across his bare skin too cool to ignore.

He slid his face toward the window, instinctively knowing it to be the source of the unwelcome sensation. It took him several attempts to open his eyes.

She stood framed by the thick edges of the open window. The gossamer weave of her nightgown fluttered, a ghostly wing in the cool moonlight. Her hair glowed silver and white against the dull darkness beyond.

"Are you awake?" she whispered.

"No, I'm still dreaming," he said. His voice was soft and smoky, a rumble of deep notes. He felt it roll across the pillow.

His silver angel turned in the moonlight that flared around her, gilding the outline of her body. It drew a luminous silhouette of her form. He could just make out a glint in her eyes, the flash of a smile.

"What are you dreaming?"

"An angel has come to ravish me in the night." He chuckled.

"Do angels ravish men at night?"

He sighed. His hand searched below his knee for the corner of the sheet. He tugged at the twisted knot, gave up, and turned to the side to look down at the bedclothes.

"From the looks of it, I think the angel has already ravished me."

Meg sat and leaned across the bed to kiss him.

"Several times," she whispered inside their kiss.

He drew her down again.

Later, they lay nestled inside each other's embrace, content. Erik might have slipped off to sleep had Meg not gotten out of bed yet once more. This time he shook off the drowsiness and came to stand beside her.

"What has you so intrigued tonight?" he asked, looking past her to the dark lawn below.

"Looking for Rénard," she said. She let Erik pull her to the cushioned chair by the windowsill. He sat and brought her down to sit on his lap. From there they had watched before as the clever fox hunted. "I haven't seen him." She sounded disappointed.

"I thought you worried about the poor bunny rabbits."

"Is that him?" She sat stiff against Erik's lap and pointed to something at the edge of the copse of trees.

Erik strained to see the varying gradations of black and gray, waited to catch the flutter of movement. A patch of darkness streaked across the lawn. A larger one gave chase. At the last moment, just as the dark shapes were nearly one, the smaller turned sharply to the side and evaded the hunter.

"Rénard must be off his game," Erik said as Meg leaned back against his chest.

"The hunter doesn't always get his prey. I'm glad that the bunny escaped tonight."

"It could just as easily have been a horrid old rat, like the ones Cook catches in the larder."

Meg shivered and made a sound of disgust.

"You wouldn't want one of those to get away, would you?" he asked as he nibbled at her ear.

"That tickles," she said, scrunching up her shoulder against his chin to brush him away.

"Well? Answer my question," he insisted. He wrapped his arms tightly around her, threading his fingers together as if they were a lock.

"I suppose not." She smiled and licked his nose, which she knew he did not like her to do.

He rubbed his face in her hair to remove the strange sensation from the tip of his nose and growled at her in mock anger.

"I'm glad you got away," she whispered. "I'm glad Verduce didn't pounce on you."

Erik didn't speak for several moments. He held her, knowing that they were both thinking of recent events.

"Erik?" she asked.

"Yes, ma petite?"

"Would you have let Verduce take you to prison?"

Erik wondered what she needed to hear from him to assuage her fears. He wondered what he could say that would not be a partial lie. In truth, he wasn't sure what he would have done had Grimaldo not come forth and confessed to the crime.

Before they assembled on the stage, Raoul had, even then, taken Erik aside and offered to help him escape. Just one sign from Erik and Raoul would have found some way to extricate him before they reached the prison. Erik had been moved by Raoul's willingness to break the law to ensure his freedom. When he had allowed the officers to cuff him, he had seen Raoul come forward, ready to act. He had stopped Raoul with a warning shake of his head.

"I was buying time. I couldn't let them take François or Mario to prison. At that moment, I was relieved that he had set his net for me and not for our sons."

"What would you have done? What if they had taken you to prison, locked you up in one of those cells again? How would you have borne it?"

"Verduce is not Leroux."

"And that would have been sufficient?"

"I don't know what you want me to say, Meg."

She twisted in his arms. He let her go. She stood beside the open window and looked up at the moon. Erik was stunned by the soft glow of the light on her skin. He could see every detail, her small nose, the sweet curve of her lips, the rounded swath of her cheek, her large dark eyes. How could he have survived without her?

"I don't ever want to see you in jail again. I'd give you up rather than see them lock you away." She turned her back to the moon and looked down at him. "Even if I never saw you again, even if you had to run to the other side of the world."

Erik reached out his hand. She laid hers inside his.

"Come back to bed," he said. "Dawn is still a way off. The rabbit's alive and well. The fox will live to hunt another day."

CHAPTER 10

The Open Cage

My heart
Is true as steel.
Jack shall have Jill;
Nought shall go ill;
The man shall have his mare again, and all shall be well.

A Midsummer Night's Dream, William Shakespeare

Victor waited until his father had closed the door solidly behind him and until his angry footsteps faded down the hallway. Then, in his native tongue, he let out a barrage of curses vile enough to soothe his wounded ego. He had not been lectured so soundly since he had taken the barouche and driven it and the horses into the pond. Although the horses had escaped injury, the barouche had been irreparably damaged. His father had smelled the cognac on his breath and threatened to have him flogged if he ever did anything again as foolish as drive a team of horses while drunk.

Of course it had been a mistake to argue with his father. The lecture had been long in coming. Victor had dreaded a confrontation. Everyone was reeling from the incidents at the theater, the death of the tenor, and his burial. If Victor had listened to his father and answered respectfully, the lecture would have ended long ago. But he had found it impossible to keep his mouth shut. They had argued until Victor had realized just how dangerous the situation had been and that his father was more worried than angry with him. Then he had restrained himself. Even though he understood his father's right to reprimand him, he resented being treated like a child.

The worst of his anger having been spent on curses and kicking harmlessly at a cushion that had fallen to the floor, Victor slumped into an armchair near the fireplace. The only mercy his father had afforded him was not to harangue him in front of the Costanzis.

"May I ask you the origin and meaning of a few of those words you just used?"

Victor leaped from the chair and turned to see Laurette climb out of a cedar armoire at the far end of the room. "God's blood," he blurted out before he could stop himself.

Laurette had one leg firmly outside the armoire, but her long and bulky skirt had snagged on something inside the large wardrobe closet. She wrestled with it for a moment, then looked in his direction. "Well? You might come help," she complained.

Victor considered bolting from the room, but he was embarrassed that she had heard him taken to task for the events of the night of the murder. He had some notion that he might erase the worst of the effects of his chagrin if he had a chance to redeem himself in the girl's eyes. So he went to help her.

"Here, let me see," he said as he pushed aside the various articles of clothing that were stored in the armoire. Among them were strange concoctions with feathers, long laces, and flashy sequins. Long flowing robes were hung beside lacy items that made him blush. He bent and tugged at Laurette's skirts. Then he followed the length of fabric to the wall at the back of the wardrobe in an effort to find where it had caught. "What are you wearing?"

Laurette didn't blink an eye. "I'm a princess," she said as she yanked at the frilly skirts that were much too long for her.

"Oh," said Victor when the girl didn't elaborate.

"There, look down there, silly, by my ankle," she demanded. He had never paid much attention to Laurette. She was several years younger than her brother François. Victor stopped and looked into her eyes. He had the strangest sensation that they belonged to someone else. The expression more than anything alerted him to the fact that she had an uncanny resemblance to her father when she used that tone of voice. "Well? Why don't you do something instead of staring at me? I really do have things to do."

"What may I ask were you doing inside the armoire?" Victor tugged at the piece of petticoat that had caught on a twisted nail in the back of the closet. Given a bit more patience, he wouldn't have torn the fabric. But the princess was struggling so fiercely that he could not unwind the hem of the petticoat from the nail. "There," he said as the fabric gave way and Laurette was able to step free of the armoire.

"Thank you," she smiled. The previous commanding tone, as well as any resemblance to her father, had vanished. She beamed up at Victor from her diminutive height. Victor found himself forgetting for a moment that she was only eleven or twelve years old. "Now, as I was saying, a few of those expressions you used intrigue me."

As he gleaned that she was referring to the litany of curses he had spat out into what he thought an empty room, he turned a bright crimson.

"My father," she continued to say, "doesn't allow us to talk that way. He keeps all the best words for himself. I have done everything I can to drag the meaning of them out of him, but he can be stubborn. Now most of the ones you used I do recognize and I know that some refer to basic biological needs while others…"

"Mon Dieu," exclaimed Victor.

"Oh that's a mild one. I'm talking about the others."

Victor put his palm across Laurette's lovely pink lips. "Please. Stop. Talking." He risked removing the palm. Underneath was the most beautiful smile he had ever seen.

"I'm sorry. I suppose Papa would be upset if he knew I was asking you to explain such things to me." She picked up her skirts and ran to the door. Victor noticed that the back of her elaborate gown was unfastened. "Oh, I was getting dressed. You and Uncle Raoul surprised me. I couldn't very well let you catch me in my bloomers, now could I?"

Getting a better look at her dress, Victor could now see that it was most likely an old gown belonging to his Aunt Meg. The cast-off clothing stored in the armoire served as costumes for the Costanzi children in their frequent theatrical extravaganzas.

Victor's fingers itched to fasten the back of her costume. But by the time he reached the door, she had already run down the hallway and was climbing the stairs. As she ran, she yelled out to someone at the top, "I'm coming! You're the King's man. Give the eye patch to Étienne." Victor leaned against the doorjamb, confused and delighted. Thirteen years old, he told himself. He would have to ask his father when Laurette's next birthday was.

"You can be incredibly dense, you know." Mario closed the door to the practice room and leaned against it. He crossed his arms and scowled at his brother.

François stopped mid note, fingers still poised over the same chords. For the past several days, he had been avoiding Mario.

"I'm practicing. I don't like to be interrupted when I'm practicing." François began to play. Out of the corner of his eye, he could see Mario framed against the doorway. After a moment, François pounded the final note of the measure, slammed the lid down on the piano, and turned on the bench to face his brother. "What is it?"

"Why have you suspended your sessions with Velia?"

"What?"

"You heard me. You're not Beethoven. Why. Did. You. Suspend...?"

"I heard you," shouted François.

"Then answer," shouted Mario. He unfurled his arms and barreled down on François. François, too, stood and met Mario in the middle of the room. Both boys glared at each other.

"This is none of your concern. Leave it alone, Mario." François's voice was quiet, but the anger was there for anyone to hear.

"Why are you so angry? What did I do?" Mario raised his hands in frustration and moved off to pace the room. "You barely give me the time of day. And Velia. Why does she burst into tears anytime I mention your name, for Christ's sake?"

François's mouth gaped open. "She cries?"

"All I have to do is ask, 'Are you and François practicing today?' and she sobs."

"Sobs?"

"I can't get a word out of her. She's not eating. She's pale as a ghost."

"Pale?"

Mario stopped pacing. He stared at his brother. He cocked his head and pointed his finger at François's chest. "You're…" He stopped and stared again at François. "It's…" He closed his mouth and sighed. "Admit it. You *do* care about her."

François stared off into the opposite corner of the room, but he couldn't mask the deep blush in his cheeks. "Of course I care. She's…she's…an…important member of the…company, and…"

"And you don't want to see her," Mario smirked.

"No, that's not it. I…"

"She's so good a singer that she doesn't need to practice."

"Don't let Papa hear you say that."

"You aren't up to training her."

"What?"

"I knew that would get your attention. So what is it? Why did you suspend the practice?"

François had nowhere to rest his eyes.

"You want her, don't you?" Mario didn't so much ask as tell François.

"It doesn't matter. She made her choice. We agreed that we'd abide by her decision." The return of anger set François once more in motion. "Now, if you could just bugger off, that would be great." He sat at the piano, lifted the lid. The lid fell back into place, and he flipped it up again. As it started to tumble back, François let out a growl of rage and pushed with both hands until the lid settled firmly into its upright position.

"Now that you've mastered the piano, would you please tell me what the devil is going on?" Mario's deceptively calm tone did little to soothe François.

"She chose. Story ended."

"Yes?" Mario encouraged with a rising lilt to his voice. "She chose you, you fool."

François glared at Mario. "Oh, really? And is that why she was kissing you in the wings?"

Mario's brows rose practically to his hairline. He blinked several times before he finally found the words he was searching for. "You ass."

François streaked across the room before Mario could prepare himself. He threw his weight against Mario, slamming them both to the floor. That was how Erik found them when he stepped inside the room, Velia DeVita close on his heels.

When both boys saw their father looking down at them, disapproval obvious in his stiff posture and cold green eyes, they unraveled their limbs and stood. Each mumbled a kind of formulaic apology to their father even as they shot darts of loathing at one another with their eyes.

"Signorina DeVita has mentioned that you've not been available for her practice sessions." Erik Costanzi fixed his gaze on François. "I told her that you were expecting her. Sessions will resume and continue. Is that clear?"

"Yes, Papa." François straightened his clothes.

"Mario, don't you have something to do?" Erik asked his other son. Mario nodded and excused himself. But before he reached the door, Erik called out to him to wait. "I'll leave the two of you to your practice," he said to François and Velia. He gave them one last look before he clasped Mario on the shoulder and led him out into the hall.

Velia stood awkwardly just inside the doorway.

"You saw me?" she asked.

François's blood plummeted to his feet. He stammered. "You heard us?"

"Anyone within twenty yards heard you."

"It's none of my concern. You're free to do whatever you wish."

"He kissed me. I didn't want him to. I wanted…"

François waited. An impossible hope rising in his chest cut off his breath.

"I like Mario. But it was you that I…"

François tentatively wound his arms around her. His mouth

drank the words she was about to say. Her mouth softened, yielded to him.

A knock on the door was followed by the sound of the door opening.

François wrenched himself away from Velia, sure that it must be his father again. Mario stuck his head in and said, "That's what I was trying to tell you, you stupid nit."

François grabbed a tuning fork from a nearby music stand and threw it at his brother's retreating head. It hit with a clear A as the door slammed shut and rebounded to the floor. He turned to Velia. She broke out into a wide smile. François chuckled.

"We should begin the practice or my father will be coming back, too," he said.

"Yes, let's begin," Velia said as she took her place beside the piano.

Down the hall, Erik waited patiently for Mario to catch up with him.

"Did you forget something?" he asked. He made no attempt to disguise the touch of sarcasm in his voice.

Mario looked up sheepishly into his father's smile. "I just wanted to give my brother some friendly encouragement."

Erik turned and walked down the hall toward his office.

"Can I assume your affections for the girl have changed?" Erik heard Mario's footsteps falter for a bare second behind him. He glanced over his shoulder at the young man.

"I don't know what you're talking about," Mario said. He could tell that his father knew it was a lie. He rolled his eyes and added, "It was never love. I just liked her a lot."

"She has nice legs," Erik said, without a hint of emotion.

Mario cleared his throat. "They're not bad."

Once inside the office, Erik indicated that Mario should sit. He slipped his mask off and threw it onto the surface of the desk. He wiped his brow and scratched the side of his face where the mask had been.

"You and I haven't spoken much lately," he said as his son made himself comfortable.

Mario's color rose slightly, but his smile remained intact. "Lately?"

"Since the argument you and François had."

Mario's expression turned suddenly serious. "There were other matters far more important to deal with. You've had a lot on your mind."

Erik couldn't disguise his surprise. He was certainly aware that all his children had been concerned for him during the final days of the investigation. But it moved him to realize that Mario was mature enough to know the relative importance of a dispute with François over a girl that he didn't really love and the possibility that his father might be accused of murder.

"I've never thought less of you than I have of François."

"I know."

"You're my son, Mario. Nothing will ever change that."

Mario nodded. He lowered his eyes, and Erik allowed him the moment to gather his emotions. "I know, Papa. I know."

"Are you going out tonight?" Erik asked as Mario rose to take his leave.

"No, I think I'll stay around. Laurette has a play she wants to put on in honor of the Chagnys. It's something based on a Dumas novel."

"Do you have a role in it?"

"Yes."

Erik sensed that he had been about to elaborate, but had decided against it for some reason.

"What role are you playing?"

Mario hesitated. He shrugged his shoulders as if it didn't mean anything. "I'm the man in the iron mask."

Erik and he shared an ironic grin. When they had both stopped laughing, Mario went on to say, "Since the Chagnys are soon to depart, we've sped up the rehearsals. Elise has a particularly important role."

"Have you heard something about their leaving?"

"Elise says her parents have mentioned returning to Paris in the next few weeks."

Erik pursed his lips together in thought. "I think they might change their plans."

"Really?"

Erik couldn't help but notice a distinct change in attitude in his son. In contrast, he now realized that Mario had been tempering his disappointment over the news that the Chagnys would soon depart.

"So you would like to see them stay longer?" asked Erik.

Mario's face turned a bright red.

"Is it the Chagny family or a particular member of the family that you would like to see remain?"

"Uh, well, it's… Victor is a great friend."

"Victor? Only Victor?"

"Who else?"

"Is Elise a good actress?"

Mario's eyes widened in surprise before he thought to look away. "Oh, I don't know. I suppose she's got a certain flair."

"I won't ask."

"Good," said Mario with some relief. "May I go now?"

"In a hurry?"

"Elise…I mean…the others will be…uh…we're rehearsing this afternoon."

"Mario?"

"Yes, Papa?"

"Caution."

For a moment Mario's face was completely blank. Then as if his father's concern had suddenly dawned on him, he scowled. "You don't need to tell me that."

"Good."

"I mean, I'm old enough to know…"

"Good."

"I would never…"

"Good."

"It's not as if we ever had any time…"

"Good."

"…alone…or together…"

"Good. I'm reassured."

"So it's not really necessary for you to…"

Erik raised one eyebrow and waited for Mario to conclude, but his son swallowed the end of his sentence.

"She's young," Erik said.

"I know."

"She's the daughter of my dearest friends."

"I know, Papa."

"She's under my care and protection. She's our guest."

"I know."

"Good."

"It's just a…a… Never mind. You don't have to worry, Papa."

"Good."

"So I'll just go. Laurette gets testy when we don't show up on time with our parts memorized."

Erik smiled. "I look forward to seeing the performance."

"Well, I wouldn't expect too much. Étienne and Raoul are playing the musketeers, Athos and Aramis."

"And Elise?"

"She's…in love with the main character."

"Played by you."

"Yes."

"Hmmm."

Mario was saved by an escalation of voices raised in anger just outside his father's office. Erik put on his mask and nodded for Mario to open the door. In the hallway stood Rinaldo, Carlotta, and Chiara Greco. The latter stared back and forth between Rinaldo and Carlotta who were both talking at once at the top of their lungs. Mario took advantage of the confusion and slipped out the door.

"Mon Dieu, quelle vie," Erik muttered under his breath. Then he raised his voice over the din others were making. "Silence! Zitto! I can't hear myself think."

Rinaldo and Carlotta grabbed one arm each and dragged Chiara Greco in with them to Erik's office. More quietly, but still simultaneously they began to explain their situation to Erik who understood enough words from each harangue to catch the drift of their argument.

"Not a word," he said to each of them. Then he looked down at Chiara Greco. She had a stunned expression on her face as if she had just witnessed a train derailment. "You and only you may speak. What are they upset about?"

"Rinaldo says…"

"Why start with him, eh?" said Carlotta. She jerked her chin in Rinaldo's direction. "He is busy. He does not have the time to deal with your…voice."

"Carlotta, I would like to be able to speak for myself if you…"

"She can practice with anyone. Like the skinny one, the girl, the little thing that practices with the son." Carlotta glanced over at Erik and nodded to him as if to encourage his participation.

"I…" Chiara's voice simply was not up to the task.

"Erik, Chiara, I mean, Signorina Greco has asked me to…," began Rinaldo.

"I won't have it," yelled Carlotta.

"Calm down, Carlotta," said Erik. "Remember your voice. We don't want to strain it, do we?"

Carlotta's hand went to her throat to soothe her damaged vocal cords. In a voice that was a husky whisper, she said, "I have a solution."

Rinaldo cocked a surprised eyebrow at her, as did Chiara. Intrigued, Erik studied Carlotta. Then he looked at Chiara Greco. In some ways, the young soprano had been a thorn in his side since the first day she arrived. Unwilling to take her on as a pupil, he had pushed her off on Rinaldo. That had been a mistake. But the solution had not been for him to become her teacher. The two of them mixed poorly. Her ego was too fragile to withstand his demands. She had made him feel like a monster. Nor had his demands succeeded with her. They had only frightened and undermined her confidence.

"What would you suggest, Carlotta?" Erik asked.

Dropping the pretence of injured vocal cords, Carlotta resumed speaking in a normal voice. She squinted her eyes at Rinaldo in defiance and then turned her attention to Erik.

"I will train her."

The silence in the room was absolute.

"Why do you not say something?" Carlotta asked. "I will train her. I know what you want. You trained me. I will train her. She doesn't like you."

Rinaldo burst into laughter, but he quickly tried to cover it with a loud and rasping cough.

Erik glanced out of the corner of his eye to see Chiara's blood drain from her face.

"I'm aware that Signorina Greco and I do not understand each other."

"Yes, yes, yes. That is it." Carlotta poked Erik in the sternum. He scowled but made no attempt to restrain her. "I understand her. I am a woman. She is a woman. A woman understands a woman. We will work. She will listen. I will train her."

"I really don't..."

Erik interrupted Rinaldo. "I think you're right."

"What?" said Rinaldo and Chiara simultaneously.

"I think Carlotta has much to give."

Carlotta's face softened into a broad smile.

"You will see. She will sing nearly as well as I do. And I will be a severe teacher." Carlotta took Chiara by the arm and led her away. As they walked down the hallway, Erik could still hear Carlotta talking. "Costanzi trained me. I wanted to kill him. He was rude and insufferable. Rinaldo is a pussy cat. He is a composer, not a teacher. You will bat your eyelashes at him, and he will have pity on you. I will train you like the Phan...like Costanzi trained me. You will see. You want to be a great singer? It takes work and pain and suffering and lots of pain and it takes suffering, too. How that man made me suffer."

Rinaldo shook his head. "Do you really think Carlotta has the patience to teach her?"

"Stranger things have happened, Rinaldo."

Erik waited until Raoul had gone to the library. Letters had arrived that demanded the count's attention. The Chagnys had already stayed several months in Rome, and Raoul had begun to suggest that Christine, he, and the children needed to return. Neither Erik nor Meg wished them to depart.

Knowing that Christine would be in the garden, Erik went to find her there.

"Christine, may I speak with you?"

"Of course." She patted the bench next to her.

"Raoul's talking about returning to Paris. I want you to stop him."

Christine laughed. "You have an exaggerated notion of the power I have over my husband. I'm afraid that if he's made up his mind, we will have to go."

Erik frowned. "If you ask him to stay, he'll stay."

"Really? You think so?" Erik seemed puzzled by her question. She could see that he was in earnest. "Tell me. Why is it so important that we stay? Aren't you tiring of our company? We've been here far longer than we had intended."

"I would be happy if you made Rome your permanent home."

Christine grinned from ear to ear. "Look at us. Could you ever have imagined it?"

Erik lowered his eyes and looked at her hand. He took it in his and brought it to his lips. "No, I don't believe I ever imagined this."

For a moment, Christine felt her heart rush forward as her memories took her back. In an effort to capture the playfulness of the previous moment, she teased him, "What secret requires that I bewitch my husband so that he will postpone our departure?"

"It's for Meg," he said. "You scolded me. You told me that I had been selfish."

Christine's smile slipped. "Did I say such a cruel thing to you?"

"No, not cruel. You made me see how much she's given so that we can be together."

"She wouldn't change a thing, you know. If she were to do it all again, she would make the same choices."

"But should I have let her?"

"Erik, listen to yourself. 'Should I have let her?' It wasn't and isn't your decision to make."

He remained silent. He still held her hand in his. He seemed to be studying it.

"What is it, Erik? What is this all about?" she asked. She was concerned by his silence.

"I have a gift that I want to give her. I would like you to be there when I do."

"When?"

"It may still be several weeks."

"Oh, I see," she said, even though she didn't. "What kind of gift is it, Erik?"

"A ballet. I've composed a ballet for Meg."

"Oh."

"You think it's a mistake?"

"No. No, not at all. I think it's a lovely idea. What made you think of it?"

Erik's face darkened. His green eyes sparked with embarrassment.

"Meg was a dancer."

"I remember. She always loved dance. I'm so glad that we had the opportunity to see her again on stage. She's remarkable."

"She is amazing, isn't she? I always told her, when she insisted that I teach her, that her true talent…"

Christine smiled at his sudden silence. "You were trying to discourage her from singing?"

"Partially."

"Go on."

Erik's green eyes softened as he remembered. "I can't," he said almost shyly.

A few moments of silence passed between them as they allowed the memories of their past to twine about them.

"What if Meg doesn't want to dance? Most dancers retire early."

"But she's in excellent form. I find her in the practice rooms almost daily."

"I'm sure she'll be moved." Christine squeezed his hand. "As long as you leave the decision to her."

"Of course," he said. "Then you'll make Raoul stay?"

372

"*Make* my husband stay?" Christine sighed. "Yes. I'll do what I can to convince him."

"Don Erik, you've changed your mind at least twenty times already."

Renata Cossa's chest heaved. Erik could see the shocking ridge of her ribcage as her lungs worked to expel and suck in the air.

She was right. As exasperated as Renata Cossa was, Erik was more so.

"The sequence makes no sense. Something...is...wrong." Erik scrubbed at the surface of his bare face as if he were trying to smooth out the irregularities of his disfigurement. He stared at Renata through splayed fingers.

He peeked at her as if he were a child dreading punishment. Renata laughed at his plight.

"Don't laugh," he said without much conviction. "What if we put several of those...jetés...in a circle?" He bounded from the small stool from which he had directed and observed Renata's performance and circled around her. "Then one of those...." The word stubbornly eluded him, even though he could easily see the pose in his mind. Frustrated, he looked as if he were about to do something foolish. When he saw Renata's expression, he stopped. "What the devil is it called?"

Renata performed a set of complicated movements, finishing with a pirouette. Defying gravity, her body spun on a single dot on the floor.

"Is that what you want?" she asked as she came to a graceful rest, arms held in an oval parallel to the ground.

He slumped his shoulders. His head hung.

"I can't do this," he muttered. "It's...it's...another world completely." With anger rising, he paced the room. "It mocks me with its silence."

Out of the corner of his eye, trapped and multiplied in the opposing bank of mirrors, Erik found his defeat played out into infinity. Just over his shoulder he saw, in equal numbers, Renata's expression of sympathy. He beat down the disappointment and schooled his features into a mask.

"It was egotistical of me to think that I could choreograph an entire ballet," he admitted.

"I'm sure with time…"

"No. Besides, I don't have time or patience. Nor do I have any talent for it. My mind works differently."

Renata sighed. She took a towel and wiped at her arms and legs.

"Erik, the music is beautiful. The story is perfect. It would be a shame to abandon it."

"Abandon it? I have no intention of abandoning it." He could tell that his scowl unsettled Renata. He turned so that his disfigurement was less obvious. "I need you to choreograph it."

Renata's face was a mask of horror.

"Me?"

"Clearly you're the best person to do it. When can you start on the staging?"

"I…I…can't."

"Don't be modest."

"I'm not, I assure you."

"You choreograph dances all the time." Erik was losing patience with her false modesty. He did not like obstacles. He did not like that Renata was presenting him with yet another. She had been enthusiastic when he presented the idea of the ballet to her. She had done everything that he had asked her to do. So why was she being difficult now?

"Those are set pieces, interludes. They don't carry the story. I can't choreograph an entire ballet."

"It's not that, is it?"

Renata paled at the grimace on his face. His eyes—once animated with myriad emotions ranging from inspiration to frustration—grew cold and fixed on her, the green slicing into her with the hint of restrained violence.

"What do you mean?" she asked. She schooled her body against the urge to shiver and contract. Somewhere in the back of her mind, she thought she knew what he was thinking.

"It's him." When she was silent, Erik knew he was right. "You're harboring that scum, DeVita."

Renata had worked enough with Erik Costanzi to know that if she backed down, he would dominate her. He would hover over her like a panther, licking its paws, and wait to attack.

"There's hope that he might gain some flexibility in his injured leg."

Erik's turned slightly to the side as if to gain a better look into her soul. He frowned, but said nothing.

Renata hesitated, waiting for him to pounce on her. Taking courage from an unexpected surge of anger, she said, "I've training that can help him. I'm working with him each afternoon." She added, "On my own time."

Erik's lips curled in a half smile. The green of his eyes sharpened. "Is that what they call it nowadays? Work?"

The allusion was not lost on her. She blushed a bright red, pulled her shoulders back, and returned his stare. "No, that's not what they call it. That's what they call my attempt to give him physical therapy that will loosen his joint and perhaps give him some confidence and self respect, without which he will not survive."

The green eyes lowered, flicked to the mirrors along the wall. He studied their reflections.

"He tried to kill my wife."

Renata nodded. What could she say to that? It was true. But had fate perhaps stepped between Adamo and his intention? Wasn't that an indication that he was meant to have a second chance?

Lost in reverie, Renata was startled by the deep throaty chuckle that Erik gave. When she looked up at him, she saw no humor in his eyes.

"You may be nursing a viper. Have you thought of that?" He studied her. "Take care, Renata. Take care of your heart, too."

Neither spoke. After a few minutes, Erik picked up the sheets of music.

"It was a grand idea," he whispered. He started toward the door. Back over his shoulder, he called out to Renata. "Remember what I said, Renata, about DeVita."

Just as Erik was about to open the door, Renata called for him to wait.

She stood with her arms folded across her chest in a protective feature Erik had learned to recognize from Meg. He waited for her to speak.

Then she bowed her head, unwilling or unable to look him in the eye. "I intend to help him."

He knew that it was useless to berate her. "All right. That's your choice."

"What are you going to do?" she asked.

"About what? DeVita?"

"No, I was thinking of the ballet for Meg."

"I'll have to think of something else." He nodded to Renata and started to leave.

"Wait, Erik. I have a suggestion."

"But where did this come from?" Meg looked up from the sheet music to her husband and back again. "This isn't an opera. There are no lyrics. The piece is...."

"It's a ballet," Erik said. Awaiting her reply, he held his breath as if the sound of air coming and going would drown out other sounds.

"This is the music," he said when Meg remained silent, her attention riveted by the score. "But you will have to choreograph it."

"What?"

"Renata says you can do it. She told me how you've been working with her on the dances. She said you have a sense of the music and the movements that allows you to see the whole."

Meg thought at first that the surge of emotion in her chest was panic. But it wasn't. It was a strange exhilaration mixed with hope and inspiration. She thought of the opera, *La canzone di cuore*, in which she had played a dancer. In the final act her character had chosen her career over love. The last steps in the dance led to her death on the stage. She now imagined the entire story again, but this time told through the body of the dancer, without words.

"You don't want me to sing?" Her voice was small, tentative.

"I want whatever you want, Meg."

She ran the tips of her fingers over his face until they rested on his lips. Her smile was too big for her face, and she saw and felt Erik's lips stretch, too, into a wide grin.

"I...I have to get started." She rushed down the corridor, halted, and then came back. "Will you play it through?"

"I'd be delighted, ma petite danseuse."

Meg grinned, rose up on tiptoe, and kissed him.

Ma chère,

> *Marcelo and I are at a loss as to how to respond to your recent letter. How could you keep from us the news of Ricci's murder and the investigation? We would have returned immediately had we known the gravity of the situation. The very thought of the Italian police snooping about the theater, interrogating all of you, the fact that they had suspected Erik of the murder is too horrid to be believed. And yet we do believe you, ma petite. I can only say that we are relieved that the case has been closed, although we are amazed that Grimaldo Tessari confessed to the crime and is now dead. Goodness knows we all wished Ricci to an early grave, from time to time, but such thoughts can be excused when they are recognized for what they are—a simple expression of our disgust with his vicious sarcasm and his grossly unfair reviews of our work. I daresay even Erik regretted his death. What grieves me now is the loss of Grimaldo. Poor man. Who could have guessed at his loneliness, his infatuation with Carlotta, his growing anger? Who can know what makes us love or hate with such passion that we destroy others and ourselves?*
>
> *Although Marcelo and I have enjoyed the hospitality of the Duke and Duchess of Lancaster, I have asked that*

we return posthaste. I needn't have asked, for Marcelo, no sooner apprised of the recent crisis, had already informed our hosts of our intention to depart. We will travel across the continent by rail. This should guarantee a relatively short transit. It will take a few days to make arrangements.

Give your dears a warm hug and kiss from us. We have box upon box of souvenirs to share. Warn Erik that the Duke of Lancaster fashions himself a composer and has given us no choice but to bring with us for Erik's perusal an operetta based on the legends of King Arthur. Marcelo has already glanced at it—I didn't have the nerve—and thinks it has potential, but in its current state it will require a good deal of revision. He fears Erik will take one look at it and toss it and our friendship with the Duke out with the day's scraps. Unfortunately Erik can be brutally honest on certain fronts, as you, ma petite, already know.

I am intrigued by your cryptic allusions to a work in which you are involved. You make it clear that you are not singing in the production. My mother's intuition cannot avoid assuming that you are returning to your first love—dance. It also appears that the decision is accepted—I dare hope, even encouraged—by your husband.

Marcelo and I are anxious to return home. Tell Signora Bruno that I look forward to sitting in the small parlor adjoining our room in the morning and hope that the gardenias we had transplanted to the garden outside my window are thriving. And please tell Cook that we would most ardently like to have her cannelloni. She knows the dish that we prefer. I have missed you all. I can't imagine why we have stayed away for these many months. Now that our return is imminent, I can barely wait to hold you and kiss you all, my dear ones.

Please do what's in your power to convince the
Chagnys to delay their departure as much as possible so
that we may spend some time with them.
    My prayers of thanks have all been dedicated to
whoever keeps watch over you and Erik.

                                        Ta mère

Madeleine leaned over and whispered into Erik's ear, "You wrote the music, but Meg did all the choreography?"

"She had some help from Renata." Erik took Madeleine's hand and squeezed it. Her eyes were bright with excitement and pride. Just beyond Madeleine, Marcelo's attention was fixed on the orchestra as it prepared to play.

"Of course, but…it's…amazing, Erik. Isn't it?" Madeleine looked him in the eye as if she would convince him even against his will. But Erik didn't need to be swayed by Madeleine's fervent desire.

"It is," he said. "But the best is yet to come. Watch." The first two acts had gone without a hitch. During the intermission, Erik had circulated discreetly on the edges of the crowds. The audience was delighted.

To his side, Raoul and Christine leaned forward to watch the beginning of the third act. This was to be Meg's big scene. During the rehearsals of the ballet, Meg's dance had been shrouded in mystery. Erik knew that she had given herself the minor role of a demon in love with the god of the underworld and jealous of Persephone. But he had never been allowed to see her rehearse. For weeks Meg had required that Erik leave the theater each afternoon for several hours. Renata and the entire company conspired against him. Even Raoul seemed complicit. Erik consoled himself by attacking Raoul with unrestrained glee during their bouts of pugilism. Raoul had insisted that they alternate this more brutal sport with the finer art of fencing. At least on the afternoons that they fenced, Raoul had a fair chance of outmaneuvering Erik.

As the music began, Erik followed Madeleine's gaze back to the stage. From the fiery and smoking mouth of hell came a host of demons—both male and female—bedecked in clinging fabrics of red and gold. The collective gasp of the audience intensified when two crimson devils, complete with curved and pointed tails, hoisted upon their shoulders a silhouette in black. A sheath darker than midnight clung to Meg's body as if it were a second skin. Her blond hair was disguised under a tight hood adorned with two pointed horns. The shock of seeing the contours of his wife's body so blatantly displayed on the stage disoriented him for a moment. Out of the corner of his eye, he caught Raoul's sheepish grin. But Madeleine watched the dance without any sign of embarrassment, engrossed in her daughter's performance.

When Erik had written the music for the ballet, he had imagined Renata Cossa would choreograph the dance and that Meg would dance the part of Persephone. He had not known if Meg was up to the challenge, but that was the advantage of asking Renata Cossa to work on it. Renata knew Meg's talents and limits. Once Erik offered Meg the chance to choreograph the ballet, the work had no longer been his.

Meg's contribution began the very first time Erik sat at the piano to play through the piece. He narrated the story of Persephone carried down to the underworld by Hades. As he played, he indicated and explained the motifs associated with each character, the movements in the plotline and in the music. Even then, during that first run-through, Meg had pointed out a maverick motif, a repetition of ominous notes that she asked him to elaborate and extend. He balked. It was his music, and he had completed it. It was perfect just as it stood. But Meg had innocently insisted, so wrapped up in the music and her ideas that she didn't notice the grim set to his expression, didn't notice his refusal to look her in the eye as she cajoled him to do as she wished.

"Go on," she had urged him as if he were a recalcitrant child. Then she stabbed the music with her finger and hummed the notes. Coming to the end of the measure, she did not stop but hummed a new rift that grafted seamlessly onto his own.

He played her notes. As he did, his tension eased. He knew how the next measure would go. He continued, adding onto her melody, weaving it back into the whole.

"Yes! That's brilliant," she had said, and he found himself grinning in satisfaction.

"Now, fierce. Make it fierce, angry," she demanded.

He looked at her, the question in his eyes. Rehearsing the motif in his mind, the notes evoked darkness, a malignant power—but not Hades.

"Is that what you wanted?" he asked when the motif had ended on a dramatic chord that still vibrated throughout the music room.

Meg collapsed onto the sofa, her arms and legs splayed in a most unladylike fashion.

"Yes. Yes. Yes. Yes. It's perfect." Then she rose again from the sofa and came to sit beside him on the piano bench. "Something softer, almost mournful in the final act. The part just before Hades and Persephone retire." Meg had stared at Erik's quiet fingers. "Go on. Play," she insisted.

No longer angry, his lips had curved into a lopsided grin. When he didn't continue, she cast him a sidelong glance and blushed.

"I'm sorry. I didn't mean to…"

"Shhhh." He put his fingers to her lips. "Whatever you want, ma petite danseuse. I want to see you happy."

Meg's fingers had outlined the shape of his lips. Then she brushed over the strange, irregular surface of the side of his face. His mask lay forgotten somewhere in the room. She teased the sensitive skin that pulled and twisted at his eye, rolling the soft tip of her finger over the rise and fall of his cheek. He closed his eyes and leaned into her caress. Only she touched his disfigured face, making him whole, wiping away all ugliness and pain.

He had taken that same hand and kissed the upturned palm, teasing it with his lips.

"Where do you want the other changes?" he had asked.

"Really? You don't mind?"

"No, I don't. Just tell me what you want."

She had seen the traces of the demon lover in his music. Between them, they had conjured the demon forth and written her song. Now, on the stage, Meg Giry Costanzi danced the role the two of them had created.

There was nothing delicate or demur about the woman who

danced on the stage. Her movements were bold and powerful, and Erik felt as if he were alone in the theater and she were dancing only for him. Stirred he gave himself over to her wild demonic dance. This was the woman who had faced him even in his darkest moments, fighting his fury with her own desire. This was the woman who had dressed as a young monk and come for her wedding night in a Parisian cell. This was the woman whom he had chased across the Italian countryside. This was the woman whose body was his sanctuary, who took as well as received, and who refused to swallow her cries of passion, the one who had borne his children, the one who had walked into hell itself to drag him back time and time again from madness and self-destruction.

The audience had risen to its feet. Erik had not heard the final note. He had only watched her as she pirouetted across the stage. The sound of applause was deafening. To it he added his own.

"Brava," he called, unable to blink the wet from his eyes, unable to hear his own voice among the din of the audience's enthusiasm. He applauded and applauded, his hands raised, his eyes fixed on her, his golden Meg, his demon lover.

THE CURTAIN RISES

Meg was a vision of light. Her hair was pulled back, revealing the gentle curve of her long neck. Several golden strands had escaped the pins and floated like ribbons down her back. She glided across the floor with her dancer's body. When she turned, he glimpsed her face. He sucked in his breath sharply. He had thought he remembered her, but his memory was a pale reflection of her true beauty.

Out of the Darkness: The Phantom's Journey, Sadie Montgomery

The Teatro dell'Opera may be in search of a new name given the amazing transformation the Costanzis have made to the playbill. Il canarino reveals hidden talents. Not only does she have a superb and expressive vocal range, as has been noted in previous reviews by my predecessor Paolo Ricci, but now she astounds her audience with her talents as co-director, choreographer, and ballerina. The musical score to The Flight of Persephone *composed by her husband, Don Erik Costanzi, shows a lightness and grace that is often only hinted at in his operas. Freed from the lyrics, the story of the beautiful young girl stolen by Hades and taken to the underworld, freely adapted from the Greek myth, soars.*

We are delighted to witness Il canarino, Meg Costanzi, in a supporting role to the artist Innochka Alexandrova invited or stolen away from the prestigious Russian Ballet. Sharing in the honors of director with Signora Costanzi, Signorina Renata Cossa performed the small but important role of the enchantress whose spell ultimately frees Persephone from the shackles of the dark lord. Handsome and athletic, Philippe Devereux, on hiatus from the National Ballet in Paris, performed the dark lord in such a way that the character was sinister, yet strangely alluring.

The ballet will alternate with An Affair with a Madwoman, *composed and directed by Sig. Rinaldo Jannicelli. This effervescent production continues to delight audiences with its tongue-in-cheek story and charming melodies. In the part of the eponymous madwoman, Signorina Carlotta Venedetti shows a flair for comedy that rivals her gift for the dramatic. We applaud the risks such unusual casting represents and congratulate Sig. Jannicelli and Sig. Costanzi for their combined artistic vision.*

All in all, long term patrons and aficionados will be pleased by these productions. They will also be waiting with bated breath the newest opera penned and composed by the enigmatic Erik Costanzi, artistic director of the company. Rumor is that the "masked genius of the opera" is working on a piece that will dazzle and delight. Promising to bring tears and sighs to the audience, the piece will enchant admirers and convert detractors. I, for one, anxiously await it. Meanwhile, the curtain is rising.

Caprice Argento